Sari Robins

All Men Are Rogues

AVON BOOKS
An Imprint of HarperCollinsPublishers

This is a work of fiction. Names, characters, places, and incidents are products of the author's imagination or are used fictitiously and are not to be construed as real. Any resemblance to actual events, locales, organizations, or persons, living or dead, is entirely coincidental.

AVON BOOKS
An Imprint of HarperCollins*Publishers*
10 East 53rd Street
New York, New York 10022-5299

Copyright © 2003 by Sari Earl
ISBN: 0-06-050354-8
www.avonromance.com

First Avon Books paperback printing: August 2003

Avon Trademark Reg. U.S. Pat. Off. and in Other Countries, Marca Registrada, Hecho en U.S.A.
HarperCollins® is a registered trademark of HarperCollins Publishers Inc.

Printed in the U.S.A.

10 9 8 7 6 5 4

For Mom and Dad
Always in my heart, my thoughts, and my deeds.

ACKNOWLEDGMENTS

I owe a debt of thanks to Nanci, the best sister and critique partner a person could ever have.

Special thanks to my husband for giving me the opportunity to follow my passions and meet my deadlines.

My gratitude to Lyssa Keusch and the exemplary Avon Books/HarperCollins team.

Heartfelt thanks to my family and friends (especially Dorothy), who continue to enthusiastically support my efforts.

"I must confess, you are not at all what I expected."

Evelyn tilted her head. "Is that another compliment, my lord?"

He stared her straight in the eye. "I don't know what it is."

"At least you are honest."

Justin shook his head. "Anything but. If I were being honest, I would confess my unholy desire to pull you into my lap and kiss you."

Her heart skipped a beat. "In ancient Rome a kiss was used as the legal bond to contracts, hence the kiss at the end of a wedding ceremony to 'seal' the marriage vows."

Taking her gloved hand, he raised it to his lips, asking huskily, "So what shall we agree to?" He leaned in close and pressed his lips against hers, his tongue lightly caressing her teeth. Surprised, she jerked back.

"I thought only rogues and scoundrels knew how to kiss like that," she gasped, only half-jokingly.

He moved his lips to her ear, deftly nibbling on her lobe and sending shivers racing down her spine. "All gentlemen *are* rogues and scoundrels, we simply dress better."

Books by
Sari Robins

WHAT TO WEAR TO A SEDUCTION
MORE THAN A SCANDAL
ONE WICKED NIGHT
ALL MEN ARE ROGUES
HER SCANDALOUS INTENTIONS

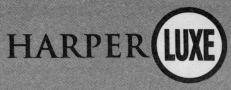

Chapter 1

London, England
1813

"**Y**ou cannot just kill the girl," Justin argued impatiently.

"Why not?" The colonel shrugged, sipping from his snifter of brandy.

Justin pressed his lips, staring down at the heavyset figure sitting deep in the leather armchair before the fire. It always amazed him how a man so callously devious could look like your most doting grandfather. Between his shaggy mane of snowy white hair tied at the nape of his neck, his broad nose, wide, thick lips, and big bushy brows, the man could easily pass for Father Christmas. He was only missing the sprigs of holly in his hair.

"She could be a complete innocent in the matter."

1

"War has its casualties," the older man commented negligently.

The fire's heat against Justin's back could not suppress the sudden chill crawling down his spine. Caught in the flickering light from the candles, the colonel's ridiculous collection of miniature porcelain goblins and ghouls mocked him from the mantel above the fireplace. With their beady eyes, rapacious mouths, and thorny talons, they seemed to take rapt delight in the ruthless conversation.

Justin ran his hand through his short hair. "I still say it's not a sound strategy. To eliminate her means we lose any opportunity of using her as a source of information."

Colonel Wheaton scratched his long white sideburns, staring into his brandy as if to discern all the world's secrets. "She's the daughter of a traitor. As far as I'm concerned, it's dangerous not to eliminate her."

"He was not murdered by one of our operatives. How can you be certain that he had turned? He could have uncovered the plot and been trying to stop it."

Justin paced before the mantel, wondering why the fire added no warmth to the elegant chamber. Frustrated, he threw on another log, and sparks flew up, dancing in the flames. The scent of cloves drifted into the room. For as long as he could recall, the colonel had always added spices to his hearth. And each of the past four winters, since Justin had begun working with the man who managed the great network of spies, he had received a bag of spices from the colonel for the holidays. As if to say, Although I deal in unpleasant matters, I still appreciate the small pleasures in life. Justin always gave the expensive seasonings to his man of affairs. He did not want that scent or any other part of these clandestine activities to enter his home.

Wheaton shifted in his seat. "All signs point to Amherst, and we cannot take any chances with his daughter. Napoleon's stratagem is set for seven weeks from now. We must do everything we can to halt that chain of events."

"Exactly. Which is why we must discern anything the girl might know. Can you imagine how much she has ascertained living with Sir Phillip Amherst and Sullivan?"

"Granted, Sullivan is still out there."

An idea took shape in Justin's mind. "He may yet attempt to contact her."

The older man pursed his lips. "Hmmm. Now, there's an interesting possibility."

"She could be the perfect lure," Justin offered enticingly.

"But how do we get the chit to cooperate?"

Justin repressed his shudder, recalling some of the colonel's previous efforts to extract information from unwilling informants.

"Don't be so squeamish, Barclay. Makes me think you're losing your edge."

Justin shifted his shoulders, careful not to let the old man see how sharply his comment had cut. When it came to the nasty games of intrigue, a man's actions bore more weight than ten titles, something Justin appreciated, despite the devious scheming. Although few had the colonel's audacity to breathe the words, some with the Foreign Office, Justin knew, wondered about his sense of duty simply because he was a peer of the realm. It was appalling and did not speak well of England's nobility.

Justin kept his voice level. "You're the one ready to cut off your nose to spite your face. I know that you and Amherst have a history. And it does look like he turned. But we have a potential catastrophe on our hands, and now is not the time to settle old scores. We must cover every corner. Hedge every bet."

The other man's steely blue eyes narrowed. He did not take kindly to criticism.

Justin sat down in the chair opposite him and leaned back, assuming a pose of ease and confidence, when he was feeling anything but. He stared at the glowing embers of the fire. His work with the Foreign Office was all his own, and earned on merit, wholly separate from his birthright. Still, he was growing weary of the twisted maneuverings, the often senseless bloodletting. He sometimes wondered how the old man was able to sleep at night, sitting in judgment as he did. It was sensible to learn everything the Amherst girl knew. There was so much at risk, and they had little enough information to go on.

"Gain her trust. Bring her back to England. Let her believe she's returning to the safety of home." Justin sipped his drink nonchalantly. "She will not even know that she's cooperating with the authorities while we use her to trap Sullivan. In the meantime, we get her to tell all she knows."

Wheaton smoothed his beard thoughtfully with his meaty hand. "The girl's been dragged halfway around the world with her accursed father and Sullivan for years. It's not like she's just going to start blabbering to the nearest fern about secrets and plots to destabilize the British economy."

"All the more reason she will want some security, some constancy in her life."

Wheaton sniffed. "Still no word from Simon?"

Justin shook his head.

"Well then, it's up to you."

"Peterman is much better suited to the job. He's charming enough to talk the unmentionables off the vestal virgin."

"He has other fronts to man. You gain her trust and get the information. In the interim, try to draw Sullivan out."

"I cannot."

"Why not?"

Justin clenched his fist, trying hard to extricate himself from this tangle. "I cannot befriend the girl. It is impossible to get near her without raising Polite Society's attention. She's the daughter of a knight, for heaven's sake. It's unseemly—"

"A young lady of marriageable age and good connections," Wheaton interrupted. "Your mother will be in heaven."

That was exactly why Justin did not want to get near any lady who was not a gray-haired matron. His mother was difficult enough without giving her something to chew. He glared. "I will not do it."

Steely blue eyes locked with his. "Then you are signing her death warrant and losing your own proposed golden opportunity to stop the conspiracy. No one else is better suited to the task, and I need you handling it. Our premiere spy has gone missing. Another turned traitor, and you want to hand the job off to someone else? I think not."

A cloak of righteous anger settled around Justin's shoulders. He had never before allowed his covert activities to leak into his private life. Yet the colonel always knew which levers to press.

"Fine. But if she is a traitor, I will handle it." No one would dare claim that he had gone soft.

"Good."

Tense silence enveloped the room, save for the crackle of the fire.

The old man set his glass on the table. "She arrives in Southampton two days hence."

"Where is she planning to reside?"

"I have made arrangements for her to stay at Belfont House."

Justin's simmering anger flared. "You presumptuous bastard."

"Calm down." Wheaton raised his gloved hand. "She's actually a distant relation of your aunt's. Her closest relation, in fact, living in Town. And we need her in London."

"You assumed that I would take the assignment," Justin charged.

The colonel shrugged. "It's not in your nature to ignore an opportunity to gather information and balance the scales of justice."

How could Wheaton claim to know him so well when he was such a stranger to himself? Was he a ruthless spy desperate for answers or the marquis of Rawlings in need of siring an heir? Or was he simply a specter of both?

"Collect the chit at the harbor. Say your aunt sent you."

"And what then?" He cocked his eyebrow. "Waltz with the girl until she sings?"

"Think of another enticing activity. She's still in mourning."

Justin stared at the callous man sitting before him. Sometimes he did not know which was harming Great Britain more, Napoleon's schemes or his own countrymen's machinations to stop him. He rubbed his hands over his eyes, inhaling the comforting scent of leather. He had to end these games spying for the Foreign Office and fulfill his obligations to his title, to his family. This madness had to end. But while Napoleon reigned, he feared it never would.

He rose and donned his hat. "Send word if you learn anything," Justin added tersely as he strode out the door. He could swear that he heard the porcelain ghouls' haunting laughter hounding his footsteps all the way down the long, carpeted corridor.

Chapter 2

Evelyn Amherst tilted her chin to the ocean's blue sky and closed her eyes. The sunlight kissed her cheeks, warmed her face, and heated her body through the dark, thick layers of her mourning clothes. A drop of sweat trickled down her side under her chemise. All good things in moderation. Sighing, she opened her parasol, immediately creating a cool haven of shade on the busy dock. She wondered how much longer she would wait before venturing out on her own to find her cousins. She frowned. Cousins she knew no better than strangers. Well, they were kind enough to welcome a long-distant relative in need of sanctuary. Moreover, she had little choice in the matter, for now.

She inhaled the salty air, trying to relish the vast greatness of the sea before she left it behind for Town life. The quay reeked of the rancid odors of rotting fish and human refuse. It amazed her that everyone seemed to just step around the mounds of waste piled high and go about their business. One and all seemed to have a purpose, even the men shouting uproariously as they tossed dice against a large stack of wooden crates. Evelyn would have liked to watch the game more closely, but the unsavory appearance of the participants and the sour odor of unwashed bodies kept her close to her piles of luggage.

Shah, her Turkish maid, perched on one of her trunks, suspiciously watching the industrious movements of the seamen. She clutched her black bag to her thick middle as if it would guard her against the English infidels. Ismet, on the other hand, seemed oblivious to the pandemonium around him. The brawny servant leaned casually against a wooden crate while picking at his darkened fingernails with a knife blade. But only a fool would take his careless pose for anything but the guarded wariness of a trained fighter.

As usual, Evelyn felt like a misfit. Even the most brutish men seemed to step around her and her baggage, respecting her haven of space amidst the chaos. Perhaps it was the severity of her ensemble that kept them away. Head to toe in mourning black. Yet she was comfortable in the severe clothing. It cloaked her with identity and, at the same time, anonymity. She was a young lady in mourning, not a woman on a mission to save her life.

So much depended on her visit here in London, her very future hung in the balance.

"Pardon me." A young man in green-and-gold livery stood submissively beside her. "My lady, Miss Amherst?"

She nodded slowly.

"The marquis of Rawlings awaits you in his carriage. If you would follow me, please?"

"Rawlings?" She pursed her lips. "I am not acquainted with such a marquis."

Ismet casually sidled closer.

"The marquis of Rawlings, earl of Hatteford."

She shook her head.

"You are to stay at Belfont House with Lady Fontaine. The marquis is her nephew. Sent to collect you."

Still she did not move.

He blew out an impatient gust of air. "He is the son of Lady Barclay, first cousin to Lady Fontaine, who is the third cousin to your mother, Mrs. Amherst."

Mollified, she nodded. "But what of my possessions?" She was loath to leave the only things that tied her to any sense of family and home.

The young man turned and gestured to three men in similar livery standing nearby. "These men will conduct your things to Belfont House in a separate carriage."

She nodded and lifted her reticule and parasol. "Ismet, Shah, *gelmek*," she called them to follow.

Heaving a large duffel over his shoulder, the burly, dark-skinned Turk rushed to her side. Her wide, squat maid hopped from the trunk and followed suit, carrying her large black sack like a shield. Together they made about as un-English a trio as ever there was.

"If you would allow me?" The liveried servant motioned to Evelyn's reticule.

"No, thank you."

He frowned but turned and moved ahead toward the carriage.

The young man led them, single file, through the

controlled pandemonium of the docks, circumventing the thick spiraled lines, assortments of cargo, boxes of squawking chickens, refuse, seamen, and other obstacles in their path. By the time they reached the waiting carriages bearing the marquis of Rawlings's austere coat of arms, Evelyn was desperate to rest her stinging feet. Her new shoes pinched her left heel and rubbed against her ankle, raising small blisters. What she would have given for her dog-eared kid slippers. But Shah had insisted that looks were more important than practicality to the English nobility, so Evelyn had resigned herself to wearing the torture devices.

The servant opened the door to the carriage, and the most dashedly handsome gentleman hopped out, his shiny black Hessians snapping smartly on the wooden dock. Evelyn's breath caught in her throat, and all thought of her aching feet flew from her mind.

He had clear, fair skin with a touch of peach accenting high, pronounced cheekbones. His straight, honeyed-wheat hair was cut short in the Greek manner, with lengthy sideburns. His long, aristocratic nose attractively offset his strong, angular jawline. All in all, his face would otherwise have seemed stunningly severe except for the boyish cleft in the middle of his chin. Devastating.

He bowed. The man moved with effortless grace that proclaimed his distinctive lineage. "Lord Barclay at your service, Miss Amherst." He looked up, and his gaze met hers.

Dear Lord, his incredible grayish-green eyes were framed by glorious thick, dark lashes. Evelyn swallowed. Then, remembering herself, she curtseyed, bowing her head so he would not see the blush warming her cheeks.

Childish ninny! she thought, staring at his shiny black boots. *You'd think I am fresh out of the nursery instead of a gently bred woman of two and twenty years!* She schooled her heart to slow and saliva to moisten her suddenly parched mouth. Since when had she become so shallow? Yes, he was attractive enough to dazzle any woman with blood flowing through her veins. But she was a woman who'd traveled the world and met men who could seduce queens into giving up the crown jewels!

She'd been too long away from her countrymen. That was it. It had been too many years around foreign strangers and snake-tongued diplomats. It was his very Englishness that made him stand out. She would look past his exterior and think of him as a . . . cousin. Exactly what he was—family, in a very extended sort of way. She needed to keep her mind on her business in London, not on her . . . ah . . . cousin.

"I say, Miss Amherst?"

She blinked, realizing he must have been speaking to her while she'd been woolgathering. "My lord."

"Welcome home."

Keeping her eyes trained on the lapel of his double-breasted gray coat, she rose. "Since I have not been on English soil for more than twelve years, it's hard to imagine calling it home."

"But it is your new home, cousin. And your family wishes to welcome your return. I trust your voyage was agreeable?"

Evelyn nodded. Pleasantries were part and parcel of a diplomat's life, and she knew when the requisite exchanges were called for. "Perfectly fine, thank you. I appreciate you coming down to the docks to meet me." Now that she was thinking of the Adonis as a relation, it was easier to ignore his appeal. She picked up her reticule from the ground where she had set it. "I'm surprised you bothered, given we are quite distant cousins, in fact," she noted, waiting to see his reaction.

"All the more reason to get to know you, as we have yet to be acquainted."

She tilted her head to look up at him. "Did you know my father?"

He blinked and stared her straight in the eye. "By reputation only. I understand he was well regarded as a diplomat in His Majesty's service."

She studied those silver-green eyes a moment longer. She could not tell if he knew the truth of her father's activities. Probably not; it was unlikely a marquis would dirty his hands in her father's world. She felt her inner walls inch higher, separating herself even more from this distant relation.

"Shall we?" He moved to take her bag, but she shied away.

"I can handle it myself, thank you."

He shrugged and motioned toward the coach.

"My servants?"

He waved to the second carriage. "Will meet us at Belfont House. Your chaperone awaits you inside."

Evelyn stepped up into the compartment and shuttered her eyes in the sudden gloom. The scent of the marquis's musky cologne and the heady stench of carnations permeated the cabin. A lanky, hawk-nosed woman sitting stiffly on one of the benches was the source of the oppressive floral odor. From her clothing she appeared to be an upper servant.

Evelyn nodded to the woman and settled herself on the opposite bench, adjacent to the door. She placed her reticule under her feet and her parasol handily against her leg, just as she had been taught.

The marquis stepped inside the compartment. He adjusted his coattails and sat down beside her. "May I introduce Miss Myrtle, your new maid, compliments of Aunt Leonore."

"I have a maid, thank you."

"Ah, but Miss Myrtle is an English maid, specially selected to ease your return to Society."

Evelyn lifted the curtain and peeked out the window. The seamen must have been gutting fish at the edge of the nearest pier, as a flock of seagulls shrieked and hovered excitedly overhead. The sky darkened, and a few of the sailors lifted their heads to sniff the wind. Evelyn inhaled deeply but could smell nothing past the overpowering carnation perfume. Her stomach roiled, and she leaned her head closer to the window for some air.

"I'm so looking forward to being of service, ma'am." The woman had an affected nasally voice to compliment her crushing perfume.

"Shah is perfectly capable of meeting my needs. She has been assisting me since I was twelve."

The only indication of the marquis's annoyance was his gloved fingers drumming busily on the head of his polished blackthorn cane. "Lady Fontaine has been quite generous in her consideration."

"I will be certain to thank her."

"I believe that she will insist."

Evelyn turned and faced him. The dark green fabric covering the inside of the coach heightened the greenish hue of his eyes. It was growing easier to ignore his appeal; they were worlds apart, and he would never understand hers.

"It will be difficult enough for Shah, with her darker skin and foreign birth. I will not abandon her to the supercilious hierarchy belowstairs simply to placate your aunt."

He straightened. "I can assure you neither she nor your man will be ill-treated."

The driver barked orders to the footmen outside, and the carriage lurched into motion. She took one last look at the great ocean waters, feeling at once a sense of loss and of inevitability. She had little choice but to proceed with her course. Returning to England, albeit temporarily, was a necessity. The pier slowly shifted out of view as the carriage turned.

She faced the marquis. "Of course my people will not be mistreated, since Shah will be staying in my rooms and Ismet can take care of himself."

"But your maid is not an appropriate chaperone when you go out in Society."

"I am in mourning, my lord."

"For only two months more. And under the circumstances, the rules will be somewhat relaxed."

She fingered the soft folds of her black woolen skirt. "Did you know that in Spain a bride wears black on her wedding day?"

"No, I did not know that." He frowned. "Have I missed something? Are you engaged to be married?"

She chuckled softly. "I think not."

"You say it as if you do not intend to marry."

"Not if I can help it."

He shook his head. "I must confess, Miss Amherst, I am a bit befuddled. You are nothing like what I had imagined."

"I assure you, my lord, you are not the first to find me so."

She leaned her head against the cushioned wall, wanting some quiet. "I will close my eyes and rest a bit, if you do not mind. It's been a long journey." The last thing she saw was the marquis's troubled frown. Good. Better to be an oddity than disdained. She sighed. Only a few short weeks and then she could finally escape her father's world. A new life, a new home, and no more worries. As the carriage rocked and swayed, she prayed that she was not fooling herself.

Chapter 3

One week later Evelyn found herself sharing tea with her newly met relations. Relatives were just like all of the other strangers she'd encountered through the years of travel with her father, she decided. Some were kindhearted and welcoming, some distinctly were not.

"You must do something about your hair, my dear," the haughty Lady Barclay chided from over the rim of her teacup. "It really is not a terrible shade of blond, and if curled properly, could be almost stylish."

"I tried already, Claire," added Lady Fontaine. "She has her mind set."

"You ought to reconsider Miss Myrtle's services as Justin arranged for you. I am absolutely certain that she can do better than your foreign woman." She patted her hand against her ash blond coiffure. "Cannot trust dark-skinned people to do anything properly."

Evelyn bit her inner cheek to keep from lashing out at the arrogant woman. Upon meeting Lord Barclay's mother, she could not help but take the self-aggrandizing, pinch-faced Claire Barclay into instant dislike. She did not know which offended her most, the lady's overbearing air or her habit of inserting an insult into every commentary.

Evelyn sipped from her teacup, relishing the bittersmooth Bohea. She studied the dark brown liquid swirling in her china cup. "This tea is divine."

Lady Barclay scowled and sent an exasperated, caustic glare at her cousin. "Cheeky," she muttered under her breath so that everyone could hear. "Doesn't know when to accept the advice of her betters."

Lady Fontaine sent Evelyn an apologetic grimace. Evelyn liked the honey-brown shade of the older woman's eyes, which were webbed by rays of fine lines. With her pleasant countenance, heavy breasts, and broad hips, she was the personification of ancient earth mother statues. Her four children seemed to adore her. The oldest, Madeline, who favored her mother, was coming out this Season in the hopes of landing a husband. Lord Barclay had a sister coming out as well. According to Lady Fontaine, Audrey was a sweet child with a pleasant demeanor like her brother's.

Lady Fontaine was quite effusive where her nephew was concerned. She ascribed the attributes of charm, intelligence, keen wit, and consideration to the young marquis. Evelyn had managed to keep her business in Town foremost in her mind and likewise to categorize the young marquis as "cousin." Thus, she'd avoided reacting like a ninny when the striking man came to call, as he frequently did. He'd been quite attentive since escorting her from the docks. Thoughtful, yet not intrusive. Since he seemed impervious to his own appeal, it made it all the easier to treat him as anything other than devastatingly handsome. She had no idea how he'd remained unattached for so long, but that was none of her business. None whatsoever. Perhaps it was the prospect of such a snake-tongued mother-in-law that frightened the marriageable young ladies away.

"You'd think she'd show more appreciation, living on the goodwill of others," Lady Barclay said as she nodded at Evelyn. "I understand you have *no one else in the world.*"

Evelyn did not need Lady Barclay's vile tongue to remind her of how precarious her situation was. "I am quite grateful to Lord and Lady Fontaine for their kindness. Indeed, in my travels, I have found that graciousness, like all the finer arts, is enhanced with application." She locked eyes with the dragon lady. "And when one does not exercise such good graces, one runs the risk of becoming unbearably cantankerous."

Lady Barclay's eyes narrowed.

Evelyn smiled sweetly, ready to slay the dragon in her lair.

Lady Fontaine set down her cup with a loud rattle. "Claire! Ah, we have the most wonderful news. Ah, Evelyn has achieved the impossible for us, and we are quite indebted to her."

Lady Barclay studied Evelyn over her teacup with her sharp green gaze, apparently deciding to pretend she had not been insulted. "Really, the impossible, you say?"

"She somehow managed to get Jane to stop biting her nails."

"I never could understand how you allowed Jane to develop such a nasty habit, Leonore." Apparently Lady Barclay had found a new target. "It bespeaks terrible failing as a mother."

"But she does it no longer," Lady Fontaine replied triumphantly. "I have no idea how Evelyn managed it, given we have tried everything under the sun to get her to stop, but Jane is cured." She turned to Evelyn. "We are so very grateful, my dear."

"It was Jane who chose to change her behavior, my lady," she stated evenly. "No one can force another to break a lifelong habit."

"Nonsense," insisted the pinch-faced matron. "Such behavior would never have continued in my house. I can get my Justin or Audrey to do whatever I tell them. Leonore was just too soft on Jane. Instead of coddling the chit, she should have beaten the girl every time she touched her hand to her face. That would have nipped the matter in the bud."

"I am sorry, Claire, but you cannot beat a child for something they cannot help but do," Lady Fontaine chided gently.

Lady Barclay harrumphed.

Sighing, Lady Fontaine slipped a plum cake off the tray and took a delicate bite.

"Your cook makes the most decadent sweets, Leonore," the snide matron droned. "No wonder you cannot keep your waistline slim." She blinked her green, cat-shaped eyes. "I have the opposite trouble. I had to take my gown for tonight's ball to Madame Vivian once again for alterations. The woman swears I am disappearing."

Lady Fontaine's cheeks colored pink, and she lowered the remainder of her cake from her mouth and dropped it on her plate. "So what will Audrey be wearing this evening?"

"It is the most divine muslin gown of lily white. Perfect for exemplifying her purity and virtue."

"In early biblical times, blue, not white, represented purity," Evelyn interjected innocently. "In fact, it was Anne of Brittany who made the white wedding dress popular. But it represented joy, not chastity."

Lady Fontaine smiled brightly. "How wonderful. My Madeline is wearing blue tonight."

Lady Barclay stuck up her left shoulder, a gesture Evelyn recognized she made whenever she was irritated with someone. She had raised it numerous times thus far in their limited acquaintance. "My, aren't you a little fount of knowledge? What of your dowry? Did your father leave you anything to assist you in your hunt for a husband? Even with our connections, you are quite the ape leader and will need all of the help you can get."

Lord Barclay swept into the room. "Mother, Aunt Leonore, Miss Amherst. May I take tea with you, or is this a chatter-broth for ladies only?"

Dear Lord, did he have to arrive just as his mother was harping on her spinsterly state? Evelyn ignored the pit of embarrassment in her belly and tried instead to focus on the pleasant view.

Today the handsome marquis wore somber navy blue, accentuating the smoky gray of his eyes. He strode across the room with infinite grace and leaned over to kiss his mother. The lady turned her cheek. He acted as if she had not moved and lightly brushed his lips on her ash blond hair.

He was so pleasantly appealing. How on earth the dragon lady had begot him had to be one of the great mysteries of the universe. His gaze alighted on Evelyn and she smiled, trying to pretend her cheeks weren't burning to cinder.

"Justin, my dear. So glad you could call. We were just discussing tonight's ball." His aunt beamed up at him and extended her hand. He squeezed it gently. The apparent affection between them added several degrees of warmth to the chilly drawing room.

Sitting down on the blue chintz sofa beside his aunt, he commented lightly, "Ah, the finer points of what gowns your daughters will be wearing. You must forgive them, Miss Amherst. The chase is on and Madeline and Audrey simply must make some poor fellows come up to scratch, even if it means shamelessly flaunting their virtue."

"By wearing white." Lady Barclay pressed her thin lips together.

"Or blue," chimed in Lady Fontaine.

"White is the color of purity," insisted the dagger-toothed dragon lady.

Barclay shrugged as he accepted a cup of tea from his aunt. "Historically it was blue, but where's the matter?"

Evelyn looked down into her teacup to hide her pleased smile.

Oblivious, Barclay reached over and selected a tart off the tray. "I wish our pastry-cook was half as talented as yours, aunt."

"Cook really has a gift." The matron pointedly ignored her sister-in-law and picked up her cake.

The dragon lady lifted her left shoulder and glared at the pastries, as if they had insulted her. Evelyn wondered if they would shrivel up and melt under the heat of her searing gaze. She reached for a berry tart.

"Justin, please convince Miss Amherst to join us this evening," implored Lady Fontaine. "She insists that being in mourning disallows her from partaking in any balls."

"We cannot have you rattling around all alone in this great house," he stated. "Of course you will be joining us. In fact, I am here to offer my services as your escort."

Lady Barclay inhaled a sharp breath.

Lady Fontaine set down her teacup so hard it chipped. "Oh, my."

"You never escort anyone, anywhere," his mother sputtered. "We have to practically drag you to fulfill your social obligations."

He sipped his tea. "Miss Amherst's companionship tempts me to be more sociable."

"It will give the wrong impression."

He shrugged, not meeting his mother's eye.

The dragon lady stood, her hands fisting at her sides. "I forbid you to allow anyone to believe that you are courting her."

"Why?"

"Well, she is in mourning."

"Second mourning. It has been over four months since her father passed."

"It does not matter, since I do not wish to be courted and am not entertaining offers," Evelyn interjected. No matter how handsome the man was, she was in no position to be socializing. Nor did she want to be perceived as hunting for a husband. She might actually catch one, heaven forbid.

"Escorting Miss Amherst does not necessarily indicate Justin's intentions," added Lady Fontaine tentatively.

"Good. Because my son needs a bit more seasoning before making any rash decisions."

Barclay tried to appear nonchalant, but Evelyn watched the small muscle jump in his jaw. "I thought you were agitated about my advancing years and my unfulfilled duty to the title, Mother."

"Do not be impudent, Justin." She resumed her seat, loudly rustling her green muslin skirts. "My George would never have conducted himself so objectionably."

His hand on the teacup was steady, but the knuckles were blanched white. Evelyn's dislike of the dragon lady flared into a seething anger. The poor man had been nothing but kind to her since her arrival, and she sympathized with anyone raised by such a vile, miserable woman. Evelyn set her tea down quietly and rose. Although she had no intention of being courted by the marquis, she could help him thorn his mother a bit.

"I am off for a stroll in the park."

He jumped from his seat. "I will join you."

"You have only just arrived," charged the dragon lady. "A servant can attend her well enough."

"Do not worry about appearances, Mother, Miss Myrtle will chaperone."

Evelyn was not happy about sharing Miss Myrtle's company, but she was looking forward to getting out of the stifling atmosphere. Moreover, it would allow Shah to continue her rest uninterrupted upstairs.

It seemed the young marquis was as enthusiastic as

she about leaving. "I will wait for you in the front hall," he said, already out the door.

The trees lining the lane were lush with the buds of spring and the rich promise of summer. Brown little puff-bellied birds flew overhead, chirping merrily in the golden afternoon sun.

"To have such a lovely haven in the midst of the city is quite splendid," Evelyn commented appreciatively as they strolled alongside a quaint little pond. They stopped to observe the ducks squawking and lapping themselves in the dark green waters.

"London offers a sundry of activities for any adventurous enough to venture forth. I would gladly show you the amusements as you accustom yourself to Town."

"Are you certain you are willing to withstand your mother's wrath? She does not like me."

"Nonsense, Mother is just . . . well . . ."

"A dragon?"

A small laugh burst forth from his throat, and he quickly coughed into his gloved hand. He peeked over his shoulder at Miss Myrtle, who was walking at least ten paces behind with a burly uniformed footman.

"She is my mother," he chided halfheartedly.

"Are you going to call me out for my impertinence? Pistols at dawn and then off to the Continent?"

He missed a step but recovered quickly, accidentally brushing against her hip. She ignored the flutter in her middle, reminding herself once again that he was her "cousin."

To ease the tension, she decided to make light. "Come, my lord, I cannot be the first to have stated it plainly."

"As a matter of fact, you are."

She grimaced. "Father always said I was a bit too free with my opinions."

He furrowed his brow. "Do you miss him?"

She watched a robin perch in the uppermost limb of a tree. The fragile branch shifted and swayed under the weight, but the tiny bird did not fly off. "How did you feel when your father passed?" she asked instead.

"He was our patriarch. Everything revolved around him. When he was gone, everything shifted, changed." He froze for a moment, staring off. Abruptly he turned to her and shrugged. "But it was not unexpected."

They continued on. Evelyn liked the way he strolled, with an inherent grace that was smooth but unaffected. Allowing her to set the pace, he effortlessly matched her steps, despite his longer stride. He really was quite agreeable company.

Pine needles scraped under her shoes. She inhaled deeply; she had always loved the scent of pine.

"Was your father ill for long before he passed?" he asked quietly.

She blinked. Ill? The vibrant man had barely been gone an hour before returning battered and bloody, with his life seeping out through a hole in his side. She could almost hear his raspy breathing as he lay dying in her arms. Although she had pressed her hand against the bandage, the warm, dark blood had continued gushing forth, creating a puddle of death. The bitter metallic stench had filled her nostrils. He had shuddered and wheezed. His eyes had glazed over and then stared off into space. The memory made her shudder as if an icy wind had run through her.

"Are you unwell?"

"No." She swallowed, trying hard to focus on the mother duck swimming along and the five tiny golden ducklings trailing behind.

He spoke more, but she could not hear his words past the memory of her father's dying request. She blinked, tearing herself to the present. "Excuse me?"

"I asked, were you close?"

"Close?" She recalled his every last breath.

"To your father?" he asked patiently.

She blew out a long lungful of air, trying to remember the days before her father was murdered and she became an orphan in more ways than one. "He worked quite a lot. Traveled. He was really quite . . . busy. There were times when he was gone for weeks at a stretch. But he was my father. My only parent. Well, besides Sully."

"Sully?"

Something eased in her chest, just thinking about the jovial, ruddy-faced man who had tried to be both mother and father to her. Her lips lifted, despite herself. "My father's man-of-affairs."

"And you were close to him?"

"Quite. He practically raised me."

"Why was he so involved with your rearing?"

"My mother, well, she was not built for being the wife of a diplomat."

"How so?"

"She hated change. Although it was never said, I knew that she abhorred living outside England. She had a fit every time we were reassigned. She could not abide by 'foreign' customs, people, even residences. She was English and wanted everyone else in the world to be."

"Families have been known to stay back in England when a husband serves."

"Not my family. My father could not bear to be separated from us."

"Still, to be dragged from place to place. It is an unsettling life. . . ."

"I did not mind. I met some wonderful people, was able to visit exotic places."

"And where is this Sully fellow now?"

A cloud drifted overhead, blocking out the sunlight. She turned and scanned the crowd, noting that Miss Myrtle and the burly footman had stopped nearby. Easily within earshot. "Do you think a storm is coming?"

"Seems fine to me." He toyed with the head of his ebony cane. "So when will I get to meet Sully?"

"I disagree. It looks like rain to me. We had best be returning. We would not want to give your mother twitching of the guts."

"Too late," he remarked offhandedly as he nodded greetings to two ladies strolling nearby.

She smiled. "Now it is you who are being wicked."

As soon as they passed, the two ladies leaned together, whispering excitedly like hens plotting a conspiracy. Oh, to be so taken with the trivial.

He spoke tentatively. "I appreciate your desire for solitude. But I would ask that you grant me the favor of your company this evening, Miss Amherst. You see, I am in need of your assistance."

"How can I help you?" she asked dubiously.

"You can shield me from the procession of marriageable young chits my mother will be parading before me. No matter what she said before, she is on campaign and I am in the trenches."

"Well, I can sympathize with your situation, not wanting to marry myself. But I really cannot see how I can be of service to you."

"Your public mourning combined with my duty as your escort will keep away most unwanted attention."

She raised her brow. "And attract attention of an altogether different sort."

"So what if the world thinks that I am interested in you? You and I know the truth of the matter." He opened his hand. "It will keep the matrimony-minded mamas at bay. And my mother—"

"— ready to drum my bonnet."

"Please?"

She stared into those pleading greenish-gray eyes. Well, the man had been quite considerate of her situation these last few days, and his mother was a dagger-toothed harpy. . . .

"Very well." It would not be too terrible to divert herself a bit with the inevitable distractions Polite Society offered.

"Thank you."

They strolled along in companionable silence.

He rubbed his chin thoughtfully. "You know, this is the first time I have ever flagrantly disobeyed my mother. I do believe that you are a negative influence on me, Miss Amherst."

"Sometimes a little transgression is good for the soul. Strengthens the blood."

"Or takes one to the devil."

"You mean we're not already there?"

They shared a little smile.

Thunder rumbled off in the distance.

"You were correct about the weather." He looked

up. Clouds were forming into gray clusters on the horizon.

She sniffed the air. "I have always had a fine sense of approaching storms." Regrettably, she had not always shown a particular talent for coming in from them.

Chapter 4

Evelyn stood at the top of the white marble staircase and beheld the glittering masses attending the Coventry Ball that evening. She soaked in the dazzling diamonds, intricate hairstyles, and colorful costumes of the *ton* and could almost hear the clank as her social armor slipped into place. Since turning fifteen she had attended various court functions around the world with her father. The languages, costumes, and mores were different, but the social particulars were always the same. She had learned at a young age that steely reserve cloaked behind a pleasant demeanor was the key to mastering any social context.

"Being the daughter of a knighted diplomat, you must have attended some marvelous balls," Lady Fontaine commented airily as she waved her lacy fan and scanned the dance floor.

The orchestra was playing a quadrille, and the dancers squared off and partnered in methodical rhythm. Evelyn was thankful no one would ask her to dance. Appreciating the added protection her public mourning allowed her, she adjusted her black bombazine gown and snapped open her black crepe fan. The heat from the masses assembled below was already climbing to the top of the stairs like smoke from burning embers.

Miss Madeline Fontaine stood on the tips of her toes, like a twittering bird perched on high, scanning the current above a stream, looking for tasty morsels to dissect. "Miss Erringston is quite the fashion with that deep flounce. And I love her hair. I will have to see if Esmie can do that style. And look at Mr. Darbon's vest. Why, it must be twenty different shades of red. How appalling." The young lady giggled.

"Shall we?" Barclay tilted his head toward the crowd.

Evelyn accepted his proffered arm, and they walked down the white marble stairs close behind Lord and Lady Fontaine.

"Quite the crush," the bright-eyed seventeen-year-old stated happily from Barclay's other side. "Lady Wellingsford will be pleased. Oh, there is Miss Abernathy." She pointed her fan across the crowded floor.

Evelyn braced herself as they dove into the sea of people. She glided along in the tide of muslin and lace, holding on lightly to Barclay's arm. She was jabbed countless times by the pins of the ladies pushing past and bumped and elbowed on every side by the hordes of loud, colorfully dressed Fancy. The air was rank with heavy perfumes; roses mixed with musk, carnations, violets, and lavender. Her stomach churned with the sickening combinations. The laughter and commentary converged into a wave of discordant clamor blaring out the melody of the ensemble. For someone used to isolation for the past few months, it was like being thrown into a bucket of freshly caught fish waiting to be gutted.

Barclay leaned close. "This must be a bit much for you. I understand the back room is usually more quiet."

She nodded, and he said something to his cousins, then disengaged from Miss Madeline and led Evelyn down a long, congested corridor toward the rear of the ballroom. The crush kept forcing her against his hard, warm body, and she tried to ignore the tension she felt at his every touch.

She was a healthy lady of two and twenty and he was an exceedingly attractive gentleman, cousin or not. Still, she did not want him getting any ideas about her. Her life was complicated enough without tossing a dashing marquis into the mix.

Evelyn let out a small sigh as they escaped the packed ballroom and entered the spacious, gold-gilded parlor. People sat or stood clustered in twos and threes, drinking and conversing quietly. A servant came by with champagne, and Barclay lifted two flutes off the tray and handed her one.

She sipped it slowly, relishing the tangy flavor and the tickle of fine bubbles on her nose.

"Señorita Evelyn? Is it you?" came a deep baritone over her shoulder.

She turned. A tall, dark-haired, olive-skinned gentleman in black formal attire sauntered up to her.

Her lips split into a wide, warm smile. "Angel!"

He grabbed her white-gloved hand and raised it to his lips. "Señorita Evelyn," he said in Spanish, "you are even more beautiful than when I last saw you."

"It's been ages, Angel!" she replied in his native tongue. Impulsively, she leaned forward and kissed him on both cheeks in greeting.

His white teeth gleamed wickedly. "The last I saw you, you were chasing away that formidable Señora Morporenda from your father."

"After I was finished with her, she didn't want to be in the same country with us."

"She was a bit of a witch."

"And what of you? How is your father? And Mercedes? And what ever happened with Señorita Isabella?"

He pressed his white-gloved hand dramatically to his chest. "Ah, my friend, she broke my heart."

She grinned. "And you have likely broken thousands since."

"Maybe a few, here and there, but I do not tell tales."

Barclay coughed into his hand.

"Oh, forgive me, Lord Barclay." She reverted back to English, suddenly aware of how excluded he must have felt. "May I introduce my dear friend Señor Angel Arolas."

Angel bowed with a graceful flourish. "At your service, my lord."

"How is it you two know each other?"

"Señorita Evelyn and I have known each other since we were . . ." He held his hand hip height. "Was it this high?"

"You were never that high, Angel," she teased. She turned to Barclay. "Angel's father is a Spanish diplomat. We have seen each other off and on for years."

"Señorita Evelyn made life bearable at the Cortes of Ca'diz. When all of the liberals were drafting the new constitution of 1812 she was trying to keep me from losing my heart."

"Is your father stationed in Town?" Barclay asked, casually sipping his champagne.

"He is everywhere these days." Angel shrugged.

"Justin?" a shrill, nasally voice called out from the doorway.

Lady Barclay stood at the door with a vapid young girl dressed head to toe in violet. Even the feathers on her turban were shockingly purple.

"On your honor, attend me, Justin. Miss Fecklesby requires a partner." Her craggy face was pinched into a disapproving scowl.

The young girl blushed beet red and tucked her chin to her chest, appalled.

Evelyn leaned toward Barclay and whispered, "Go save her, my lord. It will give me a chance to catch up with Angel without boring you to tears."

He seemed on the brink of refusing, but a trio of matrons entered the room, staring at the scene, interested. He bowed stiffly. "Duty calls, but I will return immediately."

He walked toward his mother, his back ramrod straight. The dragon lady's eyes gleamed with wicked satisfaction, the young girl's with relief.

"Let us walk outside, where we can speak more privately." Angel extended his arm.

The evening air was crisp and smelled of roses and pine. The dark, cloudless sky shimmered with stars, and the pale orb of the moon stared down at them as they strolled along the garden path. Pebbles crunched under their shoes and massaged the soles of Evelyn's feet against her thin slippers. She let out a sigh. She had known Angel for years. She could be open with him. To some extent.

"I heard about your father, Evelyn," he began in Spanish. "He was a good man. I am so sorry."

She nodded, slowly. "Thank you."

"I must confess, I am surprised to find you back in England."

"Why?"

He pressed his lush lips together. "My father told me what happened."

She shuddered. "It was . . . horrible. Every time I think about it . . . I become ill."

He stopped her with a gentle hand on her shoulder and wrapped his arms about her. He smelled of spicy, sharp cologne. She pressed her nose into the soft silk of his jacket, relishing the comfort for a moment, then slowly pushed herself away. "I try not to dwell on it. It is overwhelming, and I need to carry on, to continue."

He nodded. "I have always feared facing it, like you did. My papa . . . well, it is all part of the business, but still . . ."

Angel's father also worked in intelligence. It was something understood but never discussed.

"But you have no anger toward the English for what they've done?" he asked, gruffly.

She furrowed her brow.

He let out a long breath of air. "Papa told me that he was killed by his own."

"B . . . but that is impossible," she slipped into English.

"The British think he betrayed his country. My father does not believe it. I do not either. But who knows the truth?"

She blinked. "That's the most ridiculous thing I've ever heard."

"*Sí.*"

"How could anyone think such a thing? The man would rather have cut off his own arm than turn traitor."

"I do not pretend to understand the English. Sometimes I think they are . . ." He pointed to his forehead. "What is the English word for *chiflado*? But they are our friends and we need their help to free our country."

A cloud of confusion swept over her. How could anyone could ever believe her father disloyal? She dropped down on a cold stone bench. "It boggles the mind."

He sat down beside her. "So what do you do now?"

She shook her head, trying to clear it. "How in heaven's name could anyone ever believe for a moment that my father was untrue?" The man had given his life, in many ways had given up his family, in service of his country.

He grasped her hand in his. "Perhaps my father was wrong . . ."

She glared at him.

He shrugged. "It happens."

She shook her head again. Everything seemed distorted suddenly. Unearthly, unreal. Father had sent her to London with his last breath. *But he had told her to collect her legacy and leave, posthaste.*

"Do you have family? Protection? Does this Barclay care for you?"

"What? Ah. No." She bit her lip, lost in thought. "I have family here, but distant. I take care of myself. You know that, Angel."

"You are a young lady whose father has been murdered before her eyes. Do not be foolish. You need protection, Evelyn."

She straightened her shoulders and looked directly into those chocolate brown eyes. She just needed some time in London. Not long. If she could follow her father's instructions, then she would be all right. She had to be. "I can take care of myself, Angel."

"You English are *irracional*." He stood and began pacing up and down the shallow path bordering the bench, the pebbles crunching angrily under his shiny buckled shoes. "Your father was murdered by your own government and you think you are safe here?" He huffed and continued pacing. "You know as well as I, better than me, that this is not a game. Let me help you." He stopped short, crouching down before her. "Father is working with Wellington. He has resources. Let us help you."

Tears of gratitude welled up in her eyes, threatening to break free and overwhelm her. She could not handle his generosity; it burst through the protective shell of her numbness, making her feel as if she might shatter into a thousand pieces. She blinked back the tears and clamped down on the emotions crushing her chest.

"You are so sweet, Angel. I appreciate the offer. I . . . I have some things I must take care of. If all goes as planned, well, then all will be fine. But if I do need you . . ."

His eyes narrowed. "What are you up to, Evelyn? Do not get yourself mixed up in this business. It is too dangerous, and you have paid too dear a price already."

She raised her brow disbelievingly. "And you are not already neck deep in the nasty games?"

He growled, "My father always said you would have made a hell of a man."

"From him that is a high compliment indeed. Still, I can take care of myself just as well being a woman." She would have to.

"My offer stands. You will consider it?"

What if her plan did not succeed? What if she really was alone in the world without assistance or income? She hated the thought of having to rely on the handouts of others, but what choices would she have then? At least she knew that Angel was sincere. That he and his father had the wherewithal to help her. She blew out a long breath of air.

"I will think on it," came her cautious reply.

"Offering for her hand after only one chance meeting?" Barclay stepped closer from down the garden lane. "She is still in mourning, for heaven's sake," he declared in a mocking tone.

Evelyn's cheeks warmed. Well, she could not take it out on Barclay. He was innocent of their deadly world.

She and Angel both stood.

"I understood that Señorita Evelyn has sworn off marriage," Angel replied lightly.

Evelyn pasted a small smile on her tight lips and feigned a teasing jib. "And once I've set my mind, have you ever known me to alter it, Angel?"

"No," he replied smoothly, once again the diplomat's charming son. "But I can still try to change it."

"Is your heart broken once again, Señor Arolas?" Barclay asked, watching Angel carefully.

"I think my heart is safe with Señorita Evelyn." He bowed, his eyes only for Evelyn. "I will call upon you. Where do you stay?"

"Belfont House with Lord and Lady Fontaine, my cousins."

He kissed her on both cheeks. "Until then. My lord." He nodded to Barclay and swept down the lane, his long black coattails flying behind him.

Barclay frowned. "He seemed in quite a hurry to be off. I trust I did not offend him."

She bit her lip, lost in thought.

"Miss Amherst? Are you alright?"

"Uh, yes, I'm fine."

"You know that if you require anything, I will gladly be of service to you."

Her eyes fixed on him warily. "What would make you think that I am in need of assistance?"

"This is a difficult time for you. Returning to England. Your father's recent passing . . ." He lifted her chin with his finger, catching her gaze with his gray-green eyes. "I mean it, Miss Amherst. If you are in any difficultly, you can tell me what it is about, and I will do everything in my power to assist you."

Although her lips felt like wood, she forced a smile up at him. If he had any idea of the madcap world her father traversed. *Had* traversed. *It was dangerous for all, particularly the unwary.* He would be a guppy in a pond full of sharks. Well, not a guppy, but certainly no sharp-toothed predator. She shook her head and smiled reassuringly. "I am fine, my lord. Just catching up on old times with Angel. It made me think about . . . about before my father's passing. That's all."

He dropped his hand.

"I have very broad, dry shoulders."

"Father always said crying evidenced weak moral character."

The delicate notes of a waltz drifted into the garden through the open French doors. She took a deep breath and pushed away the fears threatening to overcome her. She needed to be alone. To think. She looked around the empty gardens. The trees swayed in the gentle breeze, and the crickets chirped in time to the music. The world moved on and so would she.

He lifted her gloved hand to his lips. "I am not a charming Spaniard, but I trust that my company does not bore you to tears."

She looked up. "Did you say something, my lord?"

"You seem quite lost to another world. Will you share it?"

"I apologize, my lord. Let us return to the ball."

She turned, and her foot brushed against a boulder lining the lane, rubbing her healing blisters. Searing pain pierced her ankle, and her step faltered. He caught her in his agile arms. All thought of her hurting foot fled as she suddenly found his silky lips pressed against hers. Her mind honed in on the contact of his mouth intimately caressing her lips, beguiling, intriguing. Heat coursed from his body to hers as he pressed closely against her. His hard form caused a wellspring of warmth to cascade deliciously from the top of her head to her toes, blanketing her body with sensual heat.

This was nothing like the ardent stolen kisses she'd shared the summer before with the brazen rogue Count Bryon. The wiry Frenchman had been all hands, grabbing, pressing and demanding. Until, that was, Sully had discovered them. Her dear Sully had turned into a bellowing giant, ready to hound Count Bryon all the way back to Paris. And he very nearly had. Since then, Sully had behaved like a mama bear with new cubs, she being the nursling.

Evelyn's arms crept up Justin's muscular shoulders, relishing the passion, the excitement, and his deliciously soft lips, just for a moment. Until the ever-hovering Sully would charge from nearby and pounce on the unsuspecting marquis. But wait, Sully was nowhere near, Father was dead. . . . A great ball of despair burrowed in her chest as the reality of her situation hit home; she was alone, truly alone for the first time in her life. She closed her eyes and pressed closer to Barclay's warmth, trying to soak in his radiance, trying not to feel so awfully alone.

He wrapped his powerful arms more tightly around her, and delicious sensations chased all thoughts from her mind. The press of his lithe body and hard thighs against hers made her body melt like wax to flame. Everything seemed to loosen within her, and the horrors were driven away by his passionate embrace. She inhaled his musky, masculine scent, relishing the pleasure of being desired, of being free from her troubles. It was momentary pleasure, but she wished this moment would last forever.

"Have you no shame?" a female voice shrilled.

Barclay tensed and broke the kiss. Evelyn's lips still tingled from his searing touch. The arms holding her squeezed tighter, then slowly released her. She looked over his shoulder. In the moonlit trees stood the dragon lady, staring angrily, and Lady Fontaine, waving her fan as if in desperate need of bucketfuls of air.

"Claire, no one saw. Do not make a scene . . ."

"Close your trap, Leonore. He is my son and I will not have him disgracing our family. If only George were here to set you to rights, Justin. Then you would not behave so appallingly."

His body turned to stone.

Evelyn tried to be embarrassed but found herself incapable of the emotion. Unlike Count Bryon's heavy-handed clinch, Justin's embrace was an amazing thrill she was not about to regret. And she was unable to pretend she was sorry just to placate a venom-toothed harpy. Unwilling to let their intimacy dissolve just yet, she whispered, "Why do you allow her to speak to you so?"

He looked down at her, and bleakness filled his smoldering eyes. "She is my mother. She's had a difficult life. . . ."

"Remove yourself from that harlot this moment, Justin."

He slowly stepped away from Evelyn and turned. "I will not have you insulting our cousin, Mother. She did nothing wrong. It was my fault. I made the improper advance. She is an innocent."

Lady Fontaine advanced quickly, her shoes crunching in the sea of nuggets. She leaned forward, urging quietly, "A hasty retreat is in order, my dears."

"What are you mumbling to them, Leonore?" Lady Barclay demanded shrilly. "Don't you dare take that lightskirt's side!"

"I was just saying how late it grows and how Evelyn and I had best be off before my husband loses his shirt in the gaming room." Lady Fontaine locked arms with Evelyn and steered her toward the ballroom, pointedly facing away from her sister-in-law.

Evelyn shot Justin a silent farewell over her shoulder, relieved to be escaping so lightly. She pitied the poor dove; he was left to deal with his witchy mother. How could anyone so amiable come from a mother that foul? She shook her head. We all had to live with the legacy of our parents. And suddenly Evelyn recalled that she needed to claim her own inheritance, or her future would be in dire straits indeed.

* * *

Justin watched them leave, not for the first time in his life thanking the heavens for his aunt's benevolent intervention. Squaring his shoulders, he prepared himself for the inevitable confrontation with his mother. Since birth she had plagued him, hounded him, and yet, deep in her heart, had always loved him. But she had granted any affection in exchange for performing as she required. Love was not gratis in the Barclay family. It required fulfilling responsibilities to Mother, to the family, to Society, to anything she found worthy. Personal feelings carried no weight in her world. The scales were measured on how you had proven yourself, *lately*.

"The fault is mine, Mother. Do not try to punish Evelyn for my improper conduct."

Her eyes narrowed. "Pray tell me you're not dupe enough to think you actually care for her."

He shrugged, not meeting her eye. "She is a fine person who has had a difficult time of it. You, of all people, should relate to losing a loved one—"

"Don't you dare try to put me in the same class as that, that vulgar missy."

"You just don't like that she won't let you walk all over her. Contrasting with most of the young ladies you deal with, she actually has a backbone."

"She has no sense of propriety. She cavorts with foreigners—"

"Who else should she associate with? She's not set foot in her homeland for over twelve years! Her father dragged her to the four corners of the globe in service of our king!" He ran his hand through his hair, exasperation edging into his voice. "How can you punish her for her father's choices?" The irony of his charge struck him in the chest like a musket ball. That was exactly what he and the colonel were doing—penalizing Evelyn for her father's crimes. He pushed aside his misgivings. If she was guiltless, his investigation would prove her such.

"She is horribly unsuitable as a wife." Mother jabbed a bony finger into his shoulder. "And that's where *your* responsibility lies. I should have a grandson at my knee, not be chasing harlots in the bushes."

"Don't get into this again, Mother. I am young yet—"

"Lord Solomon has four boys and he is two years your junior. I will not allow you to risk our future, our legacy, for some debaucher. You have no sense at all. She's after our title, our money—"

Sarcasm permeated his tone. "There's no way she could actually prefer my company—"

Her cat-shaped eyes mocked. "As I said, *no sense*. Women do not choose men for their fine conversation or their strapping form. Granted, you come from good stock and thus are well favored. But you are nothing without our title and our funds. I pray you are not foolish enough to believe she might be fond of you for anything else."

She had said the words many times before, but somehow it hurt more this time. As if now it actually mattered that someone valued him for himself. Not for his birthright, or his money, or his tricks in foiling the French. Evelyn's esteem seemed hard to come by, and claiming it would mean he was somehow worthy.

Mother stepped closer, trying for a conciliatory tone. "Certainly, if your brother George was still with us, you could dally as you wished. But life is not always as we would prefer it, and you have a duty to us. A duty to your family. To your heritage. To your sister and to me." She squeezed his hand. "I know you will not disappoint us, Justin. I have had too much suffering in my life as it is. Pray do not break my heart completely, or I might not recover."

How could he justify to her that he was doing his duty in associating with Evelyn? How could he explain to himself that he relished the lovely young lady's company, admired her pluck, and, yes, had enjoyed that kiss. He let out a long breath. He should never have taken this assignment. Mixing his clandestine activities with his private life was a recipe for disaster. Now the stew was already in the pot, the ingredients boiling and the colonel hungry for results. But suddenly it was Justin feeling the heat of the flames. Danger, treachery, passion . . . heady spices indeed.

Chapter 5

Evelyn's bottom was going numb. She shifted in the hard seat and stabbed her parasol in irritation against the wooden leg of the chair. The little man sitting across from her pushed his gold-rimmed spectacles up the ridge of his nose but pointedly ignored her and focused on the ledger on the desk before him.

Finally, after what seemed like forever, the large oak door yawned open, and Evelyn quickly stood at attention. Her black skirts rustled as she discreetly shook out her cramped legs. A head peeked out, then disappeared, and the door shut with an abrupt bang.

She pressed her fists on her hips and glared at the little man behind the desk. "Enough is enough."

He licked his reedy lips and patted the formerly white handkerchief across his shiny bald forehead for the thousandth time.

"Mr. Marlboro is a very busy man, Miss Amherst." His eyes shifted away, and he pressed the cloth to his lips. "A very busy man."

"Well, I am finished waiting on his convenience, Mr. Tuttle."

"You did not have an appointment."

She slammed her sturdy parasol on top of his desk. He jumped like a frightened rabbit.

"You can tell his eminence that I will sleep here if I must but I am not leaving until he speaks to me about my father's estate." She stepped closer and narrowed her eyes. "And unless Mr. Marlboro wishes to hurdle out his window to get home for dinner, he can and will see me."

Mr. Tuttle nervously eyed her, then the closed door to the inner sanctum. He seemed to come to a decision. The law clerk was either more intimidated by the young lady before him, or hungrier for his dinner, than he was afraid of his superior.

He sidled from behind the little wooden desk, slowly opened the door a crack, and slid inside the next room. Evelyn could not hear a word of the discussion, but after a moment, a sweaty Mr. Tuttle peeked out.

"Mr. Marlboro will see you now, Miss Amherst."

Evelyn squared her shoulders and lifted her chin, firm on establishing the appropriate rapport with the man who had kept her waiting until the sun was nigh into the west.

She stepped into a large office. It smelled of old papers, leather, and burned wax. Candles illuminated the musty room, exposing the piles of papers on every available surface, including the massive black desk behind which sat one of the heaviest men Evelyn had ever seen. She briefly wondered if the man had to pay triple for his suits, given his enormous bulk. Evelyn crossly reasoned it must have been his need for dinner that had finally driven him to acquiesce and see her. Otherwise, he probably would have remained hidden inside his cluttered cavern.

Laying hands the size of ham roasts atop his desk, he pushed himself up and nodded, jiggling his many chins. "Miss Amherst. I apologize for keeping you waiting. If you had had an appointment . . ." His voice was a thick, droning whine.

Her smile was brittle. "Ah, Mr. Marlboro, I would gladly have allowed any *clients* who actually had an appointment to come in before me, if," she added in a steely sweet voice, "that is, there had been anyone to see you in the last three hours."

He held open his hands with widened fingers that looked more like sausages than human flesh. "Papers, papers. Always need to do the filing."

Evelyn glared disdainfully at the gross mess of the room. "It seems you are well behind."

He pushed his large spectacles up his bulbous nose and picked his hat up off the rack. "Well, then. It is getting late and I must be on my way. Can't keep the missus waiting, now can I?"

"But you can keep me waiting? Need I remind you that I am a client of your firm's, Mr. Marlboro?"

"So what can I do for you?" he asked nervously while setting his hat upon his brown, curly-topped head.

She pulled her documents from her reticule and held them out. He did not step from behind his desk or remove them from her hand.

"I am here to collect on my father's estate. I am his sole heir and the documentation is all in order. The assets listed in these accounts shall be transferred to the following list of banks as soon as they open in the morning."

He swallowed. "Ah, matters such as these are quite delicate and take, ah, a certain amount of time to review and manage. . . . Papers, legal matters, and such."

She lowered her chin and glared at the troublesome man. "Do not toy with me, Mr. Marlboro. I am well aware of the legal implications, the legalese, and other aspects of these simple financial transactions. It will take three days to process the appropriate papers and then two weeks to transfer all assets to the foreign establishments. The entire matter can be resolved by the end of the month."

He licked his flabby lips. "It really is not quite as simple as all that."

"Do you represent my family's interests or not? Or shall I bring your ineptitude to the attention of the bar?"

He straightened. "There is no need to become difficult, Miss Amherst. Yes, I was your father's solicitor—"

"Was?"

"Things have changed somewhat. Given his unusual activities."

The butterfly in her belly suddenly broke free of its cage and hammered against her ribs to escape. "My father is deceased. His legal documents, all prepared by you, designate that all of his assets fall to his sole surviving heir, me."

"It has come into question whether these assets . . ." He began wringing his chubby hands, and Evelyn had to stifle the desire to scream *Spit it out!* ". . . well, whether they were ill-gotten gains . . ." His nasally drone trailed off.

She pushed down the nervous bile that had risen in her throat and lifted her chin. "Ill-gotten gains? What does that mean?"

"Certain matters have come to my attention which need bearing out before we can proceed."

"Who challenged my rights?" she demanded.

"Now see here, Miss Amherst, I represented your father for a very long time."

"Obviously not very well, or there could be no question as to the rights of his designated heir."

He let out a long breath. "My hands are tied."

"Who's challenged my rights, Mr. Marlboro?"

He grimaced at her sharp tone but did not answer.

This was becoming an exercise in futility. Someone had intimidated Mr. Marlboro, and nothing she could say would make a dent in his stonewalling.

"This is not the last of the matter, I assure you." She turned on her heel and stormed out the door. She did not deign to acknowledge Mr. Tuttle as she pushed past the swinging wooden panel and out into the corridor, where she stood quaking furiously from head to toe. She clutched her parasol and her reticule tightly, to stop her hands from shaking; her heart was hammering so loudly that she wondered if all of London could witness her anger. And her fear. Trepidation tasted bitter on her tongue as she marched down the passageway. She barely saw the dark and vacant offices as she blindly headed outside . . . to escape from the answers she had waited for, dreaded, and now confirmed.

She made her way down the shadowed, dusty stairwell, her gloved hands skimming against the narrow walls. At the bottom of the stairwell, in the enclosed threshold, she stopped and pressed her forehead against the thick, wood-grain panels of the external door. She breathed deeply, trying to ignore the dank odors of the passage while attempting to slow the racing of her heart. The tremors had left her feeling depleted and alone. Something wet slid down her cheek, and she realized that she was crying. Crying! God in heaven! That that spectacle of a man could bring her to tears! She angrily brushed them aside and sniffed. Without that money, she would lose her freedom, her independence. She swallowed. Her future. She squared her shoulders and pushed away from the wall. This was simply an obstacle to be removed. A rut in the road to be overcome. But the words sounded hollow in her heart.

She took a deep breath and pushed open the large wooden door. It squeaked loudly into the darkening twilight. She stepped out into the fresh air, inhaling the scents of evening, trying to pull herself together.

Ismet advanced from the shadows. Another man followed by his side. Where Ismet glided with the sleekness of a snake, this man moved with the lazy grace of a lion. The king of the jungle.

"Lord Barclay? What are you doing here?"

The memory of his heated embrace flashed through her mind, exorcising her troubles for an instant. She raised her gloved hand to her lips, and then dropped it. She had too much to worry about to dwell on a stolen kiss that probably meant nothing to him.

"We were concerned for you. The butler overheard your direction to the hackney driver, and I came to ensure that all was well."

She prayed that the darkness would conceal her eyes, which were likely rimmed with red. She cleared her throat. "Why would it not be?"

"Your man is not exactly the perfect escort. Why, he barely speaks English."

Ismet gave no indication that he understood. Approval swelled within her. Ismet was the keenest of men. If he did not appear to understand the language, he could not answer questions.

"How long have you been here?"

He nonchalantly swung his cane. "Oh, quite some time."

"Why did you not come up?"

"I saw the address. You are here on personal business. I did not wish to disturb you." He clicked open the gold watch hanging from the red fob at his waist. "It certainly took some time. I am glad that I did not delay you further." He snapped it closed and studied her. "All is well, I presume?"

"Fine. We should be heading back."

The wooden door behind them swung open, and the heavyset Mr. Marlboro stepped through the threshold. He raised his hammy hand to his hat. "Ahh, excuse me, Miss Amherst . . ." He stiffened. "Ahh, my lord Barclay."

Barclay nodded curtly.

Evelyn turned her head and gave the offensive man the cut direct. After a pregnant pause, he hastily turned and waddled down the street.

She turned to Barclay. "Do you know him, my lord?"

"Only by reputation. I use another firm housed in this building." He looked toward the darkening trees. "Might I suggest we move on? My carriage awaits around the next corner."

"Certainly. I do not wish to worry your aunt further." And there was nothing useful to be accomplished here.

* * *

Once again ensconced in the marquis's plush coach, Evelyn couldn't keep Mr. Marlboro's words from running through her mind. *"Ill-gotten gains."* That could mean only one thing; someone was trying to prove her father was a traitor and confiscate her wealth. But what type of evidence would they procure? Or manufacture? There were no charges against her father—he was dead. Moreover, the government could not declare him a traitor without it becoming known that he had been in intelligence. Governments were loath to claim anything except for the inoffensively neutral. So how was the matter legally proceeding? Was she simply to be swept under the rug? Or worse yet, ignored completely? She was not about to stand by and have her father's name besmirched and her fortune stolen. If necessary, she would march into the House of Commons and declare her father's innocence to the rooftops, if it would do any good. But it would not. She sighed. Which way to turn now?

"You are brooding, Miss Amherst. I pray our last encounter does not make you ill at ease in my company."

She was ripped back to reality. "Oh, that, well . . . no." Her cheeks warmed, but she resisted the urge to touch her lips. "Not at all."

"I confess I got a bit carried away." He smiled. "But I cannot claim to regret it. It was very . . . *special*."

She tilted her head, interested. "Really? How so?"

"Well, I . . ." He rubbed his chin. "If I were a lady it would be my turn to blush." Pursing his lips, he stated, "Well, to be frank, I have had the opportunity to kiss a few ladies in my time. And your kiss, well, it was . . . better than any I've had the pleasure of enjoying."

Her cheeks flamed. "Really?" It was nice to know

she wasn't the only one affected by that searing embrace. "It certainly banished all troubles from my mind."

"Troubles?"

She blinked. Had she said that aloud? She wanted to kick herself for having such loose lips, in more ways than one.

Silence filled the cabin.

"Has this something to do with the solicitor Mr. Marlboro?" he asked.

She hated to lie to him but could not dare tell the truth. What would she say? *I'm trying to follow my father's dying instructions so I have a future and am not murdered too?*

He broke the quiet. "On second thought, I apologize for intruding. It is your personal business and none of my affair." He raised his hand to the curtain and pulled it aside, allowing moonlight to filter into the plush cabin.

There was a novelty, someone not trying to interfere in her life. She studied his profile in the pale light. His strong nose added a touch of haughtiness to his features, but even in shadow the man was stunning. It was growing all the more difficult to categorize him as "cousin," and she wondered if she really wanted to keep him at bay.

Heavens! What was she thinking? She had no time to dally with a dashing marquis; her very future was in jeopardy! Father would be mad as hops at her for losing sight of her target. She needed to stay focused and not allow herself to be distracted. She needed to keep her head clear and her business in the fore. And finding a way to access her fortune was the first of her tasks.

"Please do not interpret my silence as anything but

what it is—woolgathering, my lord. I am simply rumi-
nating on some of the legal issues pertaining to my father's estate. As a matter of fact, if I may ask, which
solicitors do you use?"

"The Troutman Jones firm. They are quite good."

She filed the name away for later use. She might be
needing new legal representation. But how was she to
pay them? She bit her lip.

"They are on retainer and are available to any in the
family with legal issues."

Her eyes narrowed. "Why are you being so kind?"

He straightened. "Excuse me?"

"Why are you always trying to be of service to me?"

He blinked, as if taken off guard. "I, well, I like you."

She crossed her arms.

"I kissed you," he continued.

Her brow furrowed. "Although it was quite lovely,
what does that have to do with anything? As you well
have admitted, you have kissed many ladies."

"But that was different."

"Why?"

"Well, it's just different. They were my . . ." He
shifted in his seat, seemingly at a loss. "Those ladies,
well . . . we had an arrangement beneficial to both
sides. It was an exchange, so to speak." He continued
as if searching for the words. "Nothing was freely
given. But with you, the passion was, is, very *real*."
Frowning, he observed, "You seem quite plainspoken
in discussing such matters. Are you in the habit of accepting kisses?"

"Hardly. I just do not understand what difference the
kiss makes."

He shifted in his seat. "I like you. Everything about
you. Can it not be as simple as that?"

"Not in my experience."

He rubbed his chin, thoughtfully watching her. "It is understandable for you to be wary. And I applaud you for it. You have lived as a stranger the world over. You have no parents or protector. . . ."

She raised her brow. "Are you offering your services again?"

He straightened, ostensibly horrified. "I would not dare disgrace you so."

Relieved, she leaned back against the cushion. He was just trying to help her, and here she was questioning his every motive. Since greeting her at the quay, he had been only the kindest of gentlemen to her. She had been living in her father's world for too long. *Her father's world.* She still had Father's personal journal. He had railed that she keep it with her always. He had been so insistent. Perhaps there was valuable information inside? Information that could clear her father's name and pave the way to free her inheritance. A small bubble of excitement jumped in her belly. The possibilities whet her appetite to take action. Not to sit by and allow the Mr. Marlboros of the world to have their way. What was Sully always saying? *You are only as powerful as you choose to be.*

"If my offers for assistance offend you . . ." he stated tentatively.

She waved her hand. "I am being silly, my lord. You are all that is kind and generous."

"Do not attribute such qualities to me, Miss Amherst. Being with you is purely self-serving."

Suspicion flared again. "How so?"

"You are good company and my mother dislikes you. An irresistible combination."

She smiled, relaxing. "Ah, so much to recommend me."

"Beauty, keen wit, intelligence. What more could one want? I must confess, you are not at all what I expected." He rubbed his chin thoughtfully. "Nothing like what I expected at all."

She tilted her head. "Is that another compliment, my lord?"

He stared her straight in the eye. "I don't know what it is."

"At least you are honest."

He shook his head. "Anything but. If I were being honest, I would confess my unholy desire to pull you into my lap and kiss you again."

She shook her head, smiling. "I'm glad that Ismet chose to ride up top."

"Why? He cannot understand me." He rubbed his gloved finger across his bottom lip. "Or is it because that allows me to kiss you?"

Her heart skipped a beat. She licked her lips, nervous anticipation making her stomach flutter. "In Ancient Rome a kiss was used as the legal bond to contracts, hence the use of a kiss at the end of a wedding ceremony to 'seal' the marriage vows."

He moved onto the seat beside her, and his heat beckoned. Taking her gloved hand, he raised it to his lips, asking huskily, "So what shall we agree to?"

Her breath caught. He smelled of musk and man and was so disarmingly amiable. There was no one to jump in to "protect" her. She reminded herself that she was an adult. And with that responsibility came a certain amount of freedom. Her curiosity, mixed with a small measure of wanting that contact with another, coalesced into a sense of daring. There seemed no reason not to indulge the abandon of a little kiss, especially when the rest of her life seemed so devoid of pleasure.

And Justin was just the safe person to allow her a taste of the forbidden fruit. He was kind and so delectably handsome, with his dimpled chin and lush lashes. Where was the harm?

"Let us agree not to settle for anything," she answered, her voice suddenly a thick whisper.

"No marriage, you mean?" He leaned in close.

"Anything."

He pressed his velvety lips against hers, and it happened again. She was lifted out from the quagmire of her worries and into the most titillating oasis of pleasure. He wrapped his strong arms around her and pressed his hard body against hers. Her body melted into him, drawing closer still. His lips parted slightly, and his tongue slipped into her mouth, lightly caressing her teeth. Surprised, she jerked back.

"I thought only rogues and scoundrels knew how to kiss like that," she gasped, only half-jokingly.

He gently stroked her arms with his palms, quieting her as one would a skittish colt. He moved his lips to her ear, deftly nibbling on her lobe and sending shivers racing down her spine. "All gentlemen *are* rogues and scoundrels, we simply dress better."

The corners of her lips lifted into a smile. Justin was unlike anyone she had ever known. He was certainly nothing like the lechers and fortune hunters she had endured in the past. He was straightforward, guileless, a man simply looking to enjoy a few innocent kisses. Well, perhaps not completely innocent.

He splayed light butterfly kisses along her jawline while running his hands down her back and pressing her closer still. "I do not see the harm in exploring simple diversions between friends, do you?"

Explore. She was endlessly curious and hungered to

understand the magic between a man and woman that led so many to tragedy. She would be in London a few short weeks. She might never have this safe opportunity to taste physical pleasures without someone trying to force her to compromise her life. She leaned back and caught his half-hooded gaze. "You do understand we cannot marry?"

"I would be a fool to think that I could tempt you into matrimony with a few kisses."

She sighed, reclining.

His minty breath tickled her throat as he continued, "I would need at least ten estates, hoards of cash, a villa in Italy. Oh, yes, and five or six juicy titles to tempt you." He nibbled on her ear.

She smiled and swatted his chest. "You toy with me!"

"That is the whole point, is it not? To play freely without Damocles' sword of marriage hanging over our heads?" He traced his finger along her neck, raising tingles down to her toes. "Uninhibited safe play between friends with the true understanding that we do not press for anything more than is freely given."

Ahh, the freedom of being able to explore her passion without the fear of being trapped, without Sully's or her father's disapproval tainting the experience. To have a delightful escape from reality. It was too enticing a lure.

She licked her lips, jumping off the cliff she prayed was as secure as it appeared. She stated breathlessly, "Show me."

"By your command."

She parted her lips and waited for his intimate caress. But instead of accosting her into a clinch, he gently took her bottom lip between his lips and sucked until all thoughts of rogues and scoundrels fled from her mind. A wonderful heat smoldered up her body, engulfing her in a flaming wave of desire. With his finger, he gently tilted her head and once again pressed his open mouth to hers. When his tongue flicked inside, touching hers, shocks of lightning electrified her senses, curling her toes. She quivered with delicate joy. Wanting to be nearer, wanting more of this tantalizing touch, she shifted closer on the short bench and banged her teeth against his.

"Ouch."

He pulled away.

"I am so sorry," she mumbled with embarrassment, holding her hand to her mouth.

He smiled, pulling her back against him. "Come here, Evelyn."

His use of her Christian name was an intimate caress to her ears. She allowed him to pull her closer. She tilted her head, and when his lips met hers, his tongue intertwined with her own, playfully bringing her senses to a new level of heated awareness. She had had no idea of the intensity and passion that could be evoked from a kiss. And what a kiss. Her nipples tingled, her skin warmed, and the most glorious tickling sensation unfurled in her belly. It made her want to taste more of him. She arched her back as the smoldering heat turned into an inferno radiating from her middle and rippling outward to every extremity. She lost all thoughts except those of his heat, his touch, his caress, and the promise of more pleasure.

The driver shouted and the coach rocked to a stop.

Justin slowly disengaged from her and looked out the window. "We are here."

"Where?" she asked, dazed, with her hands still clutching his strong arms.

"Belfont House."

She blinked. He slowly unpeeled her hands and shifted to sit across the carriage. The space beside her felt cold and empty with him gone.

Sighing, she adjusted her hat. All good things must come to an end.

The door opened and the stool was set. Ismet stood patiently outside, along with the rest of the real world.

She nodded slowly. "I thank you for escorting me here, my lord."

"Justin," he whispered as he took her hand and brushed a kiss across her palm. She shivered. Flashing a devilish smile, he added, "When we are alone it is Justin."

Her face heated. She had not known that she was still able to blush after her wanton display. "Will you be coming in?"

"I will leave you here, Evelyn. I have an appointment, much delayed, I'm afraid."

The dear man had waited for her for hours and deferred his own business out of thoughtfulness for her. "I am sorry to have kept you."

He smiled. "Well worth the delay, I assure you. In fact, I might be tempted to ask John Driver to take us on another round about the park."

"Although it is appealing, I do not wish to worry your aunt further." And she had pressing business with her father's journal upstairs. She paused in the doorway. "Another time perhaps?"

His grin was mischevious, "Anything you desire."

Unable to keep the smile from her lips, she raised her brow. "Anything?"

"If it is within my power."

She withheld her sigh. If only it were in his power to

make the world a saner and safer place. Evelyn turned and stepped out onto the walkway, inhaling the scent of horse and leather. She looked down the street at the rows of fashionable houses lit by the glow of the golden moon. But Justin was able to give her a pleasurable retreat from this chaotic world. For that she was grateful indeed.

Chapter 6

J ustin jumped from his carriage and bounded up the stairs to No. 60, St. James Street. After handing his hat, cane, and gloves to the footman, he entered the dark, wood-paneled main room of Brooks, his favorite club. He ignored the elegant furnishings and well-dressed members, immediately spotting Colonel Wheaton standing by the mantel, deep in conversation with a cluster of gentlemen. He squared his shoulders and slipped into the ruse that he and the colonel were acquaintances, members of the same club who occasionally happened upon each other. It allowed them to exchange information more frequently.

"Balderdash," exclaimed Captain Hasterby. "I see no reason why the troops require such supplies."

"Yes, they can live off the land," added Superintendent Garvey. "The country has substantial resources.

No need to make ducks and drakes of us all."

General Jacobs pulled out his enameled snuffbox and helped himself to a pinch. "Wellington is avoiding additional opposition from the populace when he invades. The man's a genius."

"Yes, stunningly good plan," intoned the colonel. He scratched his long white sideburns. "It will deprive the Paris government of local support. Wellington's no fool." He looked up, and his steely blue gaze noted Justin's appearance across the room. "I am off to the gaming room, gentlemen. I feel the need for a spot of cribbage."

"I did not know that they allowed such tedious play," yawned Lord Filbanks.

Colonel Wheaton set his snifter down. "Well, I'm an old man and do not like to learn new rules. Muddles an already cluttered brain."

"I heard that Banks and Tanner were playing Ecarte," Jacobs offered. "I'll warrant the stakes are high."

The group disbanded, some of the men continuing their conversation, while others drifted toward the gambling chamber.

Justin stepped forward. "I will join you, Colonel Wheaton."

The older man nodded. "Used to do quite well against your father, Barclay. We'll have a go."

They strolled into the gaming room, and Justin's lips quirked up as they always did upon seeing the unadorned walls. Horror, if anything, distracted the players.

As they settled in with their brandies and cards, Justin marveled at Wheaton's ability, any time of day or night, to get a quiet corner table separated from the rest of the players in the large, wood-paneled gaming room. He did it without an obvious word to anyone. But by this point, Justin should cease being surprised by the crafty master of spies.

"Any news?"

"Not much." Wheaton peeked from under bushy white brows. "You?"

Justin shook his head. His lips were pressed in a firm, hard line.

"How are you faring with the girl?"

He could not quite meet the man's eyes. "She does not seem the sort to be involved."

Wheaton sniffed. "You're not going soft on me, Barclay, now are you?"

"Most certainly not," he replied, annoyed. Just because he did not wish to discuss the intimate details of his relationship with Evelyn did not make him soft. "She is new to Town, knows no one, and is without resources. Most ladies of my acquaintance would be desperate and in tears. She simply seems resolved to make it to the next day. On her own." Why should it irritate him that she was so determined to proceed without assistance? Well, for one thing, it made his task all the more difficult.

"You like her," the old man charged. "Your mother must be thrilled."

"Actually, Mother has taken Miss Amherst into dislike." He made certain not to call Evelyn by her Christian name. Wheaton was too canny by far and would read too much into it.

The old man chuckled. "Leave it to your mother to ferret out the rotten fish. Looks and style cannot hide the chit's true nature. She is, or was, Amherst's darling."

Justin looked up, surprised. "You've seen her?"

"Only from afar. At the Coventry Ball. A pretty thing. Lucky for her she favors her mother."

Justin did not recall having seen the colonel at the ball. Then again, his focus had been elsewhere. He lay out his two cards into a crib.

Wheaton turned over a card, and his thick lips bowed into a scowl. "I still think the girl might lead us somewhere. Either her or Sullivan, when he shows."

"I have seen neither hide nor hair of him, and she is watched constantly."

"Do you think he will show?"

Justin looked down at his cards, barely seeing them. He nodded slowly, thinking of the conversation during his walk in the park with Evelyn. "Assuredly. Especially when he learns that Miss Amherst's inheritance is in doubt."

"So Marlboro is cooperating." It was a statement. The colonel would expect nothing less.

"The man will do whatever we say."

"Good. Then she really is without resources."

"Except, of course, for my doting family, which you so conveniently arranged for her." Justin was finding it hard to hold a grudge against the man. The plot was brilliant. It gave him every access to Evelyn and put her completely in his power.

The older man waved his gloved hand. "She'll be desperate soon enough. Keep a tight rein on her, see if she makes any contacts, sends notices to the papers and the like."

"I know how to do my job," he growled.

The colonel ignored him.

After a few moments, Justin offered, "She did run

into an old acquaintance. A Spaniard named Angel Arolas."

"Son of Juan Arolas. The father's working with Wellington. A dangerous man if he is your enemy, I understand. Smooth with the women, diplomatic with the men, and intelligent enough for two. Glad he's on our side, for now." He nodded and flipped a card. "I'll set a man to follow the son."

Justin rubbed his forehead worriedly. "We just need more information, and time is waning. You said you did not know much. What have you learned?"

"Just confirmed that the plot has something to do with the monetary system."

"Counterfeiting?"

Wheaton scratched a bushy white sideburn. "Can't see why they'd try that again. It's never worked for Napoleon in the past."

Justin clenched his fist. "I cannot fathom that all of our sources cannot scratch up more than that. We must stop the plan from proceeding before it's too late."

"*If* we can stop the plan. The thing may already be in motion."

He stated it so dispassionately that it made Justin want to pound his fists on the polished tabletop. Instead he flipped his cards and kept his voice low. "I cannot accept the view that we are powerless to prevent it. Every scheme has its weakness, the links upon which the chain of events must depend."

"You're just like your father. If he couldn't figure something out, he would look at it a thousand different ways until he unlocked the logic of the thing." Wheaton flipped his cards. "If it held his attention, that is."

Justin shifted his shoulders. "George was the brilliant one. Not me."

"Yes, your brother was quite intelligent, but you are better at strategy."

"Strategy will get us nowhere without information."

"Move up the timetable on the girl."

"There is only so much I can do to gain her trust without raising her suspicions. She is no fool."

"Add pressure."

Justin threw down his cards, irritated with the underbelly of this business. Where was the dignity in tormenting an unprotected young lady? "I will do the best I can."

"Good. And while you're at it, get me a new deck. This one is missing a few cards."

Justin felt as if a wave of ice water crashed over him and froze him on the spot. He stared at the colonel hard, trying to assess if the man was sending him a hidden message. "What did you say?"

The old man held up the deck innocently. "I need some new cards."

Justin forced himself to relax. The colonel did not know about his brother. He took a long, deep breath and compelled his heart to resume beating normally. Colonel Wheaton seemed unaware of the effect his play on words had had on the marquis.

A gray-haired wizened chap in a sober charcoal suit shuffled over. His reedy lips split into a loose, wide grin, exposing tobacco-stained teeth. "Now here's a game I can enjoy."

Justin stood and was mortified to feel his cheeks heat. "Sir Devane." He nodded, in awe of the wise, elderly gentleman who'd galvanized the spy trade at the Foreign Office years before.

Wheaton nodded but did not stand. "Lee. How are you, old man?"

Sir Devane's hazel eyes twinkled as he responded, "Speak for yourself, Wheaton, I might be as ancient as the hills but I can still beat you at cribbage." He raised a spotted hand to his temple. "I'd always taught you, it's here that makes the difference. You don't need brawny muscles to play the game."

Justin understood all too well what game he referred to, and he was slightly put off by Wheaton's lack of respect for his former mentor. Although Sir Devane had retired before Justin had begun his service, the old gent was a walking legend for having saved the empire innumerable times.

"You may have my seat, sir, I'm off to livelier amusements," Justin said as he held out the chair for him.

Eyes twinkling, the elder gent asked, "Nothing too dangerous, I hope?" Little escaped those canny hazel eyes. Justin wondered how much the man knew. Did he still keep his fingers in the till at two and seventy years?

Wheaton sipped from his brandy, commenting dismissively, "Nothing more dangerous than chasing lightskirts. Even a greenhorn could handle it."

For the first time in four years, Justin had the sudden urge to throttle his superior. The man's disdain was wholly uncalled for and unjust. Perhaps it was Wheaton's way of motivating his troops? If so, Justin was growing tired of the tactic.

"One can never be too careful when it comes to the ladies." The weathered man dropped into the seat with a slight groan and set his gold-topped cane against the table. "They are far cannier than we ever give them credit for. Why, one of my most wily adversaries was a great dame named . . ." At the scowl on Wheaton's face, the old gent shook his balding head. "Well, that's a story for another time."

"I will keep that pearl of wisdom in mind, sir. Good evening." Justin tipped his hat and moved off. Wheaton did not even acknowledge his departure.

At the threshold of the wood-paneled room, Justin turned and looked back. Through the clouds of smoke hovering over the card tables, he watched the two vastly different men playing their game. Although far from a stripling, Wheaton still had many years left in him. Yet he was burly and gruff, while Sir Devane, a weather-beaten man arguably on the shelf, could not be more jaunty or sanguine. Not for the first time Justin wondered what it would have been like working for the legendary Sir Lee Devane. He had been known for nurturing greatness in his budding apprentices. Justin speculated on how well he would have flourished under the man's tutelage. He sighed. Well, he would never know; Wheaton was the master of espionage now.

He turned, motioned to a footman nearby to deliver a new deck of cards to the two players, stepped out the door, and strode down the thick-carpeted hallway. Justin had to admit, Wheaton was exceedingly good at his job. He was the most results-oriented person Justin had yet to encounter. An unsavory feeling itched at his shoulders thinking of Evelyn in the colonel's sights. The colonel was not a man to cross, and somehow Evelyn had managed to secure a position on Wheaton's hit list.

He could not quite imagine her threatening the realm. Still, he realized that although he knew her fresh lavender scent, the press of her soft, lush form, and the velvety touch of her lips, he still knew very little about Evelyn. Distinct from most ladies of his acquaintance, she did not like to speak of herself overmuch. Yet, just as the colonel had charged, he liked her, in addition to being physically attracted to her. Too attracted for his own good, it seemed. He was growing distracted where she was concerned—something he could not afford to do.

Stepping out into the cool evening air, he pressed his handkerchief to his lips and stared down St. James Street, wondering which way to turn. If Colonel Wheaton's sources were correct, and they usually were, there was too much at stake to lose perspective where Evelyn was concerned. He squared his shoulders and strode down the steps, heading toward Jermyn Street. Nothing like a gaming hell to loosen men's pockets and their tongues. He should be able to scratch up more on this conspiracy. His efforts had to be worth something this night. He had a job to do and was not about to play the softee, beautiful woman or not. On one matter Justin was certain both of the older men at the card table would agree; duty to England came foremost and personal feelings only complicated the matter. Justin just had to trust that it would all shake out in the end.

Chapter 7

"Devil take it!"
Evelyn crumpled the paper into a ball and angrily threw it across the room to join a heap of others. She rose and stalked over to the curtains, throwing them open. Moonlight filtered in as clouds glided past. Even the open window could not give her enough fresh air to alleviate the crushing scents of burning candles, ink, and parchment.

She stretched her arms overhead and arched her back, feeling the blood warming her cramped muscles.

"What are you trying to tell me, Father?" she whispered to the starless night.

The crackling fire answered her with a resounding hiss.

She rubbed her weary eyes and resolutely closed the curtains. No one needed to know that she was still awake at, what was it? She last recalled the hall clock tolling the hour of three. She turned and lifted a basket and gathered up the scattered papers strewn around the room. Once the floor was cleared, she crouched before the fire and tossed each paper in and watched it burn, ensuring that nothing legible of her scribblings was left. Just as she had been taught.

Once her task was done she closed her father's black leather-bound journal and removed it from her secretary. She sat before the fire with the book in her lap. Slowly, she lay down, resting her head against the soft animal skin and inhaling the comforting scent of leather. It made her feel close to her father. This was her legacy just as much as any money. His handwriting, his words, his thoughts. She lay on the thick carpeting before the fire and stared unseeingly at the dancing flames.

She forced herself to remember the great diplomat and intelligence regular her father had been. Her earliest memories were of him overseeing the clearing of the house in Madrid. Or had it been Paris? No, it must have been Madrid, because she'd been about two. She had fallen climbing on one of the trunks, and she'd split her chin. She remembered the blood and crying and being lifted into his arms. He had carried her into the nursery. White linens. Bloodstains. Many servants running with wet cloths. He had held her and made her feel safe.

With her finger, she traced the scar on her chin, feeling the jagged slash. Odd. She could not recall the pain or the treatment, only the comfort he'd given. Where had Mother been at the time? Probably already in Paris, their next assignment. Mother had had a difficult time with the nomadic life. Even at a young age Evelyn had sensed the discord between her parents. Her father had been a thinker, a doer, and a man of action. Mother had been more of an amorphous being of beauty. She had loved to sing, paint, and play the harp. Evelyn could not recall her face very clearly. Angelic, beautiful. Long golden hair, blue eyes. The scent of roses. The sound of rustling silk when she'd moved with such grace. It had been only ten years since her mother's death, but it seemed to Evelyn she could only recall the earliest memories. She seemed to have a clearer recall of her nurse. Her nanny. Her governess. And Sully. There was always Sully.

Evelyn sent a prayer out to the man who had been so loyal to her family; so much so that he'd had to leave her. A tear slid from her eye and dripped into her ear. She rubbed the sleeve of her dressing gown across her eyes. What was happening to her? She never cried. And now twice in one night? Not even when she had held her long cold father in her arms. Not when she had closed up the last house and packed up her father's belongings. She sniffed. She was just feeling so dreadfully *alone*. She needed help. No. She just needed some companionship, a reprieve from worrying about spies, the future, money and death. If father were here he would be taking her out for a ride in the countryside to slough off her melancholy. It was an exercise for mind, body, and sagging spirit.

But no joyful afternoons appeared in sight. On the contrary, it looked as if she had an uphill battle ahead of her to counteract the malicious campaign against her father's name and her fortune. She was without friends, without resources, and so desperately lonely. She rolled her face onto the cover of the journal and sobbed. She did not care that her hot tears soaked the leather. Or that wracking howls broke free from her scratchy throat. Except for the fleeting pleasure of a few kisses, she did not relish her new role as self-sustaining adult. She sniffed.

Even if these tears meant she was weak, she was going to cry anyway. Father owed it to her. And so did the British government, it seemed. A loud hiccup erupted from her throat. She shuddered as the last upswell of tears slowly diminished. She pressed her cracked lips to the cover of her father's precious journal and kissed it, reverently. If Father were here he would be sketching out a plan of action. Strategizing his next move. Prepared to *play*.

"I am only as powerful as I choose to be." Her voice was barely more than a scratchy whisper.

Laying her head back down on the damp cover, she closed her eyes, exhausted, and fell into the dreamless sleep of the half-dead.

A hand pressed her shoulder, and Evelyn swatted it away.

"*Dogmak, Arife.*"

She opened one of her swollen eyelids not more than a slit and noted Shah bending over her. As usual, the squat maid was dressed head to toe in severe black and wore a judgmental scowl on her dark face.

Evelyn slowly sat up despite the fact that every muscle in her body screamed in protest. She rubbed her grainy eyes and licked her dry lips. Her mouth tasted like stale onions. "What time is it?"

"Seven. The house is stirring, although the upstairs, they sleep on." She helped Evelyn to her feet. "I come to check on you when I get up."

They walked over to the bed. With a sigh of relief,

Evelyn slipped between the covers. She leaned wearily against the plush pillows and closed her eyes. Abruptly she sat up.

"Father's journal!"

Shah held it in her hand and was wrapping it in a long, black cloth. "I have Sahip's book. You rest. I will keep it safe."

Evelyn nodded, relieved. She lay back down and closed her eyes, praying that when she awoke things would be better. She was counting on it.

Chapter 8

With the sunshine of a beautiful day to warm her spirits, Evelyn was glad she'd let Lady Fontaine convince her to attend the fair the next afternoon. And with little Miss Jane as her escort, a smile seemed permanently affixed to her lips. The child's exuberance was infectious.

"Ooh, Miss Evelyn, they have clowns," Miss Jane squealed excitedly. "And their dogs are wearing skirts!" She pulled at her cousin's hand and dragged her through the throng toward the green lawns, where the jokers were throwing colorful balls and the costumed dogs were chasing after them.

Evelyn allowed herself to be pulled through the squawking vendors with their delicious-smelling smoked meat pies, buttery sweets and pastries until they stood on the edge of the crowd witnessing the spectacle.

A face-painted entertainer wearing a red-and-purple sack tossed colored rings into the air. Little black-and-white spaniels barked and raced to snare the rings around their heads. The crowd of mostly children and governesses clapped and laughed with each of the little dogs' triumphs.

Evelyn opened her parasol to shade herself from the glare of the afternoon sun. All good things in moderation. There were few clouds drifting overhead and the sun bore into her black mourning gown, making sweat gather under her arms and down her back. Miss Jane clutched at her hand, and Evelyn's heart swelled. With her broad-rimmed pink bonnet, matching muslin high-waisted gown and jersey half-boots, she was the picture of feminine youth.

Miss Jane was so enraptured that she let go of Evelyn's hand for the first time in an hour and deigned to sit on the grass in her new gown with the other children. Jane's governess nodded to Evelyn, then sat down beside her charge. Evelyn sighed, enjoying the moment. Her earlier reservations about attending the fair had vanished, to be replaced by delight with the welcome diversion from her worries. No one could be melancholy while watching dogs frolic.

A fresh breeze blew in, bringing with it the scents of candied apples and caramel. She scanned the crowd of upturned faces gleefully watching the entertainment. Presently, she looked over at the artist stalls, where fashionable men and women perused the creations in search of the next great painter. Her gaze locked with a set of wary brown eyes. They belonged to a smut-covered face that had not seen a washbasin in a very long time. He stood lazily and wore a dark brown cap pulled low over his face, but those sharp eyes never rested, watching her as cagily as a fox watched its dinner. He pushed away from the stall and slowly approached. He could not be more than nine, with his scrawny arms, too short pants, and overlarge hands. Shifting between the crowd that did not notice him, he made his way across the lane toward her.

She turned back to the clowns and waited. A dog barked excitedly, and the children laughed. The boy shuffled close and brushed against her skirts. She did not move a hair's breadth.

"Now see here, you little scoundrel!"

Justin grabbed the urchin by the scruff of the neck and held him high. The poor boy's legs dangled, and he swung his arms uselessly at the angry marquis.

"Put him down, my lord," Evelyn demanded, angry with herself for not noticing Justin earlier. Noting the turned heads and the interested stares, she lowered her voice. "The boy did nothing wrong. Put him down."

"You may not know that anything is awry, but I assure you this boy just picked your pocket."

"He did not pick my pocket, as there was nothing therein to steal."

"That does not mean he did not try."

The boy valiantly struggled on. His cap slid over his eyes. His voice was a whiney squeak. "I dinna take nothing!"

Evelyn stepped closer, praying the boy would say no more. "You are causing a scene. Put him down, my lord."

"Why, so he can steal someone's watch? I think not. The boy belongs with the authorities, perhaps in an orphanage where he will have some oversight, as his parents are obviously immoral or inattentive."

The cap fell to the ground, exposing greasy black hair and brown eyes widened in terror. "You canna take me! Pa needs me! I swear I dinna take nothing! I jus—"

Evelyn's heart raced with alarm, and she jammed her finger into Justin's shoulder. "Put him down this instant or I will never forgive you!"

Justin slowly lowered the struggling boy to the ground but kept his hand locked around the urchin's neck. "You are too softhearted. He would steal your bonnet from your head if it would benefit him."

"Ya canna take me from my pa, he needs me," the boy cried. "He's sick in da head an' canna work." Fat tears slid down his dirty cheeks, creating streaks of misery.

Justin's eyes narrowed. He slowly crouched, lowering himself to eye level with the boy. "What did you say?"

The boy blubbered as thick tears brimmed from his eyes, "Can't work none, for the fits."

Justin studied him a long moment. Then the distinguished marquis of Rawlings slowly pulled his embroidered handkerchief from his coat pocket and held it out to the street urchin. With suspicion the boy looked at the square of snowy white linen, then grabbed it in his dirty hand. He lifted it to his nose and blew noisily.

"Come, boy," Justin ordered. He kept his hand on the urchin's shoulder and pressed him toward the vendors' stalls.

Following close behind, Evelyn asked worriedly, "Where are you taking him?" She scanned the crowds, knowing it was futile. No one saw Sully unless he wished to be seen. She was certain it was he who had sent the boy.

They stopped in front of a stand loaded with pies. The heady scents of seasoned cooked meats wafted around them. "Two meat pies, please."

"Yes, my lord."

Justin passed the meat pastries to the boy, who grabbed them with greedy hands. As Justin paid the man, the boy scampered off into the crowd.

Evelyn let go of the breath she was holding. Pressing her hand to the pocket of her pelisse, she felt the tiny piece of parchment folded inside. She tilted her head up and studied Justin. In his finely tailored goose gray wool suit, he was the personification of devilishly attractive English nobleman. But there was something about him, a hint of vulnerability she had never seen before. It seemed some inner demons resided in that stunningly perfect exterior. She certainly knew about societal armor protecting one from being vulnerable. Perhaps she could help him understand he was not so very alone.

He would not meet her eye, so she cleared her throat and began slowly, "When I was living in Barcelona, I felt the need to do something beyond painting and sketching and attending parties."

He stiffly adjusted his sleeves and did not respond.

"So I offered to sketch and paint at St. Job's."

He shifted his shoulders and scanned the crowd, looking anywhere but at her.

She rested her hand on his arm, and he froze. His hard muscles knotted under her light touch. He looked down at her black glove against the soft gray of his coat. He stared at her hand, long and hard, considering. The muscle jumped in his cheek, but otherwise he did not move.

"So, you see," she spoke softly, "although I can never truly understand, I recognize that simple kindness is the greatest balm to ease the suffering of others' pain."

He slowly looked up. Greenish-gray eyes locked with hers, and in their smoky depths she saw his anguish and was touched by it.

"Come, my lord. Let us walk." She slipped her hand into the crook of his arm.

After hesitating a moment, he nodded and fell into step beside her.

They passed the vendors and street performers but did not see them. They came to a cluster of trees and lingered in the welcome shade. They were hidden from the sun and the crowds and the prying eyes. Evelyn closed her parasol and leaned against a scratchy tree trunk. Justin stood near, picking at the bark of the adjacent tree with his gloved hands, lost in thought.

Suddenly, he shifted and leaned against the tree beside hers. He restlessly toyed with a chunk of bark.

"Do you wish to tell me about it?" she asked softly. "Was it your father who was ill?"

"We do not speak of it," he stated harshly. He shrugged. "What would be the use?"

"To help those coping with the illness, for one."

"It was my dear brother. And he's dead, so why slander his name?"

"There is no disgrace to illness, Justin," she chided gently.

He crushed the bark in his fist and tossed it away.

"Of course there is, especially when, well, especially if . . ." his voice trailed off with distress.

"You fear that it is in the blood?"

He shrugged and looked away.

She blew out a long breath of air and watched as bunches of dark clouds gathered on the horizon. It seemed the weather was never constant in London. "I do not know what to say, other than I have no doubt that you are not mad. A bit gruff sometimes, a little too free with your kisses, but certainly not cracked in the head."

He looked at her a moment. Then his lips bowed into a slight smile, wrinkling his eyes at the corners.

She stepped closer and leaned her forehead against his broad chest. "Justin, everyone has their crosses to bear. I am just so very sorry."

He wrapped his arms about her and squeezed gently, holding her close. She pressed her nose into the soft wool of his coat. He smelled of musk and Justin, a warm and woodsy scent of which she was growing fond.

He rubbed his hand up and down her back, as if to comfort her. She understood that he was trying to soothe himself. He not only had to deal with the responsibilities of his title and family but he also had to overcome the nightmare of dealing with mental illness. And he had a dragon lady for a mother. Evelyn could give Lady Barclay a little more leeway. The woman could not have had it easy, even if she was a witch.

Justin pressed his chin against Evelyn's soft, golden hair, wondering why he had told her about George. He never spoke of his brother's illness. No one did. It was too painful. Too close. Too dangerous. Part of him was relieved to discuss it and not have her withdraw, repulsed. The other part of him felt vulnerable and afraid. What made him share one of his most private secrets with a stranger? A woman who might be involved in traitorous activities? Fear welled up in his chest. How could she use this information against him?

She snuggled closer into the circle of his arms, and his fears quelled. She was not an evil woman. If anything at all, she was likely an innocent caught up in a dangerous mess.

The faint scent of lavender always surrounded her like a bouquet. Never too much. Not perfume. Bathwater, more likely. The thought of warm water running down her naked body stirred him and made him remember that crowds were just paces away.

He gently shifted her away from him. "This is . . . indiscreet."

"Yes, how Society frowns upon human comfort."

"It was not human comfort which made me realize the danger."

"You were hoping to dispense more of those free kisses?"

"They are not free," he stated with a small chuckle. "I require you to repay me in kind."

"Let me know when the piper comes calling." She popped her parasol open and stepped away from him and the trees. "Until then."

She strolled back toward the amusements, and Justin watched the luscious swell of her derriere as she gracefully swayed down the lane. He had to marvel at the enigma of the woman who had been haunting many of his daytime moments—and the nocturnal ones as well.

She joined the audience of children, and Jane jumped up and ran to her. The child chattered on excitedly, and Evelyn listened with fond patience. He noted that even little worried Jane found harbor in association with Evelyn. He smiled. She was strong and intelligent, too independent-minded, by far. But there was a loving softness, a caring to her that made him want to bury his head in her chest and just *be* with her. Not the marquis of Rawlings or George's brother or the colonel's intelligence man. Simply Justin.

He blinked; these thoughts were so beyond the realm of his experience. It suddenly hit home: he had just poured his heart out to the lady he was supposed to be ensnaring into telling *her* secrets. Could she truly be a spy intent on destroying his country? Was it all just an enchanting facade? His heart began to pound and his mouth dried to dust. Was he allowing himself to be duped? Failing at his duty in more ways than one?

He studied Evelyn as she conferred with his aunt Leonore. They were smiling at each other, obviously enjoying each other's company. Doubt haunted him. He needed to think. He needed to sort this all out. He prayed he would realize Evelyn was not what he feared her to be. Watching the sun shimmer on her golden hair, he knew he needed to get away from her to see her clearly. He turned and strode down the lane, putting distance between himself and the woman who seemed to be turning his world on its axis.

Another set of eyes watched him go and then turned back to Evelyn with critical scrutiny. The face-painted clown slipped away from the other entertainers and casually sidled toward the entrance of the park. He studied the crowd with the guardedly trained eyes of a professional, but his mind was on the scene behind him, trying to understand what on earth Evelyn was doing consorting with the enemy.

Chapter 9

Justin ran the hard-bristled brush down Cheshire's flanks and followed it with the soft sweep of his hand. The golden-brown coat gleamed in the lamplight. The stallion neighed softly with pleasure and shifted, rustling the hay beneath his hooves. All was quiet in the stable; the laborers knew when to leave their employer to his solitude.

Cheshire turned his head and watched his master with his large golden orbs. Then, obviously bored with the distraction, he turned back to chewing lazily on his oats.

Justin squatted and rubbed his hands up and down the stallion's legs, feeling the corded muscles underneath his palms. Nothing settled him and allowed him an opportunity to reflect like grooming his horse. He knew every cleft in Cheshire's back and hindquarter, better almost than he knew his own body. He inhaled the comforting scents of horse and hay and leather and manure, trying to purge the uneasiness plaguing him.

He stood and rubbed his palm on the soft, short hairs between Cheshire's eyes, seeking solace.

"Why can't I seem to think with a clear head where Evelyn is concerned?" he asked his beloved mount. "Is she a siren, intent on enslaving me?" Recalling her loving charm with Jane, her easy smile, and her quick wit, his heart warmed. Her compassion reached so far as to include a destitute street urchin. None in his family, himself included, would have deigned to assist such as he. Picturing his mother's manner with the lower-level servants made him grimace. Consideration was certainly not her long suit. "Or am I drawn to her simply because I've finally found someone who is the exact opposite of my mother?" Attracting him to her like a moth to flame.

His position was becoming precarious. His assignment was to get Evelyn to spill her father's secrets, and possibly her own. Yet it was he who was opening up. He was the one disclosing potentially dangerous truths better left undiscovered. And he had yet to procure a shred of information from Evelyn.

He pursed his lips, considering. It had been two weeks already, and still he felt as if she were very much a mystery yet to be solved. It was decidedly odd how little she divulged about herself. Indignation pricked at him. Why had she shared so little of herself when he had ostensibly coughed up his life? Did she not trust him? He laughed aloud, but it wasn't a pleasant sound. Of course she could not trust him. It was his job to bring her down.

Closing his eyes, he rested his forehead on Cheshire's shoulder. Inhaling his mount's rich scent, he tried placing Evelyn in a category in his mind that was distinct from his feelings. He tried imagining that he was Colonel Wheaton but could not quite conceive of himself in the ruthless spymaster's shoes. Instead, he pretended he did not care for her one whit, and perused their discussions as if reading from a book. Detached, clearheaded, with everything defined in black or white.

He read through the meeting at the quay, the ride in the carriage, the walk in the park, the various visits at his aunt's, the evening she visited her solicitor, the Coventry Ball. Every time the thought of her lips, her touch, or her scent invaded his mind, he quickly flipped the page to the next discussion. Finally he came to today's chapter, the fair in the park. His mind froze above the page, seeking something but not knowing what. He breathed deeply; doubt nagged at him. Out of focus, yet somewhere on the page, was the key, just waiting for him to see it.

The boy. If he did not pick Evelyn's pocket, then why had he stepped so close? Justin had seen his hand brush against her skirts. What had she said? *"He did not pick my pocket, as there was nothing therein to steal."* Was? He hammered his palm into his forehead, damning himself for being so stupid. He had been so caught up in his own pitiful saga that he had missed the exchange. A note, most likely. He ground his teeth in frustration. He had missed the opportunity to catch Sullivan when time was critical. He had been distracted from his duty—the worst mistake an intelligence regular could make.

What was the note's purpose? To set a meeting? To arrange for passage? Perhaps to gain her some help with her funds? To solicit her aid with the plot? He had to find out Sullivan's plans. He had to stop Napoleon's scheme from proceeding. And the linchpin to all of these tasks was Evelyn.

The colonel was right. Justin had allowed her appeal to get to him, to make him lose sight of his purpose. He needed to apply more pressure. Shake her confidence, make her turn to him, put her completely in his power. He picked up the large comb and tugged at the knots in Cheshire's mane. The horse snorted, protesting loudly, and Justin realized that he was being too rough. Disgusted with himself, he threw the comb into the bucket, reset the gate, and strode from the stables. The gloves were off. He no longer had the option of being the refined gentleman. He was the colonel's man and it was time to start acting like it. Or he could close the book entirely on thwarting the French conspiracy. Something he was not about to do.

Chapter 10

❦

"**S**o you see, Miss Amherst, you must consider your future," intoned Lord Fontaine. He craned his neck and adjusted his head in the overlarge neckpiece. Evelyn wondered how he could breathe in the contraption. Turning to his wife, he said, "Leonore will gladly help you in moving about in Society. And even though it is not an enormous settlement, with our connections, you can surely secure a match."

Not enormous? It was pitiful. But that did not matter, since she would not use it.

He droned on, "You are quite pretty, if a bit old. You will do well under Leonore's fine tutelage."

Uncomfortable silence enveloped the room.

He raised his quizzing glass to his eye. "Haven't you anything to say?"

The man obviously expected her undying gratitude. Well, he was providing the roof over her head, for the moment.

Evelyn picked an imaginary piece of lint off her black skirts. "I find it interesting that the root of the word 'wedding' means 'to gamble' or 'wager.'"

The balding man blinked. "What's that, you say?"

She stared him square in the eye. "I will not gamble my future away simply to have a man's name attached to mine. I am perfectly content with my own name, thank you."

"You know that you are welcome to stay with us as long as you like, my dear." Aunt Leonore patted her green silk turban and smiled reassuringly. "Jane will be thrilled, and so would I, to have you remain."

"Remain? We are talking about her finding a husband, Leonore." Lord Fontaine sniffed disapprovingly. "I do wish you would stay with the conversation, you have the most irritating habit of losing sight of the topic before you."

She placed her hand over her husband's. "Evelyn does not seem interested in considering marriage at this time, darling. Her father only recently passed . . ."

"Not interested," he sputtered. "But she's two and twenty. And it is almost the end of her period of mourning. What will she do then?"

The man was probably terrified by the thought of having a poor relation living off him for the rest of his days.

Evelyn stated quietly, "I assure you that I will not remain indefinitely."

Lord Fontaine nodded approvingly. "Of course you won't. We will find you a match, don't you worry."

"If that is all, my lord?"

"Yes, well." He stood and held out a note. "You received this letter from your solicitor."

Evelyn knew that she should read it in private, but she was too anxious to receive news, especially after listening to the well-intentioned Lord Fontaine. She opened the note and read the lines that were barely more than a scrawl. Her heart sank.

Miss Amherst,

Regretfully, we have no progress to report other than, at a minimum, the matter will be tied up for at least another six to eight months.

> *Yours, Mr. Tuttle,*
> *Writing on behalf of Mr. Marlboro*

The frump had not even had the decency to scratch out the foul letter himself. She shoved the parchment into her pocket. She was finished with the ineffectual Mr. Marlboro.

Lord Fontaine clapped his hands together. "I will make a list of potential husbands, and we will all review it together. Can't say that I haven't learned anything being the father of four daughters. They always seem to have an opinion about everything."

Evelyn scrunched her face into a fake smile and stood. "I am going riding this afternoon, so please excuse me."

As she glided up the steps, she wondered just how much longer she would have to impose on her distant cousins. She ran into Shah in the upstairs hall.

The stout woman was wringing her hands with worry. "Arife, it is terrible."

"What is it, Shah?"

Evelyn's heart fluttered with fear as together they headed toward her chamber. What now? They entered her room, and it was immediately apparent that someone had searched the apartment. Her books were scattered on the floor, her wardrobe doors hung open, and the drawers of her secretary yawned wide. Even her papers lay spread like a fan on the wooden desktop.

A pit of anger roiled in her stomach. They had not even tried to be unobtrusive, as if there couldn't possibly be anything to fear from an unprotected, destitute young lady. Well, if she got her hands on the offensive beasts, then she would give them reason to fear her. She realized that her hands were fisted so tightly that her nails were biting into her palms. She purposefully unfurled her fingers and straightened her back.

"I am so sorry, Arife," Shah wailed. "I was told you needed me downstairs. When I went, I could not find you."

Evelyn shook her head. "This is not your fault." Thank heavens she had burned Sully's note. She walked over to the hearth and examined the grate. No trace.

Your friends are your enemies. Be wary.

Be wary.

Tell her something she didn't already know. She shook her head. At least she knew Sully was in London. Nearby. Just the thought of him being close was a comfort.

Anger gripped her in what felt like a vice of iron. "Father's journal!"

"I go check." Shah ran to her room next door.

Evelyn held her breath. She could not lose her father's diary; it would be too awful. He had been so confoundedly insistent that she keep it safe.

"It is here," Shah proclaimed triumphantly, holding the black-wrapped package high in her hand.

Evelyn let out a thankful sigh. "They probably didn't think to search your chamber."

"Or no time. I was only gone a small bit."

Evelyn put her head in her hands. What to do next? She looked up. "Keep it, Shah. Protect Father's book. I hate to have to ask you, but if you can, please stay in the rooms." She could not quantify the worth of her father's journal.

Shah clutched the package to her middle. "I don't like going below. Ismet brings my food." She nodded vigorously. "I stay."

"Thank you, Shah."

Evelyn closed the door firmly and examined her dressing table. Her jewelry was all in order. Apparently they had no interest in the meager possessions that meant the world to her. She sighed and began gathering the books up off the floor. At Shah's miserable expression she admonished softly, "Stop fretting, Shah. You did not make this mess, and there seems to have been little damage done."

A knock resounded at the door. Evelyn sent a warning look to Shah, and the maid scurried next door with the journal.

"Come."

Miss Myrtle entered. "Lord Barclay is here to see you, Miss Amherst." She looked around the room. "I will order the upstairs maid to clean your room at once."

She glared at the lanky woman and rose. "Do not be presumptuous." She brushed her black skirts. "Please tell Lord Barclay I will be down in a thrice."

Miss Myrtle stared at her a long moment and then curtseyed. "Yes, my lady."

Evelyn watched her go, suspicion haunting her mind. Miss Myrtle? Or that footman who always seemed to be watching her? There was no point in guessing. It could have been anyone. There was little harm they could do at the moment. She shook her head. She had to somehow collect her fortune and leave. To come out from the shadow of her father's business.

"Shah, help me dress, please. I'm going riding."

"You go with the handsome prens?"

"I told you, Shah, he is not a prince." Shah had taken a liking to Barclay.

"He is . . ." Shah slipped into her native tongue, *"erkek, comert . . ."*

"Yes, he is manly."

"So why do you not go to him for help?"

Evelyn looked at her beloved servant and observed that her maid's black hair held more traces of gray than she last recalled. Was she expecting too much of Shah? The woman was not as young as she used to be. Evelyn tried to figure how old Shah might be. She had begun working for the Amhersts when Evelyn was twelve. That was ten years ago. The Turkish woman had not been young even then, but with her dark skin and solid figure, it was hard to tell.

"I will not let anything happen to us, Shah."

"But you need a man. A sahip."

Evelyn blew out a long breath and squeezed the older woman's arm. "We have been over this before, Shah. I do not need a man to take care of me. We'll be alright." She heard the quiver in her voice and prayed that her claims were more than whispering protests amidst the howling wind of peril. If anything, Father had taught her that self-reliance was the only saving grace. But then again, where had that led him?

Chapter 11

As the horses meandered down the lane, slipping into the alleyway behind long rows of fashionable houses, the sun dipped below the rooftops, cloaking them in afternoon shadow.

"Where are we going, my lord?" Evelyn asked. "We did not pass this way before."

"To my stables. I wish to show you something," Justin replied over his shoulder. His stallion swooshed his tail at a nagging horsefly and increased his pace, nearing home.

Despite her growing reservations about time running away from her, Evelyn allowed her horse to be led to a small clearing, where she accepted the stable hand's assistance in dismounting. She straightened her black habit and adjusted the brim of her black hat, waiting while Justin conferred with his stable master.

She inhaled a deep breath of air, attempting to cool her trepidation over taking so long to get back to Belfont House.

She felt vulnerable being out and about while her enemies plotted against her. She kept staring into the shadows, foolishly expecting danger to jump out at her. Her heart leapt when a pigeon swept overhead. Swallowing, she raised her hand to her chest, trying to slow the hammering of her heart. Coolheadedness in the face of adversity kept one alive, Sully had always advised her. She forced herself to calm.

Luckily they were only a few blocks away from Lord and Lady Fontaine's residence. She tried to focus on the comforting scents of horse and leather and ignore the sickly sweet odor of the stable hands as they labored proficiently around her. But uneasiness made her shift in her boots. Again, she felt herself in a pool of her own seclusion, wondering just what she was doing at Justin's stables. The real issue, however, was what she was *not* doing: finding a way out of the labyrinth of securing her fortune and leaving England for safer shores.

The ride had been pleasant enough but had not erased the worry that plagued her. She needed to figure the best means of freeing her legacy, but to do so, she had to face the fact that someone was tormenting her and she did not understand why. What had Father been embroiled in that had ended his life so abruptly and placed her future in jeopardy?

She pulled herself back to the moment as Justin strode toward her and proffered his arm. He looked elegantly handsome in his brown doeskin breeches and shiny black riding boots. Even his coat was cut to enhance his broad shoulders and narrow waist. He was *comert*, manly, just as Shah had proclaimed.

Moreover, he was the kindest of gentlemen. She wished she could have met him under better circumstances. She would have liked to enjoy his splendid company without always looking over her shoulder. He deserved better, and so did she.

They walked along in silence, Ismet trailing behind. The Turk seemed to have worn a constant glower ever since Evelyn had told him about the search of her rooms. He was on edge, and she could not blame him. Yet he held no words of criticism for her conduct thus far. Instead, he asked her once again to carry a knife on her person and cautioned her to be wary. Father had always liked Ismet for his focus on action above all else. She had ignored her trusty servant's advice regarding the knife, however, believing that she ought to be safe in broad daylight with Justin. Whoever was plaguing her seemed devious but not intent on harming her person, just rattling her confidence. She pictured her nemesis as a shriveled-up rat dressing in a dark men's suit with an intricately tied, constrictive neck cloth, sitting behind a large black desk rubbing his spiky claws together in glee as he plotted mischief. Cowardly, underhanded, and afraid of being seen in the light of day—that was her enemy.

In the shade of the buildings they came upon an odd structure pocketed inside a narrow alleyway between two tall houses. The edifice was squat and square in the midst of rows of lofty, rectangular buildings. It had stubby windows and a covered entrance, shrouded in gloom.

"What is this place?" she asked warily.

Justin took out a key and approached the stubby wooden entry. He unlocked it and pushed it open. It squeaked noisily.

Frowning at the hinges, he commented, "I will have someone oil that straightaway."

He turned to her and extended his hand. She watched him a long moment. He had been remote, aloof, and a bit cool this afternoon. Evelyn had assumed that her mood clouded her perceptions, but suddenly suspicion reared in her mind.

"What place is this, Justin?"

Still holding his hand out to her, he let out a long breath. "It is my brother's private place. Was. Was his private place."

She blinked. She had been so caught up in her own worries that she had not realized that Justin was battling demons of his own. That he was reaching out to her and she was simply too preoccupied with herself to recognize his unseen struggle. She bit her lip. She was going to have to do better being a friend to this man who had opened himself to her. She recognized that his admission the prior afternoon had been some sort of breakthrough for him. That he had shared a painful family secret that tore at his gut and that he was treading on unfamiliar ground.

She slipped her gloved hand into his and followed him through the threshold. She was amazed to find herself amidst rows and rows of colorful books of all shapes and sizes. They were jammed and piled in haphazard array on tall bookshelves that spanned every wall of the narrow room. A window wedged in the corner of the ceiling provided shadowed afternoon light.

"I have not touched anything, except to have it cleaned," he commented tightly.

They stepped through a doorway and into a comfortable parlor, where a fire burned brightly in the hearth. The scent of cloves hung heavily in the air. Evelyn turned about the room, noting the mismatched plaid chairs, plush oriental carpets, and long green sofa with well-worn wooden legs. The furniture was obviously for comfort, not show. The focal point of the room, however, was the hand-carved secretary that sat in the corner near the fire. From across the tiny space, one could easily see the beauty of the piece. The intricate legs were carved in the shapes of jungle animals. Monkeys wrapped their arms around tree branches that became elephant trunks that wound around and turned into tigers' tails.

"It is magnificent," she stated as she walked toward the desk. She pulled off her gloves and crouched. She traced her fingers down the elaborate wooden legs. "What wood is this?"

"Mahogany."

"Beautiful," she breathed. The delicate giraffe's ears poked under her fingertips.

She looked up. He stood there, transfixed as stone, staring at her. Why did she suddenly feel as if she was being examined for imperfections? Was he afraid of exposing too much? Did he fear her response?

She stood. "This is a very special place."

"I had the rooms cleaned this morning," he stated gruffly. "They had not been used for a very long time. Almost five years." He turned and tossed his hat onto a chair. A line of flat hair ringed his short-cropped brown mane. She longed to ruffle it out.

He grabbed a log and pitched it into the grate, and the flames jumped and crackled. "We did not know of this place until after . . ." His voice trailed off. He shifted his shoulders and remained crouched staring into the fire. ". . . until after George died."

"What happened to your brother?"

"George was the eldest. He was the marquis of Rawlings, not me. I was never meant to be. He was brilliant. A star that shined so brightly. Mother adored him." He looked around the room with detachment. He stood and toyed with a golden clock sitting atop the mantel. "Apparently he used to come here often, to be, when he was . . . not feeling himself." He set the clock down and turned. "He must not have been feeling himself when he took a pistol and used it to shoot himself in the head."

She let out a long, painful breath. Her heart weighed heavy with sadness for him. "I am so sorry."

He sat on the edge of the sofa, his eyes staring unseeing into the fire. "It was at our estate in Bedford." He shifted his shoulders. "It was a long time ago, but I remember it like it was yesterday. We said it was a hunting accident. No one knows the truth, except for a handful of people. Where's the point in saying otherwise?"

She could not imagine the anguish of living with such pain, and such secrets. She knew too well the bitter taste of both and did not wish that on anyone. The poor man was struggling mightily with his demons. Trying to exorcise the past and free himself for living. Evelyn had noticed Justin's reserve, his apparent aversion to enjoying life too much, his reluctance to expose too much of himself in any endeavor. Did he think that he did not deserve to be happy?

He stood abruptly and held out the key. "It's for you."

She blinked. "What?"

"This place is for you."

He shoved it into her hand. The heavy metal was cold in her naked palm. "I do not understand, Justin."

"You seem in need of . . . an escape. You will not accept my assistance, yet you obviously have concerns that weigh heavily on your mind. I wanted to give you a place where you are free. A place all your own, where you can be yourself."

That was what Justin needed, not her. But as she stared at the golden key in her hand, it shifted and blurred. She raised her fingers to her face. Wet, hot tears streaked her cheeks.

"I am a fool," he said as he stepped closer and enveloped her in his arms. "I should not have done this."

She shook her head but could not move it much, as she was pressed against the soft wool of his black riding jacket. There it was again, that woodsy, musky scent. She inhaled deeply of him and cleared her throat.

Her voice was muffled. "No. It's just that, well, this is the most precious gift anyone has ever given me. To think of me and my needs so unselfishly . . . it is a testament to the kind of man you are."

His arms suddenly squeezed her so hard that she found it difficult to breathe. He released her and turned away so abruptly that she almost fell, but she caught herself on the edge of the couch.

He grabbed the poker and angrily jabbed at the flames in the hearth. "You always attribute such valiant character traits to me," he charged harshly.

"But if they suit?"

He might wish to deny it, but he was one of the most wonderfully kindhearted men she'd ever encountered.

He stabbed at the flames as if to slaughter them. "I am no hero."

She tilted her head, considering his words. Yes, it seemed that he *was* a bit of a hero to her. A quiet hero struggling to overcome his haunted past. A civilized man in a world of lies and betrayal. A friend who offered himself and demanded nothing in return.

"I am going to miss you, Justin."

He froze, the poker hanging motionless in his hand. "Where are you going, Evelyn?"

Had she just said that aloud?

She shook herself.

He turned to her. "When do you intend to leave, and where are you going?"

She sighed and sat on the big green sofa. "I do not know to both."

"Do you not like England?" he asked tensely.

Folding her arms about her, she rubbed her palms up and down her arms. "I am getting the sense that England does not like me."

He sat beside her on the edge of the couch. "Why would you say such a thing?"

She stared into the golden flames for a long moment. The fire crackled in the silent room. She realized that she did not want Justin involved in her father's business. The world she was forced into by virtue of her birth was one of trickery and mayhem. She wanted Justin to remain free, protected, unsullied by the nasty games. She should get back to Belfont House. Back to strategizing her next move. Looking around the room, she stole a moment to imagine it just as Justin meant it to be; an escape from worries. Her eyes fixed on a closed wooden door. "What's in there?"

When he did not answer, she turned to him. His smoky, gray-green eyes were watching her, considering. It was as if he were waiting for her to say something. She wished she had something more to give him, something more to share that would make him understand how much she cherished him. But she refused to endanger him by cluing him in on her perilous situation. She cared for him too much for that.

Finally, he looked away. "It's nothing. A storeroom."

"We should probably head back. I do not wish to worry your aunt." Or Shah.

"She can wait."

Perhaps it was to divert his mind or simply to make himself feel better, but he leaned close and kissed her full on the mouth, his soft lips crushing deliciously against hers. She sighed, parting her lips and welcoming the diversion herself. This, at least, she could give him. He slipped his tongue demandingly inside. For her, it was a welcome reprieve, a taste of what it might be like to be a normal woman. One who could enjoy the love of a man. She wanted to know what she was missing, to have her one chance at a tryst.

She relished his woodsy flavor. She could not identify it, but it pleased her. He shifted closer. His kisses were more demanding than before, more insistent. His tongue intertwined with hers, and it was as if he stroked her whole body with that single caress. Heat smoldered and burned from her toes to the tips of her fingers, making her yearn to be free of her clothes. She clutched at him and stroked his hard, muscled back with her palms, relishing the feel of soft wool under her fingertips. Pushing her back into the couch, he lay heavily on top of her. She tilted her head up, wanting more of his mouth. Pulling him down, she laughed into his parted lips.

He reared up. "Why do you laugh?"

"Because kissing you is the only escape I require."

He stared at her another moment and then lowered his head and kissed her soundly on the lips, stealing the breath from her mouth. He took her lower lip into his mouth and sucked it lightly. She writhed beneath him, feeling like she was on fire. He ran his hands down her waist to her thighs and kneaded the soft flesh of her buttocks. Her hips rocked instinctively in response. Heat pooled between her legs, and she felt a driving need burning her, pressing her forward, and egging her on. He pulled at her skirt and inched it up. She shifted beneath him to give him more room, wanting him to touch her everywhere. She was open to him. Safe, free, and not so dreadfully alone for the moment. She was intent on enjoying it.

He lifted his head up and, using his teeth, tore his glove from his hand. He yanked the other hand free from the leather and hovered above her on his hands and his knees, staring down at her. His smoldering eyes roved over her face, chest, then waist, then below.

"What?" she asked self-consciously.

He lowered his head and kissed her breast.

"Oh."

He moved his mouth over the soft mound and bit her nipple through the fabric.

She arched her back and moaned.

He nibbled and teased her hard nub through the cloth, and the muscles between her thighs contracted wildly.

He rained kisses down her belly, to her thighs, and she wondered where he was going. Her chest felt cold and empty without his pressure. She wanted him back up at her breasts—that was, until he slipped his hand under her skirt. She almost jerked at the smooth touch of his agile fingers on her stocking.

She froze, waiting, wondering, wanting.

He traced his fingertips up her calf, dancing around her knee, and he tickled her thigh. She held her breath.

Her heart was racing like a thoroughbred. She licked her lips, knowing that she should stop him, should run back to the safety of her staid bluestocking existence. But she was feeling reckless, free from the burdens of suspicion and worry. His hand lightly caressed her inner thigh. It was barely a touch, raising the fine hairs around her most private place.

He pressed his hand over her *there* and stilled. He was breathing in harsh gasps, and she realized that he was affected as well. That touching her brought him pleasure—or, looking at his face, was it pain? She noted the large bulge pressing against his britches, and her stomach lurched with desire. She wanted to touch him. To know the feel of a man. She reached out, but he cried harshly, "No. Only you."

Before she could challenge him, his deft fingers opened the folds of hot flesh between her thighs. Her eyes widened, and her jaw dropped. He rubbed his fingers up and down in her wetness. He watched her with parted lips, his breath coming in short puffs.

Her eyes closed of their own accord. "Oh my dear Lord in heaven."

He groaned.

He found her nub, and electrifying thrills rocked her. With his nimble hand still performing its magic, he leaned forward and pressed his open mouth to hers. His tongue felt thicker, hotter, more insistent as he dove into her mouth. She rolled her hips and moaned, wallowing in the wildness of his touch. She pulled his tongue into her mouth and sucked passionately. Pressure was building inside her, pushing her, pressing her. His slipped his finger inside her wetness and her muscles jumped and contracted, closing around him and gripping him tightly.

Her breath came in short gasps and her head was on fire. Tremors rippled from between her legs outward, bursting with intense contractions of joyous rapture. She threw her head back and screamed.

The crashing heat slowly simmered. The pounding in her chest slowed, as if she had just ended a long race—definitely a winner. She opened her eyes and blinked, sucking for air. She puffed in little breaths, trying to get more air to her tortured lungs. She could not move, her muscles felt like dead weight. Justin pulled his hand from under her skirts and sat up.

A window near the ceiling showed clouds gliding by in the small space between the tall buildings. How long had passed? Had she stepped into another time? She looked over at the man who had just altered her perception of the world. Justin.

He stared into the fire and cleared his throat. "I did not intend . . . I went too far."

She pursed her lips, considering. Too far or not far enough? She had undeniably wanted him inside her. She had never before understood the need to have a man between her thighs, the passion, the heat, the wanting of that one particular man.

"I apologize for taking advantage." He shook his head. "It's just, well, you do not want anything from me . . ."

"What do you mean?"

"You are new to Town, to this country, and excuse my interference, but you are somewhat out of your element and yet you ask nothing of me. Most people of my acquaintance want something, whether it be social, financial, or," he frowned, "otherwise."

She could not quite imagine what the "otherwise" might be.

"But you," he continued, "are so self-reliant. You offer your friendship and ask for nothing in return. I must confess, I am a bit awed by you."

She blinked. Dear heavens, she had just been lamenting her situation and he was praising her for it.

"I have no choice, Justin," she confessed quietly.

"Do not give me that tripe, Evelyn. You are alluring enough to sweep any man off his feet. You could have dukes and princes if you wanted. And here I am ruining your chances," he finished remorsefully.

She would have laughed if it were not so sad. She did not want to manipulate a man into matrimony; she could not do to another what she feared the most. She shuddered just to consider being so vulnerable, so exposed as to give another power over her. That was her greatest fear: exploitation, manipulation, and abandonment. Especially within the bounds of marriage, where the man held all the power under the law. She would not wither away in despair, as her mother had seemed to.

He slowly turned to her. "Do you hate me?" His eyes looked grayer in the darkened room. Perusing his swollen, sweet lips and his broad back, she knew that she could be with him and be safe. That if she had the opportunity to taste forbidden pleasures, then she would grasp it with all her might.

"We agreed, nothing taken that is not freely given," she stated promptly as she sat up and adjusted her skirts.

His brow furrowed. "You are an innocent—"

"Although I've never experienced anything remotely like what I just felt moments ago, have no doubt, I wanted it very much to happen." She shook her head, amazed. "It was astoundingly instinctual. It was as if my body was an instrument and you knew the exact keys to play. Extraordinary."

He stared at her a moment, and then a small chuckle rumbled from deep in his belly. "You are the one who is extraordinary, Evelyn. Every time that I think I might begin to understand you, you surprise me again."

She shrugged. "It must be my unorthodox upbringing. Too many countries, nannies, and the like. Makes me a misfit in our culture. Sometimes even I do not know what I will do."

"If our culture only fit you." He shook his head, smiling. "You seem able to dance with princes and dine with . . ."

". . . devils?"

He frowned. "Why do you speak like that? You are a beautiful woman with good connections—"

"Ugh. You sound like your uncle. 'A bit old and not much money, but with Leonore's guidance . . .'"

"He said that?"

She looked through the window and noted the darkening sky, wanting desperately to lie back on the couch and sleep or, if not, do whatever Justin did, again. She sighed. All good things come to an end.

"We had better head back." She stood and lifted her glove off the floor. "I would not want your family concluding that you should be at the top of my list of potential husbands."

What had made her say that? Once the words were out, she wished she could pull them back into her mouth and swallow them. Her cheeks heated. "I hope you do not think that I want . . . or expect . . ."

He waved his hand. "You have made your position on marriage perfectly clear."

Was that relief or disappointment itching at her shoulders? She shook off the feeling.

"Please use this place as your own. I have only one request . . ." He held out the key.

Accepting it, she squeezed the thick metal in her palm.

". . . that no handsome young men are allowed to meet you here."

She laughed. "Only hideous old ones?"

"You may not wish to marry me or any other, but while in London you are only allowed to dally with me. Agreed?"

"Agreed," she replied, smiling. "I cannot imagine 'dallying,' as you so tactfully put it, with anyone else."

As they left the little refuge, Evelyn felt, despite the darkening sky, as if the world was a sunnier place. Her worries did not weigh as heavily on her mind, and there was a lightness in her step that had not been there before. For the first time in four months she felt as if there was promise in the world, that things could not be all bad. There was some small benefit to her situation. What an odd notion, given the fact that her own government had apparently murdered her father and her legacy was in doubt.

She smiled up at the handsome gentleman walking beside her. It was clear that there were men nobly conducting everyday lives, men who did not need to face mortal danger at every corner to be valiant, to be heroes. It made her yearn even more than ever for a quiet life, without secrets, without doubts, without the constant fear of her loved ones being caught or killed. If she were the sort to marry, Justin would have been just the kind of man she would choose. But since she would not, she could at least have her chance to experience the passions of woman and man. Lord only knew there were few enough advantages to her situation, and she would use them to full effect. If only Sully would show his face and actually provide more than vague portents of doom.

Her childhood hero watched her out of the corner of his eye as he swept the muck from a stall in the nearby stables. With his cap pulled low over his face and the hunch he assumed, she did not even notice him. How could she, when her eyes were glued to the handsome marquis? Sully pushed down the temptation to pull his darling away from the rogue and throttle the man in the manure.

"Hey, you, boy," called the stable master. "Bring out the lady's mare."

He slapped the foot of a lad sitting nearby. "Ya 'eard da master. Get on it."

The boy jumped from his perch atop a stack of hay and scurried to obey.

Sully slipped into the shadows of the stable. It was too dangerous to be seen near Evelyn. Too dangerous for them both. But it was becoming more and more difficult to stay away from her when she was behaving so perilously. He had warned her, but she had not heeded him. Perhaps she did not understand that the marquis who seemed to have swept her off her feet was somehow involved in her father's murder. But all of the pieces were not yet in place, and to move now, although tempting, might prove catastrophic.

The scoundrel smiled down into Evelyn's upturned face and brushed a hair off her rosy cheek. Sully's stew-

ing blood began to boil. That his little girl would fall for
such a treacherous rascal . . . he had taught her better
than that. Perhaps it was time for some paternal interference. And silencing the marquis seemed the best
way to safeguard his Evelyn. Forever.

Chapter 12

Evelyn tossed another log onto the fire and inhaled the smoky scent of cloves. Justin had had the most pleasant mix of aromas added to the hearth. She pulled off her black shawl, for the vigorous fire warmed her face and hands in the small house that had become her sanctuary. It had been Justin's brother's haven, and now it was hers; she just prayed that she would meet a better end.

She dragged the wastebasket close and threw each ball of crumpled paper into the flames, one by one, and watched them burn. She sighed. The blaze crackled as if laughing at her ineptitude. She could find nothing in her father's writings, no indication of some unknown treacherous mission he had worked on near his death. Still, it was a joy to read his poetic prose. She had not truly appreciated what a gifted writer he had been. Always a great orator, he'd had a knack for gathering crowds around him and working them as a master craftsman builds his tour de force. He could bring them to laughter with an anecdote or have them charging off to glory with his rousing rhetoric. But his writing, it was like a gentle song. Reflective, haunting in its imagery. He had worried over her. He had consoled himself about the day he would be gone, would be a father to her no more, by making a legacy for her that was "fashioned from the teardrops of the gods." An odd description for English coin, but who was she to question his poetic license?

If only he had known that her fortune was to be incarcerated by the ever-inefficient and apparently unjust legal system. He would likely have placed it in a more secure location. Like under a mattress or beneath a rock.

She tossed another ball of paper into the flames. It ignited and shriveled into ashes in mere seconds. But she had to remember he had left her with so much more than mere money. He had always known what to say to encourage her, to make her work harder, to be the best person she could be. It was he who had taught her never to settle. Not to accept the limited role that society had carved out for women. "This is the nineteenth century, for heaven's sake," he would proclaim. "We no longer live in caves, and woman need not cater to man as if he created fire for her to cook and serve."

He'd had such fervor, such energy, but it had always been based in sound principles. God, country, and family. In that order. And yes, it had hurt that she had come last. That his duty to his king and his nation had held precedence. That was why it was ludicrous for anyone to consider that the man might have been a traitor. Which meant that someone else was. Someone who had been threatened enough by Father to have murdered him or have had him killed.

She rubbed her hands over her eyes. Her head ached from all of the twisted reasoning. Thank heavens or, she smiled, Justin, that she had a place for her distrustful musings. A place where she need not worry over being disturbed. The Fontaines thought her at the library, and she let them think this. How could it be a haven if everyone knew of it?

She scanned the small parlor, feeling an overwhelming sense of appreciation for Justin and his thoughtfulness. The glorious man was turning out to be the one saving grace to this horrid mess. And it did not hurt that the devastatingly attractive marquis had magical fingers. Her face heated and she giggled, just recalling his searing touch. But she could not dwell on that or she would not get anything accomplished.

As a diversion, she looked around the chamber. The wooden door of the storage room stared at her enticingly. She stood, curious to see what Justin's brother George had kept inside. She shook off the temptation, acknowledging that she had no right to trespass. She would not repay hospitality with nosiness. Still, a little peek couldn't hurt anything, could it?

Two knocks banged on the door.

Her heart jumped. She pressed her hand to her chest, trying to calm the pounding against her rib cage. She let out a long breath, pushing away the feelings of guilt. She had done nothing wrong.

It was likely a friend, to have been able to get past Ismet. Justin. A small thrill raced up her middle. She pat her hair and brushed her skirts. She hastily squatted down and tossed the final pages into the fire. Remembering her father's journal lying open on the desk, she quickly slammed it closed. Instead of putting it back into her reticule in the corner, however, she shoved it into one of the tall bookshelves as she strode to the door. She would easily retrieve it after Justin's visit. She just had to remember that she had promised to return to Belfont House in time for tea.

"Who calls?"

"Justin."

She smiled and opened the door wide. He was so handsome that it nearly took her breath away. From the top of his dark blue hat to the tips of his shiny black Hessians he was the epitome of the elegant English gentleman.

He hesitated in the threshold. "I do not wish to intrude . . ."

"Don't be foolish. This is your place, Justin, not mine." She stepped aside and waved him in. "I am merely a guest. You are the landlord and I had best be nice to you or you might just kick me out."

He stepped inside, and that musky, woodsy scent wafted around him. She nodded to Ismet, who was standing sulkily across the alley, and closed the door. Lord only knew what Ismet thought of her burgeoning friendship with the marquis. She brushed aside the worry. She was her own woman now, in charge of her own destiny.

He removed his hat, and this time Evelyn reached up and did ruffle his hair. He brushed his gloved hand across his forehead self-consciously. "That bad, eh?"

"No, I just couldn't resist."

They stepped into the parlor and he looked around the room.

"Are you burning something?"

She shrugged. "Was nothing. I just love the spices you added to the fire. What are they?"

"I don't know," he stated distantly. "They were a gift from a friend."

"The portly, old kind of friend?" she asked only half-jokingly.

"I would not say either of those things to his face, but yes."

She released the little tension in her shoulders. "Let me take your cape."

"Thank you." He turned. "Are you enjoying your solitude?"

She hung the soft black woolen cloak on the rack and smiled. "Immensely, Justin. It is such a pleasure not to have anyone underfoot or interrupting me."

"But I am interrupting you."

Her cheeks warmed. "I welcome the distraction, if it is you."

A small smile lifted the corners of his lips. "I brought you something."

"Really? You have given me so much already."

"It's nothing extravagant. Please sit."

Evelyn sat down on the couch with her hands folded in her lap to keep them from clapping with excitement. She'd always loved presents. Even the smallest things were a cherished surprise. Every time her father had had to journey abroad, he had brought back some memento of his travels for his little girl, and, although seeing her father had been an unmatchable treat, the little gifts had been an anticipated boon.

Justin grabbed the poker and stirred it in the grate distractedly.

Evelyn bit her cheek not to ask about the gift as she waited with feigned patience.

He put the poker back with the other fireplace tools and sat down.

At the look on her face, he stated quickly, "It really is nothing particularly remarkable. My grandmother gave it to me and I never understood why." He adjusted the tails of his coat. "Although it may be somewhat inappropriate for me to give you such a token—"

"What about our relationship has been proper, Justin?" she interrupted.

"Rightly stated. I, well, you said that you intend to leave England." It was a question, awaiting a rebuttal.

She opened her mouth but then closed it. She was beginning to have reservations about departing, but she knew that she had to follow her father's instructions. England was not safe for her, and she had no future here. She slowly nodded.

"I, well, I am duty bound to stay. So it seems that our acquaintance is destined to be short-lived." He clasped her hand in his. "But I hope that when you think back on our time together you will not hate me terribly."

She frowned. "What an odd thing to say. I cannot imagine hating you at all, Justin. I think you are one of the most wonderful people I have had the pleasure of meeting. You are honest, and considerate, and valiant, and—"

"Stop, Evelyn." He squeezed her hand, hard. "I told you, I am no hero, and it makes me uncomfortable when you set me up as such."

She searched his grayish-green gaze, seeing his discomfort. "As you wish."

He blew out a long breath of air. "Some would argue,

and I cannot help but agree, that I am taking advantage of you. . . ."

"My time with you is freely spent, and anything I give is freely given, Justin. It is the nineteenth century, for heaven's sake. I can take care of myself and make decisions on my own."

"Whatever the future holds for us," he urged quietly, "well, I do want you to think well of me." He sounded so dire and uncertain. He was feeling guilty about yesterday. Well, she would not. Her future was unsure, her legacy in jeopardy, she'd be truly damned if she did not enjoy some small pleasures in her inordinately chaotic life. Moreover, her friendship with Justin was turning out to be a blessing in her life; one she was going to relish now and cherish forever.

He reached into his pocket and pulled out a small folded cloth. He unwound the fabric and exposed a shiny gold ring with two clasped hands carved around the band.

"It was my great-grandmother's. As my grandmother tells it, she loved a man deeply, but her parents disapproved of her choice. He was a poor merchant and deemed unsuited to her station. He left England to seek his fortune and to prove himself to my great-great-grandparents." He lifted up the band and held it lightly between his fingers. The fire's radiance danced across the gleaming gold. "The man gave this to my great-grandmother before he left, a token of his love and esteem. He wanted her to think fondly of him while they were apart."

"Please tell me he returned as wealthy as Croesus and they married and he was your great-grandfather."

"He was killed when his ship sank in a fierce hurricane in the Indies."

She sighed. "It was too much to hope."

He handed the ring to her. The hard metal was tiny in her hand, and she wondered if it would fit. "Your great-grandmother must have been petite."

He nodded. "Like you."

She hid her smile. She was not nearly as tiny as he assumed, but she was not about to correct his misimpression. She tried her middle finger first but could not get it past the knuckle. The pointer finger was just a smidgen too tight. It slid over her ring finger, and although it was a bit snug over the knuckle, it fit perfectly once on.

"Vein amoris," she stated quietly.

"What?"

"The ancient Egyptians believed that the ring finger has the 'vein amoris,' the vein of love, which runs straight to the heart." She looked up and smiled. "Are you certain you wish to part with this?"

"Most ladies of my acquaintance would not necessarily appreciate the significance of the thing. I thought, well, maybe you would."

She traced her fingertip across the carving of the two clasped hands. "This pattern is what the ancient Romans used for wedding rings. For them the gold band symbolized everlasting love and commitment." She covered it with her other hand and held it to her breast. "It means a lot to me, and I will cherish it always."

He leaned forward and kissed her with such tenderness that her heart melted. He wrapped his arms around her as if she were a delicate flower. He loved her mouth with his tongue, sensually drawing out the pleasure of hundreds of kisses until they blended in one glorious asylum of pleasure.

For a fleeting moment she thought she ought to pull away, she ought not to be engaging in such wanton pleasure, but it quickly passed from her mind as he ran his hands down her chest and teased her breasts, raising the buds of her nipples until they were hard with wanting. All thoughts fled under the insistent devilment of his beguiling fingers.

She rocked her hips, pressing herself against the hard bulge of his manhood, telling him with her body what she was not quite ready to put into words. His kisses became less tender, more demanding. Suddenly he stood and wrenched off his coat and waistcoat. He leaned forward and kissed her hard, leaving her wanting more as he tugged off his cravat and shirt. She watched him with wide, hungry eyes. She had never seen a naked man before. Just like everything else about him, his body was beautiful. She reached up and skimmed her fingertips across his smooth abdomen. He sucked in his breath.

Reaching down, he slowly unfastened the many buttons of her dress. She had worn the front-clasping gown in the hopes that this very circumstance might happen here today. She was ready. Two and twenty, more than ready.

He parted the soft muslin and sat on his haunches. His eyes roved over her body hungrily, as her sheer shift left nothing to the imagination. He ran his hands over the soft silk and unclasped the stays. She sat up and pulled her arms free from the gown, and the shift fell in folds around her waist.

"You are so blessedly beautiful," he breathed.

She smiled, feeling magnificent in his eyes. "You are

like the statues in Italy, but not cold to the touch." She ran her hands down his broad, muscled chest, and fine hairs tickled under her palms.

"Hotter than Hades, at the moment," he breathed through his smile.

The hairs on his chest were sparse and brown and crept down his middle, ending abruptly at his breeches. Her curiosity overcame her trepidation, and this time she reached down and did touch the bulge that she understood was his swollen manhood. He groaned and closed his eyes as her fingertips traced his smooth, hot member.

It was fascinating. It was exciting.

It jumped under her touch.

She ripped her hand away. "It moved!"

He chuckled. "I would hope so."

He lay down on top of her, and she sucked in her breath. The touch of his smooth, warm chest on her bare nipples made her tingle all over. His open lips pressed against hers, his tongue plunging in and out of her mouth playfully, enticingly. Her stomach fluttered with excitement as their skin rubbed erotically with every light movement. She was panting, her heart was racing, and she felt as if she were on fire. As he flicked hot, wet kisses on her neck she looked over at the hearth and noted that the wood had burned down to embers. It was not the fire creating this wondrous heat. It was Justin.

He kissed and lathed her nipples, kneading them gently, tracing his bewitching fingers all over her stomach and chest. She arched her back and moaned with the sheer pleasure of it, but she wanted him down *there*, where he had been before. She spread her legs as demanding heat thrilled between her thighs, needing him. Wanting to know him as a woman knows a man.

As if heeding her wishes, he rained kisses down the curve of her belly. He sat on his haunches and lifted her petticoat. He traced his palms up her calves and undid her garters, slowly peeling off her stockings. Watching him undress her was so erotically tantalizing that it made her knees turn to jelly. Thank heavens she was already lying down.

He licked his lips and dove on her, trailing playfully ticklish kisses up her legs and settling himself quite comfortably between her thighs. Her face heated as she realized his focus. Well, it was what she wanted, but why did it suddenly feel so personal? He parted the rough hair between her thighs, and she tried to slam her legs closed. She was an enlightened woman and all, but having his face so close to *there*, well, that was just too much.

He shook his head, smiling. "I want to look at you."

"Wh . . . what's there to see?"

"You. You have no idea how beautiful you are to me." He settled between her legs once more and spread the lips of her most private place. He stared down at her a moment, his eyes ablaze with burning passion. How fascinating; his desire apparently was heightened by what he saw. She tried to relax while adjusting to the odd sensation of cool air gracing across her hot flesh. He leaned forward and blew delicately.

Hot and cold shivers raced up her body from between her legs. It was like nothing she had ever experienced before. And it was not unpleasant at all. She let out a long breath, savoring the pleasure.

He pressed his lips to the hard nub between her legs and kissed her reverently. Her jaw dropped open; she was shocked to her toes. He set his open mouth against her hot, wet place and slowly began licking her in small, tight circles. She threw her head back and clutched at the edge of the sofa, hanging on for dear life.

"Sweet God in heaven," she gasped.

She shoved her pelvis deep into his mouth and closed her eyes. It did not get any better than this. He flicked his tongue in and out of her, and suddenly she felt gentle fingers lower, exploring her sensitive places. He slipped his finger inside her, and her muscles welcomed him with a wild embrace. Her insides clung to him as he torturously slid in and out. Still, he licked her and lathed his mouth on her hot, tight nub, driving her mad with wanting. Fire coursed through her veins. Her hips pumped to some unknown rhythm as she was driving toward madness.

He plunged his finger deep inside of her again, and she threw her head back, trying to scream, but no sound came. The breath froze in her throat. It was too much, the rapture, the exquisite spasm inside her, the hammering of her heart. Everything went black with stars shining brightly behind her closed lids. Violent tremors raged from between her legs, spreading outward, making her feel as if she were in the center of a driving storm. She was tossed and thrown with the waves of exploding passion, and suddenly he was on top of her. He pushed into her and she whelped. He was so big. He pushed deeper, plunging inside of her. She sucked in a long, haggard breath and every muscle tightened, especially the one encircling his member.

He groaned, "So tight, so wet . . ."

His words made her feel hotter still. Yes, she was stretched and opened beyond what she thought possible, but she felt immense satisfaction as his manhood filled her. This was good. This was right. This was what she wanted. Pulling his head down, she kissed him. She reveled in the connection of their bodies, the throbbing between her legs, and his rocking in and out of her.

Her muscles gripped him and squeezed. He cried out. She held onto him for dear life, not knowing what to do. She felt as if she were riding an untamed stallion and clinging tightly as they raced toward their destination. Their bodies grew slick with sweat, and she relished the erotic play of skin rubbing velvety skin. Then the tremors rippled between her legs again, more quietly this time, but with delicious effect. He cried out and pulsed into her, thrusting once, then twice, and going still.

She was panting, as if having run the race of her life. But a smile graced her swollen lips; it was a magnificent rush. She tilted her head back, enjoying the feel of his seed inside of her, the intimacy. He dropped onto her with a great sigh of satisfaction.

She ran her hands down his smooth back, lost in the closeness of their bodies. She wondered if every woman felt this way when loved by a man. She supposed there had to be some feeling, some sense of caring to the physical union. More than just mating.

Mating. She had not considered the possibility of becoming with child. She tossed her worry to the wind. She knew people who tried for years to have children. It was unlikely anything could happen with just one coupling. But she hoped that they would get to do it again and again. And soon. It was too delicious for words. Perhaps she would give up eating and just live off the breathtaking diet of kisses and those crashing sensations. She giggled into his shoulder.

"What do you find so amusing, Evelyn?" he whispered hoarsely into her neck.

"I was just wondering when we could do this again."

He chuckled softly, his breath tickling the hairs on her neck. "You will be the death of me."

He pulled out of her, and she felt bereft by the loss. But he curled up next to her on the couch and cuddled close, wrapping his arm about her waist. It was dead weight, but she was not about to complain.

"So you enjoyed that?" he teased.

"Immensely." She wrinkled her nose. The heavy scent of musk, lavender, and their lovemaking filled the small room. It was an erotic combination.

He snuggled closer and pressed his nose into her shoulder. His breathing deepened, and she realized that he dozed. She smiled into his short, soft hair. He was a dear. Like a little boy after a feast. She snuck a peek down. A pink stain smeared across her lily-white thigh. She resisted the urge to clean it off. She was going to enjoy this haven for as long as possible. She laid her head back and sent a little prayer to heaven—that she remember this glorious feeling of being held in her lover's arms, sated, well loved—because she knew it would not last. She sighed. Good things never did.

Chapter 13

Justin threw his cards down, disgusted. "She is not involved, I tell you."

"Lower your voice, man," the colonel chided angrily. "My sources indicate otherwise."

Justin scanned the dark, paneled game room of his favorite club and noted the turned heads. He whispered harshly, "Well, your sources are wrong."

The older man snorted irritably. "Unlikely."

"Well, if they are so bloody accurate, why can they not tell us what we need to know about Napoleon's plot?"

"Have a care to remember who you are talking to, Justin. We do not want to make a delicate situation worse."

Justin straightened. "What do you mean by that?"

"I am just saying that if you have gotten too soft to be

able to handle the matter with objectivity, then I can hand the Amherst girl off to Helderby. I'm sure he could get her to talk."

Justin's stomach lurched just thinking of the brawny, coarse fellow that Colonel Wheaton called in for some of his more bloody questioning sessions.

He bit his inner cheek and forced his racing heart to slow. "And if she knows nothing, you imperil her and our branch. The powers that be will not be pleased to have one of their citizens cruelly used."

Wheaton shrugged and scratched a snowy white sideburn. "War has its casualties. We will recover. We are too valuable." He flipped his cards and frowned. "She has new legal representation, making all sorts of noises."

"Who?"

"A Mr. Tuttle."

"Marlboro's clerk?"

"The same. He seems to have little respect for the intricacies of governmental affairs."

"You mean he is not so easily bullied." Justin scratched his chin. He felt guilty about tying up Evelyn's inheritance. But if he helped her access her funds, then she would likely leave England. He was not about to let that happen. He would not examine his motives too closely, however, and would just assume, for the moment, that he was doing it simply to serve his government.

"Any sign of Sullivan?" Wheaton asked casually.

"I think he may have tried to contact her, but I have no proof," Justin answered uneasily. He was beginning to question his paranoia.

The colonel's eyes narrowed thoughtfully. "Time is wasting. Draw him out."

"How? I have taken Miss Amherst about, given her a

remote location for possible meetings. We have tied up her resources and threatened her future. The man is not biting."

"Place her in jeopardy."

Icicles crawled down Justin's spine. "What are you suggesting?"

"Runaway carriage, kidnapped by rogues, have a madman attack her, you surely know something about that."

Justin's body stilled. "What are you insinuating?" The man could not know about George. It was too much to be so deeply in the wily man's power.

Wheaton peeked from under bushy brows. "That you are good at manipulating a situation. Why? What did you suppose I meant?"

Justin forced his muscles to relax. This was going too far. Withholding Evelyn's inheritance was one thing, but putting her in real danger on the slim hope that her friend might jump to the rescue was too far-fetched. Too risky. He could not stomach such hazards, not with Evelyn's life. He shook his head. "There must be another source for ascertaining the information we need."

The colonel stated quietly, "Helderby."

Justin leaned back and crossed his arms. There was an undercurrent here he did not understand. Why was the colonel so adamant about this particular course? The man had always been a grand proponent of multiple strategies.

"I dislike the thought as much as you, believe me." The old man shifted in his seat. "Time is the problem. I will not have Napoleon undermine everything Wellington is trying to accomplish. It's our watch, Justin. Our duty to guard the realm. I'm not long for this station. I don't want to be remembered as the man who allowed our financial system to fall."

So the old man was planning his retirement. He was trying to preserve his legacy. Well, everyone wanted to be remembered well. Justin rubbed his chin, thinking about his great-grandmother's ring. What had made him give it to Evelyn? He was feeling mortal and a bit unworthy. He was growing more and more afraid of her finding out the truth—that he had set her up for a fall. That he had quite deliberately undermined her claim to her fortune—for what? The vague whispers of a conspiracy designed to devastate the economy seemed insubstantial compared to what he was doing to Evelyn. He was not willing to examine too closely his motives in seducing her. His feelings were too raw as far as she was concerned.

The colonel's words brought him back to harsh reality. "She is the key to Napoleon's strategy, I tell you. Do whatever you need to. Draw Sullivan out. But make it happen, or I will do whatever it takes." Wheaton sniffed. "You know how I hate having my back up against the wall, Barclay, and I am feeling a bit pressed lately."

Justin was feeling a "bit pressed" as well. But it was not his mother or his duties or his superior that troubled him, but his own disgust with himself about Evelyn. She was, by far, the most amazing woman he'd ever had the good fortune to know; and it was all based on lies. Well, not all of it. Unmindful of his mission, his heart was growing fonder of the lovely lady every day. He tried to tell himself he had no claim to her, had no right to her affection, but his feelings were having other ideas entirely.

He shook his head. He'd be damned if he was going to endanger her life, or worse yet, allow Helderby to lay his vicious hands on her. Just the thought enraged him. "I do not see the benefit to imperiling someone's life for uncertain gain."

"If you have a better idea, I am open to hearing your suggestions."

Justin scowled. "I will think on it."

"You have two days, Justin. I will not settle for anything less than success. And if you are unequal to the task, I will find someone who has not lost their sense of duty to the Crown." Wheaton flipped his cards. "My game."

Chapter 14

Justin tugged at a knot in Cheshire's tail, intent on untangling the snarled hair. He was attacking the knot with his fingertips, taking care not to take out his anger with himself on Cheshire. How on earth could the stallion's tail have become such a knotty mess in such a short time? Entangled, ensnared. He rubbed his aching temples. He was not such a complete fool as to miss that he was thinking of himself.

He could not allow Helderby anywhere near Evelyn, yet he wondered how in heaven he was going to continue on with the nasty charade. It tore at his gut that he was using her so disparagingly, even if she was somehow caught up in this mess. He could not seem to accept the pretense that she might be a threat to his nation. More likely, she was just an innocent bystander to her father's intrigues. She should not have to pay for her father's betrayal or her association with her friend Sullivan. And if the piper came for pay . . . he did not know what he would do.

He rubbed his eyes. He would have to find a way to prove to the colonel that she was not involved. Yet he could not pretend that he was acting honorably. He was so confoundedly disgusted with himself for his conduct thus far. Tying up her inheritance, using his aunt and uncle to pressure her, playing to Evelyn's goodness, her sympathy about his brother to try to trick her into disclosing information, using his brother's cherished place to try to get Evelyn to lower her defenses or, better yet, to ambush Sullivan. Worst of all, using her own incredibly sensual passion to ensnare her. And to top it all, taking her innocence. Despite her protestations about marriage or her decision to give herself freely, Justin felt an overwhelming sense of duty to the woman who trusted him so implicitly with her virtue.

He blew out a frustrated breath of air. He was the one feeling captured, almost enchanted, by Evelyn. He could not seem to get the scent of her out of his nostrils. That light lavender mixed with the heady aroma of her desire. She was so confoundedly sensible and intelligent and ridiculously beautiful. And completely uninhibited in her passion. He knew of no other woman like her and realized that he never would. She did not use wiles or trickery or games. She simply was. And that straightforward recipe was proving irresistible to him. He dreaded the possibility that she could discover his treachery. That she would despise him. Moreover, it chilled him to the bone that the colonel considered her so easily disposable.

A ripple of coldness ran through him, distracting

him from his troubling thoughts. The hairs on his neck lifted, as if something was very wrong. He dropped Cheshire's smooth tail, suddenly wary in this place that had always been his haven. A knife whizzed by and slammed into the wood of the stall where his head had just been. Thinking quickly, he crouched low, swiftly searching the darkened stables for his assailant. He listened, trying to hear any indication of the scoundrel over the beating of his racing heart. Cheshire nickered and shifted uneasily.

Justin slipped into the next stall and then out through the gate. His boots crunched on the matted straw. He hunkered down behind bales of hay, trying to quiet his breath so as not to betray his new location, and scanned the shadowed space. Carefully reaching for the pitchfork leaning against the wall, he'd barely grazed the wooden handle with his fingertips when a heavy body crashed into him from behind. Only the soft straw gave some relief to the jarring crash that shook his senses. Meaty hands gripped his shirt, but he tore free and rolled away, lunging for the pitchfork. He grabbed the wood in his hand and whirled to face his attacker.

The man had covered his face with black paint, but his beady eyes gleamed from beneath a low hat like dark diamonds with evil intent. He was beefy and broad, with a square jaw and large hands, and he had at least two stones' mass on Justin.

Justin balanced the tool, gripping the wooden handle tightly. He quickly assessed the distance and then pounced, putting his full weight behind the strike. The burly man twisted around, but the metal spikes ripped into his back and shoulder.

"Goddam!" he roared. He wrenched the fork from

his back so forcefully that it threw Justin off balance and he crashed into the wall. Justin spun and stood just as his opponent barreled down on him, pounding him. Justin's head slammed into the wooden gate, and stars swam before his eyes. He slumped to the floor, tasting hay and manure.

The door to the stable slammed open into the wooden slats. Suddenly his attacker was gone. Justin lay on the matted floor and listened, trying to catch his shaky breath. All he could hear were the snorts and neighs of disturbed animals and the innocuous sounds of the night. He slowly lifted his head. The stable door swung freely in the wind.

He spit out a stick of straw, flattened his palms on the floor, and pushed himself up. He stood and dusted off his clothes. Every muscle of his body hurt. Walking over to Cheshire's stall, he stopped and stared at the knife protruding from the wood, then grabbed the handle and yanked. The blade ripped free. He turned it over. It was a classic Japanese tanto shape, the point exactly in line with the spine of the blade and the belly curved. This was a serious weapon, and it left Justin no doubt the threat to him had been real. But not lethal, apparently. If his assailant had been intent on killing him, he had lost his chance when Justin had lain dazed on the floor. The first knife shot had been close, but a master would have had no problem with such a throw.

That meant that this was probably an exercise in intimidation—something Justin knew quite a bit about. He flipped the well-balanced blade in his hand. Was his burly attacker the infamous Sullivan, warning him away from Evelyn? Or had his other inquiries raised some hackles? Regardless, for the moment it meant that he was aiming in the right direction and needed to intensify his efforts. He lifted his coat off the back of the stall door and slipped it on. Carrying the knife in his hand, he strode out the door. He had entered the stables a man in doubt, and he was leaving it with a renewed sense of purpose. He would find the collaborators and end their machinations once and for all. Napoleon's plot would be halted. By so doing, he also hoped to exonerate Evelyn. And if he could not prove her innocent, well, he prayed that she was not an enemy of the state, for he would leave no traitor standing.

Chapter 15

The midday sun was high in the sky as Evelyn walked down the long alleyway toward the shelter of her new sanctuary. She hoped that Justin decided to "interrupt" her today as he had the day before. She could barely sleep last night for running the deliciously intimate events on the long green couch through her mind. Justin was turning out to be much more than simply an eye-catching gentleman; he was kind, noble, and, in her mind, the personification of Eros, the Greek god of erotic love.

Her delightful musings were interrupted by the sounds of a scuffle. She turned. Three brutish men, all armed with knives, circled Ismet.

He shouted to her, *"Kosmak!"* Run.

She was torn by her desire to help him and her need to protect her father's journal. She clutched her reticule to her middle, as if the journal inside would tell her what to do.

Her brawny servant pulled a long dagger from his sleeve and another from his boot. He faced his foes with a wicked grin.

Her heart was pounding like a stampede of wild horses. Without thought, she tossed her reticule to the wall and pulled her blade free of its scabbard under her cloak. The men paid her no mind. Well, she would give them reason to fear. Ismet's eyes flashed anger at her disobedience, but he was not about to argue with her now.

She slowly stalked behind the small wiry fellow with the stained yellow coat. She had never killed a man, but this was a time of firsts for her.

Ismet lunged at the largest man, and all hell erupted. Evelyn dove for the back of the wiry one's knee with the bottom of her boot. He yelped as his knee folded underneath him. He snarled at Evelyn and swiped his blade in the air. She jumped back.

Ismet swung and parried, easily avoiding the larger man's knife. It was a long, ugly thing with a stained blade. The two men circled Ismet, jumping in and out with military precision. Toying with him. Their movements were fast and meticulous. Despite their disheveled clothing, these men were well trained.

The wiry fellow jumped at Evelyn, spinning around, trying to grab her from behind. She swept her cloak in the air, leaping out of arm's reach. The fellow on the side stepped away and moved to assist his compatriots. All three rounded on Ismet, hounding him. Ismet feinted and struck, slicing his knife through the burly one's arm. The man cried out and dropped his blade.

Evelyn jabbed at the wiry one's back, cutting through his yellow coat to the flesh underneath.

"The bitch cut me!" He twisted away, grabbing over his shoulder at his bloodied back.

She licked her lips, breathing hard.

The big one swung his fist at Ismet while the second man slipped behind him and jammed Ismet's head with the hilt of his dagger. Ismet dropped to his knees. All three men turned on her.

Evelyn spun on her heels and fled down the alley, screaming at the top of her lungs, "Help! Help me!"

The men raced after her. She dashed past her sanctuary and around the next corner and barreled into a broad, wide figure. She fell flat on her bottom, the wind knocked right out of her. Her knife clattered away. She twisted around and jumped up, struggling for breath.

"This is no time to be sitting on your duff, Evelyn," a deep voice commented.

Her heart swelled. "Sully!"

"Get behind me, if you would, my dear."

He coolly cocked his pistol and aimed toward the broad chest of the largest man. The three attackers skidded to a stop, uncertain. Evelyn slipped behind her beloved friend and peeked from under his arm.

"I will shoot," Sully remarked quietly.

"And I will shoot her," came a harsh voice from the rear. Evelyn turned. Behind her stood a large, square-jawed, big-fisted man in a long black overcoat, pointing a gun at her head. Her mouth went dry.

Sully pursed his lips. "Helderby, I presume?"

"H . . . how? Never you mind, you bloomin' bastard. Put the gun down or you'll have her brains all over your fine coat."

Sully tilted his head. "As you command." Evelyn

knew that tone of voice. It meant anything but submission. She tensed. Sully held up his gun as if surrendering. He slowly turned, and, with lightning speed, shot Helderby. The three men jumped on him, jarring his aim. They ripped the empty pistol from his hand and pummeled him with their fists.

"Alive! He's to be taken alive!" Helderby roared, clutching his bleeding shoulder.

Sully could not beat off the three men.

"Run, Evelyn!"

This time she obeyed. She shot past the skirmishing men and raced back down the alley from which she'd come.

Justin was striding toward her, flanked by three brawny footmen.

"Justin!" she screamed breathlessly. "Help Sully! Attacked. Go help." She pointed behind her.

He grabbed her shoulders. Shoving her toward the house, he shouted, "Go to my brother's, now! I will take care of this!" She lifted her skirts and ran. Thank God for Justin. She just prayed that he would get there in time to save Sully and that he would not be injured.

She raced back to where Ismet had fallen. He was gone. Her reticule lay on the ground by the wall, hidden in shadow. She grabbed the handle and ran back toward the house. Midstep, she pulled out the golden key. She was rasping for air and her chest burned as if a knife were lodged in it. She dashed back to the house and tried to insert the key in the door, but her hands were trembling too badly.

She bit her lip and took a deep breath. She arched back and tried to glimpse down the alley but could see nothing beyond the corner. She listened breathlessly but could barely hear anything above the clamoring of her heart. She used two hands to get the key in the lock and turn it. Heaving the door open, she charged inside and slammed it closed. She turned the lock and grabbed a chair to bar the handle. Her eyes scanned the long, tall bookshelves, longing for some magical weapon to use to save the day.

She yanked her father's journal from her bag and shoved it into the bookshelf. She stared at it a hesitant moment, and then pulled it out. Removing four or five books from the shelves, she slid her father's precious diary in back and reshelved the volumes.

A loud knock pounded the door. "Evelyn! Are you alright?" It was Justin.

She removed the chair and whipped open the door. He was whole and fit. Thank God! She ran into his arms and hugged him close, pressing her nose to the soft wool of his gray coat.

"Sully and Ismet?" She looked up hopefully.

"Sullivan is badly bruised, but otherwise fine. Ismet, no one knows where he is."

She peeked past Justin but saw an empty alley. "Where is Sully?"

"In custody."

Bile rose up in her throat. It was as bad as a death sentence.

With his arm tightly wrapped around her, he pushed her inside and closed the door. He walked her into the parlor as her mind reeled with the implications of Sully's arrest. Justin seated her on the couch and crouched before her.

"Evelyn. . want you to be frank with me." He squeezed her hands between his. "Do you know why your friend Sullivan is wanted by the authorities?"

She shook her head. "What are they charging him with?"

"Treason."

Her stomach lurched. Oh, God, no. She closed her eyes.

"Evelyn. You must tell me. Do you know anything about a plot against the Crown?"

At least they had not murdered him in the street as they had her father. There would be a trial, if unjust, and she might have another chance to save him.

He shook her gently. "Listen to me, Evelyn. Did Sullivan say anything to you at all about Napoleon or banking or the monetary system? Anything at all?"

She opened her eyes and blinked. "Why are you asking me these things?" A ball of anxiety roiled in her gut. "You, you did not help them, did you?"

"Please just tell me what you know," he pleaded urgently. "We haven't much time and must stop the plot from proceeding before it's too late."

We.

The room rushed in and out of focus, suddenly clouded in white. Justin was talking to her but seemed to be speaking from down a long, dark tunnel. Then waves crashed in her eardrums, muting him altogether, and her queasy stomach lurched and heaved. She twisted away from him, and the contents of her breakfast rushed up through her throat and splashed onto the worn oriental carpet.

Someone was holding her hair back as she coughed and sputtered. Tears sprang to her eyes, and she thought she might die from the pressure in her head.

A hand pressed her forehead and a handkerchief was shoved in her sweaty, gloved palm. She raised the cloth with shaky hands and wiped her mouth. A glass was placed in her fingers, and she clutched the brandy to her chest. She took a small sip, swooshed it around her mouth, leaned over the grate, and spit. She sniffed and took a long, hot swallow of the fiery liquid. It burned the whole way down. She welcomed the pain. It made everything more clear.

She dropped the glass, and it rolled across the thick carpet. The same carpet where she had kissed the despicable man standing before her now.

She stood, and her legs wobbled like jelly. She drew herself up. *"Carry yourself like a queen,"* her father had told her; *"it is like a cloak of protection when you are feeling most vulnerable."* When she turned and headed for the door, Justin grabbed her arm.

"Where are you going?"

She stared down at his gray-gloved hand as if it were a poisonous snake. Her free hand clenched, and before rational thought came, she reached back and smashed her fist into his nose.

Blood splayed out and he let her go, reaching for his face. "What . . . ?"

In a voice she did not recognize, she railed harshly, "Do not lay your filthy hands on me ever again."

She lifted her skirts and sprinted out the door, dashing past the surprised eyes of the burly footmen, and raced toward Belfont House with one thing on her mind. Shah.

Ismet was gone, Sully was arrested; heaven help her if she did not save her loyal servant. Fancy and street vendors alike stared at her as she charged down the avenue, but she did not heed them. Her throat burned and her chest was on fire, but she was not about to be taken in or lose the only friend she still might be able to help.

She banged on the heavy oak doors of Belfont House, rasping for air.

The butler opened the door. "Egad! Miss Amherst!"

She tore past him and headed down the fashionable hallway to sprint up the stairs two at a time. She burst through the door to her chambers, swallowing to bring some moisture to her parched mouth.

"Shah, *gelmek*," she panted. Her body was drenched in sweat and she felt so hot that she thought she might combust while simply standing.

Shah stood wide-eyed in the doorway to her room. Evelyn grabbed her hand and dragged her out the door. Ever-quick, Shah did not need to be told twice. They raced back down the hallway together and barreled down the stairs.

Lady Fontaine stood at the bottom of the stairs. "Faith have mercy! What happened to you, child?"

Evelyn could not imagine how awful she must look, but she didn't care. One more landing and then out the door. Escape.

Lady Barclay stepped out from the drawing room and into the hall, a wicked glower on her sharp face. "She looks as if she rolled in mud. How appalling!"

Then *he* bombarded in.

Evelyn froze midstep, and Shah barely stopped herself from catapulting down the stairs.

His face was bloodied, his nose already enlarged to twice its normal size. Two dark welts were forming under his eyes. At least she'd hurt him a little: Lord help him if she got another crack at him.

"You must listen to me, Evelyn!" he pleaded, but it sounded more like a command.

"Justin! You're hurt!" The dragon lady pounced on him, dragging at his arm.

He shoved her off and stepped up the bottom stair. "You have to listen to me!"

"Can't a man have any peace in his own home!" Lord Fontaine said as he stepped into the hall, scowling. His eyes widened. "Gadzooks!"

Evelyn was betting that the bastard's family didn't know about his auxiliary activities. It gave her an advantage, little as it was.

"Lady Fontaine, I need your help," she exclaimed.

Justin froze midstep, beseeching her with his eyes.

"Anything, child," Lady Fontaine offered worriedly.

"I beg of you, please tend to Lord Barclay." She glared daggers at the villain. "It seems he's been fist-fighting, and the sight of his hideous face makes me ill."

"Fistfighting?" The dragon lady turned on her son. "Have a care, Justin! Have you no sense of duty to your family or your title? Like a common ruffian, you behave!" Her left shoulder was inching up huffily. "The chit is right, you look positively horrid."

"Come, Justin, we will clean you up." Lady Fontaine turned on her nephew.

"I say, Barclay." Lord Fontaine peeked through his monocle. "You must confine your tussles to pugilistic science. And certainly not in front of the ladies. Too much for their delicate sensibilities."

"Go upstairs," Justin ordered Evelyn, glowering at her as his mother and his aunt tugged at his arms, directing him to the drawing room.

"Of course, my lord." She scrunched her face into a fake smile and curtseyed, which was quite a feat, standing on a stair and holding Shah's hand while all she really wanted to do was rip his lying throat out. Or perhaps tar and feathers might be a suitable punishment.

She turned and calmly stalked up the stairs, with Shah following close behind. As they reached the top of the landing, Evelyn lifted her skirts, and she and her trusty maid sprinted the length of the hall to the back staircase.

"Evelyn!" Justin bellowed. Footsteps thundered after them.

Shah and Evelyn flew down the servants' staircase and tumbled into the kitchens, frightening the cook into dropping a platter full of stewed beets. Sloppy purplish-red liquid splashed all over the wooden floor. Evelyn and Shah skidded through the mess, grabbing for purchase as they went. Evelyn clutched the cutting table for balance and pushed off, propelling them toward the back door. Plates crashed, people yelped, but they charged on and barreled out the servants' door and into the fresh air of the sunlit garden. Out the gate and into the crowded street they ran, racing away from treachery, running as if the devil himself was surely after them. For that was what *he* had become to her, evil incarnate.

Chapter 16

Justin raked his hands through his hair for the thousandth time as he paced the well-appointed drawing room. Magnificent oils lined the walls, and he glared at the olive-skinned faces in the portraits, wishing that they would stop staring at him. The clock chimed for the third time since his purgatory had begun, and he wondered if he could chance a dash up the stairs. But he did not know which room Evelyn occupied, and the two huge footmen by the door looked ready to eat him for midday snack. Lord only knew what Señor Arolas had said to the servants on his way out.

The door swung open, and the tall, raven-haired, olive-skinned gentleman glided inside. He walked with a natural grace even Justin had to begrudgingly admire.

Justin straightened, trying to contain his annoyance that Evelyn had run away from him and into the arms of the handsome Spaniard. "Well?"

"Brandy?" Arolas offered casually, his singsong Spanish accent making it sound like an illicit invitation.

"Will she see me or not?" Justin demanded, barely disguising his impatience.

The tall gentleman poured himself a snifter and delicately sipped from his glass. "I have known Señorita Evelyn since she was, how you say, chubby." He held his hand in front of his waist, as if Justin were an imbecile. "She had cheeks as big as plates, Mediterranean blue eyes, ah, and that white, white English hair." He sighed and shook his head. "For as long as I have known her she has always loved to eat." He waved his hand dramatically. "Good food always found a place on her plate and in her stomach. But now." He frowned. "My chef can find nothing to tempt her. She will touch not a thing." He glared at Justin. "I wonder what makes her so ill that she cannot stand the taste of simple pleasures?"

Guilt swept over Justin, but the conniving Spaniard could not make him feel any worse than he already did. "She did not tell you what happened?" he ground out through clenched teeth.

The man shrugged dramatically. "Sully is arrested, I heard."

Another sore point. The colonel had refused to allow him to interrogate the man, claiming that Justin was too soft for the exercise. As if there were sport in torturing a caged man. Now he was impotent to stop the plot or exonerate Evelyn. He was ready to kick up a riot with his frustration.

"I need to see her." Justin forced himself to unfurl

his locked hands. "Can you not convince her to speak to me?"

"Have you not yet comprehended? No one can make Señorita Evelyn do anything she does not wish to do." Arolas smiled, and his white teeth gleamed like a predator with dinner in its sights. "Perhaps if you explained the situation I might be able to offer some advice or be more persuasive?"

Justin pursed his lips, grasping for the slim opening to try and learn anything helpful. "It's complicated."

Arolas gracefully reclined in one of the large wing chairs and stretched his long legs out before him, like a lion relaxing languidly after a kill. "I have no appointments this afternoon more important than my dearest Señorita Evelyn."

Hearing the man wrap endearments around Evelyn's name made Justin squirm. Were they sharing more than just a roof over their heads? Did the bastard whisper to her in his suave native tongue while . . . ? Justin's gut clenched, and he fisted his hands to control his emotions. He licked his lips, for his mouth had suddenly gone desert dry. "How is she? I mean, are you taking good care of her?"

"I will always appreciate my Señorita Evelyn. For I value the friendship between us." He asked indolently, "Something you did not do?"

Charged silence enveloped the room.

"I can only surmise that you somehow were involved in 'apprehending' the fierce Sullivan, thereby betraying our Evelyn." Arolas raised his dark eyebrow inquiringly. "Simply a guess, of course."

Justin drew himself up. He would not allow himself to be toyed with for the Spaniard's amusement. He turned on his booted heel and strode toward the door. "Just take care of her, Arolas, or you will answer to me."

Suddenly the Spaniard sprang from his seat and pounced on Justin, gripping him by the cravat. "As good a care as you and your government have taken of her?" he whispered fiercely.

Arolas's brandy-scented breath brushed against Justin's cheeks, but he hung motionless. He could not defend himself against the truth. He was guilty of lies, betrayal, intimidation, and more. As he stared into the man's glittering dark brown eyes, he saw his guilt reflected therein. The knowledge tasted vile on his tongue. Well, he could warn her, at least. "She has dangerous enemies," he ground out, though his breath came in short gasps. Although it pained him to say so, he suggested tightly, "It would be best if she left the country."

Arolas's dark brown eyes narrowed, and he asked in a steely, sweet voice, "Are you threatening her?" The cravat tightened.

Justin could barely shake his head. "I would never hurt her."

"Ha!" Arolas released Justin so quickly that he stumbled to the floor. "You English are *chiflado*!"

Before Justin could rise, the man spun on his heels and strode out the door. Justin put his head in his hands. How had he sunk so low?

Arolas charged back into the parlor. "I forget. She wanted you to have this." He nonchalantly tossed something. The golden ring landed with a quiet thud on the carpet beside Justin. He picked up the small band and stared at it for a very long time. He did not know how much time passed as he sat there staring at the golden orb, but when he looked up Arolas still stood there, watching him with calculating eyes. "It would take a supremely devoted man to undo the damage you have done," he stated with oily smoothness.

Harsh jealousy tore at Justin's gut. "And are you assuming the task of consoling Evelyn?"

Arolas smiled wickedly. "I would jump at the chance to do anything for my Evelyn." His eyes narrowed. "Anything."

Justin wanted to hate the man, but he could not find it within him, for Arolas could give Evelyn what he could not—a home without the lingering shadow of betrayal. He stood, brushed off his britches, and straightened his wrinkled coat. Curling his fingers around the ring, he grumbled, "There is no need to gloat."

Arolas studied him, weighing whether he was worthy and finding him wanting. "Did you ever meet Señorita Evelyn's father, Señor Amherst?"

"No."

"He was a great man." Arolas sniffed. "There are not that many these days, so when you meet one, well, he makes an impression." He waved his hand dramatically. "He was an eloquent speaker. His words would bend your thinking, so subtly that you would not even know that it was he who had changed your mind. He was principled." Arolas frowned. "Sometimes too much. His country always came before anything else, including his family. So the idea that he would ever put anything before his homeland, well, it is ludicrous."

Justin felt as if he were staring into a mirrored pool containing a vast store of knowledge but he did not know what questions to ask the oracle. Or whether he would get a straight answer. He licked his lips. "Do you know . . . what Sir Amherst was working on before he died?"

Arolas's teeth gleamed white against his olive skin. "Diplomacy, of course."

"Evelyn was not involved in her father's 'diplomacy,' was she?"

Those dark brown eyes glittered. "What do you think?"

"I would bet my last farthing she was not."

"Why? Because she is a woman?" He said the word as if it was a high compliment, not a mere circumstance of birth. As if spying was a dirty sport. Well, it was.

"Because she's not devious. Intelligent, astute, yes, but her mind does not twist with devilish cunning . . ." Two could play at wide-eyed innocence. ". . . like what I assume one would need to be involved in the Intelligence business."

"You sound as if you care for the lady."

Justin shifted his shoulders, not wanting to face how strongly his feelings for Evelyn had become. "I hold Evelyn in the highest esteem."

Arolas raised his brow. "Not exactly a declaration of love. But then again, you could not love her to have betrayed her so."

Justin was so filled with shame that he could not meet the man's eyes. Only his need to do something to help Evelyn kept him from wanting to crawl into a hole and lick his wounds in disgrace. Since she'd run from him the day before, he'd felt as if someone had ripped out his heart and run a loaded carriage over it. But he was not about to expose his pain to the bloody Spaniard.

He asked through clenched teeth, "Can you help me or not?"

Arolas strolled lazily over to his brandy, lifted the snifter, and sipped slowly. Staring into the glass as if contemplating the brownish-gold liquid, he stated quietly, "Let us suppose that Señor Amherst never faltered from his 'diplomatic duty' to his country, and let us also assume that his death was, shall we say, ill-timed, for argument's sake, of course."

"Of course."

"Then, let us also suppose that Señorita Evelyn never partook in her father's activities, as you suggest." He pursed his lips, "That would indicate—"

"—that we have a traitor in our midst," Justin finished for him.

Arolas shrugged nonchalantly. "All presupposition, of course."

"Of course." Justin rubbed his chin. "But what does she have that someone wants?" Besides her beautiful, earth-shattering smile.

"Her legacy?" Arolas offered.

"I would assume *the authorities* have covered that corner," Justin replied guardedly.

"So it must be something else. Perhaps something she knows but does not know she knows?" Arolas tilted his head, studying Justin once more. "Why did you come here today? You knew she would not see you."

"I had to try." Justin looked away. "I have a duty toward her."

"Ah, so with you, like Señor Amherst, duty comes first. You English. I will never understand you. You are so honor-bound you forget the simple pleasures in life. The love of a good woman, the hug of a small child's arms around your neck. You miss so much."

"I do not see your loving family crowding about you," Justin replied stiffly.

The confident gentleman shrugged. "All in good time. And do not think that I will place *anything* before them."

Justin bowed, facing Arolas again. He was impressed by the man, despite the fact that he was jealous of the bastard to the core. What he would give to switch places. To be the one coming to Evelyn's rescue, consoling her, making things right. "If we have nothing further to discuss, I will bid you farewell."

"And you as well. I confess, my lord . . ." It was the first time he had properly addressed Justin. ". . . you are not like the other 'diplomats' I have met."

"How so?" Justin asked, intrigued.

"You do not seem to have the same taste for it, the blood, I mean. You seem to actually have some semblance of remorse. An unhealthy trait for a man in the diplomatic field, I might suggest."

"Well then, it's a good thing I'm not a diplomat, Señor. I am merely a man attempting to do the best he can to fulfill his duties."

Arolas smiled wickedly. "Aren't we all?"

Chapter 17

Perspiration lined his brow and soaked his armpits, his breath came in harsh gasps, and his heart banged against his rib cage with his efforts, but Justin stuck the pitchfork into the hay for the hundredth time in an hour and flung the heap into the loft. He was trying to sweat the self-loathing out of his system but could not get past the odor of manure and rotten fruit wafting around him.

He did not know which was worse, the idea of Evelyn hating him forever, or the thought of her living with the smooth, princely Spaniard. The man probably had a harem in every capital, and . . . Justin tossed away the idiotic musings, even more disgusted with himself.

He had more important things to consider, like the health of his great nation and the likelihood of a traitor in their midst. If Sir Phillip Amherst was not a turncoat, then who was? The mighty Sullivan? Conjecture was useless without more information, something Wheaton was ensuring he went without. He wanted to scream in frustration but instead heaved another load of hay and tossed it onto the pile.

The eerie glow of lamplight cast ghoulish shadows up in the loft, and he wished they would rise up and materialize so he could have something to slaughter besides his sense of self-worth.

He paused to wipe his clammy brow with the sleeve of his shirt. The only sounds in the darkened stables were his rasping breath and the nighttime rousing of the slumbering animals. His soft hands pinched and burned with blisters as his station decried the manual labor he was relishing so piercingly tonight.

He deserved the pain. It was nothing compared to what Sullivan must be facing. Justin only hoped that the man's actions warranted it. It would be the only saving grace for this chaos; otherwise, he was the unbidden tool of a traitor within his own ranks. He was beginning to question the existence of a targeted French threat to the monetary system. The facts were not adding up to anything remotely equal to menace. Nothing, so far, justified what he'd done to Evelyn.

He stuck the fork in a pile to resume his penance when he heard boot steps pounding past the front of the stables. People rarely traversed the alley this time of night. Heaving the tool, he jumped down and silently strode to the door, leaning against the rough wooden slats to listen.

"The Spaniard's outside with two men. She's inside the little house." A scratchy voice sniggered menacingly. "Alone."

The sweat froze on Justin's face like a film of ice. He counted at least six, no, seven sets of boots clomping past, heading toward his brother's sanctuary nearby.

His heart pounded while he waited until they had passed, and then he lunged for his coat. He dug in the pocket, pulling out his only weapon. One pistol, one shot. It would have to do. He hoped that Arolas and his men were well armed. Rushing out the door, he grabbed a small whip coiled on a notch on his way and prayed he was not too late.

He heard the grunts and scuffle of boot steps before he could discern the shapes of fighting men. He rushed forward, barely making out the skirmishing bodies. In their wisdom, the authorities had not bothered to waste good light on the back alleyway. He easily spotted the gracefully catlike Arolas as he whipped his sword back and forth, keeping three of his attackers at bay.

Justin did not recognize any of the other men. He squared his stance and uncoiled the whip, snapping it tautly against one of Arolas's assailant's hands, lashing the knife right from the man's grasp.

"Goddam!" he railed, and turned. Square jaw, big hands, black-painted face. So Mr. Sullivan had not been his attacker the other night in the stables. The burly man roared and launched himself at Justin. Justin spun on his booted heels and, using the pistol butt, whacked the man on the back of his shoulder. The brute screamed with agony. Before Justin could congratulate himself for his deductive reasoning, Arolas shouted as he held off two knife-wielding attackers, "Two men got past—Evelyn's inside!"

Justin raced past clusters of combatants and through

the threshold door to his brother's sanctuary. The flickering glow of lamplight lit a scene out of his worst nightmare. His blood chilled in his veins.

Through the corner of his eye he took in the ashen-faced man lying slumped against the bookshelves, a knife protruding from his belly. But Justin's gaze was glued to the bastard pressing Evelyn into the couch with his beastly body while he tugged open his breeches. A meaty fist clamped around her neck while she screamed and fought wildly, her arms and legs flailing ineffectively against his greater bulk.

Justin jumped on the bull and grabbed his shoulders, ripping him off her. The man whipped around, backhanding Justin into the wall, jarring him so hard that his teeth rattled. The bastard lumbered over to Justin, terrorizingly near. Justin whipped up the pistol and fired. The blast was so deafening that his head spun. Blood splattered everywhere and the man fell backwards, a circle of red gore where his chest had been. The room shook with the shock of the bull's slow crash to the floor. Smoke billowed from the spent pistol, and the acrid scent of gunpowder filled Justin's nostrils.

He swallowed, trying to clear his head. He looked over at Evelyn. She was staring at him like he had grown two heads. Well, one could argue that he had. She tugged together her tattered clothing and heaved herself off the green couch, heading for the door.

"Evelyn! Don't go out there!" he screamed, and it sounded like an echoing whisper in his ears. He pushed himself up to follow, but she charged back inside in a thrice. Her chest was heaving, and her eyes were wide and frightened.

She ran past him and ripped open the door to the

back storage room, peering frantically inside. He knew there was nothing useful in there, just some bizarre sketching and watercolors. He grabbed the whip off the floor where it had fallen and was about to go out to help Arolas when he saw the gun in the other fiend's hand.

Despite the knife in his chest and the deathly hue to his skin, the man's hand barely shook as he aimed it at Evelyn's back from his perch on the floor. She turned, and her eyes widened even more.

"No!" Justin screamed, and threw himself forward. A thundering crack resounded for the second time in the small room. Pain seared his chest worse than the fire of God's wrath. He crashed headfirst into the far bookcase, ramming his skull with a hammering jolt. The shelving tumbled down on top of him, and his last thought as the heavy bookcase crashed onto his body was, *It's not fair, I still had so much left to do.*

Chapter 18

❝I cannot even stand to look at the man's face," Evelyn cried, pounding her fist on the scratchy wooden tabletop. "There's no way I'll nurse the vile bastard back to health so he can try to kill us once again!"

"Justin Barclay took a bullet for you," Angel countered.

Evelyn ran her hand through her tousled hair, realizing it had been days since she'd last had a bath. The frantic escape from London to this remote village in the country had not allowed time for grooming. "Perhaps it was another of his deceptions. The man seems a master at manipulation." His betrayal still burned hot in her heart, making her quick to discount any decent thing he might have ever done, including save her life.

"Or perhaps he has grown to care for you."

"Harrumph! The man does not have a feeling bone in his body." Just the thought of his lean muscular physique and how she had allowed him to touch her made her want to spit nails.

Angel's handsome features hardened as he rose from the wooden stool. "We've been over this before, Evelyn. We took him along with us because he is our most critical source of information. I'd bet my last farthing he knows who's behind the scheme against you, who may have killed your father."

"It's not worth learning any possible information he may know. I cannot do anything about Papa now, and claiming my inheritance is just not *that* important." She crossed her arms. "Mr. Tuttle can chase after my legacy, on the unlikely chance that I can still claim what is rightfully mine. Once it is safe to travel, I intend to be handily out of the British government's reach."

"What about Sully?"

She swallowed.

He pressed, "Sullivan has disappeared from Newgate, last seen being herded out by six guards. No one knows where he is, or even if he is alive."

She ignored the searing pain tearing at her heart. Sully had to be alive. She did not think she could handle another loss. She rubbed her hand over her eyes to keep the unshed tears from spilling free. This was a nightmare, but all too real. She shuddered and took a deep breath, knowing she would do anything to save Sully.

"I will find out what he knows," she stated flatly.

Angel stared at her hard, his chocolate brown eyes narrowing. "Take good care of him, Evelyn. Although he is somehow involved in the government plot, he is still a marquis and an earl and he has no heirs in his line. He can be very valuable to us, if the need arises."

"Sully is worth fifty of him."

"Perhaps to you, but not to the English."

The specter of her father lying dead in her arms flashed through her mind. She shuddered, pushing away the thought. "I've never tended someone with a gunshot injury. Perhaps we can retain the doctor's assistant or someone from the village to care for him."

"The doctor removed the bullet; you just need to keep the wound clean and the fever away. Moreover, we need to keep as low a profile as possible. You need to be the person hearing his tales, no one else." Evelyn recognized the tight, resolved look on Angel's handsome face. His mind was set. Besides, he was right; although she would hate every minute of it, she was best suited for the job.

Sighing, she looked around the spartan kitchen that would be her home for the foreseeable future. "Very well. Shah and I will tend to him."

"Remember, the doctor seemed equally concerned about the head injury." He donned his long black cloak and black hat. "The caretaker is paid through the end of the month. He and his wife will leave provisions every other day by the end of the lane. They have no interest in coming closer."

"What did you tell them?"

He smiled, but it was not a jovial thing. "They are good Christians who've fallen on hard times. They need the money but do not want to know about the sin transpiring in their cottage."

She grimaced. "The only sin transpiring here will be me drawing out the knave's toenails if he does not tell me what I need to know."

Angel leaned forward and kissed her on each cheek. "Take care, Evelyn."

She laid her hand on his arm. "Angel?"

He paused, then squeezed her hand. "I know, *caro*. I know."

She pressed her lips together to keep from crying. She nodded stiffly. "Thank your father for me as well."

"He would like the men who murdered your father to see justice, as much as I would, perhaps more."

"I fear I've given up on justice. I just want Sully safe."

He strode toward the door and opened it wide. The cool country air drifted in. An owl hooted in the distance.

Angel paused in the threshold and turned. "Remember, Evelyn, the marquis is the key to unraveling at least part of this mystery and may prove to be our final gambit. He might even turn out to be an ally, in the end."

She shivered. "He has no honor; no matter the odds against us, we are better off without him on our side."

"It seems we could use all the help we can get." He stepped through the doorway into the cold black night and slammed the door closed behind him.

Evelyn rose from the rickety chair and barred the entry. She leaned back against the rough wood grain and wrapped her arms around each other, hoping to fortify herself for the task ahead.

No use putting off the inevitable. She pushed away from the door and strode to the adjacent room.

The chamber smelled of the odd poultice the doctor had left behind. She could discern mint and linseed in the mix; the mint was probably to cover up the other unpleasant odors.

Two candles rested on each of the side tables to the bed, illuminating the body lying prone and lifeless under a brown woolen blanket.

At Evelyn's entry, Shah got up from her chair in the corner.

"He has not woken?" Evelyn asked.

The stout maid simply shook her head. A dark scowl lined her features. Shah had been hard-pressed to believe that the marquis had betrayed them. Instead she had clung to the supposed fact that he had saved Evelyn's life, a fact Evelyn found equally galling and unbelievable.

She stepped closer and leaned over his still form. A layered white bandage wrapped his head, contrasting with his bruised and ashen face. With his eyes closed and his features softened with sleep, he looked almost harmless. But she knew better.

Shah hung back in the corner. Evelyn knew she was not comfortable looking after a man but was prepared to assist in any way she could. Evelyn did not know how she had been so fortunate in her friends.

She peeled back the blanket and stared at his naked body, trying to see him as an object to be tended, not as a man she abhorred. His pale skin shone in the candlelight as she perused his lean, muscular body, her eyes resting on the bandages encircling his broad chest. Blood had seeped through the layers near his right side, staining the white in an egg-sized circle of red. "I suppose I will have to clean the wound."

"The doctor said to change the bandage in the morning," Shah supplied. "That it might bleed some was expected."

Evelyn yawned, accepting any excuse not to touch him. "Right, then. The morning it is." She checked the thin leather strips binding his wrists and lowered the blanket further to examine the bindings at his ankles.

She kept her eyes far from the private area covered only with white men's drawers.

The doctor had scoffed at restricting the wounded man, insisting that he would be as weak as a newborn, but Evelyn was not about to take any chances. She and Shah were alone in this house, and he was as clear an enemy as ever she'd known.

Evelyn dropped the blanket, rubbing her hands over her eyes. "Go lie down. I'll tend him if he wakes."

"You need rest too."

"My head is racing too much for sleep. You go on."

Knowing it was useless to argue, Shah drifted out of the chamber to the bedroom next door. The accommodations were anything but lavish, but Evelyn was thankful they at least had a few rooms, some semblance of privacy for when the man awakened.

The doctor had suggested that it might take weeks for the marquis to recover. Evelyn prayed it was not even close to that time. She just needed him conscious enough to answer questions and yet not be a threat. Anything beyond that was a problem. No matter what she had told Angel, she was not prepared to nurse the man back to health. The authorities might deem the man worthy of a trade, but a knife in the back would be all she could expect once the marquis was back in his domain.

She went back to the kitchen and sat at the rough wooden table. She placed paper, ink, quill, and blotter before her, thanking Angel's foresight for her purgatory in this place. He was generous to her in all ways. She did not know how she would ever repay him.

Blotting the quill, she began the task of sorting the crazed web of her thoughts to set herself a strategy for the days to come.

What we need to know:

1. Where is Sully?
2. What do you want from him and from me?

She scratched her nose. That question presupposed that the marquis was behind the whole scheme, which did not fit the facts. She had to begrudgingly admit that if he was behind the matter, he would not have interfered with the attack the other night. Which meant someone else was orchestrating events.

3. Who do you work for/with?
4. What is their goal?
5. What is their weakness?
6. Do you make a habit of seducing your victims, or was I a special case?

She blinked. Where did that question come from? She rubbed her eyes. She must be more exhausted than she thought; she was allowing her anger to overshadow her purpose. Father had always said you need decent sleep to keep a clear perspective.

Sighing, she pushed aside the papers and went to the bedroom where the marquis lay. She propped a pillow in the wooden chair in the corner and sat down, glaring at the man who lay at the heart of this tangled fabric, slumbering as if he had all his days to rest. She hoped he had a nightmare.

"He sleeps too long," Shah commented worriedly.

"I agree." Evelyn paced the room. It had been three endless days of sitting on pins and needles watching the man, who did not rise to consciousness. He had barely responded when she had changed his bandages. She could only imagine the pain from his wounds; that he did not complain or even moan vested her with unknown fear. Evelyn had removed Justin's bonds, realizing that her own safety was the least of her worries now.

"We must eat," Shah commented while drifting out of the bedroom.

The small sick-chamber reminded Evelyn of a cabin on a ship, but a vessel that had lost its moorings. The wind had died, the sails were flat, and the crew waited desperately for the promise of land. She felt as if she and Shah hung on simply to endure the next squall, their spirits were so low.

Justin's ashen face, bloodied body, and shallow breath terrified Evelyn. Foolishly, part of her wondered if all of the hatred she'd directed at him had somehow manifested in his poor recovery. Could the powers that be have somehow interpreted her loathing as a death wish for him? She hoped not. She cleaned him, cared for him, and watched over him. What else was in her power?

Evelyn found herself doing something she had not done in a very long time: praying. She crouched on her knees before the small window in Justin's chamber, somehow sensing that God would be outside on this glorious day, rather than in the stale, malodorous chamber. Evelyn could hear Shah in the kitchen, probably saying a few prayers of her own.

Evelyn pressed her forehead to her clutched hands, not knowing what to say to the heavenly father. It seemed odd to beseech the Lord to save Justin, the man she hated with an abiding passion. Would God sense her incongruent feelings on the matter? Could He read her heart when it was so befuddled with hatred, anger, fear, and the quiet cries of desperate longing?

As her thighs cramped and her knees burned raw, she finally concluded her course would be to ask the Lord to sort things out as best as He saw fit. But to save Sully, take care of Shah and Ismet, and, finally, to help Justin. She hated him, yes. But she sincerely did not wish for him to die. She could not imagine this world without him. She could not ignore the good deeds he had done in his life, including saving her life and winding up in this terrible state. The memory of his throwing himself in front of the discharging bullet played through her mind, over and over, making her feel as if her ties to Justin were not nearly severed. There was still much between them, no matter how hard she wished to deny it.

She rose on shaky feet, more certain of herself than she'd been in days. Evelyn swept into the kitchen. "Get me some water from the stream," she ordered Shah. "Do not heat it. We will bathe him and then try to wake him."

Wringing her hands in her apron, Shah nodded. Her usual scowl had deepened even further, if that were possible.

Together they washed his body with icy water. He did not wake. They tried shouting, shaking him, propping him up, to no avail. They even tried sticking pins in his feet. Nothing evoked a response. Evelyn was growing frantic. If he died, how was she going to return his body to his family without setting the authorities upon them? If he died, how could she help Sully? If he died, how was she going to ever know why he betrayed, and then saved, her?

The dark cloud that hung over the isolated cabin did not abate, even when Angel sent a message reporting that Ismet was all right. There was still no word on Sully.

Evelyn began reading to Justin from her father's journal. Somehow saying the words out loud gave her comfort and added some semblance of beauty to her strained world. If only the ghost of her father would appear with some brilliant insight, showing her a way out of this sordid mess. If only the words she read off the page would give her the answers she so urgently needed.

She read long into the dark nights, her voice growing hoarse. At least it helped keep her sane, and perhaps Justin would find his way out of his dark warren of oblivion.

"I warrant Evelyn's heart is larger than the great ship that brought us to this godforsaken place. Today she adopted four pitiful, motherless kittens despite the fact that the staff has not yet recovered from the mongrel she brought home last week. They mew all over the residence and smell worse than the Thames." She grinned to herself, recalling her father's feigned disgust; she had spied his lips bowing into a smile. Even though he'd hated to admit it, he'd found the little darlings just as adorable as she had. He had just liked to pretend to be gruff. Sighing, she read on, "All hell broke loose when she attempted to bathe the filthy pests. Yet, I cannot rebuke her. She is diverted and concurrently entertains the staff. No small blessing there."

She turned the page. "The tension here is thicker than butter but my efforts are slowly but surely proving fruitful, and I know with half a chance—"

"Arife?" Shah entered. The lines of her face had deepened, and shadows fanned her dark eyes. "You must take a break."

"I want to bathe him again." Evelyn set aside the journal and rose. Stretching to get the blood back into her aching limbs, she added, "You sleep, I'll do it."

"I do not see the benefit, but I will get the water and cloth."

"Then will you rest?"

Shah nodded. "As you say. But I have prayed much to Allah, and I fear our efforts are lost on this marquis. The man has gone to brighter places."

"He's a strong man and will fight back. He just needs a little prodding."

"The kind of push we are powerless to give, I'm afraid." Shaking her head, Shah left the room.

Sitting next to him on the small bed, Evelyn traced the cool cloth along Justin's broad, bare shoulders and down his muscled arms. Even in ill health the man managed to appear virile. His limbs were long and strapping, his shoulders and chest brawny, his waist tapered and firm. Her gaze traveled to the blankets draped at his waist, and then moved back to his upper torso. No use thinking about what's down there.

Despite the fine dusting of golden-brown hair, his skin was pale in the flickering candlelight. One could almost believe him a ghost, if not for the heat radiating from his skin like a hearth with dying embers. If he had a fever, it was low and intense, not blazing.

Brushing the damp cloth along his brow, she smoothed back his short honeyed-wheat hair, exposing his broad forehead. His face had been handsomely defined before, but now it was reminiscent of a stone-chiseled masterpiece. His skin was like alabaster, high-lighting the refined cheekbones, aristocratic nose bordered by hollowed cheeks, and dark beard with a cleft peeking through. The whiskers encircled his pink lips, which were open and chapped around the edges.

Molding the damp cloth about her finger, she leaned forward and traced his open lips, trying to chase the dryness from his mouth. A hand gently wrapped around her wrist. She gasped and her heart skipped a beat.

"Justin! Thank heavens!"

His thumb gently caressed the underside of her wrist, sending shivers racing up her arm.

She yanked her hand away as if burned and jumped far from the bed.

He mumbled something unintelligible. With her heart caught in her throat, she realized he must be in that hazy dream state floating haphazardly between the real and imagined. Still, this was an exciting development after days and nights of no progress.

Stepping back to the bed, she leaned over and gently shook his arm. "Justin?"

When he gave no response, she pressed her hand to his forehead. Was she imagining it, or was he warmer than he'd been just a moment before?

She sat down beside him, lifted the discarded cloth, and swept it across his brow.

His arm slowly coiled about her waist, heavy and locked.

"If this is your idea of a joke, Justin Barclay!" She shook his shoulder more forcefully, but he did not wake. His muscled arm lay heavily around her middle, not in an uncomfortable kind of way. Still, it was a bit too intimate to bear.

She pried her fingers below his forearm, only to have it tighten.

"Wake up, Justin."

He mumbled something unfathomable, and the arm around her waist slowly pulled her on top of him, squashing her breasts against the bandages of his brawny chest. She lay frozen, not wanting to hurt him, yet not wanting to be in his power either. Should she call for Shah? She certainly wasn't afraid he would harm her; for all his misdeeds, he would never laid a hand on her. She didn't believe he would start now. Still, part of her was fearful of him.

Taking a shaky breath, she realized she wasn't exactly afraid of him, but of the hodgepodge of emotions he stirred in her breast; hatred, pain, bitterness, longing, desperate hope mixed with fear. He had ripped out her heart in the worst kind of betrayal but then saved her from being assaulted. The blasted man had taken a bullet for her. She could almost hate him for it.

"Justin," she whispered. Then clearing her throat, she asked, "Are you awake? Please wake up."

With no response from him, she lay frozen, waiting for something, wondering what to do. His warmth radiated up her body, making her recall the pleasure of lying beside his hard-muscled form on a worn green couch not so very long ago. Everything had been so different then, yet her body still recognized her former lover. She closed her eyes, trying to force away the recollections, but Justin's spicy-woodsy scent pervaded her senses, making the memories rush to the fore. Passionate, ardent kisses. Flesh rubbing against hot, wanting flesh. The heat, the ache to have him between her legs, filling her, sating her desire. Her body flamed, hungering for him still. It was appalling. She was mortified by her weakness, by the fever coursing through her flesh for him. She needed to get away from the bastard before he truly came to.

She wiggled slightly, praying he would think this was only a dream. A fiery, erotic fantasy of latent desires transforming into unbridled passion.

Dear Lord, she had to get away from him.

She decided to try sliding down his torso to the bottom of the bed, as his hold was firm, yet not painful. She squirmed, trying hard not to put pressure on his injury.

A small groan, barely more than a whisper, escaped his lips. She froze. Had she hurt him? His arm still held her locked against him, heavy and unmoving. With his eyes still closed, he slowly moved his free hand to her hair. Clutching a fistful of her tresses, he pressed them to his nose.

Heavens, was he smelling her hair? This was growing farcical!

"Uh, Justin, my lord—"

Suddenly he pulled her face to his, meeting her mouth with awkward precision. He pressed his smooth lips to hers, causing her squirming to escalate. She had to escape!

With a firm grasp on her hair, he tilted her head and opened his mouth, daring her to deny his kisses.

She checked all movement, terrified she might actually respond. With her heart hammering faster than any smithy, she decided to reason with him and pretend this was all a funny, horrid mistake.

"Justin?" she tried speaking into those silkily delicious lips. "Now that you're awake, my—"

His hot, thick tongue slid inside her mouth, making

speech impossible. Her body flamed and unconsciously pressed closer, hungry for more. Of its own accord, her tongue entwined with his, eager and wanting. He was on fire, and she wanted to jump into the flames. Blood rushed to her head, sending all thoughts of freedom from her mind. His scent, his touch, his fevered passion trapped her and she wanted him to throw away the key. Her hips reflexively pressed against his hard member; her body yearned for him.

She pressed fiery, wet kisses to his ear, along his handsome jaw, aiming downward.

"Oh, Rachel," he breathed into her hair.

It was as if someone had dropped her into an icy pond. Her passion turned to frosty humiliation. Evelyn pushed out of his arms, uncaring of his injury. Pressing her hand to her mouth, she stood over him, stiff with mortification, horrified by her behavior, by the wanton reaction he had unknowingly ignited in her. She was pitiful beyond redemption.

A frown puckered his brow, but his eyes remained closed. "Mother? I thought you'd gone to see the queen."

His head rolled from side to side. "George! You're back. Good, we've missed you."

She stepped closer and pressed her hand to his brow. The simmering heat had intensified into a raging conflagration. Fear clutched at her heart; she had more to worry about now than her lascivious behavior. The man was burning up with fever.

The words tumbled from his lips, weak and barely sensible, "Don't go . . . hunting. . . . Please stay . . . with me." His voice pitched in panic. "George!"

She grabbed the cloth, dunked it in the now tepid water, and squeezed it over his forehead.

"George!"

Her mouth had dried to dust; she was fearful for him and yet mindful of her own role in this mummery. "Shh," she soothed. "George is dining at his club. He'll be back shortly."

His brow relaxed. "George," he sighed. A small tear trickled out the corner of his eye and rolled down his chiseled cheek. She brushed it away with the cloth. Her heart twisted over his pain for his brother. For all the lies and betrayal, the grief of his brother's loss was very real.

She brushed the damp rag over his neck. "George is at his club having the lamb with mint jelly. And crème brûlée for dessert."

The tension fled his body. His head rolled to one side, and he appeared to doze.

Raising her hand to her mouth, she let out a long, shuddering breath. Swallowing hard, she gathered the bowl and cloth, intent on getting more cold water from the stream. And getting away from Justin Barclay. She felt raw, her insides glaringly exposed during the awful incident.

Not wanting to rouse Shah, Evelyn quietly donned her cloak and left through the kitchen door. Crickets chirped merrily in the brush, and the birds began their morning song. The first golden rays of dawn gave the hint of a glorious day to come. Evelyn barely took it in as she stumbled toward the stream.

Inhaling the woodsy scent of oak trees and green shrubs, she tried to ignore what had just happened in the cabin, instead focusing on the fact that Justin had finally wakened. Well, not quite wakened, but certainly showed some signs of life. An ostensible miracle, one for which she needed to be thankful. Yet, the memory of Justin's passionate embrace and her wanton response made her belly turn over with mortification.

She rubbed her hand over her eyes. She must be well and truly exhausted. Drained to the point of losing her sense of reality. That must have been it. She'd been so tired, unable to help herself. It had been a natural response to a virile male. She was not to blame, nor was he. He had been out of his mind, and, in some sense, so had she.

The air was crisp and damp with the dew shimmering off the mossy ground. As her shoes crunched along the rocky path, she tried to make sense of her world and exactly how to deal with the mystifying marquis and her traitorous body. All business, that was the ticket. He was her prisoner . . . well, her patient, and needed to answer all of her questions. Answers. They would finally have the answers they needed to help Sully. To help her and those she cherished out of this horrid mess. The thought reignited her sense of purpose.

"In my business, clear thinking, keeping your eye on the prize, that's the way we win," her father had explained. *"Emotions muddle one's perceptions and are a luxury a good emissary cannot afford."*

She needed to keep her mission foremost in her mind. To take the passion and emotion Justin evoked in her and set it aside forever. Well, perhaps not forever, but as something to ponder on in her dotage, if she ever made it that far. For all her protestations about wanting to be free of her father's world, it looked as if becoming part of it was necessary in order to survive. She needed to be like her father—coolheaded and willing to do whatever was required.

Feeling back on track, she paused to watch two russet-bellied birds playfully circle and dive. They twittered with cheer. She felt as if the dark clouds hanging overhead had split and a ray of sunlight had pierced through the gloom. A small glimmer of hope, but a glimmer nonetheless.

"But there's a problem with hope," she whispered to the wind. "With it comes the distinct possibility of disappointment."

A crow squawked in the distance in apparent agreement.

Chapter 19

Shah raced in from Justin's chamber, a hunk of cheese and a knife still in her hands. "I heard him. Allah be praised. He's awake."

Evelyn rushed into the room, praying he would not recall anything about the prior night.

She and Shah clutched hands as they stood over him, waiting breathlessly for another sign.

He licked his dry lips.

Evelyn sat beside him. "Bring me some water, Shah."

The trusty maid raced from the room to return a moment later with a pitcher and a cup of water.

"Drink, my lord." Evelyn and Shah gently propped him up, and he sipped from the mug she held for him.

He shuddered and slowly opened his eyes a red-rimmed slit. He looked at her and then Shah, speaking slowly, "Who are you?" His voice was thick and scratchy.

Evelyn blinked. This was the last thing she'd expected. "You don't recognize me?" she asked, uncertainly.

"What happened to me?" he asked slowly. "My head's pounding and my chest is on fire." His glassy eyes traveled the stark room, then locked with hers. His gaze filled with alarm.

Suspicion kept her voice flat. "We've been praying for your recovery, my lord." Her answered prayers did not mean that she was about to fall for another of his ploys.

Slowly raising his hand to his bandaged head, he watched the women warily. "Who are you?"

"I'm hard-pressed to believe you so conveniently lost your memory when it's finally time for you to speak the plain and naked truth." Her cheeks warmed as she realized what she'd said.

Something flickered in those gray-green eyes. Awareness, perhaps? Fear of being forced to spill the ugly facts? She hoped he was not remembering anything about the night before.

"Tell me who you are, at once!" he demanded hoarsely, but he winced in pain, seemingly from his own raised voice.

If he kept up this nonsense she was going to tear every hair from her head. Or better yet, from his.

Ignoring him, she held out the cup. "Here, drink more," she urged.

Licking his lips, he accepted more water from the cup and then dropped his hand palm upward, seemingly exhausted from the limited exchange. His lids lowered, and in a moment he appeared to be asleep.

Evelyn watched him for long moments. Was it her

imagination, or was there more color in his sculpted cheeks? His golden-brown beard blanketed his jaw and dimpled chin, and with his head bandaged, he appeared almost like a dashing pirate. She mentally shook herself. Coolheaded business. Answers. That was his only role in her life. She forced herself to recall that this was the man who had given her the taste of forbidden pleasures, granted her the dream of a saner future, only to dash her hopes against the jagged shards of his betrayal. She needed to keep that in the forefront of her mind.

She turned to Shah. "Let's cook him some soup. He'll be hungry when he wakes again."

The twittering of birds nagged at Justin's consciousness, along with the undeniable scent of . . . cooked onions? Raising his hand to his aching temple, he eased off the bandage and gently traced his fingertips over the egg-sized bump adorning his head. It was tender to the touch. What the hell had happened to him?

He peeled open his eyes, but the bright light of an afternoon sun glaring through a small window caused him to cover his face with his hand. Lord, just moving hurt like the dickens. His breath caught at the searing pain that felt like a heated poker jamming into his chest. He repressed a groan; he felt so bad he'd have thought he was ready for the undertaker.

Trying to force his memory to resurface, he could only recall the hazy specter of George eating lamb with mint jelly. Now he knew he was going daft. But wouldn't it be wonderful if that were really true? He pushed away the pathetic musing, focusing instead on determining how he had been injured and come to this forsaken place.

The room was sparse, with his single bed, two side tables, and a rickety wooden chair against the unadorned wall. The floorboards were swept clean, and a straw broom sat in the corner by the door. He listened but heard no voices, just the clattering of dishes and the movement of people. How many were they, and were they friend or foe? Even with the door and the small window as possible means of escape, he doubted his wretched body would be able to get the job done.

His belly growled, and he chastised it to silence. Food would have to wait. He swallowed, feeling more parched than any desert. A jug sat on the table beside him, adjacent to a ceramic cup. Out of the shadow of his recollection formed the memory of a stout, dark-skinned woman and her blond-haired, blue-eyed companion. They had given him water to drink. Were they the servants of his enemies?

He was loath to make a sound, but the water beckoned. First, he needed to assess his injuries. Taking a deep breath, with his fingertips he felt the wraps around his torso. They were neatly done. He could smell linseed and mint. Likely a concoction for treating a gunshot wound. He'd been shot and had had his head banged in. But by whom? A memory beckoned but drifted out of his grasp. The lovely miss golden hair and her companion? It seemed as if they'd been treating him, but appearances could be deceiving.

Frustration brimmed forth. He was useless without his memory or a weapon. He was alarmed by how weak he felt and how little he recalled. He could remember nothing of a pistol confrontation or of the women ministering to him. He closed his eyes, trying to force his memory to return. The horrific pounding in his head intensified, clamoring to a crescendo loud enough to make his teeth clench.

"Are you alright?" came a melodic voice.

He slowly opened his eyes. A robin's egg blue gaze met his own. A recollection brushed the edges of his vision. Moonlight on golden hair. The sounds of a waltz in the distance. Small pebbles underfoot. And a deliciously sweet kiss.

"I kissed you," he murmured.

Her porcelain cheeks reddened, and she eyed the door nervously. "Nonsense. You must have been dreaming."

"It was at a ball. You were wearing . . . black." His gaze traversed her dark, tattered gown.

Relief flooded her features. "Oh, yes, that. At the Coventry Ball. But that was ages and *ages* ago."

A faint bouquet of lavender reached his senses, and sudden insight flashed through his mind. "You're Evelyn." He smiled, quite proud of himself.

Crossing her arms, she asked dubiously, "So now you remember?"

This was not exactly the welcome he'd hoped for. "You are Evelyn Amherst?"

"Yes."

"And where are we?"

"Reading is the closest town." She met his eyes. "How far is your estate in Bedford from Reading?"

"Two days' ride." With a change of horses and no bullet wound.

"We've made you some soup. I'll be back in a thrice." Frowning, she turned and abruptly left the room.

We. He took a deep breath, letting the images come to him. He was remembering, and it was not at all pleasing. Not by half.

*   *   *

Squaring her shoulders, Evelyn carried the soup and bread into Justin's chamber. He was wrestling with the covers, and the covers were winning.

"Lie still or you will loosen your bandages," she chastised. "Or worse yet, injure yourself further."

He inched himself up on the bed, exposing the white wrappings encircling his broad chest. A small oval of red stained the snowy bandages. He fell back into his pillows, seemingly exhausted. But peach colored his chiseled cheeks, and his gray-green eyes sparkled. The man was unquestionably on the mend. He demanded testily, "How about telling me how the hell we got here?" Recovering indeed.

She placed his soup bowl and bread plate in his lap, careful not to touch him. "My, aren't we snippy upon awakening." She sent a cynical prayer of thanks that she'd never had the opportunity to slumber with the bastard.

"Sorry," he replied, scowling. "But between the aches in my body and what I am finally recalling, I'm feeling a bit put out."

The floorboards creaked as Shah entered and moved to the corner. Wringing her hands in her stained apron, her eyes flew from Justin to Evelyn and back again, concern warming her dark brown gaze.

Between bites he motioned to her. "You are Shah? Turkish, right?"

Shah beamed at him. "We have prayed for your recovery, and Allah has answered." She nodded. "Can I get you anything else, Sahip? More water?"

Evelyn waved her off. "He seems fine for now. Certainly well enough to eat and answer some questions."

"He only just woke," Shah countered, eyeing her re-provingly.

"We've waited long enough for this lying turncoat to tell us everything he knows."

He grumbled, "I'm no turncoat and I'd appreciate a bit of water." He nodded to Shah. "Yes, please."

Shah poured him a cupful, and he drank it down like a man who'd just traveled the desert. He helped himself to two more cupfuls before consuming every drop of the soup.

"Are you ready to talk now?" Evelyn asked evenly, standing at the foot of his bed with her arms crossed. She was chomping at the bit to get down to business. The sooner she exposed the facts and got away from Justin Barclay, the better off she would be.

He nodded and set down the empty bowl on the side table. His spoon clattered loudly in the tense silence.

Leaning back against the covers with a sigh, he stated, "I was not lying, Evelyn. And I will answer any of your questions. Although I have a few of my own." Shifting the bedclothes around his bare waist, he looked up, saying, "If I recall correctly, I was shot and the bookcases fell on top of me. I assume a doctor examined me. I'd like to know what he said about my injuries."

She had to begrudgingly admit that it was not an unreasonable inquiry. "He said it was fortunate we got the bullet out. He said you'd be weak. That if we were lucky you'd avoid infection. And it looks like you have, so far. But you did have a fever and were a bit delirious." She tried to stop her faithless cheeks from heating.

"Did I say anything terrible?"

She couldn't help herself. "Who is Rachel?"

He chuckled. "I really must have been fevered."

"Well, who is she? An agent? Mistress?"

Shah slipped out the door. "I go cook."

"My old governess." Shaking his head, he commented wistfully, "I haven't seen her in years. She was my very first—" His words abruptly stopped and his brow puckered. Tilting his head, he studied Evelyn.

Suddenly a loose thread that needed snipping on her sleeve drew all of her focused attention. She rolled its end in her fingers and pressed it down. "Well, no matter then." She cleared her throat. "So how are you feeling now?"

He seemed to consider her a long moment, finally speaking slowly. "Well, there's the carriage rolling over my head. And the gaping hole in my chest." He licked his lips. "But they are nothing compared to the ache in my heart."

"You can stop pretending now." Her hands clenched. "You've accomplished your goal; Sully was taken, I am completely alone."

He shifted uncomfortably. "I know I've wronged you, Evelyn. But if you only knew how much I care—"

Ignoring his declaration, she let out a long breath. Making certain to stay at arm's reach away from him, she turned and dragged the wooden chair from the corner to the side of the bed.

"Does my remorse count for nothing with you?" he asked roughly.

She adjusted her black skirts, noticing how dirty and drab they had become. She was having trouble looking at him. You would think he'd at least want to don a shirt. "We need to know why you trapped Sully. Why do you want him?" Sudden insight dawned on her.

"For that matter, why did you have my father murdered?"

"I did not kill your father, Evelyn. How can you believe that?"

She met his gaze levelly. "I don't know what to believe where you are concerned."

"Well, let me tell you the truth." He implored with his eyes. "For all of the convoluted plotting and scheming to entrap you and Sullivan, you cannot understand how much you've come to mean to me."

She set the information aside as one would a trivial letter. "Your feelings are neither here nor there. I need to know who you work for and what is your intent. That is your only usefulness." The words sounded harsh even to her own ears, but her anger made them feel justified.

He pursed his lips. "Do you have any feelings for me at all, Evelyn?"

"Emotions are immaterial. Sully is in trouble and that is my only concern."

He nodded slowly. "So you claim." He said it as if he did not believe it or was unwilling to. Well, it was not her problem. Getting answers was.

"Who do you work for?"

"The Foreign Office."

"What is your immediate mission?"

"To stop a conspiracy targeting our monetary system."

"Connived by whom?"

"Supposedly Napoleon," he paused, "and your father."

"Stuff and nonsense. Father would have rather slit his own throat than bring harm to his country."

"What was he working on when he died?"

"When he was *murdered*"—she let the word hang in the air—"Spain was firmly committed to the alliance. So he was bolstering the bonds with Prussia, Russia, and Sweden. Napoleon's spies were everywhere, trying to ignite discord. We were based in Sweden, and he traveled frequently between the three countries, keeping everyone steadfast, unswervingly devoted to the campaign."

"You are certain?"

"Absolutely."

"What about Sullivan?"

"You are barking up the wrong tree, I tell you!" Her patience was growing thin. "My father would've given up his life a thousand times for his king! The fault lies with your masters, not my family!"

"I fear you might be correct," he stated quietly.

She hid her surprise; she'd finally gotten through to him. Rubbing her hands over her eyes, she asked quietly, "So what do they want from us?"

"I don't know. I was supposed to get you to spill your father's secrets. Or get Sullivan to come out of hiding."

"You se—" She swallowed hard, ignoring the pain perilously near her heart. "Seduced me to get my defenses down so I would tell you . . . what? What secrets could I possibly hold?"

He studied his fingernails. "Supposedly you knew of the plot against the Crown." He looked up. "Do you?"

She laughed. She would not have thought it possible just a moment before. "If only you knew how preposterous that sounds. The last thing in the world I want to do is become part of my father's horrid world." Staring out the window, she became serious. "I'm running from it just as fast as I can, Justin. Except it seems to hound my every step. Oh, I understand the dirty business is necessary for the health of the nation. But it's certainly not good for my own health. I'd like to live to see my twenty-third birthday."

"On that point we can wholeheartedly concur." Rubbing his hand against his temple, he stated quietly, "This means I've been duped into placing Sullivan in Wheaton's hands—but for what? If not for the French plot, then what were you supposed to know? Or what were you supposed to reach for if all of your resources were seized?"

Her hands clenched the sides of her seat. "I should have known you were behind that as well."

He grimaced. "Guilty as charged."

Heavy silence enveloped them. It seems they were both pawns in a deadly game of cat and mouse, in which she had been the cheese. But to what end?

"Who is Wheaton?" she asked.

"He supervises the spy trade at the Foreign Office."

"Has he turned?"

Justin shook his head. "He would never betray his country."

"Isn't murdering an English emissary betraying your country?"

"I don't understand any of this. It doesn't make any sense." Wincing, he raised his hand to his temple again.

Her brow knit, almost feeling the ache herself; his anguish was so evident. Although she had exceedingly mixed feelings about the man, watching him suffer was a pastime she did not relish. "Does it hurt much?"

He replied through clenched teeth, "Only when I think. Or breathe. Or speak . . ."

Wanting to do something to stop his distress, she offered, "I'll get you more broth."

"No, I just need to sleep." His voice was strained.

Watching him struggle to lower himself in the bed, she stood. "Let me help you." She gently held his shoulders and eased him down. His nearness and that spicy scent recalled memories she wished to exorcise forever. So instead, she focused on adjusting the pillow under his head and covering his bare chest with the blanket. If she really wanted to make him unappealing, she'd have to raise the cover to the top of his head. And send him to another country. She was just going to have to fight her body's impulses; they seemed oblivious to danger even when it bussed her on the lips.

Before she could move away, he grasped her hand. "Thank you, Evelyn."

"For what?"

"You can't hate me terribly to have nursed me so."

She swallowed, hard. "You cannot tell me what I need to know if you are dead, can you?"

A small smile lit his smooth lips. "Keep telling yourself that, Evelyn." And with that disturbing comment, he closed his eyes and released her.

Chapter 20

Evelyn could not sleep. She lay on her pallet, staring up at the timbers bracing the roof of the small cabin. Thirty-four posts. She'd counted every one, five times over. She was exhausted, but sleep evaded her like an elusive ghost taunting her with a naughty prank.

"Catch me if you can," she whispered into the darkness. The moon hung shrouded in clouds, sending little light through the small window. The gloom perfectly matched her black mood. It had been two days of questioning Justin and getting few answers. They'd both surmised that the French plot was likely a cover-up for something else, but what, they did not know. All in all, if it weren't for Justin's improving health, Evelyn would have counted the last two days as a resounding failure.

She was feeling tired and irritable, yet restless energy infused her every time she had the opportunity for sleep. So she'd undertaken the lion's share of Justin's care, allowing Shah time to rest. Not that the trusty servant put her feet up much, between cooking and cleaning.

Evelyn had to admit—she was better suited to the nursing than she would ever be to cooking and cleaning. Moreover, forcing herself to be around Justin would eventually drive out the memory of his touch. That's what she kept telling herself, anyway. It was deplorable how skittish she was around him; as if she'd never nursed a virile man she'd been intimate with! She almost giggled to herself at that thought.

What was decidedly not amusing was his response to her discomfiture. He tried to pretend he did not notice, yet somehow he always needed her help whenever he wanted to move. She'd almost caught him smiling a time or two but had yet to nail him. Lord, he was so much easier to deal with when he was unconscious.

She flipped over on the bedding, wishing someone would knock her over the head so she could finally rest. Trying for something uplifting, she tilted her ear toward the window. If she listened really hard, she might just be able to discern the creek bubbling past. But she could not hear much over Shah's thundering snores emanating from the pallet across the room. Evelyn envied her ability to sleep so deeply that an earthquake wouldn't wake her.

Evelyn heard a scraping in the room next door. She rose onto her elbow, listening intently. Someone was definitely in the kitchen. But she had not heard the door open, so it was likely their unsettling guest. Did he have no respect for the feelings of others? It was bad enough they were tending him slavishly, could he not at least let them sleep in peace?

She scrambled up, adjusted her skirts, brushed her hand across her braided hair, and tiptoed into the next room, ready to let her patient know who was in charge of this outfit. If he did not sleep, he would not recover. If he did not recuperate, they could never get back to London. Part of her wished she would have the excuse to stay in the beautiful countryside, but she was unwilling to admit that to Justin or anyone else.

A single candle sitting on top of the stove illuminated the small kitchen. Justin sat at the table with a feast of apple and cheese on a plate before him. A black wool blanket tightly draped his waist, but otherwise he wore nothing to cover his naked state. You would think after days of seeing him undressed she would grow immune to his appeal.

He looked up when she entered. "Sorry if I woke you."

"You should be in bed," she chided, gently closing the door to her room. At least someone ought to sleep this night.

"I'm hungrier than a bear."

Eyeing the last shreds of their provisions, she replied, "You certainly eat like one." Turning her back to him, she tossed some timber into the stove. "If you don't sleep, you cannot recuperate."

"I cannot sleep when my body aches like Napoleon's cavalry used it for target practice."

"If you'd just take the laudanum—"

"No," he interrupted briskly. "I told you I want my head clear."

"No need to be prickly about it." She slipped into the

rickety wooden chair across from him and inched it back a notch. She certainly didn't need to be on top of him. Her cheeks warmed, and she fiddled with a corkscrew lying on the rough table.

"You try being pleasant with your body screaming at you in agony."

She harrumphed, mumbling, "I'd like to give you some agony."

Hurt flickered in his silver-green eyes. Evelyn looked away. She knew she was behaving badly, but she seemed unable to help it. She felt so out of control where *he* was concerned. Her anger simmered below the surface, bubbling up at his every conceived infraction. Here she was, tending him hand and foot, while he should be paying for his crimes. She'd always known there was no justice in this world.

Uncomfortable seeing Justin in his half-naked state, Evelyn let her eyes drop to the table leg. Staring unseeing at the wood, she listened to his every movement, glaringly aware of him. That awareness pricked her indignation and made her want to scream.

The silence stretched long.

"We need to get you some decent clothes," she finally remarked, turning her attention to her skirts. Could her attire get any shabbier?

"I know it's horribly indecent, but I kind of like being so free," he replied, inserting a piece of cheese into his mouth. "I'd never realized how liberating not being slave to so many layers of clothing could be. I never could have imagined surviving without my valet. And here I am, doing quite well, if I do say so."

"How very un-English of you." She watched him skin the apple and slide a sliver between his glistening lips. She ripped her gaze back to her hands in her lap. "Shah is uncomfortable around you."

"And does my bare flesh agitate you, Evelyn?" he teased.

She ignored him and the sudden tingles unfurling in her belly, letting her scowl speak for itself.

"You've certainly seen it before," he added playfully.

Heat warmed her cheeks and stirring memories flashed in her mind. But she pressed her lips together, forcing herself not to react to his baiting.

He leaned forward. "And stroked it."

She crossed her arms, swallowing, thankful it was anger, not embarrassment, heating her cheeks this time. "If you say one more word—"

"And kissed it—"

"That's enough!" she cried, trying to keep her voice low, yet desperately wanting to end his maddening dialogue and the desire he stirred within her breast. "How can you be so proud of yourself for duping an innocent miss into flipping her skirts? I'd never have figured you for a debaucher of maidens, but you certainly played the part better than any actor traversing the boards on Drury Lane. Perhaps your true nature finally shines through!"

Leaning forward, his face was a mere hand's width from hers. The scent of apples warmed his breath. "I've tried every conceivable way I can think of to make amends, but you jump down my throat every time I even try to tell you how I feel. I've apologized. I've answered every bloody question you've thrown at me." He hammered his fist on the tabletop. "Every time you have to touch me you're more skittish than a newborn colt. As if I were going to maul you—"

"Like you haven't before!"

"I never laid a hand on you without your express permission. Hell, *invitation*!"

She jumped from her seat, and the chair flipped back to the floor with a crash. "Do you want to know why I jump every time I go near you? Because just the sight of you makes me want to scream!"

Justin tried to hide his satisfaction; he'd finally got a rise out of her after two days of listening to her protestations about feeling naught as far as he was concerned. He'd grown tired of her claims that emotions had nothing to do with their circumstances. As far as he was concerned, they had *everything* to do with their situation and the simmering passion between them.

He smiled wickedly. Her breasts were heaving, her blue eyes were flashing, and her cheeks flushed red. She was dazzling. And his blood was boiling for her. He played his trump card. "You certainly weren't screaming when you kissed me. And I was half-dead with delirium."

Her mouth worked, but no sound came. Finally she sputtered, "I, that, I . . . it was not me!"

"It certainly wasn't Shah. With the silky tresses and the scent of lavender. One might say you were mauling a helpless invalid."

"I could kill you," she growled.

"Find a spot in the queue." He stepped around the table, edging up against her. She stepped back, stopping at the wall. "I just wish you'd get it over with and stop acting like a cantankerous witch. If I close my eyes I might actually think I was at home with my fractious mother."

She seemed to be trying hard to show him that he did not intimidate her. She leaned forward, nose to nose with him. He detected her lovely lavender fragrance, as well as a hint of cloves on her breath. "I'm no bloody dragon lady, but perhaps there's something she and I have in common. We both hate you! I despise you for everything you've done to my family and to me. For allowing others to manipulate you into hurting us! You're pathetic!"

Her words ripped at his most vulnerable core, making him see red. Between his hunger for her and his anger at himself, all sense of decency fled. He pressed his burning heart next to hers, wanting her to stop the pain from tormenting him. He was so much larger than she, pinning her soft, pliant body to the wall.

With one hand, he grabbed her wrists and locked them against the wood above her head. "Look into my eyes, Evelyn. Tell me again how much you despise me, the unknowing instrument of your enemies—"

She writhed against him, attempting to break free. Yet even now, she was obviously trying not to harm his injury.

His free hand slipped to her shoulder, and she froze. "What? No more words of loathing? I find it odd that for all your vicious charges, you have yet to say anything scathing about my performance between the sheets, Evelyn." His hand dipped lower, gently grazing across her breast. She inhaled sharply, her body frozen, her head leaning back against the wall and her eyes smoldering.

His fingertips glided over her nipple, circling the precious nub. It hardened and, seemingly of its own accord, her warm bosom pressed deep into his palm.

Her body wanted him; warm, soft, and so deliciously feminine. Her excited heartbeat pounded against his hand. She pushed against him, but her attempt at escape lacked force and seemed half-hearted at best. Still, she looked ready to scratch his eyes out.

He dipped his head, pressing his mouth to the soft wool covering her breast. A small groan escaped from her lips as he tenderly bit the nub.

Her breath was coming in short pants. "This means nothing," she murmured in a throaty voice. If looks could kill, he'd have been tarred and feathered by now.

Her denial of the naked truth made his body fire all the more. Reaching his hand down to her thigh, he nibbled tenderly on her neck. "I know you want me, Evelyn." He massaged the delicate curve of her derriere, grinding her into him, making her feel how much he wanted her.

She suddenly stopped moving. Turning her head, she whispered, "Let me go before I harm you."

"You cannot hurt me any more than you already have, my love." He brushed little kisses on the nape of her neck, teasing, licking, and nibbling up to her ear, all the while kneading her luscious buttocks.

His mouth moved to hers, pressing first one corner of her lips and then the other. "Kiss me, Evelyn."

"No."

"You know you want to."

"No. I don't." But her body belied her words. Her flesh was fevered. Her back arched, pressing her hips into his, and her legs slowly spread, welcoming him into her heat.

He pressed his mouth against her velvety soft lips, nibbling tenderly for purchase. He drew her lower lip into his mouth and sucked gently, just like he knew she liked it.

"Make love to me, Evelyn," he breathed into her honeyed mouth.

Slowly her lips softened. Her body relaxed, and a

small sigh escaped from those lovely lips. He dove in, feeling a sense of exultation. She finally acknowledged she wanted him! At least part of her had to care. Her soft, supple body melted into his. Those well-formed legs clutched at his thighs, welcoming him into her innermost sanctum.

He was like a starved man at his first meal. He sucked on her tongue, running his hands up and down her gloriously curvaceous body. The chafe of her woolen gown against his exposed skin teased his senses. He gripped her waist as she writhed against him, her hot, soft flesh hardening his member to iron. He could not recall ever being so aroused.

Her tongue captured his and claimed it in a dance that assaulted his senses. The once tender kisses turned hot, wet, and passionate, sending all thoughts of triumph from his mind. Escaping his locked hand, she grabbed the back of his neck, pressing the kiss tighter. Her fingertips twined in his short hair, teasing the back of his neck. She laved his tongue, ardently pressing her pelvis into his, rubbing against him in wanton pleasure.

Softly biting his earlobe, she whispered, "Lay back onto the table."

His breath caught. Lord, let this not be some terrible ploy. He eased his body off hers. She pressed him back onto the scratchy tabletop.

With infinite slowness, she lay down the length of him. It was his fantasy come to life in the woman of his dreams. She pressed her lips to his, and he surrendered to her passion. Writhing against him, she moved her wet, open mouth to his neck, sucking, licking, while sliding her hips up and down his engorged staff. She was hotter than Hades.

Panting, she tossed aside his blanket, yanked off his smalls and ripped up her skirts. She was moving so quickly that he barely had time to breathe.

She mounted him with a harsh groan. She was hot, tight, and wetter than he'd ever imagined. Reaching up, he gently squeezed her exquisite breasts, molding them into his hands. Through the thin wool of her gown he caressed her nipples, teasing them to tight buds.

She rode him hard, grinding her hips into his with escalating ferocity. In the flickering glow of the candlelight, he watched her. Her head was thrown back, her eyes closed, her cheeks red, her breasts heaving, and her lush lips parted in rapture. She was the most magnificent woman he'd ever laid eyes on.

Her pace quickened. He gripped her buttocks, trying to hang on. His heart was pounding like horse hooves and his breath was coming in short gasps. She was going so fast, driving him so hard, that he couldn't hold on. His hips lifted off the table, plunging into her, challenging her to take her fill.

She came with a loud moan, gloriously pulsing her innermost muscles around him in a heated rush. He pumped his hips harder, throbbing into her, feeling his existence crash into shattering pieces. With a final thrust, he poured his seed inside.

The world slowly came back into focus. She lay atop him, warm, wet, and soft. Her heart still raced in crescendo with his. Breathless, she peeled herself to a sitting position, squeezing him inside her. Still joined to him, she pushed her golden hair from her face, staring down at him, uncertainty filling her sparkling blue eyes.

"That wasn't supposed to happen," she stated

huskily. She shook her head. "I didn't mean for it to happen."

"It's the only thing between us that makes any sense to me," he replied gruffly. He traced his hands down her arms. "Nothing else does."

"Oh, no! You're bleeding!" She jumped off him so swiftly that he felt bereft. She ran from the room, returning quickly with fresh bandages, a jar, and a bowl.

Now that he was back to his senses, his body was aching from the stimulating exertion. His back burned raw from the wood grain. His head was hammering so hard that it made his teeth clench. But it was nothing compared to the searing pain in his chest. Still, he did not want her ever to hesitate to love him so thoroughly, as she'd just done. "It's alright," he managed to bite out.

"No, it's not. So don't pretend to be fine," she chided, chewing on that lush bottom lip. With her eyes never straying from the wound, she commented, "I never should have, we never should have . . ."

He grabbed her arm. "I'd walk through fire to have you mount me like that again, so don't think a gunshot wound is going to slow me down."

She looked away, her cheeks tinging a delicious rose while she tried to hide her pleased smile. "Well, let's forget about . . . *that* for the moment and concentrate on removing your bandage and re-dressing that wound."

He tried to think of a witty rejoinder, but the thundering in his head amplified to an earth-shattering roar, making speech impossible.

She eased him up and helped him walk to his room. He dropped onto the bed, biting his inner cheek so as not to groan. She sat down beside him and, with his stilted cooperation, slowly unwound the cloth. The scents of lavender and sex wafted around her in a heady bouquet. Once free of the bandage, he lay back down, relieved for the rest.

He was irritated by how much the coupling had taxed him. He peeked down at the odious injury, which was burning as if the air licking his flesh were burning cinder. It was small, oval, and ghastly enough to make his head swim. He rolled his face away and clenched his teeth, intent on not revisiting his repast all over his lovely nurse.

"Are you alright?" she asked worriedly.

"Fine," he snarled. "Just please be quick about it."

Her hands were skillful and gentle as she wiped away the old medicine and lathed fresh poultice on him. An icy fire raced up, and then down, his body, raising bumps along his skin. The poultice smelled of mint and linseed. . . . He focused on the mint as his stomach lurched and his head reeled.

Suddenly a cold, wet cloth was set upon his forehead, easing his discomfort. He opened his eyes and captured her concerned gaze. She took another damp cloth and slowly brushed the coolness across his upper chest. Relief flooded through him, and he relaxed.

"I don't know what I ever did to deserve you," he breathed.

She did not answer as she stroked the wet rag along his bare arms.

He wanted to tell her how much she meant to him. How he'd like to stay hidden in the country with her forever. Instead he asked, "How long do you suppose we're safe here?"

"I don't know." Her manner had once again cooled, but that could not undo what had just happened between them. "Angel was supposed to come this afternoon or next. Hopefully he will have news."

"I'm sorry I don't have more information for you, Evelyn. I wish I knew all the answers to your questions."

"Shhh," she coaxed. "Get some rest, Justin. We've had about as much excitement as I can handle for the moment."

He smiled, barely able to keep his eyes open. His head felt like it weighed ten stone as it pressed deep into the pillow. "Now that's the kind of excitement I like . . ." His words were a mumble, but his lips remained lifted at the corners as he drifted off to sleep. She did not hate him. He did not fool himself into thinking all was sunshine and roses between them, but she did not hate him, not nearly.

Chapter 21

Justin woke near dawn; at least he thought it was close to morning. It was hard to tell, with the rain pouring down so hard that the rooftop seemed to be drumming a symphony. The light was still dim, and the air smelled fresh and damp. He loved a hearty English rain. It washed away all the soot a London street could harvest.

He adjusted his shoulders, feeling the painful after-effects of his nocturnal activities. Despite the fact that his body ached liked the dickens, nothing could eclipse the budding joy in his heart. Evelyn still had feelings for him. He wanted to shout to the hilltops with happiness.

Despite her harsh words, she had to care for him to make love to him with such ardor, to nurse him with such tender dedication. Given that kernel of hope, he intended to fan the flames of that tiny ember into a con-flagration that would bind her to him forever. He had taken her innocence, she had saved his life; he owed her that much. He owed that much to himself. He would do everything in his power to make things right with her.

He had to find a way to repair the damage he'd wrought with his recent chicanery. No matter that his role was unwitting, he had played her cruelly, and this he could not forgive. He must free her from all treach-ery, restore her funds, and save her and her innocent loved ones. The problem was, he could not tell the guilty from the blameless, given his lack of information and mobility.

As soon as his body healed, he would remedy Ev-elyn's situation. He only prayed that before then he had the chance to bond her heart with his. Now that he had tasted the intoxicating fires of her passion, he recognized how bereft his life had been. In the quiet of the dawn, the memories washed over him. With them came emotions pounding his heart like an anvil hammering a suit of ar-mor that refused to take shape. Duty had always driven him; he had known nothing else. In his family it was the most cherished success. Now he understood there was much more to life than fulfilling others' expectations.

Awareness of his mortality overwhelmed him. He could no longer afford to be the specter of the man he wished to be. There was too little time; life was too pre-cious. He would make the most of his imperfect exis-tence. It was time for him to lay claim to his life based on his needs—not his mother's, Wheaton's, Society's, or anybody bloody else's.

Evelyn was the key to his metamorphosis. She'd shown him that thoughtfully challenging others could be a healthy thing, driven by a strong sense of self. She knew who she was and what she wanted in life. He could not have admired her more. Evelyn never pretended to be anything other than what she was— strong, independent, intelligent, and kind. And she did not let anyone knock her self-worth, a trait he longed to emulate.

"Oh, you're awake." Nervously brushing her hand across her fair hair, the lovely lady pervading his thoughts glided into the room. "Would you like something to eat?" She carried a small candle, encircling her in a golden halo.

He smiled. Despite the drab gown and shadows under her eyes, she looked radiant. He decided when this mess was over he'd buy her a hundred gowns, in dazzling rainbow colors. No more black for Evelyn Amherst. "Actually, I'm feeling quite content this morning."

With her eyes never meeting his, she set the candle on the side table. Keeping her head averted, she drew the broom from the corner and frenetically swept the room in hasty brush strokes. The clattering downpour barely covered the swoosh of the broom.

"I don't believe the floor needs cleaning right now. Why, you can barely see."

She shrugged, not answering or meeting his eyes.

"Is something bothering you, Evelyn?"

The broom abruptly stopped midstroke, the straw bowing as she pressed her weight onto it. "I, we need to talk about . . . well . . ." Her cheeks blushed an enchanting rose, and she seemed at a loss.

"Evelyn, have you slept at all this night?"

She shook her head in the negative. "I couldn't. I kept thinking about what I, well, what we . . ." Her blue gaze met his. "I can't believe my behavior. I'm mortified . . ." Wringing her hands on the broom handle, she murmured, "By what I said, what we did . . ."

He could not keep the corners of his lips from quirking, just thinking about her wild side. "I certainly did not mind."

Dropping the broom into the corner, she replied, "Well, I did."

"What are you saying?"

"I'm saying I'm not proud of the things I said last night—"

"Oh, about my mother hating me?" He waved her off. "I know she doesn't. She drives me to distraction with her attempts to manipulate my life, but she really does care. Nothing anyone can say will change that."

Evelyn peeked at him out of the corner of her eye. "So, you didn't believe me?"

"The same way I didn't believe it when you said you hated me."

She scowled. "I certainly find myself horrifically angry with you—"

"You didn't seem so angry when you pushed me onto the table," he interrupted.

"Shh," she chided, glaring at the open doorway. "Shah might hear you!"

"The woman must sleep like the dead, not to have heard us last night." Extending his arm, he beckoned, "Come here."

She shuffled closer with obvious hesitation.

He grasped her hand in the circle of his palms and squeezed it gently. "I have no explanation for what's happening between us." It was not precisely the truth, but it wasn't exactly a lie either. "But don't ever think there's anything sordid or shameful regarding how we feel about each other."

"That's just it," she countered, her blue gaze shimmering with misery. "I don't know how I feel about you. It was easy when I hated you. Black and white. But then you saved me." Shaking her head, she frowned. "And now you tease me and kiss me and well . . . you never did tell me why you saved me that night at your brother's."

A hearty laugh erupted from his throat, and he kissed her palm. How he loved her scent. "I couldn't let you go and die after all of my convoluted attempts to ensnare you!"

"Ensnare?"

"I wanted you to like me. Enough to share your secrets with me. But you never did. Instead I found myself liking you very, *very* much."

"There's the rub; I didn't tell you anything because I didn't want to involve you. It's bad enough that I have to live in the shadow of my father's world. I wanted to save you from it." She pulled her hand from his grasp. "When all along you were mixed up in the nefarious games."

"I regret many things, Evelyn. But I will not apologize for fulfilling my duty to my country."

A wistful smile flashed across her features. "That's what Father used to say."

The rain pounded down the roof, reminding Justin of marching soldiers. "Stopping Napoleon is our most urgent responsibility. I will do whatever it takes to help make that happen. I was under the belief you were aiding the enemy. It was all a bit muddled at the time. But my intentions were true, although, I must admit, grossly misguided."

She met his gaze. "I seem to be the one confused where you are concerned, Justin. But emotions have no place in this nasty business. They can play no part in saving Sully."

"I used to think that emotions were a liability when it came to the spy trade, Evelyn. I don't feel that way any longer. If I hadn't grown to care for you—"

"I'd be dead," she finished for him.

He grasped her hand and pulled her back to the bed.

Licking her lips, she ventured, "But I wonder where these feelings can take us. When this is over, pray we all make it out of this mess alive, I want my freedom. I never want to deal with subterfuge, lies, or government chicanery again. I want a secure future, on my own." She shook her head. "I intend to leave these shores, Justin, never to come back to England."

That was very bad news indeed. She was a strong-minded woman, unused to changing her mind.

"This is too much contemplation before breakfast," he chided gently, wrapping his arm around her shoulders and drawing her to his chest. She went willingly enough. Her luscious body molded against him, and a small sigh escaped her lips. He pressed his lips to her silky tresses. "We will do the best we can, for the moment." He tilted her chin, and he brushed his mouth across hers. "And for the moment, the best thing I can think to do is kiss all thoughts of spies and treachery from your mind."

He nibbled on her lips, and they parted. He kissed her tenderly, savoring her sweetness.

Pots clattered in the kitchen. Was it his imagination, or were they exceedingly loud? Shah was no fool; he just prayed she was on his side in this skirmish to win Evelyn's heart.

Evelyn slowly extricated herself from his embrace. "I'll go help Shah with breakfast."

Watching her glide from the room, he could only thank the heavens for this opportunity to be closeted away in the country with Evelyn. In his condition he could not do much to help untangle the espionage mess, so he might as well take advantage of this time to change the tide of her feelings regarding England and regarding him. For if she left him in the end, all he'd have would be his duty, and that wasn't near enough at all.

Chapter 22

Two days passed, and for Evelyn it was like an isolated harbor perched in the eye of a storm. All was quiet, yet not at peace. Tension permeated the air despite the idyllic setting. Her relationship with Justin was evolving, yet she could only let her emotions go so far. She knew the time would soon come when she would leave him and these shores, and she did not plan on taking a broken heart with her. She resolved to enjoy this haven with him, preserving a lifetime of memories in a few short days. For that was all, she feared, they would ever have.

She'd been so hesitant to leave Justin this morning, as if everything would magically end just as it had so abruptly begun again between them. In his condition he could not go far, yet she worried that altering the chemistry of their respite even slightly might bring reality crashing down on her head.

But Angel had been gone far too long. She had to find out if he had left word for her at the local inn. Lamentably, he had not. So she and Shah spent some time in town making a number of necessary purchases. She had to admit, no matter how much she enjoyed the view of Justin's strapping form, it was time to obtain some decent clothing for him. Heaven only knew when they would have to leave their sanctuary in the woods and how quickly they would have to go.

Shah trudged along beside her on the beaten track, barely saying a word on the journey to town and back. She tilted her head, eyeing the clouds sweeping past. "A storm comes."

Evelyn pulled her hood closer. The scent of damp hung on an agitated wind. "Yes. I can smell it."

"Perhaps Señor Arolas will come before it pours."

Evelyn did not respond. A million things could have delayed Angel, but with Wheaton and Helderby on their backs, too many things could have gone wrong. Evelyn had questioned Justin extensively about Colonel Wheaton, the man she ventured was the key to unlocking this treachery. Wheaton seemed a nemesis without discernable weakness. According to Justin, his loyalty was beyond reproach, he had never married, had no family to speak of, lived modestly and looked after his men. Yet he was a coldhearted leader, one who viewed everyone as expendable.

Evelyn shuddered in the sudden chill. No doubt, if his own men were a means to an end, Sully was nothing more than a cheap instrument in obtaining his goals. Whatever those goals might be.

Justin had far less to say about Helderby, and Evelyn knew he was trying not to frighten her. All he would say was that the man was like a barely tamed beast and Wheaten held the leash, quite loosely at times.

"If Angel does not come," Shah asked as she stepped over a rut in the trail, "will we go to the marquis's estate in Bedford?"

"I don't know what we'll do." Besides her great concern over her dear friends, how could she possibly stay with Justin in his exacting world of rules and propriety? Somehow she doubted Lady Barclay or anyone else in Society would welcome her presence as Justin's . . . what? She was his friend, his lover, and his partner in trying to get to the bottom of Wheaton's games. But unless she married Justin or became a kept mistress, two things she would not do, there was no place for a woman like her in English Society.

On the rocky path, their shoes crunched loudly in the silence of the woods. Evelyn's footsteps hastened as the door to the lodge came into view.

Shah opened the entry, and they stepped inside the shadowed cabin.

"Justin?" Evelyn called, anticipation pooling in her belly.

He stood in the threshold to his room, one hand holding up the blanket at his waist, the other hidden from view. His honey-wheat hair had grown longer, sweeping across his brow and emphasizing his eyes. They'd shaved his beard the day before, and with the peachy color in his handsomely chiseled features, he looked like a Nordic god. A snowy bandage still covered his muscled chest, but the sight of his bare shoulders made her belly flip and her body simmer. He was a feast for her eyes and her senses.

Pulling out the pistol he'd been holding behind his back, he set it onto the tabletop. "I'm so glad you've returned safely. Any word?"

Mutely, she shook her head. A sudden shyness overcame her; you'd think by now she would have grown accustomed to his dazzling looks. Part of her prayed she never did; as long as they had this time together, she longed to enjoy every last bit of it.

"Well, at least you got to go shopping," he teased. "I'm told it can uplift any female's spirits."

She raised her brow questioningly.

"Oh, yes, how could I have forgotten?" He smiled wickedly. "You are not the typical female."

Playing at being put off, she dropped her parcels onto the wooden chair. "I'm glad you noticed." But she could not hide her smile.

"I notice everything about you, Evelyn. Everything." His glorious eyes smoldered and her breath caught. She was devastatingly aware of his magnetism; it lured her to him so that she might cavort in the shimmering waters of those grayish-green pools.

Shah ripped open a brown paper package, wrenching Evelyn back to the moment. Inhaling deeply, Evelyn pulled her eyes from Justin's gaze. She had to keep reminding herself that they were not alone.

Beaming knowingly, he looked over the many parcels, inquiring, "And how was your excursion?"

Mischievous once more, she made a face. "Horrid." She unfastened her cloak and hung it on the wall hook. "The salesclerk kept pressing me to purchase Pimpernel Water—you know, to improve the skin." She raised her hand to her flawless cheek. "We've all been guilty of not donning our bonnet properly, but I had no idea my cheeks were so blotchy."

He grinned, seemingly delighted with her humor. "I have that problem myself."

"Blotchy skin?"

"Not wearing my bonnet."

They shared a smile. Her cheeks warmed and she asked, "How do you feel?"

"About sixty years old now."

"I thought you were looking a bit beyond your prime."

Unwrapping the paper on the largest package, she pulled out a long black cloak.

"You shouldn't have," he jibed. "I was just lamenting the fact that I would have to become civilized once more."

Her lips quirked and her cheeks burned. He had not been overly civilized the night before. His eyes sparkled, as if he could read her thoughts.

"Go try on the clothes," she admonished, pushing him toward his room.

"I'll need help."

"So does Shah," she replied. 'With luncheon."

As the women prepared the meal, Evelyn could hear the floorboards creaking as Justin moved about his chamber. The temptation to peek in on him was overwhelming. Wiping her hands on a cloth, she commented self-consciously, "I'll go check on Justin. To see if the clothes fit."

Shah nodded, not looking up from peeling the potatoes. "When I'm done here, I'll go gather more herbs."

Evelyn had to admit, her trusty maid was no fool, but neither was she judgmental. Evelyn recalled that Shah had been wed once, but she rarely spoke of it. Apparently it was not a good marriage, and the man had died before any children were born. The only time Shah referred to it was when counting her blessings. Still, she did not begrudge Evelyn her relationship with Justin, something Evelyn was becoming more and more thankful for with each passing day.

Evelyn knocked lightly on the door.

"Come.

"I struggled with the coat a bit," he commented, adjusting his sleeves. "But I did bearably well, given I had no assistance."

"If you'd had my assistance, you probably wouldn't have gotten past your undergarments," she teased, a bit shocked by her boldness.

"Thank goodness you're not my valet. I'd never leave the house."

"You look wonderful." The clothes did not fit him as perfectly as did his fine tailored London attire, but the navy wool suit made him appear brawny and dashedly handsome.

"I'm glad you think so. You know how much I like to impress."

Reaching for her, he wrapped his strong arms around her waist. Brushing a tendril of hair away from her face, he curled it about her ear, sending shivers racing up her spine. He sighed into her hair. "It's almost hard to care about the intrigues going on outside this little pocket of the world when you are near."

She frowned, reminded of her disappointment today. "I wish I knew what was taking Angel so long."

"I know you're worried, darling. But if he can get here, he will." He pressed a tender kiss to her temple.

The leaves rustled outside, and the first spatterings of rain drummed on the rooftop.

"Shah wanted to collect more herbs," she mumbled. As if reacting to her thoughts, she heard the heavy kitchen door open and close with a thud.

"It's only sprinkling," he commented, looking out the window. "I love the rain, and so does my dear friend, Mr. Oak."

She raised her brow, amused. "Your friend?"

"He kept me company while you were gone. I told him all about my lovely nurse and her inventive remedies."

Evelyn's cheeks warmed and she replied, "In some Eastern countries a bride plants a tree in her yard as her wedding nears. She might decorate it with colored ribbons to express her joy. Legend has it the bride would live as long as the tree."

"In Bedford there is a big oak that must be three hundred years old. Its trunk is fatter than a horse's rump, its roots gnarl the ground paces all around, and it's got a hump stuck right in its center." He playfully squeezed her middle. "Would you like to live to be three hundred years old?"

She huffed, "I am having enough trouble with twenty-two." Grazing her cheek across his fuzzy jaw, she added thoughtfully, "Still, it would be a joy to plant a tree, water it, watch it grow every day. To be able to see the roots take and deepen, tighten around the soil as if laying claim to its eternal corner of the world."

"Roots do grant one a sense of balance. You would

do a place well if you stayed long enough to plant the seeds of your brightness."

She shook her head, bringing her thoughts back to reality. "I was talking about the tree."

"I am talking about you. Staying in England. I would protect you. . . ."

"Shh. Enough talk about that." Not a day went by that he did not try to convince her to trust him with her future. She was coming to wait for his offer. Although she knew she would refuse, she enjoyed being sought after so enthusiastically.

"If you would leave England, then where would you go?" he asked, pursing his lips, apparently accepting her rebuff.

"Italy."

"Why?"

She let out a long breath and looked out the window, lost in the memories of golden villas, shimmering cobalt blue waters, and delectable feasts that seemed to last for days. "It's a beautiful country. But the primary reason would be for the people. Some of them certainly like to bellow a lot, but deep at heart they are wonderfully gracious. I was eighteen on our last tenure there. I became ill, and the neighbors could not have been more helpful."

"Is that where you collected those dastardly kittens your father complained of?"

She tilted her head to see his features, suddenly feeling vulnerable about him knowing of her father's journal.

At the look on her face he continued, "Between the leather-bound volume you're always reading and the stories I recalled, it did not take much to piece the puzzle together."

She felt silly for being so secretive. "I have found nothing in it that would lead to murder."

"It's certainly a logical starting place. I wonder, does anyone else know of its existence?"

"I don't know."

He shook his head. "If someone wanted the journal, they could have simply blackmailed you for it."

She raised her eyebrow. "I marvel how your mind always slinks to the dark side."

"It was why I was so useful to our government. And," he murmured as he dipped his nose beneath her hair and nibbled on her earlobe, "why I will be useful to you now."

"Let me show you how you can be useful to me," she replied, wanting to end all talk of intrigue and of the future. They had little enough time together; she wanted to enjoy every precious moment of it. Taking his hand, she led him to the bed. "As your nurse, it's my opinion you need to lie down, my lord."

"I always follow the nurse's orders."

He drew her down on top of him and kissed all thoughts of the outside world from her mind.

Pulling back from his embrace, she stated breathlessly, "Let's get these cumbersome English clothes off you." Unwilling to wait, she pressed small kisses on the nape of his neck as she yanked off his coat.

"Not exactly pulling his toenails out, are you?" a deep voice boomed from behind.

Tearing her lips from Justin's neck, Evelyn looked up. "Angel!" Mortification swamped her senses, and she rolled off Justin and fell onto the floor like a sack of potatoes. Her cheeks burned to cinder, and she could not find words to save her life.

"I guess you've decided what side Barclay plays on," Angel said as he swept off his hat and rainwater dripped to the floor. His black cloak shimmered, wet, and his raven hair was matted down with damp. "I'm going to have something to eat. If you'd care to join me?" He strode out of the room, his boot heels clipping loudly on the floorboards.

"I didn't hear him come in," Justin supplied, sitting up and adjusting his coat. "Why am I suddenly glad for these many layers of English clothing?"

Fixing her dress as best as she could, Evelyn murmured, "Not exactly a hero's welcome for Angel." Guilt burrowed in her belly. While Angel had been out facing danger, she had been safe and dry, and cavorting with Justin.

She walked into the kitchen, unable to meet her dear friend's eyes.

"Just so you know what you're doing," he commented to her, while he devoured the stew as if he had not eaten in days.

Shah stood over the stove, her back to them.

He tore off a hunk of bread. "I had no luck when lady love crossed swords with intrigue; perhaps you shall fare better."

She did not know to what he was referring, but she replied defensively, "He's mending well."

"That is apparent."

Sliding into the seat across from him, she pressed, "He answered all my questions and seems really committed to helping us."

"I wonder if you should not be the one committed, *caro*," he said quietly. "Just a short while ago you were ready to skin him alive for his betrayal, now you love him?"

Her back stiffened. "I, I never said I loved him. He's intelligent and good company and . . . well, he's on our side."

Angel snorted.

She shrugged. "I don't see the harm."

"Where's the harm, indeed?"

Justin strode in, removed a stool from the corner, and sat beside Evelyn. She was glad for his presence; just his company made her feel more secure. Still, she did not like the questions Angel raised in her mind. Looking at the handsome man she'd come to cherish, she tried to push away her qualms. Of course she could trust him. But doubt still lingered.

"I want to thank you, Arolas, for all of your assistance." Justin extended his hand. "Evelyn tells me you helped dig me out from under that bookcase, obtained medical care, brought me here, and provided all of our provisions. I cannot tell you how much I appreciate your efforts."

Angel's hand did not meet Justin's, nor did his eyes ever lift from his bowl. "It was for Evelyn. Not for you."

Pulling his hand back, Justin accepted the rebuff with aplomb. "For your labors on Evelyn's behalf, I am eternally grateful."

Shah set bowls before Evelyn and Justin. "Join us, Shah," Evelyn urged.

Justin stood and offered her his stool. "I'll get the chair from my room."

The four of them sat in tense silence, everyone seemingly intent on their food. Evelyn waited breathlessly for Angel to break the silence with news about Sully, but she wanted to give him a chance to eat before rushing him. He looked exhausted. Dark shad-

ows banked his chocolate brown eyes, and his beautiful olive skin was marred with grime. His tangy
cologne tickled her senses, and she was surprised to
find herself comparing it to Justin's natural woodsy
scent.

She sent a prayer of thanks Angel was fit and whole
and back to her. "I'm so glad to see you, Angel," she
commented, her eyes suddenly burning with unshed
tears. "And so thankful you are well."

He reached across the table and squeezed her hand.
Justin watched the movement and then looked away.

Leaning back in his chair, Angel ran his hand
through his black wavy hair. "You've lost more weight,
Evelyn," he commented disapprovingly.

Evelyn didn't care about her weight, instead asking,
"Have you found Sully?"

"You know I would have told you by now if we
had." He frowned. "We followed the trail to a house by
the piers but then lost it. Someone is moving him about."

Evelyn's heart sank, and then fluttered. "But he's
alive."

His usually smooth voice was gruff. "Seems to be."

Justin leaned forward. "Was the house at the pier on
Longston Street?"

Angel raised his brow. "Yes."

"It's a safe house used by my branch."

An excited itch trailed up Evelyn's spine. "Where
would someone take Sully now, Justin?"

He scratched his chin. "Well, there are at least five
safe houses in London proper and a few in the outlying
districts."

She clenched her hands, anticipation coursing through
her. "We can get the list and check them one by one!"

"You are not going anywhere near London," Angel countered. He nodded to Justin. "Barclay's mother has been screaming to the rooftops over her son's disappearance." He turned to Evelyn. "And the authorities have issued a warrant for your arrest in his kidnapping."

She blinked but then waved him off. "We can bring Justin home and they will drop the charges."

"And you will be arrested, Sully won't be found, and all will be lost," Angel challenged.

"But then, what can we do?" she cried. "We need to get Sully back!" She pursed her lips. "Perhaps we can do a trade, Justin for Sully . . ." As she realized what she'd said, her cheeks warmed, and she bit her lip. "Simply to get Sully back, Justin, and you do wish to go home. . . ."

He scowled. "I am not a side of beef to barter. Besides," his voice clipped, making her feel even guiltier, "they will arrest you anyhow."

"But you will be returned, whole and well. . . ."

Angel's and Justin's eyes locked. An agreement seemed to flash between them.

"What?" she asked, annoyed.

Angel's voice softened. "Barclay is right, *caro*. They will arrest you. That is the whole point of this exercise. They want you."

Frustration gripped her, and she shook her fisted hands as if beseeching the heavens. "But why?"

"Ask him." Angel pointed to the marquis.

"Bloody hell if I know," Justin countered, rubbing his temple. "But I do know that it's not safe for you to venture back to London."

"But I have to find Sully!"

Angel smiled affectionately at her. "You were always

the one to jump to the fight. But you have to let me do it for you this time."

Justin was eyeing Angel warily but Evelyn did not have it in her to deal with his resentment.

"Is there any other news?" Justin asked tersely.

Angel shrugged. "Ismet is well. There is rumor in the streets of some conspiracy, but it seems to have no substance."

"We believe it's a ploy," Justin replied. "To get me and the members of my branch to do Wheaton's bidding."

"We?" Angel queried.

Justin scowled. "Evelyn and I."

Angel seemed to consider this a moment. "Do you, Barclay, think Wheaton has turned?"

"I just can't see Wheaton serving anyone other than Mother England."

"Did you know the men who attacked us?"

"At least one, Helderby. A bloody brute who would cut his mother's throat if there was gold in it for him. But Wheaton has a hold on him, at least for now."

Evelyn shuddered, suddenly chilled. "So where do we go from here?"

"We will consider our options in the morning." Angel raised his arms over his head and stretched, yawning. "When Ismet arrives."

Evelyn could barely contain her enthusiasm. "Ismet is coming here? But why did he not arrive with you?"

"We were followed. He's routing the pack in the opposite direction."

"Yet he's heading here in the morning?" Justin's voice grew strident. "How can you lead those men here?"

"Ismet knows what he's doing," Angel rejoined.

"You have much faith in a man who lost in his last encounter with Helderby and his men."

"If I recall correctly, Barclay," Angel retorted in an icy tone, "you were part of Helderby's men at the time."

"So I know how dogged they can be. We have to leave here at once! Evelyn is not safe."

"We have no choice in the matter," Angel countered. "We have but one horse and we're not splitting up."

"How in heaven's name do you expect us to leave?" Justin hammered the tabletop. "Whenever it is you do decide we're going."

"Ismet will bring a coach. He knows what he's doing." Angel sent Evelyn a hard stare. "Unlike others in our party."

Justin held his peace, but dissatisfaction shimmered off him in waves.

Evelyn eyed the men worriedly. "We are all on the same side, boys, remember?" she chided. "I'll set up a pallet for you in Justin's room, Angel. You look like the walking dead."

He made a face. "You were always so free with your flattery."

Justin stood. "If you'll give me a moment."

"Certainly." Evelyn nodded.

Justin turned and closed the door to his room behind him.

"Be nice, Angel," Evelyn chided. "The man took a bullet for me. Or have you forgotten so quickly?"

"That does not mean he won't slit my throat in the middle of the night."

Evelyn studied her fingernails, not wanting to argue with her dear friend. Once Angel had time to get to know Justin better, he'd realize his suspicions were un-founded. Justin was not the enemy.

Shah poured Angel some water as they sat in tense silence.

A horse neighed outside, followed by a man's deep command, "Haya!" and the charge of hoof beats.

Angel jumped from his chair. Dashing to the door, he tore it open and stepped out into the pouring rain. "The bloody Englishman is stealing my horse!"

Evelyn rushed beside him. Her heart was in her throat watching Justin's disappearing form as it raced on horseback down the rocky trail. She was shocked speechless.

Angel commented bitterly, "Your lover seems to have plans of his own that do not include you." He pushed her back inside the house. "Grab your things together, Evelyn. You and I are leaving! Shah, when Ismet comes, be ready to go. Barclay won't have gone far by then. Still, you'd better be ready to depart immediately."

Shah quickly began gathering up supplies.

Evelyn dropped into a chair, trying to make sense of Justin's abrupt departure. Her head was numb, but a piercing ache was escalating in her chest, perilously near her heart. He wouldn't betray her again. Would he? She didn't think she could bear it. Her mouth had dried to dust, but she managed to ask, "Where are we going?"

"Away from here. Let's pray your judgment is true regarding your marquis, for otherwise, well . . ." His voice trailed off, and the look in his dark eyes sent chills racing down Evelyn's spine. "Let's just say, the man won't get away so easily next time."

"Why would he leave me?" she whispered.

"Only he knows the answer to that question, *caro*," Angel replied, dragging on his still-soaking cloak. "But be certain I'll ask him the next time I see him. If I don't kill him first."

Chapter 23

⌒⎯⎯◯◯⎯⎯⌒

Justin tore through the rain-scored blackness, his battered body barely able to hold his seat as the stallion raced down the rocky lane. Resolution filled him; he needed to get Wheaton off of Evelyn's back. He had to get the warrant for her arrest quashed and find out where Sully was being held. He could do none of those things from his bed in the cabin, no matter how much he longed to stay there.

He could not imagine Evelyn's thoughts at the moment. He only prayed his efforts were successful and she would eventually understand his motivations were true. Arolas never would have let him go. The man didn't trust him worth a stick. Lord only knew what he was telling Evelyn at the moment. Guilt and fear made Justin kick his heels, pressing the tired mount to the end of his endurance. He just prayed his own fortitude would stand the trial of making it to Reading. If he could get there, he would do something he had not done in his life: brandish his peerage like a shield against intimidation and as a sword to get what he wanted—quick transit to London. He would use every resource available to him to make things right for Evelyn; it was the least he could do.

It took far too long by Justin's impatient estimation to press the company of men hounding Ismet into altering its course and assisting him instead. By the time he was ensconced in a rented coach and on his way to Town, Justin's head pounded to the beat of the horse hooves towing the carriage down the London thoroughfare. His bullet wound ached so badly he thought he might just vomit from the pain.

Finally, the carriage bumped and jerked to a stop. The door squeaked open and the stool was set. He swallowed the bile in his throat and was relieved when his butler, Stanley, poked his head inside.

"My lord! Thank heavens you are back!"

Justin reached out and grabbed the man's proffered hand. To his shame, he hobbled out of the coach. His sister, Audrey, flew down the residence's steps and crashed into his chest, causing stars to sparkle before his eyes. "Mother feared the worst! But I just knew you'd be back, Justin!"

Inhaling a shaky breath, he affectionately patted her soft shoulder. "I'm glad to be home as well, Audrey. I just need to get inside the door." Servants and Fancy alike had come out of the nearby homes and stood on the steps gaping at the long-awaited return of the kidnapped marquis. Justin was not about to give them additional fodder by passing out on his doorstep. He straightened his spine and gently wrapped his arm about his sister's shoulders, an outward sign of affection covering up his weakened state.

Together they mounted the stairs, and Justin was thankful that his legs did not betray him. Once inside the vestibule, he let out an inward sigh of relief.

"Justin! Thank heavens you've returned!" Mother came bustling down the magnificent stairs, replete in muslin and lace of the darkest green to match her cat-shaped eyes. Her ash blond hair was coiled tightly at the nape of her neck, and an odd, long black ribbon was draped from her shoulder to her waist.

His man, Sylvester, slipped behind his master, giving Justin a chair in which to rest. Justin dropped into the seat with a groan.

"Don't dally in the foyer, Justin," his mother charged. "Let us go to the blue room for refreshment. We must celebrate your homecoming."

"I am off to bed in the moment," he countered stiffly.

Her catlike eyes watched him suspiciously. "What is wrong with you?"

"Besides the gunshot wound to my chest?"

She raised her fan to her lips, and her porcelain cheeks went pink.

He raised an eyebrow. "What did you think had happened to me?"

"I, well, we . . ." She eyed the servants lingering about. "We can discuss it upstairs." She clapped her hands. "Come. Come."

Her irritatingly supercilious commands were the last thing he needed now. He replied forcefully, "I am off to bed. I will call for you when I am ready to speak with you."

She blinked. "Don't be silly, I wish to confer with you now."

He raised his hand to his aching temple. "And I wish for you to stop bellowing."

She sputtered. "Bellowing . . ." Lifting her shoulder, she admonished, "At least have the good graces to visit me in my rooms, son."

He knew it wasn't the time or the place, but it was as if another had taken control of his tongue. "It's my *wife's* apartment, and you were supposed to have vacated it over a year ago."

He wondered if his mother's face might turn purple, she was so provoked. "I did move out, I just continue to put the chamber to use," she replied defensively.

"Well, it's high time you finally moved out of my space." He inhaled deeply, measuring the pain and wondering if he was ready to confront the stairs to his bedroom. "Since I hope to finally persuade a lady to marry me soon, you will remove your things at once." He looked up at the astonished crowd of hovering servants. "Ah, Mrs. Searles."

The wiry, gray-haired lady stepped forward nervously. "Yes, my lord?"

"Help my mother remove *all* of her personal items from my lady's chambers. The marchioness's study can likewise be cleared out. Mother can use the second drawing room at the end of upstairs hall."

A pall hung over the awestruck servants.

When no one moved, he urged, "Well, get on with it."

"Yes, my lord," Mrs. Searles murmured as she kept her eyes far from her mistress and hurried toward the stairs.

Mother stood there, her face pinched with fury. Thankfully she kept her barbed tongue silent.

"Help me to my rooms, Sylvester," Justin muttered. His man rushed to obey, a new respect flashing in his muted brown eyes, quickly replaced by stoic deference. In the hushed quiet of a household on the brink of unstoppable reform, together they managed the stairs, one painful step at a time.

"What's with mother's black sash, Sylvester?" Justin asked a few hours later, after having slept like the dead, then consuming two bowls of stew.

"It was your mother's, ah"—he coughed into his hand—"standard. To mark your kidnapping."

Justin barely suppressed a groan. Leave it to Mother to make this into a fashion drama. "What is the rumor belowstairs about my ordeal?"

Sylvester's sunken cheeks reddened, but he answered deferentially, "Word is that you were taken involuntarily by Miss Amherst. That she was trying to . . . to . . . tempt you into marriage."

He snorted. "I should only be so lucky." It made him sound like a bloody cuckold. And made Evelyn appear the desperate lightskirt. He could only imagine the licentious conjecture about Town.

"All of the staff was interviewed by the authorities, and your mother went so far as to retain Bow Street Runners to try to secure your release." He licked his lips. "I do not wish to intrude, but if you would like I could rectify the tongue-wagging . . ."

So Sylvester was dying for juicy tidbits himself. Well, everyone would have to wait. The rumor mill was the least of Justin's problems now.

A knock resounded on the door to the outer chamber, and Sylvester stepped into the next room. He returned announcing, "Mr. Stanley informs me that a Colonel Wheaton requests an audience."

"Help me get dressed, then send him into the up-stairs drawing room." Justin was not about to see the man in his dressing gown or in his bedroom. He needed to speak from a position of strength. The colo-nel was one to assail any sign of weakness.

Thirty minutes later Justin stepped over the thresh-old, watching the master of spies with a wary eye. The older man was standing before the drawing room win-dow, peering outside. The afternoon sunlight shone on his snowy white hair, making it appear as if a halo sur-rounded his large head. He turned. "Ah, Justin. How are you, my boy?"

Justin damped his irritation at being called "boy." It was a tactic designed to set the tone of their meeting. Well, two could play at that game. He stepped gingerly inside, careful to appear nonchalant as he gracefully slid into one of the high-backed chairs. Sylvester slipped unobtrusively into the room, carrying a silver tray with two brandies.

Justin accepted his and sipped, welcoming the rich, fiery liquid's intensity. "How are you faring, old man?"

The colonel pursed his thick lips and stood over him, nodding his head at the offer of brandy. "So the chit wound up being the rascal, just as I'd said."

"Last I saw her, she was procuring me medical atten-tion after one of your men shot me." At the look on Wheaton's face, Justin leaned forward and scoffed, "What? You didn't believe that prattle about Miss Amherst trying to seduce me, did you?"

Wheaton's lips moved silently. "Well, we . . . she disappeared, you disappeared . . . my men were killed. It was not a far-off notion."

Justin chuckled, probing to see if his suspicions were true. "I was the one doing the seducing, remember? And to what end? We're no better off now than we were before. And this French plot seems nothing more than smoke and shadows."

The old gent shrugged, ignoring the lure.

Justin sipped from his drink. "What have you learned in my absence?"

Wheaton sat down in the opposite seat as Sylvester quietly slipped from the room and closed the door. "Regrettably very little. Napoleon's plot is set for next week and all we know is that the financial system is the target."

So the colonel was going to stick by his stance that the French conspiracy was the real threat. "You learned this from Sully?"

The older man's steely blue eyes narrowed. "*Sullivan* has yet to cooperate, but he will."

"Helderby couldn't handle the job?"

"Sullivan is a tough nut to crack, and Helderby was injured." His smile was oily. "But you know quite a bit about that."

Justin tried not to fidget under that icy gaze. "I still don't understand why you tried to kill the girl."

"We were trying to capture her, some of the men got a bit . . . ahead of themselves."

"I trust you believe all of this gamesmanship is worth it."

"We have Sullivan."

Justin sipped from his drink. "Where are you holding him?"

For the first time in Justin's memory, the colonel's ruddy cheeks reddened. His blue gaze shifted away. "Safe, for now." His gaze flicked back to Justin. "So the chit has been nursing you this whole time?"

"She took off, just after the doctor came. Left me quite laid up. She seems to bear me some ill will. I wonder why?"

"By the by, I don't appreciate you assuming command of my men. They were in pursuit of some nasty fellows I believe are connected to the plot."

Justin's tone was cool. "I would have thought you would be pleased to get my mother off your back. As well as securing my safety, of course."

"Of course."

Justin swirled the drink in the cup. "I'll have to get that warrant quashed."

"Why?" Wheaton shrugged. "We'll use all of our resources. She can't hide forever, and when we do get her, we'll have our answers."

"I'd no sooner allow my mother to don that silly sash as have that unnecessary warrant remain outstanding."

The old man scowled. "I like hedging my bets, Justin."

"And I like keeping my pride intact. Besides, she did not seem particularly knowledgeable on the spy trade, as far as I could tell. . . ." He let his voice trail off, shadowed with doubt.

"In your sickly state, I'd venture you couldn't tell much." The colonel snorted. "But I know she'll lead us straight to what we need." Leaning forward, he watched Justin closely. "She and the Spaniard are quite the hot number, it seems. He's disappeared too, you know."

It was Justin's turn to look away. He would not let

the jealousy searing his gut distract him from learning what he needed to know. "I'd grown bored of the chit already. I really don't believe she can be useful to us."

The colonel ignored this remark and sipped from his drink. "I'd hazard Amherst might have left something behind for his daughter to follow the trail."

"Trail to what?"

If Justin had not been watching closely, he would have missed the flicker in the colonel's eye. "Napoleon's scheme, of course."

"Of course." Justin's mouth had suddenly gone dry remembering Evelyn's father's journal. *"It is more priceless to me than a cache of diamonds,"* she had said. He stood, thankful his legs were supporting him. "Well, I don't want to keep you, Colonel. Thank you for checking up on my welfare."

The colonel did not rise. "So you are recovering well?"

"Stronger than a stallion." *On its last legs.*

After a long moment, Wheaton scratched a snowy sideburn and stood.

They faced each other, each measuring the other, almost as if squaring off for a duel. The charged air shimmered with unasked questions. Part of Justin grieved the distrust that had developed between them. For all of Wheaton's coldness, Justin admired the man greatly. Conceivably when all was said and done, the air could clear and Wheaton could be vindicated for all his misdeeds. Justin supposed it depended on whether one believed the ends always justified the means.

For Justin, there was no excuse for Wheaton's abuse of power. So the loss of faith between them was perhaps the only end to their four years of working together. It was sad, given they were on the same side, supposedly.

Without another word, Wheaton spun on his heel and strode from the room.

After the colonel crossed the threshold, Justin counted to fifty and then dropped unceremoniously into the chair with a loud thump. His exhausted body almost shook from the effort it had taken him to keep it together throughout the interview.

Reaching into his pocket, he pulled out the note he'd taken from the cabin just a day and a half before. He'd felt no compunction pilfering Evelyn's list; it was a reminder of her and of the task before him.

He read, " 'What we need to know. Where is Sully?' " Justin rubbed his chin, thinking out loud, "Probably at one of the safe houses." But Wheaton was suspicious, so the usual spots might not be used.

" 'What do you want from him and from me?' "

"Answers to some questions. Trail to something." Justin wished he'd drawn more from the colonel. He looked at the empty threshold, considering the prior interview. He'd never known the colonel to stray from His Majesty's service. But something was not adding up. He shook his head. No. Wheaton would not betray his country. It was unimaginable. "Then what's the old codger after?" he asked the vacant chamber.

Justin skipped to the last question, reading it aloud. " 'Do you make a habit of seducing your victims, or was I a special case?' " Brushing the parchment across his lips, he whispered, "You are a very special case, darling, and I'm not about to let Wheaton or anyone else hurt you. On my honor."

Folding the paper and slipping it into his coat pocket, he called, "Sylvester?"

His man popped his head inside the room. "Yes, my lord?"

"Bring me my writing instruments."

"Yes, my lord."

"And don't forget my seal." He was going to have to get busy, and there was little enough time. He wondered where Evelyn was, and he prayed that she was not taking matters into her own hands, for no one knew better than Justin the colonel's tenacity. The man was like a tiger with a foot in its jaws, eating its way upward until nothing of a man or woman was left.

Chapter 24

Evelyn was shaking so badly that she thought her teeth might fall out from their clattering. She was chilled to the bone, and no amount of firewood could draw out her frostiness. She scooted closer to the raging flames in the hearth and held out her frozen hands. At least the carpet under her bottom was plush.

"You need to get out of those wet clothes," Angel barked as he strode into the chamber with leopardlike grace. He dropped an ivory dressing gown onto the enormous bed. "Here, put this on."

She eyed the silky confection warily but knew that she would catch her death if she did not do something quickly to ward off the chill.

"I'm going to get us something to eat and drink." His dark clothes were plastered to his lean body, and his black hair had curled up around his ears. "Lock the door behind me. Three knocks, remember." With that, he opened the door a crack, peered down the hall of the fancy inn, and slipped out the door.

After firmly turning the brass key in the lock, Evelyn yanked off her sodden shoes and set them by the fire to dry. She tugged at her drenched garments, taking off everything, down to her damp chemise. She unfastened her stays and peeled the last vestiges of her sodden clothing from her skin. She slipped on the silky nightdress, wondering how Angel had managed to procure such an expensive and personal garment on such short notice.

Thunder clamored outside, followed by a flash of lightning so bright it illuminated the entire chamber, even through the thick drapes. She shuddered and moved back to the fire, tucking her feet under her bottom, praying that they would thaw. She sat hunched so close to the flames that the heat's radiance wrapped her in a toasty blanket. After a few long moments, she realized that her teeth were no longer chattering.

In the silent chamber she listened to the pitter-patter of the raindrops hitting the windows and the muffled sounds of horses neighing and carriage wheels rolling by on the cobblestone street below. She wondered if she should light the candles on the side of the bed, but she was unwilling to move from her warm spot by the fire. The firelight cast gloomy shadows around the spacious room and across the thick carpet where she sat. She wondered how much such a well-appointed room cost for the night. Certainly more than she had to her name, she thought glumly. She was indebted to Angel once again, with no means of ever repaying him. Yet now she was even worse off than before.

She'd been a fool twice now where Justin was concerned. Not that Angel took her to task over it. He mostly kept his thoughts to himself, but his silence was reprimand enough. She felt torn from the inside out, hoping beyond hope that there had been some dreadful mistake. Or that she was misreading the situation somehow. Yet even if Justin had had good intentions supporting his actions, she could not forgive him for taking off without at least discussing them with her.

Moreover, he had put himself in dire risk haring off on horseback like that. His wounds had healed well, but not nearly enough for a pounding dash on horseback through a rainstorm in the dead of night. He could have fallen off his horse and be lying in a ditch half-dead somewhere. Part of her wanted to kill him for his bravado. Part of her wanted to skin him alive for being so inconsiderate of her feelings. Mostly she wanted to crawl into a hole and mourn the loss of her faith in him and in her judgment. Once again she'd been a reckless cully to trust him. She supposed she had a weakness for the dashing marquis—one she would regret until the day she died. She just prayed that day was none too soon.

Evelyn inhaled deeply, trying to find something good about the situation, and all she got for her efforts was a coughing fit from too much wood smoke in her lungs. She felt sodden in spirit as well as body. Pressing her hand to her burning chest, she shook her head.

God, she was pitiful.

Three knocks banged on the thick pine door to the chamber. She stood and tiptoed to the entry.

"Angel?"

Three more knocks came. "Open up, Evelyn." She'd know that smooth inflection anywhere. She turned the key in the lock and yanked open the heavy door. Angel stepped inside, carrying at least ten different parcels. While she locked the entry, he stepped over to the table in the corner and laid out his cache.

He unwrapped the first bundle and set out a hunk of cheese; another bundle was a loaf of bread. Another held apples. With a flourish he unwrapped what was obviously his most favored prize, a bottle of reddish-brown liquid. He tugged open the cork, tilted his head back, and took a mighty swig. She watched the Adam's apple in his olive-skinned throat jump with each gulp.

He licked his lips. "Beverage of the gods."

He held the bottle out to her, and she took a hearty sip. She coughed and sputtered as fire lanced down her chest straight to her hollow belly. Her eyes teared, her nostrils flared, and her chest burned. It was like tasting liquid smoke.

"Quite the strong tipple," Angel commented, smiling. He reached for the bottle and took another swill.

Evelyn sat down on the carpet by the fire, feeling warmer on the inside and out. She watched silently as Angel tore a hunk of bread, sliced some cheese with a shiny silver knife, and held them out to her. She shook her head. Food was unimaginable; her stomach was roiling.

He frowned disapprovingly but ate the food himself. After a moment, he commented, "You do no one any good if you are feeble."

"I am not feeble, I'm simply not hungry."

He munched on in the silence-filled chamber. The fire crackled and hissed.

She stared into the golden flames. "Do you think they are safe?"

"Ismet will take care of Shah. I pray you're not including the bloody marquis in your concerns."

"Of course not." She buried her head in her arms, abashed once more. She heard the rustle of clothing and peeked up. Angel's dark coat and silk vest were draped across the armchair by the window. He stood by the bed wearing only his shirt and pants. The white linen was stuck to his lithe form, and his breeches were like a second skin. He had the body of an Adonis. Heat flashed from her cheeks to her hairline, and she pressed her face back into the fold of her arms. For the first time she realized her situation. She was half-naked and alone in a luxurious inn with an attractive man. For a moment, she disregarded the fact that the man was Angel.

He dropped a pillow onto the carpet and lounged beside her by the fire. Leaning up on his elbow, he stretched his legs toward the flames and wiggled his toes. She looked away. No matter how dear their friendship, eyeing his bare toes was a bit too intimate for her liking.

"Are you still cold?" she asked.

"Not with this to warm me." He raised the bottle to his lips, then passed her the drink. She took it from him and sipped slowly. Her eyes teared again, but the fiery liquid warmed her down to her soles.

"Not too much, *caro*," he chided softly. "You have not eaten, and we would not want you to become ill."

Her cheeks reddened. It seemed she was in constant

need of his guidance these days. She licked her lips, tasting the smoky brandy on her breath. The firelight played across his handsome features, adding a golden glow to his olive skin and chocolate brown eyes. His raven hair curled tightly around his ears, and she just had to ask, "Were you speaking of Isabella when you said you'd had no luck when intrigue crossed swords with love?"

He stared into the flames a long moment. "She was working for the French."

"How did you know?"

"She was trying to seduce my father."

"But he's happily married."

"What has that to do with anything?"

"But she was with you."

"Father and son, an interesting arrangement, don't you agree?" he replied, bitterness cracking his usually velvety voice. "At first I did not believe Father when he warned me against her. I thought he was jealous. That he wanted her for himself." His laugh was a harsh bark. "Can you imagine me believing that Father wanted something I had?"

"She was very beautiful," she replied softly.

"She was a scheming bitch."

"But you loved her."

"I loved someone who did not exist." He took a swig of the brandy and turned away, his features cast in shadow.

It somehow made her feel better that she was not the only one with poor judgment in matters of the heart. She pursed her lips. "Have you sworn off marriage?"

"That is your favorite pastime, Evelyn. I am simply intent on enjoying the amusements women have to offer without becoming entangled in their trickery."

Was that what Justin had wanted from her? Amusement?

Angel commented slowly, "You claim you do not love the marquis. Yet somehow you always seem to wind up back in his arms."

"How can I love someone I don't trust?"

"How could I love someone who didn't exist?" Watching her through hooded eyes, he murmured, "If only we could find love where it finds us."

The fire crackled and sparked as they sat in silence, each lost in their own musings.

He stood so suddenly that she had to cram her neck to look up at him. "You take the bed." He pulled the coverlet off the mattress, and it slid noisily to the floor. "I will sleep by the fire."

Nodding, she stood and stepped over to the bed. Staring down at the thick mattress, she turned. "Angel?"

He sat on the carpet before the hearth, his broad back facing her. "Yes, Evelyn?"

She needed to say the words. "You mean so much to me. I, I don't know what I'd do without you."

"I know, *caro*." He rolled over and tugged the blanket over his shoulder. "Go to sleep."

Lying beneath the scratchy wool blanket, she realized that she'd changed in the last few weeks. Gone was the maidenly girl who'd thought that seduction was a lighthearted game to be played in relative safety with a friend. Feelings were not without peril, and apparently neither was she when it came to matters between the covers. She grasped that although there were people capable of enjoying the pleasures between the sexes without emotional attachment, she was not one of them. That in opening her body to Justin, she had opened up a small corner of her heart. A corner that had flickered with girlish hope but was now dampened by cold reality. A lonely corner that, when she probed it, still burned with his betrayal.

Thunder boomed in the distance. Shuddering, she shrugged the rough cover higher to her neck and nestled her face deeper into the feather pillow. Before, she had always been afraid of being in another's power. Now, she realized, power came not just from the bonds of matrimony but from intimacies as well. Intimacies that led to emotional hazards she could not afford to risk.

Gentle sleep weighed her heavy lids closed, but her mind still struggled with her newfound insight. It was a lesson well learned now, never to allow a man to control her physically, emotionally, or legally. She had once imagined that there were gentlemen with whom she could be safe, but Justin's words came back to haunt her. *"All men are rogues and scoundrels."* But then again, a gentleman lay on the floor by the fire, giving her his protection without asking for anything in return. *Perhaps not all men are rogues and scoundrels*, she thought dreamily as sleep fogged her exhausted brain, *the good ones are just few and far between.*

Justin watched the lightning flash across the window in his study and prayed that wherever Evelyn was, she was safe and dry. Sighing, he looked back down at the letter on his desk, dipped his quill, blotted it, and continued scratching out the missive to Doctor's Commons.

"I think that I've been exceptionally patient with you, Justin, and I've just about had enough of your heavy-handedness," his mother chided from the doorway. The single candelabra lit in the room sat on his desk, barely illuminating her by the threshold. Yet he could not miss the silly black sash still wrapped around her thin frame.

She glided into the study, her red silk dress swooshing with her every step. "I have not pressed you for answers, even though you owe me them. I have allowed you your petty little desire to order everyone about, yet I am your mother and I demand the respect due me."

He scratched out the next word and examined his work. "Respect cannot be insisted upon; it is earned."

She crossed her arms. "If George were here, he would set you to rights."

Justin dropped the quill to the desktop and stared at the woman who had tormented him with George's death for years, as if he had been responsible for his brother's descent into madness. One thing was for certain: George would never have put up with half of his mother's malicious tactics. "Well, George is not here," he stated mildly.

Scowling, she raised her hand and patted her ash blond hair. "If only you were more like your brother."

"I am sorry, Mother, but I do not have the inclination to put a pistol to my head."

She hissed, her catlike eyes flashing daggers. "For shame!"

"No, Mother, shame on you. You toss George's death about like some sort of chalice signifying your martyrdom." He stood, squaring his stance for a confrontation for which he had little time or patience. "George is no longer here, due solely to his own actions, which you seem to forget, and you are left dealing with me. It might not be what either of us wants, but it is all we are left with. Since you've chosen to interrupt my work, I suggest you state your needs and be gone. What can I do for you?"

She sputtered, her gaunt cheeks coloring white, then pink. "I, I require some answers. . . ."

"Don't we all," he mumbled under his breath. He sighed. "What do you wish to know?"

Watching him nervously, she replied, "You said something about marrying a lady. I want to know your intentions."

He looked down at the letter on his desk and then up at her. "You will meet my lady wife when I am good and ready. Not a moment before."

"But I am your mother and must prepare her, I mean, for her."

"I will not have you poisoning the most important relationship in my life." From the look in her eyes, it was clear that she understood his implication that his maternal relationship did not rank.

"Not every woman is worthy of the Barclay jewels."

"The woman I love is worth everything I have," he spat back, "including the Barclay bridal gems." He leaned forward, bracing his fists on the tabletop. "And why do you continue to wear that ridiculous black sash?"

She lifted her left shoulder, as she'd always done when on the defensive. "I was worried for you. It is my right as a mother to care."

He felt like laughing, so comical was her reply. "If you truly cared, you'd be asking after my health instead of demanding my intentions."

She scowled, guiltily. "You seem fine enough to rant at me."

Dear Lord in heaven, had she always been this awful? What had Evelyn called her? Lady dragon. Well, the designation fit. He stared down at the papers before him, astonished that he'd ever put up with such twaddle. Now more than ever he had no time for such nonsense and could not have his mother interfering with his delicate plans. He came to a decision. "Mother, I realize that you have your needs and they must be met." *Or you'll muddle up everyone else's existence.*

She harrumphed. "I'm glad you see the error of your ways."

"Most assuredly. So much so, I am sending you off to the fort in Wales, where you can satisfy your need to be queen of the castle."

"But . . . that's so far away, and Audrey is coming out this Season, and . . ."

"Aunt Leonore and I will take care of Audrey. You have your wants, and they must come first. I absolutely insist, and I will not take no for an answer. Stanley!"

"Yes, my lord." The man must have been hovering by the door, listening to every word. Good. Let everyone understand who held the reins in this household.

"I want the servants to pull all the stops to get my mother packed and out of the house on the morrow."

"The morrow . . ." she sputtered.

"We will move heaven and earth, my lord." The butler was having difficulty containing his delighted smile.

"Excellent. I want nothing to interfere."

"It is my pleasure to serve you, my lord."

Justin nodded, once again focusing on the papers on

his desk, effectively dismissing them both. His mother gave a curt nod of her head and glided from the room, looking as if she'd eaten a sour grape.

He reread his missive. *Your Grace, I write to you on a matter of the utmost urgency. . . .*

Chapter 25

Sully knew he was dying, and he was not much put out by the thought. The gut-wrenching aches all over his body had faded to a distant roar of pain, and the piercing shards no longer tore at his chest every time he breathed. He heard a faint wheezing sound and realized that it was his wretched body struggling for air through his smashed and broken nose. He'd grown almost accustomed to the bitter metallic taste of blood in his mouth and no longer could find the energy to care about what it was exactly his tormentors wanted from him. He felt the oddest floating sensation and welcomed the blessed blackness.

Consciousness winked out. He floated along until black turned to gray and gray into shadow. In the distance, a hazy glow of lantern light peeked through the swirling fog. The light bobbed and swayed, accompa-

nied by the sound of shuffling boot steps and the clank-
ing of a rattle. It must be a Charlie, prowling the district
for unrest, Sully realized. But this was Seven Dials. No
watchman dared go out alone in the deadly London
neighborhood for fear he would never make it home
alive. In this brutal quarter a man would be killed simply for the coat on his back or the boots on his feet.
Someone was whistling. It was a hauntingly familiar
tune. Curious, Sully followed the receding light as it
ebbed through the gloom.

The dense fog suddenly parted, and he stood before
a large wooden door lined with metal bars and hinges.
A board hung high above the threshold, squeaking
loudly as it swung in the vaporous wind. He shrugged
his coat closer, warding off a sudden chill.

Although the paint was faded and scarred, the sign
clearly depicted a rose and a crown. The Rose and
Crown. Sully stared at the closed doors to the familiar
backwater where the ale was weak, the barmaids surly,
and the customers categorically belligerent. A mighty
gust of wind blew at his back, pushing him forward.
He opened the door and stepped out from the gloomy
night into dimness of another kind. Darkness lined
with lingering shadows.

"Ah, there you are, my good man."

Phillip sat at the second table on the right, healthy and
affable, with a long dark coat draped across his chest
and a tall tankard of ale sitting on the table before him.

Sully stepped forward, thrilled to see Phillip alive.
He gripped his dearest friend's muscled arm. "Phillip!
Holy Jasus, you're a sight for sore eyes!" Suddenly a
memory filtered into his consciousness. A pool of death
drowning his dear mentor. His darling Evelyn draped
in mourning black. Pain, agonizing shards of torture

piercing his legs, tearing at his chest. He could not breathe. Just as quickly, the recollections faded into nothingness, leaving behind only a fuzzy feeling of discomfiture.

"Sit down, my old friend," Phillip invited as he waved an elegant hand at the seat across from him.

Sully could barely contain his joy as he dropped into the rickety wooden chair. "By Gad, it's good to see you again."

A wiry barmaid shuffled over, her ratty hair a mass of snarls. She pushed a clump of dark tangles from her eyes, exposing a haggard face with slashing scars lining her hollowed cheeks. "Drinkin'?"

Phillip waved her off. "He'll not tarry."

She shrugged and shuffled off to the bar.

"But I'm so thirsty," Sully complained, eyeing the large tankard. He couldn't remember the last time a drink had passed his parched lips. "Just a nip to ease my throat." He grabbed for Phillip's tankard, but his friend negligently swatted his hand away.

"You don't tip from this particular spirit, Sully. It'll be the death of you." Phillip leaned forward; his familiar, striking face, which reminded Sullivan so much of his Evelyn, was banked in earnest appeal. "Listen to me, Sully. We don't have much time and I need you to go back. Leave this place and get on with your business, *our business.*"

Sully leaned back, and the wooden chair screeched in protest. In the dim light, he took a long, hard look at his beloved mentor, a whisper of doubt unfurling in his belly. "What is this place, Phillip?"

"I need you to get on. Evelyn needs you, and so do I."

Chills slithered up Sullivan's arms and raced down his back. "Where are we?"

Phillip looked away and lifted the tankard. He gulped, not meeting his friend's eyes.

"Phillip?" Sullivan pressed his lips together, fear roiling in his gut.

His friend dropped the mug and looked up. His wise brown eyes met Sully's, and he slowly shook his head.

And he knew, he just *knew*.

A weight of sorrow tinged with fear pressed down on Sully's chest. He noted now what he had not noticed before. The blood at the corners of Phillip's mouth, the ghostly tinge to his cheeks. Sully leaned over and pulled at the cloak. Blood covered Phillip's torso, stemming from a hole in his side. He looked under the table. Phillip's chair sat in a wide pool of black blood. "You're dead. It was real."

"Go back and finish our business. There's justice to be done."

"Why? Evelyn seems to have found a new life. We've taught her well, she can take care of herself." He looked down. Surprisingly, his body showed no trace of assault. Was it poison that had brought his end? He tried hard to remember, but nothing came, only a sense of nothingness, of being lost.

"I need you to go back, Sullivan. *Now*."

Phillip only used his proper name when he was really pressing. Still, Sully demurred, "Even if I did, what could I possibly do at this point? I must be in sorry shape indeed to be meeting up with you here."

"Remember when you came to me that first time? Albert had just died, and you thought you had no purpose in life. That there was nothing left worth living for."

A smile tugged at Sully's lips as he recalled being so lost. Phillip, however, had helped him find his way.

"You showed me how to serve others, my country. How to be part of something bigger than myself."

"Yes, and we were a great team, you and I. We could change the positions of monarchs, sway petty-minded bureaucrats, bring peace to a world that sometimes felt mad in its chaos."

"And look at what good it did us." Gazing at Phillip's wan face, soberly he choked out, "You're dead."

"Come, Sully, you never give up, and even if I'm not around to keep you in line—"

Sully snorted and crossed his arms. "I was the one who kept you in line, Phillip." It was a familiar refrain between the comrades.

His friend smiled, and it was a warm, wonderful thing.

Sully ran his hands up and down his thighs, feeling the thin wool of his pants. He suddenly felt driven, itching to take action. He needed to be somewhere, doing something. *Now.*

"Off you go now, Sully. Evelyn needs you, and I just cannot let that bastard win."

"But what about you?"

"I've got to move along." He looked down at the tankard in front of him. "But I think I'll have one more nip before I go."

What was that whistling? He looked over his shoulder at the door.

In the distance came a gruff shout. "You fool! You were supposed to get answers from the man, not send him to his maker!"

He turned back and Phillip was gone, the skeletal wooden chair sitting empty. The tankard of ale had vanished.

A flash of white blinded him, tearing away the veil of darkness and crashing reality down on his head. His skull ached; each breath was piercing agony, and the jolts of anguish tearing at his arms and legs made him long for unconsciousness.

He opened his swollen eyelids a slit and saw the glow of lantern light hovering over his head, beneath a burly, dark-swathed arm.

"We cannot move him in this condition, and yet two safe houses have already been compromised." He heard the crack of a hand on flesh. "You've got the finesse of a bull in heat, Helderby."

Helderby. Sully gritted his teeth and almost smiled. He had a debt to repay and could almost taste the vengeance on his bloodied lips.

"And tell me what good he will be to us dead if the Amherst girl won't cooperate."

Evelyn. He tried to place that voice, but it was growing harder to keep conscious.

"I'll call for the doctor. Stay away from him, do you hear? There's too much riding on this for you to muck the whole thing up with your ineptitude."

As a cloak of blessed sleep dropped over Sully's awareness, his last thought was a benediction of thanks to his mentor, who'd always shown him the way.

Chapter 26

Justin awoke from his nap with a cold sweat blanketing his entire body. Chills crept up and down his spine as he recalled the terrifying nightmare about Evelyn. His muscles were clenched tight, and his breath was coming in short gasps. Awake, he thanked heaven for the familiar pierce in his chest and the throb in his temple; they took him back to reality. Staring at the inlaid woodwork on the ceiling of his bedchamber, he waited for the beating of his heart to slow from a canter to a trot.

Gradually he sat up, unclenched his hands, and inhaled a shaky breath. In his dream, Evelyn had been a traitor, come to destroy his country. The colonel had charged him with killing her to save the lives of countless Englishmen. Justin had held the gun pointed at her heart, being called upon to do his duty and murder the one woman he knew was his salvation. She had stared at him, unflinching, her sparkling blue eyes contemptuous of his betrayal. His finger had slowly been pressing down on the trigger when he had suddenly snapped out of the dream.

His mouth tasted like rotted cheese, and he leaned over and took a sip of the tepid tea by his bedside. He pulled the chamber pot from under the bed and spit. This was a nasty business indeed.

He leaned over and yanked open the drawer to his nightstand, wanting to see her handwriting on the single page he'd taken from the cabin. He always kept it near. Something clattered and rolled to the front of the drawer, undulating slowly to a stop with a clank against the wood. He lifted out the metal. A shiny gold ring with two clasped hands carved around the band.

"What the . . . ?"

His grandmother's love token. It was a reminder of all he had done to Evelyn and all he yet still owed her.

"Whatever the future holds for us," he had told her. *"I want you to think well of me."*

How could she think well of him when he had accomplished so little to help her thus far? He was getting nowhere with his sources, was deplorably unable to get the warrant quashed and still had no idea where they held Sully. The magistrate who'd executed the warrant for Evelyn's arrest had suddenly become ill, and no other person seemed able to handle his matters. He would have thought his title could have garnered him at least that minor accomplishment.

Finally, desperate and hoping beyond hope that Wheaton was still honorable, Justin had tried to convince the colonel that Evelyn was not involved in anything nefarious. It had made no difference in the old man's determination to see her arrested, yet doing so had exposed Justin's partiality. If he'd had any doubts before, Justin now knew that Wheaton would not trust him with any information regarding the conspiracy, Sully, or Evelyn. For all intents and purposes, Justin had been cut loose and was alone in his quest for justice.

A wave of fear blanketed his heart so painfully that he fell backward on the solid mattress. He could not fail. Closing his eyes, he remembered Evelyn's soft skin, her fresh lavender scent, and the tinkling harmony of her laugh, and he recollected her misty gaze when she spoke lovingly of her father and Sully. She was the most remarkable woman he had ever known. He refused to let her down.

Sitting up, a feeling of sureness in himself cast all of his doubts to the wind. He slipped the golden sphere into his pocket as a talisman of his mission and the woman who held his heart.

"Ah, pardon me, my lord, but there are two men waiting to see you downstairs." Sylvester stepped deeper into the chamber. "Misters Clontz and Montag."

"Who?"

"They are the Bow Street Runners retained by my lady to . . . ah . . . assist in your return."

"Really?" An idea took shape in his mind. Perhaps all of his cards had yet to be played.

Sylvester's cheeks reddened. "Although it is not my place to say, my lord, I might add that it seems the men have not yet been paid for their services."

Well, Justin knew a way to allow them to earn their

keep and then some. "Help me dress, Sylvester. We've much to do."

Always efficient, his man rushed to obey.

Evelyn held the golden ring up to the light, marveling how such a tiny thing could come to mean so much. But exactly what, she was not sure. Was it a forerunner to another betrayal? Did it mean Justin wanted her to think well of him after he'd scarred her heart beyond redemption?

"It's a trap, I tell you," Angel voiced her fears as he paced the small square of the room, his booted feet making the floorboards creak with his every step.

"How did he find us?"

"The pub is a rendezvous point used by many. He took a chance leaving the message there."

"Justin told me they'd had men following you before. Perhaps they observed you frequenting it then?"

"Regardless, I will not return there again." He scowled. "And don't fret, I took extensive precautions making my way back here."

The candlelight in the cheap, barren room shimmered on the gold ring in her hand. She was tired of the tangled web of her emotions, tired of this relentless second-guessing. She wanted to know once and for all whose side of this madness Justin played on. She had doubts about his allegiance, doubts about his honor and, yes, doubts about his treachery. Part of her could not accept his betrayal. Hope lingered, making her want to tear her hair out. She would go mad if she did not brand him friend or foe once and for all. And if he was the enemy, so be it. He would lead her to Sully or die for his failure.

A sense of inevitability settled over her. She dropped the ring onto the scarred tabletop and watched it slowly undulate to a clattering stop. "I think we should meet him."

Angel waved his hand. "You are not exactly thinking with a clear head when it comes to the marquis, *caro*. No. Too much depends on trusting him."

"You just finished telling me how we couldn't continue searching the safe houses for fear that the authorities will lie in wait for us. What choice do we have?"

Scowling, he ran his hand through his raven hair. "I am beginning to think we'd be better off departing the country."

"I will not leave Sully."

"He would not want you to place yourself in peril for him."

"He's not here to have a voice in the matter. I'm an adult making my own decisions. If you feel you cannot abide by them, I thank you sincerely for your help and will not think any less of you if you leave." She held her breath. She wanted him to know he was not beholden to her, yet the thought of being alone . . .

He growled deep in his throat, reminding her more than ever of an angry leopard. "Do not speak foolishness, *caro*."

Relief swamped her as she let out a long breath. "We will meet Justin at the appointed place."

"And if it's a trap?"

"Let's hope when the man took a bullet for me it meant more than a mere strategy." Sighing, she rubbed her hand over her eyes. "I must confess, part of me yearns to believe he had his reasons for leaving."

"It is not inconceivable."

"What?" Her mouth almost dropped open.

He shrugged. "Even if he had claimed to be able to stop Napoleon himself, I never would have let him go."

"What are you saying?"

"It was the only way he could get back to London. To do good or mischief."

"How do we find out which?"

"We meet him." Angel scratched his chin as he did when deep in thought. "Yet we do not have to come into the encounter as lambs to the slaughter."

"Well, there's no need to take unnecessary chances." Resolve flooding through her, she asked, "What do you have in mind?"

Ghostly gray fog swirled around the damp mausoleum, and for the tenth time in an hour Justin wondered at his choosing such a morbid place to meet Evelyn. He shifted on the hard cold marble, squinting his eyes into the gloom as he caught a hint of movement in the corner of the crypt. He lifted the low-lit lantern, illuminating only about two paces forward. Against the white marble a rat peered up at him, wrinkled its whiskers, squealed, and scurried off behind the tomb.

The bell in the nearby church chimed the hour of two, and he was glad he had thought to wear his warmest cloak for the rendezvous. He pulled the wool closer around him and sniffed the stale air that was barely freshened by the thin slits near the ceiling. Peering through them, he could see only the black night. Even the moon deigned to take cover this grim night.

He ignored the nervous flutter in his middle and prayed that Evelyn trusted him enough to come. She was late. It did not bode well. He stood, anxious to move and warm the blood in his numbing legs. He paced the oblong antechamber, his boots scraping along the stone floor.

The slight scuffle of footsteps on gravel emanated from outside. He shifted closer to the slit on the high wall. The stone pressed cold through the thin leather of his gloves. The exterior metal gate creaked as it was pushed open. His breath caught in his throat and his heart hammered. He pulled the pistol from his pocket, ready for anything, but praying he was being overcautious.

Three clanks hammered against the iron-studded door. He stepped close. His voice was a hoarse whisper. "Who goes there?"

"Angel Arolas and Evelyn Amherst," came the smooth inflection of the Spaniard.

Justin unbarred the heavy door and stepped back, his pistol unwavering in his hand. The heavy door groaned open. Two black-cloaked figures stepped inside. The one on the right wore a long, dark mourning veil.

Justin's heart sank. Anger etched with deep remorse as he held up the pistol and accused, "What do you take me for? A fool?"

Arolas's wary eyes scanned the chamber and then settled back on him. "What do you mean?"

"That's not Evelyn."

The Spaniard swiftly pulled his gloved hands from inside his dark cloak, a pistol in each one. The figure next to Arolas shrugged off the black veil and cloak. Instead of Evelyn, her man Ismet stood ready with a long, menacing dagger slicing through the air with a hiss.

"We needed to know this was not a trap," Arolas commented tightly as he balanced on his toes, ready for a confrontation. "Is it?"

Justin had to begrudgingly admire the defensive tactic. Anyone who did not know the graceful glide of Evelyn's step or the fact that her head came just to Justin's shoulder might have missed the ruse. Although jealous to the core of the handsome Spaniard, a part of Justin was thankful Evelyn had such vigilant friends.

"This is no trap. I have a man in a coach by the eastern gates. Otherwise, I am alone in here." He did not bother to mention the Bow Street Runners in the crypt next door. He eyed the fighting men warily, realizing there was only one way to proceed. He slowly uncocked his pistol and relaxed his stance.

With Ismet watching, Arolas turned and paced the chamber with catlike grace. He peered into each corner of the crypt and behind the central tomb. The man moved with the natural agility of a predator. Apparently concluding that all was as it should be, Arolas leisurely put his firearms in the inside pockets of his cloak.

Ismet nodded to the man, then silently slipped out the heavy door. It closed with a grating thud.

Justin could just barely hear Ismet's soft footfalls on the mossy grass outside. "Is she coming?" He slipped his pistol into the exterior pocket of his coat.

"In a moment."

They waited in silence, an owl hooting off in the distance.

Arolas said softly, "An interesting place to meet, yet ingenious. Quiet, away from prying eyes, we can hear anyone coming near."

Justin accepted the tribute with a nod. "There is only one entrance." He tried to ignore the jealousy nipping at his gut as he imagined the Spaniard and Evelyn together. Even he could recognize that the Spaniard was too good-looking by half. Guardedly, he asked, "How is she?"

"She is strong, our Evelyn."

He did not miss the possessiveness in the man's voice. "I heard that two of the safe houses were compromised. It was you."

Arolas shrugged. He stared hard at Justin. "You said in your missive you could return Sully. Where is he?"

"I don't know."

"Then how—?"

"I will explain everything when Evelyn arrives."

The exterior gate squeaked. Justin's heart began to hammer once more, and he realized that he was gambling his entire future on the lady's delicate footfalls that trod near.

The iron-studded door groaned open, and a black-cloaked figure stepped inside. He would know that graceful glide anywhere. A wave of relief swamped him till he felt light-headed. "Evelyn," he breathed.

She slipped off her dark hood, and he soaked in the sight of her. Her coiled golden hair barely shone in the dim lamplight. Her lush lips were pressed tight and dark circles still banked her eyes, yet the brilliance of that blue gaze pierced his heart.

The corners of his lips rose, but he was too overwhelmed to smile. "I'm so glad you came."

She was eyeing him as if to discern all his secrets

from his gaze. "I see you did not kill yourself in your mad dash for escape."

"I'm sorry for leaving you so abruptly, Evelyn, but Arolas would never have let me go."

"In my country, when a man steals your horse, he owes you something of equal value in return." Arolas's dark eyes glittered. "Your life, perhaps?"

"We have yet to ascertain if that will be enough," Evelyn added bitterly.

Her anger tore at his heart, but he had to try to convince her he was true. "I apologize. But I had to go. It was the best course of action available to us, and I was not about to let you talk me out of it or let him stop me."

"Us?" Arolas raised his brow. "We do not know of whom you speak."

"I had to try to get the warrant for Evelyn's arrest quashed. The only way to do that was to appear whole before the magistrate who granted it."

"And is this done?"

"I am having difficulties."

"Aren't we all?" Arolas countered.

"I also had to try to convince my superior that Evelyn is not involved in any French plot. And to endeavor to find Sully. I could do none of those things traipsing around the countryside while we tried to keep a Spaniard, two Turks, and a couple of English gentry from being captured. We were too obvious, and yet to return to London was too risky for Evelyn. I had to go alone."

"Yet I am here," she murmured. "At risk."

"And I cannot deny it: I'm so glad to see you," he offered, trying to show her with his eyes what he was having difficulty explaining with words. She was the reason for his every action, his raison d'être these days.

"I presume you had no luck with Wheaton." Arolas waved his gloved hand.

Evelyn looked up, hope flashing in those robin's egg blue eyes. "And what of Sully?"

"I do know for certain that Sully is alive. Helderby has him at one of the safe houses. I'm working on finding out which one."

"We are trying the same tack," Evelyn replied quietly. Straightening her shoulders, she asked, "You said you could help end this mess. Help recover Sully . . ."

He waved to the white marble steps. "If you would have a seat?"

She eyed him warily, yet let him take her hand. He thanked the heavens for these small measures of trust. He led her to sit on the hard stone steps, never releasing her small hand. The heat of her grasp warmed him on so many different levels that the cold stone on his bottom barely registered.

Arolas negligently flipped open his long cloak and sat on Evelyn's other side.

Justin began, "I have considered our situation in a thousand different lights. There is only one way to expose Wheaton and ascertain if there is a real threat to the realm or if he has gone rogue." Justin prayed that he could be as persuasive as he needed to be. "Wheaton claims there is a French plot in the works. We cannot take the chance that he is right." He swallowed, knowing Evelyn was perceptive enough to grasp the intricacies of the matter. He hoped she would likewise appreciate what he was about to divulge. "Besides administrative matters, the Alien Office handles many sensitive, secretive matters pertaining to France. They are beyond Wheaton's control."

Arolas rubbed his chin. "I'd heard rumors, but . . ."

Evelyn shook her head appreciatively. "Even Father never spoke of it." She blinked, comprehension dawning in her lovely eyes.

"Few are aware of its clandestine operation. Or of its power. You must contact the Alien Office and offer to trade me for Sully."

The Spaniard fisted his hands. "We've been over this. Before anyone can make sense of this mess, Evelyn will be arrested on the kidnapping charge, and all will be lost."

Justin played his trump card. "Not if she is immune from prosecution."

Arolas inhaled a sharp breath. "Are you suggesting what I think you are suggesting?"

"Yes." Justin clenched his fist. "Do you have any issue with that?" He prayed it wasn't pure folly to fantasize the Barclay bridal gems adorning Evelyn's lovely neck.

The Spaniard eyed him critically. "Are you sincere?"

"Deadly. I'm willing to bet the rest of my life on Evelyn."

Arolas blew out a long breath, considering. "In that case, I have no issue."

The relief on Justin's tongue tasted sweet. One down, one to go.

Evelyn squeezed his hand. "I'm not following. What are you suggesting?"

He caught her brilliant blue gaze, stating softly, "As my wife no one would dare prosecute you for my kidnapping. You will be protected, and we will have time to get our answers."

Her whole body stilled. Her hand was dead in his grasp. With his heart pounding, he rushed on, "We will insist that they bring Sully to the exchange, ensuring that he is whole. I will arrange for the appropriate members of the Alien Office to be there at the meeting, and Wheaton will be forced to answer to them for his actions. If there is a French plot threatening our nation as he claims, then we will fight that battle with additional forces. But you will finally know where you stand and be free from this terrible game. It also will make them have to go through the proper channels if they are going to charge Sully."

"And if, on the slim chance Evelyn knows something to help stop the French conspiracy, she will be able to impart the information without being indicted." Arolas tilted his head in salute. "The plan has merit."

"Can't you just go to this Alien Office and insist that they step in?" Evelyn ventured, pursing her lush lips.

Arolas shook his head. "Politics, *caro*. No one can challenge the master of spies unless he is caught with his hands dirty."

"I can't imagine Wheaton betraying His Majesty," Justin stated quietly. "But what he's done to you in the name of security . . ." He pounded his hand on his thigh. "This is the only way to get all our answers. The French plot, Wheaton's actions, Sully's charges, the warrant against you—" He reached inside his breast pocket and pulled out the parchment. He was thankful his hand did not shake when he held it out to her.

"What is it?" she asked, eyeing the document warily.

"A special license. We have little time. The colonel says that the French plot is set for next week." Justin watched Evelyn closely, yet he could not read her, as there was so little emotion in her lovely features. It was as if she'd frozen from the shock of his offer.

Arolas reached for the document. The paper crackled as he opened it and read. After a moment, he said, "It appears in order, *caro*." He looked up. "But what about the future? Evelyn's situation?"

Justin squared his shoulders, verbalizing what he dreaded to say. "I know how Evelyn feels about marriage. . . ." He caught her gaze. "After you're safe, I am prepared to obtain a divorce, if that's what you want." It was his most fervent hope that she would not want it.

Crickets chirped in the funereal silence. A rat scurried across the room.

"Divorces are rarely granted," she stated while looking down and adjusting her black skirts. "They are expensive and publicly humiliating. Everything about you, me, your work in the Foreign Office, will be subject to public scrutiny and scorn. Your reputation and your family's social standing will be irreparably damaged. . . ."

He squeezed her hand. "It does not matter so long as you are free."

She turned her head away. He held his breath. If she rejected his offer, he had hit a stone wall from which he feared he just might not recover. He could not stomach the idea of her running for her life as Wheaton and his men hunted her down.

"There are few other options, and we can save Sully." He was determined to convince her. "It's the only way."

Arolas grabbed her free hand. "It is a good plan, Evelyn. You will be protected."

Evelyn looked down at her hands, one in Angel's grasp and the other in Justin's. Two very different but remarkable men who seemed to believe that this was the best course of action. She inhaled a shaky breath. *Theoretically* it was a good plan. It seemed that Justin could be trusted not to surrender her to his government. But could she entrust him with such power over her life, legally, physically, and—the most thorny— emotionally? She did not miss the irony that every- thing appeared to hinge on accepting the one thing she feared most in the world.

Justin stated softly, "To 'wed' literally means to 'gamble' or 'wager.' I'm hoping you lay your bets on me finding us a way out of this maze."

She was caught again in the enchantment of those greenish-gray eyes. She felt his magnetism like a lure pulling her into his warmth, to soak in his passionate fires. Remembering how she had melted against him, she prayed her body and her instincts were sound. Re- calling the bitter tang of his betrayal, she marveled at how she could even consider trusting her own judgment where he was concerned. What a fine pickle she was in.

She could not help the ironic smile that tugged at the corners of her lips. "Heavens, what Byzantine quan- daries we face." She chuckled. "It's almost as if some- one is setting obstacles in our paths, by design." She dropped Angel's hand and rubbed her tired eyes.

Angel commented wryly, "It fits, don't you think?"

"How so?" she asked.

"As the wedding lore authority, you should know that in the Scottish Highlands, it is the man who faces the trials, as it should be."

She smiled at her friend. "All for a woman's kiss."

"What are you talking about?" Justin asked.

She turned to him. "In the old custom of creeling, the bridegroom must carry a large basket of stones throughout the town searching for his bride. Only if she comes out and kisses him can he drop the weight."

Angel leaned forward and faced Justin. "How much weight can you carry, my lord?"

Justin straightened, his mouth pressed in a firm line. "As much as it takes."

It seemed as if an accord had been reached between the three of them without her actually agreeing to anything. Evelyn felt it like a web around her chest spun so tightly that she thought she might not breathe. Dropping Justin's hand, she stood, needing to move. She rubbed her suddenly sweaty palms together; even the leather of her gloves chafed. She licked her desert-dry lips. "Well then. Where do we go from here?"

"We have the special license, we can be married at any time or place of our choosing," Justin offered. "Fortunate for us, my local vicar is in Town for a family service."

"How opportune," she mumbled under her breath. Funeral, most likely.

"A christening, I'm told." He stood smoothly. "I have him waiting at a small chapel near Charing Cross."

"You expected me to say yes?" She looked up, surprised. Had she laid bets she would have wagered against a wedding that day.

He shrugged his broad shoulders. "I had hoped."

Angel jumped up. "Let's go."

"My, you're in a rush to see me leg-shackled."

He beamed a wicked smile. "This is a treat I never expected to see—Evelyn, the ultimate naysayer, getting married. I only wish my father were here to witness this. He would not believe it."

She crossed her arms. "And will you tease me so mercilessly when I am in the midst of an ugly divorce?"

Justin scowled. "No need to make this into a bloody drama. The carriage awaits at the eastern gate."

Angel headed to the door. "Just so long as it is you and not me in that chapel, *caro*."

She swallowed hard and followed him out the door into the gloomy night, toward the dreaded parson's mousetrap.

Chapter 27

Evelyn alighted from Justin's carriage, thankful to be out of the stifling enclosure. While Justin and Angel had seemed perfectly at ease discussing strategies and options as the coach had rolled its way toward the chapel, she had barely been able to breathe in the airless cabin. Her stomach had lurched with each rut in the road, and she'd felt as if those Scottish creeling stones had been bearing down on her shoulders with their odious matrimonial burden.

Inhaling deeply, she relished the crisp night air. Cedar trees lined the external gate of the little house of worship, guarding it like sentinels. Tilting her head back, she stared up at the ancient chapel. Even in her apprehensive state, she had to admire the simplicity of its design—a single spire poking up at the moonless night as shadowed clouds grazed by. In one of the tall windows a whisper of lamplight shimmered through the skeletal outline of the diamond-shaped glass.

Justin opened the gate, which squeaked with protest at being disturbed. Evelyn swallowed and strode through. Gently grasping her elbow, Justin led her toward the tall wooden doors.

Inside, the dusty air smelled of mold, timber, and beeswax. Two small rows of wooden benches lined the sanctuary, with a short aisle leading up to the pulpit. In the corner by the altar sat a frumpy, heavyset man in a long brown cloak with a lamp lit at his feet. He was nearly bald, with a crown of white cresting large ears. He pushed his glasses up his bulbous nose and stood. Peering into the darkness, he shifted from foot to foot nervously. "My lord?"

Justin propelled Evelyn forward, down the short aisle, up to the platform. Her mouth went dry, and her heart began to pound so loudly she thought the spired rooftop might quake. "Vicar Rece. Thank you so much for waiting on our arrival." Justin said it as if he had feared the man would not appear.

The cleric peered at Evelyn, his brown eyes squinting tightly. "Black? I've never officiated at a wedding where the bride was in mourning." His shifting intensified. "Highly improper, indeed."

"As I explained in my missive, these are unusual circumstances." Justin drew the license from his pocket and handed it to the minister. "Everything is in order. We can proceed with the wedding ceremony."

Her nervous stomach flipped over.

The cleric sniffed and leaned forward, holding the document to the lamp on the floor. His lips moved silently as he read. "You're certain she's of age?"

A nervous laugh burst from her mouth and she coughed into her gloved hand. At the moment she felt as old as the ark.

"Yes, Vicar Rece." Justin's voice was growing thin with impatience. "Everything is in order."

The cleric straightened and scratched one of his chins. "Black."

"In Spain a bride always wears black at her wedding," Justin countered irritably.

She turned to him, surprised. "How did you know that?"

"You told me when we first met. I recall everything you've ever said to me, Evelyn. Even when you told me you had no wish to marry."

The vicar looked up from the license. "What's that you say? She does consent, doesn't she?"

Justin turned her to face him and asked solemnly, "Do you, Evelyn?"

It was as if a pit had yawned open underneath her feet and she hovered on the brink, barreling down into nothingness. She licked her parched lips and wondered if she could excuse herself to find a cup of water, or perhaps a glass of wine, or some of that fiery brandy of Angel's. She frowned. "Where's Angel?"

"We do need our witnesses, my lord," Vicar Rece intoned judiciously.

She stepped out of Justin's grasp and strode to the door.

"Wait!" Justin charged in a harsh whisper.

"I'm just going to call—" The heavy wooden door was yanked out of her hand with a loud squeak.

A hulking brute shrouded in darkness grabbed her arm and jerked her outside into the chilly night air. His sickly-sweet unclean smell pierced her nostrils, and it was the final straw. Her nervous stomach lurched. She gagged, and her last meal from the cheap inn gushed from her mouth all over the thug's black coat.

"Ugh! You bitch!"

His steely grip on her arm loosened, and Justin plowed into the man's chest. She spun out of the conflict, landing hard on her knees in the soft earth by the chapel steps.

Shadowed men encircled them, the dark outlines of their figures offset by the lamps they held. Squinting up, she raised her hand to ward off the bright lights, when a heavyset man moved close enough for her to discern in the glow. She blinked. Father Christmas stood before her, holding out his white-gloved hand. He wore formal attire, down to his black buckled shoes.

"Miss Evelyn Amherst. So glad finally to make your acquaintance."

Justin stepped between them, huffing hoarsely, "She's done nothing wrong, Colonel."

"And I'm a witch's toad." He frowned, and the snowy tufts of his brows bowed low over his steely blue eyes. A chill crawled down Evelyn's spine. This was not the jovial legend of her childhood; this was a man to be feared.

She spit the sharp taste of vomit from her mouth and slowly rose. She eyed the men warily, spying a glimpse of Angel struggling between two burly oafs. He caught her eye, and her heart burned with indignation. She turned on Justin. "You bloody bastard," she hissed and slammed her fist into his torso so hard her knuckles throbbed.

Grabbing her arm, he cried, "You don't believe I knew about this?"

Her voice had thinned to ice. "Didn't you?"

"If you would join me in the carriage, Miss Amherst." The colonel waved toward the front gate, where a line of coaches waited. They were surrounded; there was no way out other than to follow the bastard's lead and wait for an opportunity.

She lifted her skirts and stalked to the entry, her chin lifted high, her gaze staring forward.

"Evelyn!" Justin raced by her side. "I didn't arrange this."

His superior held him back with a firm hand on his arm. "Your job is finished here, Barclay. We have everything we need, thanks to you and your very cooperative vicar. You can find your own way home, I'm sure."

"Don't do this, Colonel," he pleaded. Then a harsh edge infused his cultured voice. "There'll be hell to pay if so much as a hair on her head is harmed."

"I'm on my way to meet the piper now," the old man intoned as he followed behind Evelyn.

She stopped and turned. "Angel Arolas has done nothing wrong."

The colonel smiled a grandfatherly smile, and Evelyn barely held back her cringe. She would not show this bastard her fear.

"Aiding a wanted criminal is a triable offense. Let's see how well you cooperate, and perhaps he'll make it to the magistrate." He tsked. "Terrible how men keep getting lost on the way to court these days."

She clenched her hands and willed her armor to fall into place. Instead of the familiar clank inside her head, all she heard were the rattling of chains as the vicar locked the chapel doors.

After a nail-biting carriage ride, Evelyn contained her surprise when, instead of a grisly dungeon, she was led into a spacious drawing room where a raging fire flamed in the hearth. The heady scent of spices drifted up from the flames—the same aroma Justin had burned in the grate at his brother's place. Her teeth clenched, her anger was so raw. She mentally shook herself. She needed to be thinking about escape, not lamenting her mistakes.

"Brandy?" Wheaton waved to the bar.

She nodded curtly. She needed something to expunge the stale taste of bile from her mouth, and she did not mind taking from the despicable bastard; given half a chance she'd take him for everything he had. She stepped over to the hearth, feeling no warmth from the billowing flames.

"Here." He held the glass of brownish liquid out to her. She glared at him and did not move. There was only so much contact she was willing to subject herself to. Shrugging, he set the glass on the side table. She stepped over and raised it to her cracked lips. The fiery liquid slithered down her throat into her hollow belly. It brought minimal relief from the anger, couched in fear, that roiled in her stomach.

Looking up, she examined the rapacious faces of the porcelain ghouls hovering on the mantel. She shuddered; only a sick person would keep such vile curios.

Wheaton dropped his heavy bulk into the deep armchair by the fire and motioned for her to sit across from him. She did not pay heed.

"Where's Sully?"

"Sullivan is in my care. In fact, I had to call a doctor to monitor his progress."

"Progress from what?"

He scratched a snowy sideburn. "Seems Sullivan came face-to-face with a hard object."

The only hard object sat in the armchair before her. "What do you want?"

"Justice."

"You are not exactly a good judge of it, given you are imprisoning two innocent men without allowing them the benefit of due process."

"I am detaining you as well."

She let out the breath she had been holding. So they didn't have Ismet or Shah. She'd suspected as much when she could not glimpse Ismet anywhere near the chapel. That also meant her last hope against hope that Justin was not in league with this bastard melted away, since Justin was not arrested either. Well, she had wanted to know what side he played on. Now she knew. She pushed away the hurt; she had no time for it now. Anger was all she could afford.

She leaned over Wheaton in the chair, a burst of self-confidence coming from some unknown source. "How dare you speak of justice when you are the epitome of engorged arrogance?"

His white cheeks reddened. "You don't know what you're talking about."

"You toy with others without regard for the faith entrusted to you by your country." She edged closer, wanting him to feel her wrath. "Does His Majesty know how you trample on the rights of your fellow Englishmen to feather your own nest?"

"I am claiming what is rightfully mine, earned, by the way, in service to my country!" Spittle flew from his lips, and she felt a small sense of satisfaction that she was able to rouse him so easily. Perhaps he was not the impervious archfiend he appeared.

"What utter nonsense. You are a travesty of an Englishman," she retorted, her voice laced with scorn.

His face turned a fascinating shade of purple, and he seemed to shake from head to toe, his fat lips quivering. He raised his fisted hand to her, but the menace was lost as it shook wildly. Swallowing hard, he blew out a long breath. Seeming to get a hold on his emotions, he shook his head, suddenly smiling. "I did not realize how disquieting it would be to speak with you face-to-face. I must admit, you have more mettle to you than I expected from Diedra's daughter."

He knew her mother? She turned and stepped away from the mantel, trying to hide her shock.

"Oh, yes, your mother and I were quite close growing up." He reached into his coat pocket and pulled out a white linen square. He patted it across his beaded brow. "In Bloomsbury our houses stacked up side by side. We could not have been *closer*."

She did not like the insinuation in his tone. "What does that have to do with why you are abusing your office?"

He leaned forward angrily. "I am not abusing anything, you randy-faced chit! I am doing what should have been done years ago. If only your bloody father had not been knighted." Crazed violence shone in his steely eyes. "If only the dratted bastard had never been born!" His hatred was palpable; it rippled off him in waves.

She realized that she had unconsciously edged backwards into the flanking bookcase. She forced herself to step forward and attempted to regain that swell of confidence. "If he had never been born, then this country, no, the world would have been a much poorer place. He was a peacemaker," she declared proudly.

"He was a thief!"

"He would not have stolen to save his own skin!"

"He pilfered my life!" He shoved his big bulk up on shaky legs and stomped to the mantel, leaning hard against the marble. "He stole my wife. My knighthood. My treasure." He wiped his hand across his eyes. "My Diedra." He blew out a shuddering breath. "You look so much like her, it's uncanny."

Silence enveloped the eerie chamber.

She peeked toward the entry, wondering how hard it would be to make it out the back door. The colonel seemed too ungainly to follow a twenty-two-year-old racing for her life.

"But you are Amherst's bloody babe, and whether you know it or not, you have what's mine." He turned, hatred glittering brightly in his eyes as he stepped menacingly toward her. "I had hoped throwing the truth in his face would have brought me some redress. But the only satisfaction I got was from putting a bullet in his gut. I trust you won't push me so far."

Shock pierced her heart at his cold-blooded confession.

"Step away from Evelyn, Colonel!" Justin stood in the threshold, the pistol pointed at Wheaton unwavering in his grip. Relief and distrust warred inside her. He was her adversary, yet there he stood, acting as if he were her champion.

"So the boy finally grows to be a man." Wheaton held up his meaty hands in surrender. Still, he sidestepped closer to her.

"Don't make me shoot, Colonel!" With Justin's eyes trained on his former superior, he called over his shoulder, "In the drawing room, Mr. Clontz!"

Evelyn slid along the bookcase, away from Wheaton, and stood by Justin's side.

"Did he hurt you, Evelyn?"

She shook her head, relieved but uncertain. "Angel? Sully?" It was too much to hope.

"I wanted to find you first." His mouth was pressed into a firm line.

"I hate to disappoint, but I cannot stay to blow the gab." The colonel stepped toward the bookcase.

"Sit down in the seat by the fire, Wheaton," Justin ordered.

Wheaton jumped in the opposite direction, grabbing one of the volumes from its shelf. A section of the bookcase slid open with a hiss. The colonel stepped through, amazingly fast for a man of his age and stature.

A boom exploded near Evelyn's ear. She opened her eyes, and smoke wove through the chamber. Her ears were ringing from the report, and the sharp scent of gunpowder filled her nostrils.

Justin raced to the concealed exit. "Bloody hell!" He ducked his head and charged through.

"Justin!" With her heart in her throat she ran after him, into the darkest pitch. Something crashed into her head with a horrible crack. Pain pummeled her skull, stars shimmered in her eyes, and then all went black.

Chapter 28

Voices whispered in the darkness, but Evelyn had no wish to leave the safety of her comfortable cocoon. She inched deeper into her slumber, ignoring the world that pressed against the invisible wall of her cozy sanctuary. To her chagrin, her senses slowly rose to wakefulness anyhow.

The sharp scents of spirit of turpentine and camphor teased her nose, making her cognizant of the fact that someone had been diligently cleaning against bedbugs. She shifted slightly under the soft blanket; how she loved a firm wool mattress. The silky smooth sheets under her palms brought understanding that this was a fancy establishment indeed. Her brow furrowed. Was she indebted to Angel even more for yet another night in an expensive inn?

But what were whispering strangers doing in her

leased room? And why did her head ache as if a sea-
man had used it to crack open a drum?

"My lord, she wakes!"

Heavens, did he have to bellow? Her head pounded
horrifically and her ears rang. This was not fancy
hostelry. She was in a luxurious bedchamber with
strange servants scrambling about. She heard soft footfalls on thick carpeting and felt a presence standing near.

Excitement bubbled in her middle, blended with no
small sense of relief. She'd know that woodsy, masculine scent anywhere. Still, her warm feelings were
tinged with fury. Justin had betrayed her, had he not?
Or had he saved her? Her muddled brain was having
trouble discerning between fact and wishful thinking.

She pried open her eyes. Her vision was filled with
the familiar features of the handsome man who was at
the center of her confusion. Swallowing, she took her
fill of his striking good looks; the dimpled chin, pursed
smooth lips, sharp, high cheekbones, and smoky gray-
green eyes. A thin fuzz of golden hair blanketed his
chin, and black circles shadowed his worried eyes. The
way he watched her apprehensively, as if fearful of her
reaction to him, brought to the fore the mishmash of
her emotions.

She cleared her throat. "Ah, what happened?"

He spoke quietly in his succinct, cultured voice. "The
colonel had traps set. The first one trounced me." He
raised his leg and showed her the ivory bandage that
had been out of view. "And you, regrettably, suc-
cumbed to the second."

The confrontation in the drawing room rushed back
to her. Justin had shot at his superior, had placed himself on the line, to help her. Why would he do such a
thing if he had been the one who had arranged her cap-

ture? She recalled the colonel's words, *". . . the very co-operative vicar."* So Justin had been true all along. The certainty hit home, and deep in her heart a little voice gave a cry of joy.

She raised her hand to her throbbing head. "What hit me, an anvil?"

"A useless cannonball."

"So that's the explosion resounding in my head." She shifted up slowly. "Obviously he found a use for it."

"A bloody nasty use," Justin mumbled under his breath as he gently helped her sit up. Even through the fog of her pain she was aware of his masculine strength and the power of his attraction. He called to every feminine instinct within her.

Clearing his throat, he offered, "You gave us quite a scare. You've been unconscious for some time."

She quibbled, "I was due for a holiday."

"Not one from life, I presume," he replied somberly.

Motioning to a hovering servant, Justin accepted a steaming mug and passed it to her. Herbs floated in the warm greenish-yellow liquid. Evelyn sniffed. Chamomile, mint, lemon, among other things.

"I cannot afford to be beef-brained," she said as she handed back the cup. "There's too much left to do."

"But you're in pain," Justin countered.

"Nothing I can't handle." Straightening her shoulders, she repressed a wince. "We need to find Angel and Sully."

He grimaced. "I've searched every safe house in London, without finding a trace of either of them."

"On that?" She pointed to his injured foot.

"It's nothing I can't handle," he echoed back grimly.

She let out a long breath. *So Justin was The Real*

Scratch. She could not quite face her combustion of emotions, so she pushed them aside for examination later. Sully and Angel came first. "Then we will just have to search the entire country. Whatever it takes to find them."

"Oh, I hope we don't have to travel by coach," came a familiar lilting Spanish accent from the doorway. "My back is aching from that nasty trip from Wellington's camp."

"Señor Arolas!" Evelyn exclaimed, but razor-sharp pain pierced her temple from her own loud voice. She lifted her hand to her throbbing head but smiled through the ache. "Here come the Titans!"

"Don't think I can save the world, Evelyn. I was little enough help to your father." The elegant older gentleman sauntered into the room, a scowl marring his handsome features. He was an older version of Angel, but with curly silver hair instead of black and at least two stones heavier than his son. Still, he had that same darkly attractive countenance and catlike grace, which made Evelyn miss Angel even more.

"I came as fast as I could."

"How did you know, Señor?" she asked.

"I contacted him." Justin hobbled forward with his hand extended. "Señor Arolas, I'm so glad you could come. We're in the Briers and need all the help we can get."

The men shook hands. "So Wheaton has Angel?"

Justin blinked. "How did you—?"

The older gentleman shrugged. "I have my sources. And I can tell you this, Angel is not involved in any French plot."

"I've come to the inevitable conclusion that the

French conspiracy is nothing more than a subterfuge to give Wheaton access to Evelyn, Sully, and whatever it is he's after."

"The scalawag does not appear to worry overmuch about the authorities," Evelyn pointed out. "Why did he even bother with the ruse?"

"The old double shuffle," Justin replied. "With everyone loyal chasing the wrong target, he pursues his own with impunity." His gaze turned bitter. "I can't believe what a cat's-paw I've been!"

"You thought you were saving your country," she commented. "Besides, if you hadn't been involved, Wheaton would have had my hide by now."

Señor Arolas rubbed his chin. "So you were the infiltrator, my lord?"

"Yes."

"A logical plan, given the family connection and your role with the Foreign Office."

"How do you know so much about me?" Justin questioned.

"I asked a friend."

The scope of Señor Arolas's influence hit home; the only friend with that kind of knowledge could be Wellington himself.

Silence enveloped the elegant chamber. A servant slipped a chair behind each man, and they sat by Evelyn's bedside.

"So what happened to the plan?" Señor Arolas adjusted his legs before him. Even in this odd situation, Evelyn had to admire the fine cut of his elegant clothes and his graceful manner. The men in the Arolas family had incredible flair.

Justin's style was quite different, but somehow equally appealing. Wincing, he adjusted his injured foot. "The trap worked. Wheaton captured Sully but apparently did not get what he wanted. So he went after Evelyn."

"And got my son." Señor Arolas scowled. "So what does the fiend want?"

"I don't know," Justin admitted.

"Vengeance," Evelyn whispered. "He killed my father." The coldness in her voice surprised even her.

Señor Arolas's features darkened. "Now he's got a double debt to pay for abducting my son."

"He believes that Father stole from him."

"Stole what?"

She bit her lip, trying to remember what the knave had said. "His wife, my mother. Ah, his knighthood and . . . some sort of treasure."

"What kind of treasure?" Justin leaned forward eagerly.

She slowly shook her head.

"So he was the one," Señor Arolas spoke softly.

That really got her attention. "What are you talking about, Señor?"

Arolas cleared his throat. "Your father had confided in me, and, well, at this point, you are old enough to learn the truth without it devastating you."

She swallowed. "What is it?"

"A diplomat's life can be difficult, especially on one's family." Guilt flashed through his cocoa brown eyes. "We do it for our country and, let's be honest, for ourselves. But it means sacrifice." He shrugged. "Phillip knew Diedra was not happy; still, he was distraught when she confessed to having had an affair." He watched her closely, surmising, "You don't seem surprised."

"I've always suspected she had been untrue to Father. Even at a young age, one hears things not meant for tender ears. Odd as it may sound, part of me had felt glad she'd found some happiness in her life, the rest of me could never forgive her for causing my father so much pain." Her lips curled in disgust. "I'm just appalled that she chose to flout her marriage vows with such a loathsome villain."

"Apparently they had been childhood friends and had almost married," Señor Arolas explained. "Evidently Wheaton pursued her for years after she wed, intent on winning her back. I don't know exactly when the affair occurred, but she ended it, too overwhelmed by guilt."

"Probably regained her sanity," Evelyn retorted.

Justin shook his head. "If she ended the affair years ago and your father was knighted many years back, then why did Wheaton kill your father now? And why is he coming after you?"

"Even though you have a splendidly diabolical intellect," Evelyn commented dryly, "you cannot try to decipher the mind of a madman." His eyes locked with hers, and she suddenly realized what she'd said. Her cheeks heated as a sense of horror overwhelmed her. She prayed he could not believe that she'd ever compare him to his disturbed brother!

His lips slowly lifted into a grin that flooded his eyes with radiance. The affection she saw in his gaze made her hollow stomach flip over, and caused her to long to melt in the embers of his smoldering greenish-gray eyes.

Señor Arolas coughed into his hand, breaking the spell. "So, ah, I understand that Angel was captured at a church. What exactly were you doing at a church at five o'clock in the morning?"

"Evelyn and I were about to be married," Justin supplied, watching her carefully.

Señor Arolas sputtered, "You must be jesting! Evelyn's sworn since she was eight years old that she'd never marry."

She blinked as insight flashed through her mind. "I remember Mother and Father having a terrible row when we were in Italy. Mother had just returned from an excursion to London. I must've been about eight years old." She felt as if a veil had been lifted from her eyes. A mourning veil. "That certainly explains a lot."

"But you must have changed your mind about marriage, given you were about to wed." Señor Arolas nodded approvingly.

"The warrant was for my kidnapping," Justin supplied. "If we were married . . ."

"She could not be charged." Señor Arolas seemed disappointed. "But obviously the man no longer needs the cloak of his office to conduct his illicit dealings."

"Apparently he's growing more desperate," Justin concluded. "Which means that Angel and Sully are in ever more danger."

Evelyn fisted her hands. "What can we do?"

Señor Arolas rubbed his chin, looking off into the distance. "Give him what he wants."

"What?" Evelyn shrieked, leaning forward so quickly that her head felt like someone had ripped it open. "I'll be damned if I'm going to let that bastard win."

Justin shook his head, resolution lighting his eyes. "Señor Arolas has not yet explained what we will do to Wheaton once we've given him what he wants and he's given us Angel and Sully."

"Oh." She leaned back. "How do we give him what he wants when we don't know what it is?"

"We ask him," Señor Arolas stated quietly. "I might not be a Titan, but this old Spaniard still has a few tricks up his sleeve."

Chapter 29

Evelyn stared up at the dilapidated dwelling that looked exactly like every other one of the squat row houses on the grimy street, marveling that her refined mother could have come from such humble beginnings. Well, her mother was not exactly turning out to be the angel she remembered.

"Are you certain you wish to do this, Evelyn?" Justin asked, standing by her side, eyeing the residence askance.

"My wishes seem to have little enough to do with reality these days," she replied, squaring her shoulders.

His fine carriage horses nickered and shifted in the narrow street, and the contrast between Justin's fancy team and the neighborhood was not lost on anyone in the vicinity. The coach probably cost more than leasing the entire block for the year. Hard-faced working men and women scurried past, eyes aimed to the ground.

"I'm being serious, Evelyn."

She let out a long breath. "Wheaton will not have seen the notice in the papers as of yet, and so we have time on our hands until he responds. Ismet and Shah are Lord knows where. . . ." She sent him a plucky little smile, when she was feeling anything but. "We need to find out more about Wheaton and what he wants, and this seems the best way to do it. You're the razor-sharp thinker; don't you agree?"

"I can question the residents. You wouldn't stay at home, but you can at least wait in the carriage. . . ."

"For the hundredth time, Justin, I appreciate your concern, but you can stop worrying about my feelings. I don't believe I can learn anything more disillusioning about my mother than that she tumbled with a murderer."

He grabbed her arms and made her face him. His brilliant eyes shimmered with concern. "No one can deny you're made of sturdy stuff, Evelyn. But why torture yourself?"

She raised her gloved hand to that dear face. "I need to do this, Justin. I need to take action, do something to help my friends."

He watched her with a glowingly affectionate gaze that sent shivers coursing from her hairline to her toes. Ever since he had come to her rescue and she was finally free from doubt, her feelings were solidly in line with her physical reactions to the magnificent man. It was all a bit overwhelming, to say the least. She had no time for facing all of the feelings wrapped up inside of her, just aching to break free. And it was too much to hope that she ever would.

"Very well," he murmured. He gave her arms a final squeeze for support and released her. Although it was what she had wanted, she suddenly missed his touch.

They faced the washed-out door that had once been white but now was a scratched shade of gray. Justin led her forward. Remarkably, he walked with only a slight limp.

The liveried footman raised a gloved hand and knocked. They waited a few long moments, staring at the colorless wood.

"Someone is definitely home, my lord," the footman offered as he stepped aside. "I saw a face in the upstairs window."

Finally they could hear a shuffle of feet and a bolt being shifted. The door opened a crack, and a brown-haired, mop-topped woman peered out. "Lawd in heaven, yer the spittin image of yer mother, may she rest in peace."

The door creaked open wider, and a plump, dowdy woman in a soiled apron stepped aside to allow them to enter. "Welcome, welcome."

Silently, they walked inside.

Evelyn blinked in the sudden gloom. The quarters smelled of cooked leeks and beer. Its low ceiling gave one a sense of enclosure, but otherwise, it was clean enough, with a family room entry, kitchen, and additional rooms toward the rear.

The woman rubbed her chubby hands nervously on her apron. She was platter-faced, with deep-set eyes, round, rosy cheeks, a button nose, reedy lips, and no evidence of chin. "I'm Dora. Dora Plum. You probably don't remember me, I was yer mother's maid her last year."

A faint memory whispered on the edges of Evelyn's vision. "I believe I recollect you being with us, but it's a bit hazy. I'm sorry."

The woman kept running her hands on her grubby apron. "Well, you were quite young, and you stuck to yer father pretty well, and that man of his."

"Sullivan?" Justin asked.

She nodded and bit her lip, her worried brown eyes flashing to them and then away again.

Evelyn hoped to ease her concerns. "As you've already surmised, I'm Evelyn Amherst, and this is Lord Barclay."

"Yer father always said you'd be back and that I was to give you the run of the place."

Evelyn's brow furrowed. "Why would he say such a thing?"

The woman waved toward the ramshackle furnishings in the family room. "Have a seat. I'd take the brown chair if I were you, my lord. It's the sturdiest."

Even though Evelyn would have liked for him to rest his injured foot, Justin seated her in the brown chair and stood behind her. "Thank you, but I'll stand."

Evelyn eyed him disapprovingly but dismissed the notion of being a mother hen for the moment. "Please tell me what else my father said, Mrs. Plum." She leaned forward, fascinated by this glimpse into her background and anxious for a morsel of connection to her father.

The woman's ruddy cheeks blushed pink. "I never married."

"My mistake, Miss Plum."

She patted her mousy hair. "Not a problem. I always knew a man wouldn't be takin' me for a wife, but I do fine well enough, thanks to yer father." Her worried brown eyes suddenly flashed to Evelyn's black gown, and she sputtered, "Dear Lawd in heaven, don't say it's true." She shook her head and sniffed. "I'd wondered why you'd come, and now I know."

She yanked out a cloth from under her apron and sniffled into the rag. "He was a good man. Set me up when he didn't owe me a thing. I'd only worked for yer family for a year or so. He was a blessed soul." She began to bawl, and to Evelyn's dismay, started to bellow uncontrollably. Her howls and moans reverberated through the small parlor.

Concerned, Evelyn leaned forward. "Can I get you something, Miss Plum?"

The bawling intensified as Miss Plum waved her off, bellowing even louder, "Oh, yer just like him. Good, fine, decent, kindhearted. . . ."

Justin spoke softly, "We're here simply to find out more about Mrs. Amherst and the neighbor next door. We've no interest in turning you out."

The bawling ceased abruptly, and those beady eyes watched them warily. "No fooling?" She blew another sniff into her hankie for good measure.

Realization dawned, and Evelyn felt like a pudding-head.

"Do we look like we're ready to move in?" he quibbled in a soft voice, without a shred of disdain.

Evelyn asked, "What was your arrangement with my father?"

The rag promptly found its way back under Miss Plum's soiled apron. "When he gave me the lease for life, he made me promise three things," she replied in a tone that was coolly composed once more.

She ticked off the items on her stubby fingers. "First, keep the place up for him, which I was glad to do. I was never a lagabout. Also I was supposed to inform him 'posthaste' if anything happened to the place. Even the smallest things he wanted to know."

Miss Plum nodded solemnly. "I have to say, when I asked if my mother could come live with me in her last days, he was most accommodating. And then when I let him know that she'd died, well, he posted the nicest letter and sent a little something to help with the funeral expense. I had Rector Arnold read it to me, and even he said it was one of the finest condolences he'd ever come across. He even took some of the words for his sermon that week."

She leaned forward conspiringly. "T'be honest, I keep hearing those words in most of his sermons since. But, getting back to it, the final thing was that if you ever come back, and he said you would, I was to give you anything you wanted and give you the run of the place." She stood. "Whew. I don't remember the last time I said so much at one time. I need a nip. You want anything?"

Evelyn blinked. "No, thank you. I'm fine."

"Did Sir Amherst give any indication of what Evelyn might want upon her return?" Justin asked quietly, judiciously eyeing the room and its environs.

"Not really, although I figured she might want to see the memorial for her mother. Lovely notion, to have a tribute for eternity." She shook her head. "Now, there was a love-match if I ever saw one."

Justin sent Evelyn a meaningful look, and she rose. "Would you show us, please?"

Nodding, the stocky woman led them to the back threshold, through the tidy kitchen and out the rear door to the miniature square of dirt that was considered a back garden. In the corner in the ground by the weather-beaten wooden fence was a rectangular marble headstone, not more than a hand span across and high.

Evelyn peered down and read aloud the inscription on the gray stone, "And the gods rained teardrops of splendor from the heavens, yet wept for your burden, my darling. I love you, always." A swell of sadness built in her chest, threatening to bring her own mortal tears. Her father should have been a bard.

Justin coiled his arm around her shoulders and hugged her to his side. The solid warmth of his body and his caring comfort gave her a wholly different sense of belonging. She did not belong at this dwelling. She might not belong to this country, but part of her had found a little pocket of space inside Justin's heart, and that was a place she yearned to call home.

She gently unwrapped his arm. Hope was something she had to distrust, for with it came heartache. She cleared her throat and faced the portly woman. "What can you tell us about the neighbors, Miss Plum?"

Miss Plum waved to the matching square of dirt in the adjacent yard. In contrast to Miss Plum's neat garden, it was littered with refuse and scarred with castoffs.

Scowling, Miss Plum shook her head. "It's a cryin' shame to have such a mopsie with wee children. Why, she has a brood of four, each with a different pa." She scratched her mousy brown hair. "Rector Arnold's been trying to help her, but the wanton is set in her ways."

"Actually, we are interested in learning about one of

the prior tenants, Miss Plum," Justin interjected. "Mr. Wheaton."

"Oh, him? He was a nice boy and he grew up to be a decent landlord. Too decent, if you ask me. I can't believe how he allows that light-heeled woman to stay next door. She can't possibly meet the rent, seeing as how she don't work a decent job and she can't seem to keep a man around long enough to do things right. Wheaton should set her out on her bottom."

Evelyn could not keep the tinge of irritation from creeping into her voice as she asked, "If he set her out, wouldn't that mean four young children would be on the street as well?"

Miss Plum blinked and her round cheeks went pink, as if she suddenly realized that she might find herself out on that same street if others shared her ungenerous attitude.

"Can you tell us anything more about Mr. Wheaton, Miss Plum?" Justin asked coolly.

Evelyn knew him well enough to discern his impatience with the woman, but he managed to put business first, and she would follow his example. "Yes, have you seen him recently?"

Eyeing them warily, she said, "He comes around every couple of months. To collect the rents, I'm sure. I've passed him on the street a few times and he always says good day. He's never forgotten where he came from, that one, even though he's bettered himself, by the look of it. I heard he's a military man."

"Did my father ever mention him?"

"Not that I recollect."

Sighing, Evelyn stared down at the memorial to her mother and realized that it was positioned in the far corner of the garden so that the inhabitants of the neighboring house could not see it. She wondered if Father had done that on purpose, for the tribute to be his alone, untainted by the memory of the deceitful cad next door. She turned away, suddenly feeling unclean. She did not want to know more about her mother's faithlessness, nor did she want to explore Wheaton's villainy. She just wanted peace for herself and her loved ones.

That thought brought Angel and Sully back to the fore and resolve flooded through her, more potent than any tidal wave. "You were right, my lord, this is not a good use of our time. Good day, Miss Plum. Thank you for being so gracious." She hoped the woman took the hint and was kinder to her neighbors.

"You go on," Justin suggested. "I'll be with you in a moment."

Surprised, but anxious to be away from this place, Evelyn drifted into the residence.

Miss Plum tracked closely behind her, muttering, "Yer certainly quite kindhearted. . . ."

Watching the women move off, Justin missed Evelyn's rejoinder, but he was certain Miss Plum would think twice before sharing her malicious opinions again. Leave it to Evelyn to set others to rights without demoralizing them. She amazed him more and more with each passing day. He was in awe of her steadfast dedication to others, her astute intellect, and her earnest compassion. He feared that his days with her, however, might be numbered.

The irony of his situation did not evade him. This tangle was a dangerous game indeed, but while it waged on, Evelyn was by his side, sharing her deliciously refreshing humor, her melodious voice, her cherished smile. Justin was determined to unravel the complex web his former superior had woven around the woman he held so dear, entangling him and the entire branch. Yet in disentangling this dastardly maze, Justin would do the thing he most feared in the world: set Evelyn free. Once her friends were safe and her inheritance secured, there would be nothing to keep her in England.

He repressed a shudder. He could not imagine life without her. He could barely recall his life before her, other than that it had been loveless and wan. She sparkled, she laughed, she worried over her loved ones like a mother hen, and it gave him no end of pleasure that she counted him in her brood to cherish. But he needed more than lighthearted affection; he wanted her to love him enough that she could not bear to leave him. Even if she would not walk down the aisle with him, staying by his side would be enough.

Thinking of the reason Evelyn found the idea of marriage so repugnant, he turned and looked down at the memorial. While keeping his weight off his injured foot, he squatted down awkwardly before the small rectangular marble. Hessians were not exactly known for their give, and an injured foot did not help.

"And the gods rained teardrops of splendor from the heavens, yet wept for your burden, my darling. I love you, always."

Balancing on the ball of his good foot, he traced his gloved fingertips over the inscription. Something was nagging at his consciousness, hovering on the edge, never coming clear. "'And the gods rained teardrops of splendor . . .'" he read. *What burden did they weep for?*

Evelyn's mother's rootless life? Justin rubbed his temple. It would come to him eventually; he just needed to let it go.

He rose just as a set of sharp blue eyes topped by a dirt-smeared forehead and scraggly blond hair peered over the edge of the wooden fence.

A squeaky voice shrieked, "Holy! You've got the greatest set a gallopers a man's ever seen!" The man in question could not have been long out of leading strings. His head barely came to the top of the fence.

"You've an eye for horseflesh?" Justin countered, amused, eyeing the filthy clothing and hole-poked shoes.

"Won't be before long and I'm gonna be a cavalry officer!"

"Really?"

"Pap says he's gonna get me a horse. All me own fer when I grows up and can be in a regiment. I bet he'll get me one as fine as yers, maybe even finer!"

"Your father sounds like a military man."

"Not me father, me Pap," he replied with the impatience of a young whelp dying to crow. "The king himself told me Pap what a crack job he's done in battle."

Truth slipped into place in Justin's mind, as it always did when pieces of a puzzle found their address. "Colonel Wheaton is your . . . grandfather?"

"D'ya know him?"

"Oh, he's very famous," Justin assured. "Everyone's heard of his daring exploits on behalf of king and country."

Pride shone from those recognizable steely blue eyes. "Ya don't say!"

A slender woman with dirt-blond hair and a haggard

face stepped out the rear door to the boy's house. A howling, butter-toothed baby was perched on her hip. She was the spitting image of her father, the colonel.

This bit of intelligence about Wheaton revealed more about the colonel's character than any of the man's actions thus far. Another piece of an exceedingly mystifying puzzle that Justin was determined to crack.

Adjusting the babe on her hip, she shouted at the boy, "Lee! Don't be pestering the fancy gentleman."

Lee. Justin almost smiled as information shifted in his mind. So Wheaton had sired a child out of wedlock, set her up in his childhood home, and, in return, had probably asked that she name her own first child Lee, in homage to his former mentor. The man who had seemed so without ties was tangled up indeed.

"Oh, he's not bothering me at all," Justin commented, noting how nervously she watched him. Trying for an amiable tone, he offered, "I am Lord Barclay, who are you?"

Her blue eyes slid away. "Miss Edwina Thomas, my lord. Come, Lee, stop bein' a nuisance to the fine lord." She slipped back inside without another word.

As the boy scrambled jauntily inside the house after his mother, Justin marveled at being so young, so brash, and without a care. At having a grandfather who did not acknowledge you to the world. Wheaton had probably considered their existence a potential weakness to be exploited by his enemies. Was Justin cold-blooded enough to take advantage of Wheaton's Achilles' heel? He wondered. Perhaps if he could use the information without targeting the struggling family . . .

The breeze picked up, bringing with it the sour odors of the refuse next door. Justin shuddered, yanking his gloves tighter on his hands and wishing the gods would not play him for such a fool. He would do the best he could for the woman who held his heart in her tender hands. He would erase the worry from her brow, give her a respite from these dastardly machinations, and set her free. If only she did not take his heart with her when she left.

Chapter 30

"**N**o, Justin. You cannot go," Evelyn insisted. Fear was like a fever splintering across her flesh, making her want to scream, but she kept the panic from her voice, focusing on being convincing instead. "I cannot abide you placing yourself in peril. You've barely recovered from your last encounter with the colonel."

Steely resolve infused his handsome features. "It's the only way he agreed to meet."

Señor Arolas nodded, assuring her, "I don't think Wheaton will hurt him. He needs to tell us what he wants, and he'll use Barclay to communicate. That's all. Moreover, I know it's only a gut feeling, but the men worked side by side for four years, the marquis knows his comrade."

Crossing her arms to stop them from shaking, Evelyn scoffed, "If he knew the man so well, we would

308

not be in this tussle. The knave would be behind bars, where he belongs."

Justin had the audacity to smile. "I'm glad you've so much confidence in me."

"I cannot afford to lose another of my friends," she bit out.

Justin's smile faded to a scowl. "As *my friend*, you don't have much say in the matter. I will meet the colonel at the appointed place and time."

She glared at him, her anger lying more with the puppeteer maneuvering their strings than with Justin. Her stomach was clenched in a knot no laundress could unwind. She tried once again, "There must be another way."

"I know you're worried, Evelyn, but I have this well under control," Justin soothed. "And I'm going into this with a strategy of my own."

She withheld her groan.

"Ye of little faith," he chided, trying not to look hurt.

She stepped over to him and rested her hand on his arm. "There's not enough faith in the world when it comes to your safety, Justin." She willed him to see the affection behind her arguing. "I fear for you," she whispered softly, for his ears only.

He kissed her forehead as one would a younger sister. "The plan proceeds as we discussed."

This was unacceptable. Pasting a brittle smile on her lips, she turned to Señor Arolas. "Señor, if you would excuse us a moment?"

"Certainly, my dear." He strode from the room, smiling a wicked grin. The door banged closed with a hard thud.

She turned on Justin. "I don't want you to go."

"What we wish for seems to have little connection

with reality these days," he echoed her remark from the day before as he slipped into a large armchair by the hearth. He could not hide his wince as he adjusted his bandaged foot.

She faced the fire, praying for an answer from the fanning flames. Thank heavens it did not burn with those spices the colonel seemed to favor. Instead, the natural scent of wood smoke filled the lavish drawing room, reminding her of the enticing scent of the stubborn man sitting in the chair behind her.

She turned and crouched before him. "Please, Justin. You admired the man for years. It's too difficult for you to see him as he is, a vile monster."

"Just because I am trying to understand his motives does not mean that I don't loathe him for what he's done. And what he's become."

She grabbed his hand and squeezed. "He will use you against me."

"He has Angel and Sully, he doesn't need me." He stared into the blaze as if to discern the truth behind these treacherous games. He asked quietly, "Would he, ah, have much more to bargain with if he did happen to try to use me as leverage?"

She rubbed her hand over her weary eyes. Lord, if the colonel only knew how much she'd grown to care for Justin in their short acquaintance, she might as well just fold her cards now.

At her lack of response he grimaced, mumbling, "I guess there's my answer."

She rose and, without rational thought, dropped herself down on his well-muscled thighs, where she snuggled into his lap.

He quickly wrapped his steely arms around her and

hugged her close to his chest, nuzzling his face in her neck. "You smell delightful."

Sighing, she cuddled closer. "So do you." In the past days she'd found herself leaning toward Justin, surreptitiously seeking out his scent, in their various conveyances, at mealtimes, in the study, virtually anywhere. Now she soaked in his flavor at her pleasure and relished the radiance of his warmth, which comforted her as no mere fire could.

He rubbed his hands up and down her arms, sending delicious shivers chasing down her spine.

Raising her hand, she lightly brushed his hair, loving the velvety feel of his locks. She rested her forehead against his chin and whispered, "I cannot stand the idea of anything happening to you."

"You mean other than what already has?" he countered lightheartedly. "I've been shot at, had a bookcase fall on my head, been booby-trapped into damaging my foot."

"It's a wonder you've made it through all that as whole as you have!"

He curled a loose tendril around her ear, raising the delicate hairs on her neck. "But I'm not whole. I've lost my superior, my faith in following orders, in doing my duty . . . and I've lost," he swallowed, "I've lost my heart."

Shivers raced up and down her spine, and tears burned her eyes. "Then for the love of God, don't go to this meeting."

The arms encircling her tightened, then relaxed. He ground out, "It's for the love of my country and for you that I must go." He moved to shove her away, but she pressed herself deeper into his embrace.

She pushed back against those muscled arms, not letting him thrust her aside. "I am not toying with you to get you to do my bidding, Justin."

"Why else would you do it, if you don't love me?"

"I didn't say I don't love you."

"Your feelings are quite evident," he replied bitterly. "Since returning from the country we've been nothing more than—"

"We've been a bit busy, Justin," she interrupted. Sighing, she shrugged. "But it's more complicated than that."

"It seems pretty apparent. I shouldn't have hoped you'd reciprocate my feelings."

"That's not it, Justin. I have feelings for you galore." Grabbing his dimpled chin in her hand, she pressed her nose to his. "But what I feel for you terrifies me down to my toes. I'm afraid to trust what I feel because it causes me too much hope!"

Those greenish-gray eyes watched her warily. "I don't understand."

She blew out a long breath. "Neither do I. All I know is that when you are near, I feel . . . giddy. My stomach does these annoying little flip-flops, my cheeks heat at inappropriate moments, chills seem to live under my skin, and yet I feel warm all over."

"Sounds like a fever," he quibbled, his minty breath tickling her cheeks.

"Oh, worse than any fever; I want to dream."

"What's wrong with dreaming?"

"It brings hope, which eventually leads to betr— pain."

"Betrayal. You were going to say betrayal." He shook his head. "I cannot fathom what I was thinking in deceiving you as I did."

She looked away. "You thought it was in defense of your country—"

"Don't defend me, it only makes it worse!" It was his turn to make her face him. He tipped her chin with his finger. "And don't lie to me. I know you still have not forgiven me."

"But I have. My heart just cannot seem to get past the hurt." She felt it like a hole burning in her chest, so piercing it brought tears to her eyes. She pressed her hand over her breast and swallowed. "It hurts, and there doesn't seem to be much I can do for the pain, other than to ignore it and move on."

"Ignore it and move on," he repeated, bitterness infusing his clipped tone. "Well, I cannot ignore it. It's too real, too magical. Do you have any idea how you've transformed my pitiful existence? It's as if my life were a painting, half-done. Incomplete for lack of color until you crashed into it with your joy, your courage, your laughter—" He captured one of her teardrops on the tip of his finger and brought it to his smooth lips. "And your tears. You make me feel more alive than I've ever felt in my lifetime, Evelyn. I cannot ignore it any more than I can ignore the beating of my heart."

She sniffed. "You should have been the bard."

They held each other close, cherishing the comfort in the chaos of their emotions and their madcap world.

He cleared his throat. "I want you to know that your inheritance is free from legal challenge." He asked quietly, "Can you ever forgive me?"

"In many respects I already have."

"But not in all?"

The fire crackled as the clock on the mantel chimed three times.

She toyed with the brass buttons of his sea green coat. "Part of me feels silly for not being able to just toss my anger to the wind."

"Most folks would not be able to look me in the face for the things I've done to you. In contrast, you nursed me back from death's door."

"I did that for selfish reasons. I wanted your help to save Sully." She raised her hand to that dear face and pressed her palm to Justin's scratchy cheek. "I think the reason it hurts so much is that I care so much." She frowned, trying to articulate her feelings. "I've never loved a man, I mean in that way, but I seem to love quite strongly when I do care for someone."

"Are you saying that you don't love Angel?"

"Not that way."

"Not what way?"

"You are beginning to make this feel like a tooth extraction," she gibed, only half-jokingly. She blew out a long breath. "If you're going to make me say it, I've never felt for anyone else what I feel for you." It was true. If she ever did consider marriage, Justin would be the one man to tempt her down that hallowed aisle.

He grimaced. "Well, I guess that's something."

"So I cannot convince you not to meet Wheaton?" she asked.

"No."

"Then kiss me and make me forget about the vicious games for a few moments. Justin, make me forget. . . ." She brushed her mouth across his velvety lips, willing him to understand how much he meant to her. His arms tightened around her and he parted his lips, claiming her mouth with gentle insistence. Those glorious hot chills infused her body from her hairline down to her toes. His tongue caressed her teeth, explored her mouth, and loved her tongue with such tender ardor it melted her heart. Justin Barclay tasted like the sweetest nectar of the gods, and she wanted to drink every drop he had to offer, for it would be over all too soon.

Evelyn could not recall the last time she'd ever felt so dreadfully alone. The world was crashing down around her ears and there was not a blessed thing she could do about it. Sully, Angel, and—her heart contracted—now Justin were all at the mercy of that vile monster, Wheaton.

She sat on her knees before the large bay window of her bedroom in Justin's house, praying for the safe return of those she loved. It was all that was in her power to do. Staring off into the moonlit night through the billowing open drapes, she watched the stars flicker and the sliver of moon disappear behind the windswept clouds.

"I'll never do this again," she swore aloud. "I'll go mad from all of this waiting." Better to be out there, at risk with the others, than left behind. She whispered, "Better yet, all of us should be home asleep in our warm beds on a night like tonight." Well, if her friends did not have that benefit, then neither would she.

A sense of foreboding overwhelmed her. "Please, dear Lord, please take care of those I love. And let Wheaton get exactly what he deserves." She hoped her prayers would make some small measure of difference, for they could use all of the help they could get.

That night, the little boat rocked and swayed in the lapping waves of the foul-smelling Thames. Justin pulled his woolen cloak tighter around his shoulders and nodded for Señor Arolas to push him off.

Despite the half-moon perched in the starry sky and the low-lit lantern resting at the bottom of the boat, he could barely see past five paces in the gloom.

"Good luck, Barclay." Señor Arolas waved as the craft drifted out into the torrent. "I'll meet you at the far pier."

Wheaton's plan had been explicit and, just as Justin had expected, brilliant. He and the colonel were to meet midstream, exchange information, and float down to the next pier, where Justin would disembark to reveal the colonel's demands. Wheaton had innumerable means of escape.

What the colonel had not counted on was Justin bringing along the passenger hunched over in the seat across from him in the rickety little boat. The lamp at his feet barely illuminated the old man's thin, pallid face.

"How are you doing, sir?" Justin asked, worried for the frail gent.

"You're the one who's got to row this pile of wood, Barclay," countered Sir Lee Devane. "I'm just taking a little moonlit cruise."

Justin's admiration for the elderly former master of spies had only increased since meeting with the man that afternoon. The old gent had taken the news of Wheaton's betrayal hard, yet after an episode of mourning, he'd explored every avenue, sought out every fact as if sifting through glittering jewels, relishing each morsel for its significance. Justin could tell the man missed the spy trade enormously and, despite the abysmal circumstances, was ready to jump right back into the game.

The only fact that had seemed to unsettle the old fellow was learning that Wheaton had a grandson who was his namesake. "About six years old?" he had asked.

"Yes, sir," Justin had replied. "What's the implication?"

"I'd helped him get out of a tight spot about that time. I suppose it's his way of saying thank you. After making it through that sordid mess, well, I'd never have thought he'd turn on his country." The old gent had shaken his head. "It just does not add up."

The muddied waters swirled around the hull of the little craft, high and rushing from the recent rains. Lights flickered in and out of view as they raced along, helped by Justin rowing on the long oars that had come with the borrowed craft.

"I see another boat," claimed Devane in his craggy voice. "Two lamps, just as he'd said."

Justin peered over his shoulder, spotting the other craft. He set the oars into their sockets and waited as the boat drifted downstream.

Two hulking figures draped in shadow hovered in the opposite boat.

"You were never very good at taking orders, Justin," came a familiarly disdainful voice.

"I insisted, Wheaton," Devane replied jauntily. "I felt the need for some fresh air."

"Well, you can't get any here, old man," Wheaton retorted. "This river smells as if the whole of London pissed in it."

The two boats bumped together with a resounding thud.

Helderby handed Justin a rope. "Tie us up."

Justin would have liked to have tied up the bloody thug and his master and demanded some answers. Instead, he silently knotted the twine through a hook, binding the crafts.

Joined, the two boats drifted downstream in the speedy current. The water lapped loudly against the paired bows, banging them together. Helderby moved close, pitching the crafts. The lout smelled of ale and grime. He moved his beefy hands up and down Justin's coat, searching for weapons, and then he checked Devane. He motioned to Wheaton and then sat on the far bench, watching them guardedly.

"Nice rendezvous point," Devane commented as if they were at a ball. "From the Scarelli incident?"

"It was my inspiration," Wheaton rejoined.

"Tell me what you want from Evelyn," Justin growled, impatient with the games.

Devane sent Justin an admonishing look but added, "Yes, it seems that you are in need of something that only the lovely Miss Amherst can provide. Something about vengeance, I understand."

"I'm only asking for what is rightfully mine," Wheaton answered defensively.

"What do you believe you deserve?" his former mentor asked.

"You mean besides the gallows?" Justin murmured.

"How'd you like to be the one soon meeting your maker, Justin?" the colonel retorted. "It's not a comfortable position, I can assure you."

"Do you fear prosecution?" Devane asked, interest interlacing his question.

"The only thing I fear is not meeting my goals."

"Which are?" Justin prompted.

"Amherst stole my wife, my knighthood, and my treasure. Since I cannot get the first two, I insist on the last. I deserve it."

"What did you do to merit Diedra's love?" Devane

queried. "Or the king's designation? What makes you believe you are that worthy?"

Even in the gloom, Justin could make out the redness infusing the colonel's pale face. "If that bloody knave Amherst had never been born, it all would have been mine!"

The old gent shrugged. "Perhaps, perhaps not. Water under the bridge at this point, if you ask me."

"Well, no one's askin' you!" retorted Helderby. "Enough chitchat, let's get on with our business! We want the jewels!"

Wheaton sent a warning look to his hired dog. "I'll do the talking, Helderby. You seem unable to communicate other than with your fists, which will lead us absolutely nowhere!"

The burly oaf grunted but kept his peace.

"I'd always suspected the sultan of Kanibar gave Amherst something special after the kidnapping episode— a fact I confirmed right before killing Amherst."

Devane hissed, "How could you?"

"The man had plagued me for long enough; I was not about to let him have the final triumph and outlast me on this earth." Wheaton grinned, and it was an ugly thing. "Besides, killing him had an added advantage; I found out about the magical necklace of Kanibar. It's so powerful, it's bloody legendary."

"And where is this necklace?" Justin asked.

"That's what I need you to find out. Amherst swore to the heavens that his daughter didn't know anything about it. And Sullivan doesn't seem to know anything either. But someone has to know how to get their hands on it, and I'm betting the chit can figure it out, even if she doesn't think she knows where it is."

Devane shifted in the seat, using his gold-topped cane for leverage. "I'm disgusted with your actions, Wheaton. Why would you risk everything for a piece of jewelry?"

Wheaton's hands began to shake, and it looked as though he wanted to throttle his former mentor. "It's so powerful, kings would start wars over it! I deserve it!"

"Evelyn didn't deserve to have her life ripped apart over a bloody necklace!" To his horror, Justin's voice had risen to a shout. "For a lousy piece of jewelry you perverted my allegiance to my country into a mockery!"

"Bloody sappy," Helderby mumbled.

"Shut up, Helderby." Wheaton scowled.

Justin was ready to jump the bastard, but Devane stopped him with his long cane. The old man shook his head.

The waves lapped loudly against the bows in the tense silence. After a long moment, the old gent eyed his former apprentice carefully, and then pushed himself up with his cane. The little crafts rocked with his every shuffle forward. "What's really going on, Tristram?"

At that moment, Justin realized that he had never known his superior's Christian name. He was so thankful he'd thought to bring along Devane.

Wheaton looked over at Helderby and then tottered closer to the other craft. He leaned near his former mentor. "I'm dying," he murmured so softly that the echo was barely carried along in the muddy waters.

"And this is how you choose to go out?" Devane huffed. "Destroying a lifetime of exemplary service with murder and mayhem?"

Wheaton snarled but kept his peace.

The elder gent leaned on his cane, his eyes wide with disbelief. "Dear heavens, you're cross because you wanted to meet your maker with a bullet or a poisonous dart or while safeguarding the king."

The colonel hammered his fist into his chest. "You're damned right I did! My bloody body betrayed me!"

"What's wrong with you?" Justin asked, fascinated by the depths of this man's diseased outlook.

He coughed. "Cancer. I even went to that new Cancer Hospital. The butcher of a surgeon wants to try to cut it out, but I'll hire my own undertaker before I let him carve me open like a bloody turkey."

"I can't blame you there, given that few survive the surgery," Devane agreed. "But to destroy everything in the name of settling up long-dead scores that are ill-founded at best . . ."

"It's not *just* about old scores," Wheaton replied defensively. "The necklace is supposed to be magical. I've done some research, and the thing's been known to heal the sick. . . ."

"You cannot believe that!" Devane scoffed.

"It's not just about me. The bloody quacks have raked me through the coals, taken everything I own. I have nothing left to leave—"

"Ah, you mean to take care of Lee and Edwina and her brood?" the old gent charged.

"How—?" Wheaton's shaking intensified. "You can't hurt them! They have nothing!"

Devane waved his hand. "They have you. And if you'd have come to me I would have provided for them—"

"Enough with the damned chitchat already!" Helderby roared. "Give us the blasted necklace!" He pulled a pistol from under his dark cloak and aimed it at

Justin's chest. They were so close that even in the darkness Justin could discern the black hole of the barrel.

"Put that thing away, you idiot!" Wheaton jeered. "If he had it, we wouldn't be meeting here in the first instance!"

"I'm tired of following your stupid plans! A whole lot of bloody nonsense from a useless dying bastard." With a flick of his wrist, Helderby triggered the lever, and a shattering blast shot from the firearm. Wheaton flew backwards, crashing into the water with a titanic splash.

With lightning efficiency, Devane whipped his gold top from his cane and ripped a sword free. He swung it through the air with a hiss, cutting the rope connecting the two crafts. Justin quickly shoved the other boat away and snuffed out the lantern before Helderby had the chance to grab another pistol.

The lout stood in the rocking craft, screaming, "I'll get that bloody bitch and her bleeding necklace! Don't think you can protect her from me! I've still got those two blokes and I'm not afraid to kill 'em!" His figure faded into the darkness as he was swallowed by the gloom.

Gurgles could be heard from paces away, and Justin yanked the oars from their sockets and heaved toward the place where the colonel had fallen.

Devane leaned against the bow, searching for his former apprentice. "Tristram! Tristram!"

They scoured the vicinity vainly for what felt like hours, finally giving up after an exhaustive hunt.

Funereal silence pervaded the craft as Justin rowed them toward the pier, each splash of the oars like a hammer crashing into his heart. Sweat lined his brow and his underarms as he knifed the oars through the murky waters. His palms burned and his back ached, but it was the despair in his heart that caused his grief. He had accomplished little this night other than to unleash Helderby on Evelyn's dearest friends.

"The poor sop thought he had it coming to him," Devane commented.

"He had a lot more coming to him than a ball in his chest and a muddy death."

The elderly gent eyed Justin with interest. "What do you believe he deserved?"

"To be stripped of his commission." Lift, heave, drop. The water splashed. "Public trial. The gallows." Lift, heave, drop. The water splashed.

"So the humiliation would be his retribution?"

"That and a swing in the hangman's noose."

"And what of Edwina Thomas and her brood? Should they be made to pay?"

Slicing the oars through the foul-smelling water, Justin shook his head. "They cannot help who they're related to."

"Yet Wheaton had Miss Amherst pay for her father's supposed crimes."

"Wheaton had cracked."

The older gent nodded, sighing. "Diseased in mind, body, and spirit."

"The man played me for a fool," Justin cried bitterly. "I'm so bloody angry with myself for not seeing it sooner."

"How could you have known?"

Guilt and anger fused together, making Justin see red. "My brother was sick in the mind. I, of all people, should've noticed the signs." His hands tightened, and the rough wood bit into his palms. "For both of them."

Devane leaned forward. "And what would you have done had you known?"

Justin shouted, rage making his aching arms shake with his exertions. "Something!"

"Ah, to believe so much in one's own power. It's a gift and a great burden."

To Justin's amazement the elder gentleman withdrew a white linen handkerchief from his pocket and raised it to his craggy eyes as tears spilled out the corners. "I loved that fool like a son. You don't think that I'm blaming myself for not being there for him? For not helping him as he descended to his doom?"

"What could you have done?"

"Held his hand." Devane sighed, a haunted look overwhelming his saddened eyes. "One thing I've learned in my long life, sometimes it's just as important to simply be there when times are tough. It makes all the difference in the world."

Chapter 31

Justin hobbled down the long, carpeted hallway, every muscle in his body throbbing. In tandem with the torrent of pain, his every limb shook with exhaustion. It had been a terrible night, and this morning was about to get horrifically worse. He was going to have to break the news to Evelyn that he'd unleashed Helderby on her beloved friends. His legs felt as if they had anchors attached to his boots, weighing him down and keeping him from making it to his final destination, Evelyn's bedchamber. He almost cackled at the notion of wanting to avoid the one place he'd been dreaming of entering for weeks.

Finally he stood before the awesome portal, slowly raising his hand to knock lightly on the wood. He waited a breathless moment and then knocked again, this time with more insistence.

"Evelyn?"

Stanley had informed him from his perch by the front stairs that Evelyn waited in her bedchamber. She had insisted that Justin report to her posthaste upon his return.

Fear clutched at his gut. He ripped open the door and frantically scanned the room. The fire had long since burned down to ashes, the drapes billowed in the wind of the open windows, heralding the shimmering dawn, and Evelyn was nowhere in sight. Justin's heart flipped in his chest. He charged over to the window to peer out into the burgeoning morning. As the birds chirped cheerfully, the sun's golden rays rose over the city in anticipation of a new day. Justin wanted to scream at the bloody birds to stop their incessant merriment; doom was at hand. His dearest Evelyn was gone.

His mouth was parched dry, and his blood was pumping so powerfully that he thought it would explode through the top of his hammering head. He turned to race downstairs and sound the alarm, when he spotted her pale dainty feet, lying near the bed.

"Dear Lord in heaven!" He ran to her and lifted her in his arms. "Dear God, please don't let Evelyn die!" He pulled her onto his lap and pressed her face to his chest. "Speak to me, Evelyn!"

"I can't breathe, Justin," she mumbled.

"Is it poison? A wound?"

"You're crushing my face with your coat." She pushed slightly away from him and blinked. "You're back."

Relief flooded through him so powerfully that he almost forgot to breathe himself. "I thought . . . Why were you lying on the floor?"

"I was praying." Rubbing her eyes, she yawned. "I must've fallen asleep."

He suddenly realized that she was clad in a thin nightdress of the sheerest cotton, and even with her shift he could discern the exquisite outlines of her womanly form.

"I'm so glad you're alright," she murmured and raised her hand to his face, tenderly stroking his rough, whiskered cheek.

For a moment, he could not speak; he was so overwhelmed by the events of the night and by his relief that she was well. Closing his eyes, he turned his mouth into her palm and kissed it reverently.

She wrapped her other hand around the base of his neck and pulled his lips down to hers. It was a tender reunion, joyfully welcoming. He loved her so intensely he wanted to weep; there were not enough ways in the world to show her how much.

He savored her honeyed mouth and relished the gentle caress of her tongue with his. The scent of lavender floated around her like a flowery cloud, giving him a respite from the Thames's stench of blood and grime. Although he knew it was folly, he cherished this moment, for he feared the moment he would have to tell her what had happened. As he stroked her back, he could feel her shapely curves beneath the flimsy nightdress, making him want her so powerfully that he pushed aside all misgivings and gave himself to the joyous passion of their pressing lips. She was sweeter than any gift of the gods; she was his Evelyn.

Her fingers laced through his hair, gently massaging his tightly corded neck. He felt the tension in his body ease; his relief was so profound that tears burned his weary eyes.

She pulled back and stared at her damp hand, then at his face. "Are you crying?"

He swallowed, hard. "I'm just so glad to be back," he murmured hoarsely.

She smiled. "No happier than I. Although you smell like a trough." Still, her arms tightened around him, making him feel loved.

A sudden hunger overcame him, for life, for her love. He would grab this moment in time and savor it. He lowered his mouth and found those silky lips. A small moan escaped her, and he captured her mouth in his.

Pressing hot kisses along her nape, he made quick work of her fastenings, dropping the soft nightdress to the floor. His eyes feasted on the sweeps and valleys of her curves.

"You're magnificent," he murmured, lowering his head to her luscious breast. His lips grazed the nipple as his hand cupped the delicate flesh in his palm. He sucked gently, relishing her heat and the fires she ignited in him.

His other hand caressed down to her waist, over the generous curve of her hips, to her rounded bottom, kneading the soft flesh. How he loved the feel of her.

Her back arched and she writhed beneath him.

His lips found the valley of her belly, trailing hot kisses down to her ivory thighs. She was panting. "Please, Justin." She spread her legs, inviting him. He needed no further prompting.

Pressing wet kisses inside her thighs, he tasted the sweetness of her innermost core. She moaned as he slid his finger inside her. She was burning hot with desire. He pressed his lips to her tight nub. She was panting, grabbing at the bedding over her head and pressing her eyes tightly closed. Her back arched and she cried out. Her muscles spasmed around him and she came in a heated rush.

His motions stilled and he gave her a chance to catch her breath. He pressed small kisses on the curve of her belly, on the thin lines of her rib cage, on her bountiful breasts, tracing up her neck and finding her mouth once more.

His body joined hers, and it felt like a homecoming. She was pliant and warm, and she wrapped her legs around his hips, pulling him deeper inside. His exhausted body found new vigor. He pumped himself into her, loving her with his body as much as with his heart. With a final thrust, he spilled his seed inside her. His heart was beating wildly and his breath still coming in short gasps, when he slowly withdrew and pulled her into the crook of his arm. Panting and spent, he savored a moment of contentment, never wanting it to end.

Somehow he found the strength to utter the words, "Wheaton is dead." He almost couldn't believe it himself.

She froze.

"Helderby shot him."

"So it's over," she whispered.

"Helderby got away . . . swearing he would continue Wheaton's quest."

Abruptly sitting up, she moved away from him and wrapped her arms around herself. Not looking at him, she clenched and unclenched her hands. "Quest for what?" she cried.

How he longed to extinguish the torment from her brow. He hated that she wouldn't meet his eye. Yet he couldn't blame her; it was all his fault. Sitting up, he adjusted his clothing. "A bloody jeweled necklace."

She blinked. "You're serious?"

"Deadly. Wheaton claimed it had some sort of magical powers, was worth a fortune—"

"I don't have this necklace you speak of!" She turned to him, those sparkling sky blue eyes imploring. "What are we going to do?"

A lightness infused his chest. She still wanted his help. She didn't wish him to disappear for his blundering.

At the look on his face, she grasped his hand and squeezed. "Stop bludgeoning yourself, Justin. This is not your fault."

"At least Wheaton, cracked as he was, played by some semblance of rules. Helderby is a beast, and I've unleashed him on Sully and Arolas."

"Do you think he'll kill them?"

"They are no more important to him than his next beer, perhaps even less so."

"Then we will just have to kill him first," she stated grimly, determination permeating her beautiful features.

Reaching over, he ran his calloused hands over her silky, golden hair. "You shouldn't have to bear it all."

Turning her head, she pressed a kiss into his palm. "None of us should."

A hard knock pounded on the door.

Justin threw Evelyn's nightdress to her and called out, "Give us a moment." She quickly pulled on the clothing.

Straightening his garments, Justin rose and strode to the door, saying, "Whatever it is, I'll take care of it."

Stanley stood just outside the threshold. "My lord. There's a man downstairs requesting an audience. A Mr. Tuttle."

"At this ungodly hour?"

"He says it's vitally important."

Clenching his hands, Justin murmured, "It had better be. Let's go."

"Not with you, my lord. He specifically asks for Miss Amherst."

"We will both be down in a few moments."

Stanley nodded and marched down the hallway. Watching him go, Justin realized he could not worry about the rumors belowstairs; they could not get any worse.

He stepped back into Evelyn's chamber.

She spun, adjusting the wrapper around her lovely shoulders. "What could Mr. Tuttle want?"

He shook his head, mourning the end to their intimacy.

Gliding across the room, she leaned up and wrapped her arms around his shoulders. "Don't look so glum, darling." She kissed him lightly on the lips. "Perhaps it's good news."

Smiling determinedly, she swept toward the door. Justin had to marvel at her. No matter what got her down, she was always ready to find the light at the end of the tunnel. She never let herself be overburdened. . . . Again, that pesky thought nagged at his consciousness, nimbly slipping away before revealing itself. He rubbed his temple, impatient for it to come, yet unable to press his weary mind further.

He straightened his aching shoulders and fairly stumbled toward the door.

* * *

The bald little man was shaking with apparent anxiety as Evelyn strode into the drawing room. In an instant Evelyn took in his disheveled brown coat with a long tear at the elbow, his drooping left stocking just below his knee britches, his scuffed brown leather shoes, and his skewed gold-rimmed spectacles. As usual, he appeared ready to jump like a frightened rabbit.

"What happened to you, Mr. Tuttle?"

"I did it, Miss Amherst," he stated proudly. Only then did she note the squared shoulders, the confidence gleaming from behind his smudged eyeglasses, and the quirk of his grinning, reedy lips.

"What did you do, Mr. Tuttle?"

"I found the letter that pig Marlboro was keeping from you."

"Say again?"

He hobbled toward her, and the sagging stocking slipped down to his ankle, exposing a milky white calf with a long red slash of blood. "I knew Marlboro was holding out on you, even though he got the go-ahead to release your father's estate. I confronted the bugger, but he brushed me off. So tonight I broke into the office and found it." His hand shook as he reached into his coat and pulled out a thick beige paper.

"What is that?" Justin limped into the room. He looked so weary that Evelyn was tempted to make him get off his aching leg and into bed, but she knew he'd get little sleep there. If anything needed to be done, Justin would be the first to volunteer. His bravery knew no bounds, and she could not have treasured him more for it. Her heart warmed, thanking the heavens for his safe return. She just prayed she could keep him alive and well until the end of this vile treachery.

Her thoughts were suddenly diverted by the sight of her name scratched boldly across the parchment. She rushed forward. "That's Father's handwriting."

The man blinked up at Justin from behind his spectacles and thrust the paper behind his back. "Ah, can I assume, my lord, that you've altered your position regarding Miss Amherst's rights?" The poor soul was no match for the marquis physically or in social standing, yet he stood tall, bravely challenging Justin for her.

Justin nodded curtly. "Miss Amherst is under my protection. My *only* concern is that she receive everything due to her."

Mr. Tuttle seemed to consider this for a moment, a gleam of sweat shining across his bald brow. "I must admit I was surprised to learn that Miss Amherst was residing here, and then when I heard about her funds being released, well . . ."

She stepped forward. "Lord Barclay is on my side, Mr. Tuttle, and I am thankful to be able to include you in the ranks of my champions as well."

He pushed his spectacles up the ridge of his narrow nose and positively preened. " 'Twas nothing, Miss Amherst. Just as you'd said, an injustice needed to be righted. I was just doing my part." He pulled the letter from behind his back and handed it to her.

She noted that the paper was still closed with her father's impressive seal securing the back. She slowly took the crinkled parchment and held it to her chest, bowing to the man. "I am grateful to you, Mr. Tuttle, for risking so much for me."

"It was well hidden. It took me hours to find, and by then the night watchman was roused. He called his dog and I had to run for it. Had a nasty scrape with some bushes, but it was worth it. I'd just love to see the look on Marlboro's face when he hears that his precious cache was compromised."

She smiled warmly. "You play the hero well, Mr. Tuttle."

His pale cheeks tinged pink as he tried to suppress his grin. "'Twas nothing, miss."

"Any word from my father is precious to me."

Justin nodded. "I also thank you, Mr. Tuttle. Your efforts will be rewarded, and Marlboro's deceit will be repaid as well."

The little man looked fit to burst. "Ah, thank you, my lord, Miss Amherst."

Evelyn slid her fingers under the paper and broke open the familiar seal. "Why would Marlboro keep it from me and yet not open it?"

Mr. Tuttle patted his shiny forehead with a yellowed handkerchief. "I'd venture he was covering all corners in case the, ah"—he eyed Justin curiously—"*authorities* changed their mind regarding you."

Justin seemed ready to chastise the little man, but instead only nodded. "My regard for Miss Amherst is not fickle, Mr. Tuttle. I had been under mistaken notions that have since been rectified. No one will interfere with Miss Amherst's affairs again."

Evelyn hastily sent him an affectionate smile but could barely contain her anxiety as she quickly scanned the cherished scrawl of the long letter.

My dearest Evelyn,

If you are reading this missive, it means I am dead. I suppose it's too much to hope that I went peacefully in

*my sleep, but alas, that is not the death of a soldier.
And no matter the terminology, diplomat, emissary,
spy, I lived my life as a soldier on behalf of my country
and would likely die as such.*

Justin stepped close and rested his strong, comforting hand on her shoulder. She pressed her hand to his,
glad for his nearness and support. She read aloud, feeling he had the right to know. " 'In passing, I pray that I
not only left you in considerable financial well-being,
but also gave you some semblance of guidance for
your life hereafter. There are few people in this world I
regard as highly as you. Thus, it is with great sadness,
and yet hope, that I pass on to you a burden I have carried these many years.' "

The hand on her should squeezed. "Burden! Of
course!"

She looked up.

Justin's incredible eyes sparkled with excitement.
"The necklace is in the memorial. It's not a memorial to
your mother, but to you!"

Her brow furrowed, unease filtering through her.
"But why would he leave a memorial to me?"

"Read on and I bet we'll have our answers."

She raised the paper once more and then lowered it.
"Teardrops, gods . . ." Exhilaration filtered through
her; they might actually be able to save Sully and Angel! Salvation was within reach. "In ancient Greece, diamonds were considered teardrops of the gods. You're
right, Justin! There were hints and snippets of it in Father's journal. It must be there! We can get the necklace and trade it for their lives! Heavens, we might
actually win!"

Justin beamed down at her. "As if you had any

doubt. You can climb mountains if you set your mind to it, Evelyn. I've come to know that."

She threw her arms around his neck and hugged him close, so blessedly thankful she could help her friends.

He wrapped his strong arms around her and kissed her forehead. "It'll all be over soon, darling." There was a catch to his voice.

Mr. Tuttle coughed. "Ahem. I hate to intrude, but after all of this chicanery, I'd suggest we read the rest of the letter and find out why your father went to such pains to hide the thing—before uncorking any champagne, that is."

She blew out a long breath and nodded, reluctantly pushing out of Justin's embrace. "Always the voice of reason, Mr. Tuttle."

Sighing, she raised the parchment and read, " 'Thus, it is with great sadness, and yet hope, that I pass on to you a burden I have carried these long years. It seems like ages ago when the sultan of Kanibar gifted to me an ancient and magnificent necklace of the finest diamonds in gratitude for saving his firstborn from a terrible death. It was reputed to have legendary qualities, magic, some said, to turn a spurned heart, to garner friendship, and other such nonsense, in which I placed little credence. Still, its history and reputation gave it significant value, and I was grateful.' "

Justin coiled his arm around her waist. Her heart warmed, and she smiled to herself, continuing, " 'I had the mythical necklace with me in Paris on the ill-fated night when I happened upon a young Frenchman, an officer in the army who had recently been released from arrest but who was still out of favor with his government. Although he was poorly clad, ill-fed, and in disfavor, a brilliance shined from his owl-gray eyes, evidencing a brightness of intellect, of magnetism rarely seen, but found in great men. I was charmed.' "

The arm around her waist tensed into iron. Justin murmured, "A charismatic officer with owl-gray eyes can only be Napoleon."

She swallowed but read on, " 'Over many a brandy, we spoke long into the dark night, and it was sometime near dawn when I showed him the magnificent necklace. It was an action I have grown to regret. Since then I never again showed the precious jewels to a living soul. I try to console myself by saying, who could have known that a starved officer would soon crown himself emperor and try to dominate Europe? But I, of all people, a man in the profession of assessing character, should have recognized the mad thirst for domination that lay within him.' "

"There were few who could have predicted how powerful Napoleon was to become," Justin commented grimly.

" 'It was just two years after that fateful night in 1795 when Bonaparte contacted me about the necklace. The man has hounded me since. As rumors of Josephine's infidelity circulated, he grew more insistent, but it soon became a crazed quest for supremacy, to harness the necklace's supposed power or possibly to use it for desperately needed funds. I do not know, nor do I care. All I know is that the necklace must never come to be in his hands. He is our sworn enemy and we cannot allow anything to benefit his cause.' "

She took a shaky breath. " 'It is with you that I entrust this great responsibility, and I have all the faith of a proud, loving father that you will protect it as did I, until the mad Corsican is finally defeated. You will find it at your mother's former residence, according to the ancient Greeks. All my love to you always, Evelyn, and may the Lord grace your days.' "

Her throat had swollen shut, and hot tears slid down her cheeks. A great weight settled on her chest, and she felt as if she might not draw breath. Justin enveloped her in his brawny arms and hugged her close, else she might not have been able to stand. She could not quite sort out the implications of her father's monumental trust, his enormous faith in her, and the heavy burden he had placed upon her. She could not rationally face the conflict between needing to do what she must to save her friends and following her father's last wishes.

"We will first get Sully and Arolas back, then I'll cut off Helderby's or anyone else's hands before they take that bloody necklace," Justin growled.

From within his embrace, a small bubble of laughter erupted from her choked throat.

He looked down at her, concern marring his handsome features. "What is it, Evelyn?"

She sniffed, shaking her head. "Wheaton, Napoleon, Helderby, all these praetorian men after a piece of woman's jewelry. It's almost comical."

"Typical, actually," huffed Mr. Tuttle.

Perplexed, she peered at him from within Justin's arms.

The little man pushed his gold spectacles up his thin nose. "Men are always after something. The necklace could have been anything, just something to reach for, to give them an antidote."

"To what?" Justin asked.

"That unsettling feeling in your gut when you think you might just not be good enough after all. To make someone feel complete . . ." His voice trailed off.

Heavy silence enveloped the chamber.

"My father trusted me to keep the necklace safe. How can I do that once I've given it to Helderby?"

Justin squeezed her arms. "I will kill Helderby and every man who gets within reach of the thing."

She lovingly brushed her hand through his short hair. "I appreciate your sentiment, Justin, no matter how impractical."

"Give this Helderby fellow an imitation."

She turned to look at the amazing Mr. Tuttle.

"Excellent notion," intoned Justin. "He's never seen it—no one has if it's been buried all these years. Leave the necklace in its safe hiding place for now."

"But where will we get an exquisite jeweled necklace this late in the game?" she asked. "We cannot trust Helderby to keep Sully and Angel unharmed for the time it will take to find something."

"The Barclay jewels will do nicely, I think."

She blinked. The enormity of Justin's offer staggered her. "Your aunt said that they've been in your family for hundreds of years. That they are worth a king's ransom."

He shrugged, not meeting her eye. "They're not worth more than your safety, or that of your friends."

Resolution was within reach, but everything came at a price, it seemed. "But they are for your bride," she whispered. "Every Barclay bride has worn them for generations."

Finally his stormy eyes met hers, and the torment she saw within them twisted her heart. "We might as well put them to some use, as I will not marry if it's not to you."

The world stopped, and Evelyn was caught up in swirling mists of gray-green tempests. It would be so easy to give in and fly with the flow of those storm clouds. But to fall was madness beyond imagining.

Mr. Tuttle rubbed his hands together gleefully. "Well, it's settled then. Let's find this Helderby chap and set up the exchange."

Justin stepped away, leaving her feeling bereft. "I'll contact Devane."

Evelyn felt the sudden urge to toss her father's letter into the fire. She didn't want Justin betting his future on her. The diamonds seemed integral to his family life, to his marriage. He deserved a family who loved him, a woman who was not harnessed to her past, expecting betrayal at every corner.

The image of gorgeous young urchins with wheat-colored locks and greenish-gray eyes racing with puppies at their heels flashed through her mind, but she pushed it away, the pain too fierce for her to manage. She could never make herself so vulnerable to another. It would give him too much power to hurt her.

"Is there any other necklace we might use besides the Barclay bridal gems?"

"It's our best course, Evelyn," he stated coolly as he headed toward the door. "At this point, our only one."

Staring at the empty threshold, she slowly nodded. She would accept his sacrifice, but she would repay him. No matter what happened, she would find a way to make amends. Just so long as it did not involve a minister, a license, and a trip down an aisle.

Chapter 32

Just as the blood ran through his veins, the pain flowed with Sully's every waking moment, as natural as his every breath. He welcomed each piercing ache, as it reminded him afresh of the debt he owed his captors—the brutish Helderby, the pretty marquis, and the conniving Wheaton. Sully did not care about the others. They were nameless muscles working toward their next payload. But Sully cared quite a lot about "the Traitorous Three." Nurturing the fires of his hatred warmed the pain, making it almost pleasurable to imagine decimating his enemies with similar grief, tenfold.

In the shadowed darkness of his cell, by the light of the flickering moon through the slit of a window, he continued to needle at the binding at his wrists, the dried blood having hardened the knots to stone. After what must have been days toiling over the bands, he had felt that smidgen of "give" that heralded burgeoning escape. That tiny yield had provided him with more hope than a charging cavalry. For he didn't want rescue, he wanted sweet retribution by his own hand.

He pushed away the worry about Evelyn, over the fact that his captors had not been to see him in what had to have been almost forty-eight hours. That did not bode well for his value to them, nor for his plans for revenge. Not that the pretty marquis was one to dirty his hands and deign to visit his captive. No, he was more intent on mauling defenseless young ladies. Sully's simmering anger steeped, and he willed the fury into his fumbling fingers, knowing that soon his hands would be encircling the throat of that very same peer of the realm who had stolen Evelyn's kisses.

The only times he felt his spirits falter were when the memories flashed through his mind; Evelyn's tenth birthday, when she was too ill with fever to enjoy the festivities but insisted that everyone celebrate without her. Her beaming grin while learning to ride her first pony. The triumph lighting her sky blue eyes the first time she beat him at chess, though in truth he had let her win.

He wondered if she had identified the mythical necklace Helderby and Wheaton were after. He had certainly never seen or known of it. It hurt his pride that his dear friend Phillip hadn't seen fit to share the secret. But if Phillip had kept the necklace hidden, it must've been for good reason. Sully trusted that it was so and prayed that Evelyn did right by her father and kept it safe. For Sully was not ready to let the Traitorous Three win in this dastardly game. He would give them each a slow and painful death first.

* * *

Helderby could barely contain his excitement as he ambled down the dusty corridor of the Largo safe house sheltering his "guests." The jeweled necklace was about to be his, *all damn his*. No bloody sharing with any damned dying colonel; he couldn't believe he'd put up with the bugger as long as he had, but he congratulated himself on overcoming the bastard. He was his own man. Takin' care a business was his profession, and he was damned good at it and about to be a might richer for it as well.

His only regret was that he'd not had a go at the Amherst hellcat. She was a tasty morsel. Perhaps after he'd got his hands on the prize she'd be more interested in coming along for the ride. And for once he wouldn't even have to pay for the poke. The thought lifted his spirits and his cock, and he almost cackled with glee.

Approaching the cell, he assumed the snarl he saved for ordering men about. Nodding to Jako, who was sitting in a chair by the end of the hall, he growled, "Any trouble?"

The muscle man shook his shaggy head. "Naw a bit. Ate not a thing but drank the lot. I'da thought he'da given me some excitement, given the bloke was supposed to be some sorta spy. But he was like a pup just waitin' to be fed."

Helderby felt a swell of smugness that he'd managed to conquer the mighty Sullivan. Well, Helderby had shown him who was boss, and old Sullivan was not about to forget it. Nor was the colonel, from the bottom of the bloody Thames. Helderby still recalled his own shock when he'd pressed the trigger and killed the man who'd been leading him about by the nose for years. Well, Helderby was tired of taking orders and didn't need some dying old man telling him what to do. He was smart enough to get the necklace on his own and enjoy all of the take for his fast thinking and slippery fingers.

He inserted the iron key in the recently installed lock and almost snorted at the extra precautions they'd taken for this past-his-prime spy. Still, he entered the room tense and wary, ready for anything.

The foxy stench of feces and blood assaulted his senses and he smiled; those odors translated into money for Helderby. In the sliver of fading daylight, he discerned the lifeless clod lying on the cot, facing the wall, just as he'd been the last time Helderby had been to visit three days before. Not taking any chances, he inched closer while yanking his trusty knife from his sheath.

"Sullivan! Wake up! Yer ransom's about t'be paid."

The man didn't move. A flush of anxiety lanced through Helderby's gut, as he feared the bugger might be dead. He sniffed, anticipating the stench of death, but perhaps the man was not yet ripe. Helderby wondered if the Amherst chit would know the difference.

"Damn it all to hell," he grumbled, stepping nearer and jabbing the man's shoulder with the sturdy hilt of his blade. Sullivan didn't move a hair. Helderby peered over the bloke's shoulder and shouted, "Sullivan, man! Yer about t'be freed. Wake up, man!"

Still he did not move.

So Helderby rolled the man onto his back and stared at his lifeless face, cursing the rotter for being so blastedly weak. Then his eyes widened at the wrenching pierce of his own dagger being thrust deep into his belly. Only when the knife took a vicious twist in his gut did he scream. The bloke was on him faster than a whip, stuffing a pillow over his head and sweeping his feet right out from under him, toppling him down onto the wooden boards.

Sully pressed his whole weight onto the pillow, smothering Helderby's screams. He knew the guards would hear the scuffle inside the small chamber and the hammering of Helderby's boots as he thrashed about on the floor. Yet Sully was willing to take his chances against any of the muscle men, so long as the first of the three traitors bled himself to death. Despite his vengeful fantasies, Sully couldn't afford to give the henchman his due and would deliver the oaf a swift justice. Perhaps Wheaton and the marquis would provide a greater sense of retribution. Still, death was death, always a nasty business.

As Helderby kicked and thrashed on the floor, his powerful muscles flailing about to find purchase, Sullivan yanked back the pillow and with exacting precision quickly gouged holes in Helderby's neck and groin. Despite his hulking size, it would take the foul beast mere minutes to die.

The stink of blood, sweat, and urine pierced Sully's clogged nose, and he felt little satisfaction in knowing the bugger had sullied himself in his last moments. The writhing slowed and the screams deadened to pitiful moans. Without looking too closely, Sully leaned forward and gave the final death thrust.

He stepped away from the still-twitching corpse to stand beside the door, his aching back pressed hard against the scratched wall. His heart was pounding, his every breath a harsh burn, but he was ready to escape this hellhole, and he was not about to let Evelyn hand anyone that blasted necklace.

Sully raised the bloodied knife and waited, stance wide, for leverage as the wooden door eased open with a piercing squeak. He lunged just as a shape entered the room; he grabbed the man's arm and flung him over Helderby's lifeless form. He then swung himself to face the open doorway, ready for the next attacker. The threshold was glaringly empty.

He whipped around, warily facing his lone assailant. Despite the blackened eye, tousled hair, unshaven whiskers, and rumpled clothes, the man had the same insolent grace as his father. "What the hell are you doing here, Angel?"

"Rescuing you." With a grimace Angel shoved himself off Helderby's corpse and straightened his sleeves. "But I see you're doing fine on your own."

"How did you find me?" Sully asked, cautiously scanning down each side of the corridor.

While checking Helderby's body for weapons, Angel stated, "Actually, I've been a guest of this fine establishment myself. Locked up downstairs. When they came to get me tonight, I decided to make my own exit."

"What about Evelyn? Was she captured as well?"

Angel yanked a pistol from Helderby's pocket and checked the sights. "She was taken, but apparently is now free."

"How could you have been so careless?"

"I made the mistake of trusting Barclay."

Sully stared hard at the young Spaniard. "Don't get any ideas about settling the score with that pretty sod, he's mine."

"I'll queue up right behind you. I've no love lost for the bastard."

As the men cautiously slipped out the door and

down the hallway, Angel whispered, "Helderby was set to meet Evelyn at dawn at the park off Portman Square. She was going to barter something for our lives."

"Not if I can bloody help it," Sully muttered. "Where's Wheaton?"

"Dead."

Sully sniffed. "Two finished, one to go." He peered down the shallow wooden stairs. "How do you know so much?"

"I gave my guard an offer he couldn't refuse; information in return for his life. That and he was to grab his friends and take off. I was very convincing."

Sully eyed the promising youth, who had grown into a remarkable young man. "I'm sure you were. Do you know where we are?"

"Clueless. But we have to be near enough to Portman Square for Helderby to have had us there by dawn."

Sully raised the bloodied blade as he headed down the wooden stairs. "Let's move along then: I have a score to settle, and I'm growing tired of waiting for Barclay to come to me."

Angel let Sully lead as they slipped down the darkened stairway and across the main room without encountering a single assailant. As he warily watched every doorway, Angel was proud to guard the older man's back. Sully had been his boyhood hero, a man who was so loyal to the Amhersts that he would follow them to Hades, yet who always kept his own counsel and his sense of independence.

As they tiptoed to the rear door, the scent of ale and cheese filled the small kitchen. A cook's knife lay beside a hunk of cheese and loaf of bread on the table. A small wooden stool had been toppled over on the floor.

The back door swung open in the evening breeze.

"This is too bloody easy," Sully commented suspiciously, inching toward the exit.

Pressing his back to the still-warm cooker, Angel peeked out the threshold and then cautiously followed.

Outside, a tall, lithe figure slipped out of the shadows of a large tree and stepped into their path, his body cloaked head to toe in black. He moved with a fighter's efficient grace as he blocked the threshold.

"Sully?"

"Ismet." Sully stepped closer and squeezed the man's shoulder. "Any more out front?"

The Turk shook his head. "Another came out and they took off."

"How the hell did you find us?" Respect imbued Angel's voice.

"I'm sorry it took so long. Only when Wheaton was dead did I trail Helderby. I wanted to slit his throat but feared that if I did, I'd never find you. So I waited and tonight he led me here."

"Good thinking, Ismet." Sully nodded. "You did it by the book."

"Make sure to give me a copy when this is all said and done," Angel commented.

"Let's be off." Sully swept toward the door. "I'm anxious for my appointment with the pretty marquis."

As Sully crossed the threshold, Ismet laid a hand on his arm. "Miss Evelyn is with him."

Angel froze, and Sully looked up at the tall Turk. "What do you mean, *with*?"

"She stays with him in his home."

"What the bloody hell is she thinking!" Sully growled.

"She's not," Angel countered, scratching his chin. "Unless . . ."

"Unless what?"

"Unless she is as much a prisoner as we. Granted, in a gilded cage."

Sully shook his head. "But if she has whatever it is he wants, then why is she giving it to Helderby in exchange for us?"

"Dissention among the ranks?" Angel offered.

Sully brushed off Ismet's hand and stomped out the door. "I don't give a bloody fig what's happening within his foul gang, I just want him dead. We can sort out the bloody details later."

Angel hid his surprise. Sully had always been the one to analyze things before cautiously making a move. Still, he was older and wiser and Angel would follow his lead, even if it led down a hazardous path.

Chapter 33

The sun hovered on the brink of morning as glittering, golden-orange rays peeked from behind the London rooftops. Leaves rippled in a breeze that carried little relief from the stench of the grubby London streets.

Evelyn waited on the edge of the dew-drenched grass, nervous energy causing her to shift from foot to foot on the path of the shrub-bordered park. The gravel crunched noisily under her dog-eared kid slippers, but she was too edgy to stop. There was enough sunlight to discern the dew pebbled on the leaves of the tree branch hanging over her head, yet it was still not bright enough to see the entrance to the park in the gloom-shrouded dawn.

"All will be well, my dear," Sir Devane commented from his perch on the bench behind her. He puffed negligently on a thin cigar, the smoke billowing in small clouds around his skeletal face. Although his hunched form was unmoving, those canny hazel eyes scanned the environs with ceaseless activity.

Evelyn, on the other hand, was finding it hard to stay in one place. She kept leaning forward, trying to get a better view of the corner of the lane where Helderby was set to turn up. With Justin waiting faithfully at the meeting place, she wished the only things Helderby would be turning up were his toes.

Her heart skipped a beat every time she dwelled on the fact that Justin was risking his life for her friends yet again. "Justin should not be alone," she muttered.

"For the hundredth time, my dear girl," Sir Devane chided kindly, "he is not alone. The two Bow Street Runners are with him, and I have men set about the entire perimeter of the park. Helderby was a fool to accept our rendezvous point. A lesson that will cost him dearly."

Evelyn fingered the handle of the pistol in her pocket, fear making her mouth as dry as dust. "It's still too risky."

With a slight groan, Devane awkwardly shifted in the seat and adjusted his gold-topped cane. "I know you wish you were with him, but you would only distract him. He would be too concerned about your safety to have a care for his own."

"He'd better have a care for his own or I'll kill him."

Birds twittered overhead and a rabbit hopped from behind a bush, the sudden movement causing Evelyn to catch her breath. She pressed her hand to her racing heart. "A lot of good I'm doing waiting over here, even a bunny makes me jump. At least there I'll be wary enough to keep lookout."

"You remind me quite a bit of your father, you know."

She turned to stare at the weathered old gent, thankful for the distraction. "How so?"

"He was never one to leave business to others. He preferred to leap into the fray and give it his best shot, whether or not he was the right man for the job."

"But things usually turned out well for him, did they not?"

"He was the best darned agent I had in all my years. He and Wheaton."

Evelyn crossed her arms and hugged herself. "Justin told me how you grieve him, but he was a viper."

He sighed. "I grieve the fact that a good man twisted into such a fiend."

Horses' hooves clattered, and a harness jingled in the distance.

Evelyn hopped onto the bench for a better view of the entrance to the park. "A black coach. One driver. His face is covered."

With swiftness that belied his age, the elderly gent dropped his cigar, grabbed his cane, and stood. "Let the games begin."

Evelyn glared down at him. "This is not a bloody game! Lives are at stake! I'm tired of the unnecessary bloodletting, the endless stratagems. This is life and it's meant to be lived by a code other than kill or be killed!"

"You are right, of course." He adjusted the top of his cane. "But for the moment, kill or be killed is an appropriate tactic."

He held his hand out, and she took it and stepped down. Soundlessly they moved behind the large oak near the bench and paused. The rhythmic sounds of hooves grew louder as the carriage veered down the adjacent path, heading toward the open square, where Justin waited.

Evelyn dropped Sir Devane's hand. "I'm sorry, sir, despite my promise, I cannot skulk here like a useless dump while everyone I love is at risk." She lifted her skirts and raced toward the corner of the lane.

Her heart contracted at the sight before her eyes. Sully jumped out from the coach, Angel close behind. Sully was badly bruised and battered, but he was alive and whole. She wanted to scream for joy. Angel looked none the worse for wear besides a blackened eye and his usually impeccable clothes rumpled and torn.

Before she could shout her welcome, Angel raised his pistol and shot Mr. Montag in the shoulder, sending the Bow Street Runner flying backwards in a spray of gravel.

"No!" she screamed.

Sully swung a bloodied blade with deadly efficiency, cutting down Mr. Clontz, who dropped with a cry to the dirt.

"Arolas, what the hell are you doing?" Justin shouted, barely swerving out from under a deadly thrust of Sully's vicious blade. Angel tossed aside the pistol and whipped a knife out from under his rumpled coat.

Her dearest friends circled her lover, the mad gleam of hatred glittering in their determined eyes. Evelyn ran in between the combatants, but Sully shoved her aside. "Get the hell out of here!"

"Stop this at once!" she cried.

She raced back into the fray, but it was Justin this time who pushed her away. He watched the men warily, a knife in his hand. "Go back to Devane, Evelyn!"

Sully hesitated. "Devane's here?"

Evelyn saw her opening. She grabbed Sully's fighting arm and yanked down hard, trusting that Sully would not hurt her. "Devane helped set the trap for Helderby!" Thankfully Sully did not shove her away, but the muscles under her hands were knotted with tension, the knife gleaming wickedly with dried blood. "Where is Helderby?"

"Dead," came Sully's stark reply as he shook her off and swiped at Justin. Angel circled around to Justin's opposite side, forcing him into a close confrontation. Sully's deadly blade sliced with a hiss; Justin deflected the blow, but Angel flicked his blade, cutting a long line of blood across Justin's cheek.

Evelyn threw herself in front of Justin, praying they would not slice through her to get to him. "Stop it! It's over!"

"Get off me, Evelyn! I can't fight like this!"

"Fancy that, being protected by a woman," Angel sneered, trying to grab Evelyn's arm. She kicked him in the knee, and he cursed. Sully yanked at her shoulder, but she held on to Justin with all her might. They moved back, seemingly setting up for another pass.

"You'll have to get through me!" she shouted.

Seemingly out of nowhere, a thin, cool blade hovered near her eye. She froze, rancid fear tearing the breath from her throat. If she moved a hair's breadth, she would be blinded.

"I've seen many family squabbles, but this one's a first." Devane's craggy voice pierced her consciousness, but she could not tear her eyes from the pointy tip of the long blade.

"Put it down, Devane," Sully ordered, his voice catching.

The sun's golden rays gleamed off the edge of the blade, making her eyes water. Evelyn swallowed, fear and shocked confusion lancing through her veins, making the blood pound like foghorns in her ears.

"What are you doing, Devane?" Justin asked stiffly. Evelyn could feel his heart hammering against her back.

"Doesn't anyone know how to follow a plan?" came Señor Arolas's deep baritone from somewhere on the left. Gravel crunched as he stepped closer, but Evelyn did not dare turn her head. "I do hope you don't intend to slice into Evelyn's eye, Devane. I would not take it kindly."

"Tell your son to drop his weapon, Señor, we are all going to have a chat," Devane stated coolly. Beside the slight sounds of shifting in the gravel, no one seemed to be following instructions. Bile threatened to rise in her throat, and Evelyn willed herself to be calm. Devane was a docile old man, wasn't he? And he was supposed to be on their side.

"What is the one thing you men have in common?" the elder gent asked nonchalantly.

"Me?" Evelyn squeaked.

"My dear girl, you're sharp, just like your father. So if I imperil you, it forces the men to stop and listen." His voice hardened. "Sit down and drop your weapons. You too, in the coach."

"Do what the man says," Señor Arolas ordered.

Weapons immediately clattered onto the gravel. Evelyn almost sighed with relief. She heard multiple shiftings in the tiny pebbles and assumed that everyone was following Devane's orders. She was thankful, yet that pointy blade still hovered near her eyelid, so close she was afraid to blink for fear it'd catch.

"I am going to ask Sullivan some questions. Please

be prompt and truthful in your replies, or Miss Amherst might be donning one of those fancy patches pirates love to wear."

"I'll see you in hell first," Justin growled.

Devane ignored him. "Sullivan, is Helderby dead?"

"Yes."

"How?"

"Diced and gutted."

"Do you know what he was after?"

The silence was broken by the shriek of a scavenger bird.

The blade quivered, and Evelyn's heart contracted. "All right, then," Devane continued. "We'll get back to that later. Why are you attacking Barclay?"

"Because he's a traitorous blackguard and I'm going to gut him much more slowly than I did his accomplice."

"How do you believe he betrayed his country?"

"Killed Phillip. Set me up—"

Angel interjected, "Ambushed me and Evelyn! Father, you must stop this—"

"What if I said you had your facts wrong?" Devane interrupted.

"I'd tell you you'd lost your wits," Sully snarled.

The blade quivered. "Alright then. We'll put the pesky little facts aside and cut right to the chase. . . ."

Evelyn inhaled a sharp breath at his words.

"Miss Amherst, please inform Sullivan why he should not kill Barclay."

"Ah . . ." She swallowed, staring at that silver spiky tip. "He's honorable?"

"You'll have to do better than that, my dear, your eye and your life are at stake."

Her heart hammered and she licked her lips. What

games was Devane playing? "He's on our side. He was duped by Wheaton into coming after us?"

"Not bad, but you left out the part about how much you care for him. Now tell me, Sullivan, how do you think she would feel if you gutted her beloved?"

"She'd get over it quickly enough," Angel stated grimly.

"Would you have preferred that someone had murdered Isabella?" Señor Arolas challenged.

"It would have been a public service," Angel replied stonily.

"Who's Isabella?" Justin growled.

"A traitorous bitch who deserved to die," Angel retorted. "Now put down that blade, Devane!"

"Give us our answer, Señor Arolas. Is Barclay a traitorous man who deserves to die?"

"Although it appears that Barclay is upstanding, I have yet to hear my son's side of this matter," Señor Arolas hedged.

As Devane continued, the blade quaked, and Evelyn held her breath. "Then let's assume he is not a traitor—"

"Lies and supposition," Sully charged. "You know me, Devane, and you should trust what I'm doing."

"I trusted Wheaton, see where that got us all." The blade shifted a smidgen as the old gent stirred in his shoes. Evelyn suddenly feared the man might inadvertently impale her. He went on, "Barclay trusted him as well. He followed orders, not knowing that those orders were being given by a man who'd lost his mind, lost his will to live, and lost his sense of right from wrong."

Evelyn grit her teeth; she'd had enough of these games. "Sir, if you don't intend to slice open my eye, I'd like you to remove that bloody blade. I'm tired of all this nonsense."

A flicker of air sliced through the breeze and her heart stopped as the blade moved. Her shoulders sagged as the sword dropped out of her line of sight.

Justin let out a long breath and grabbed her arms.

She looked up, surprised no one had moved. That's when she noted the rows of Devane's armed men surrounding them.

Devane bowed. "You called my bluff. Well done, Miss Amherst. Let's hope next time it will be over a card table instead of a mêlée." He slipped the sword into his cane, locking the head with a loud click. "Now, I'll venture you all have many questions, but I, for one, am famished and would prefer a more civilized venue to elucidate the facts of this dicey affair. Let's be off then, shall we?"

Chapter 34

~~~ ∞ ~~~

Hours later, after having sorted through the facts and cleared the air, Evelyn, Justin, Sully, Angel, Señor Arolas, and Sir Devane stood around Devane's drawing room drinking brandy and smoking cigars, quietly celebrating the conclusion of the dastardly game. The mood was light yet somber. No one could forget the reason for the gathering, yet an aura of rejoicing hung in the air, too powerful for any lingering qualms.

"I'm pleased with Miss Amherst's decision to house the remarkable necklace of Kanibar in the British Museum. It will certainly be much appreciated, as well as safe there," Devane said quietly to Justin, excitement shining from his sharp hazel eyes. "My real concern lies with ascertaining how much damage has been done to the branch and rebuilding it."

359

Justin nodded distractedly, his mind on the conversation occurring three steps away near the tall windows. Señor Arolas was talking about returning to Wellington's camp, while his son Angel intended a trip home to Spain to visit his mother. Evelyn did not seem to be offering any insight into her future plans.

Devane droned on as he puffed on his thin cigar, sending a cloud of pungent white smoke into the chamber. "I'm hoping to convince Sullivan to stay in London and help with the task."

The afternoon light played softly around Evelyn's lovely hair, giving her a golden halo. Her eyes were sparkling as she looked fondly from Sully to Angel and back again, as if she could not get enough of the sight of them. At one point her sky blue gaze lit upon Justin, and she smiled warmly, as if to include him in her circle of those she cherished. Sully touched her arm and murmured something in her ear. Her melodious laugh tinkled throughout the room like a playful caress. Justin's heart contracted; how much longer would he be able to have his dearest near?

"Perhaps that Ismet fellow who just left would be interested in assisting as well." Devane nodded sagely. "We cannot focus on Wheaton's betrayal, but must think of the future, Barclay."

The future for Justin seemed bleak indeed without Evelyn in it. The light she beamed on his miserable existence would soon be brightening other shores. His heart began to pound and his palms became damp with sweat. Devane's lips were moving, but Justin heard no sound beyond the crashing of waves roaring in his ears. His world had irrevocably changed the moment Evelyn had swept into his life, breathing fresh air into his stale existence. There was no turning back from the transformation her association had wrought in his soul, from the inexplicable revolution she'd led in his heart.

The room rushed out of focus as the past and the future collided together into a picture of what his wan life had been and what the promise of a brighter future could be. But that promise would all turn to ash if he allowed it to, something he was not about to let happen. Resolution flooded through him, carrying with it the knowledge of the man he had become and what he needed to do. He opened his mouth and shouted, "I need more!"

Conversation ceased, and all eyes turned to him.

Gazing at him uncertainly, Evelyn stepped forward. "Ah, the bar is over there, Justin. I'm certain Sir Devane wouldn't mind if you helped yourself."

He strode over to her and looked down into those sparkling blue eyes. "I'm not talking about the bloody brandy. I'm talking about us. Being your ally is not enough for me. Hell, even being your—" he paused, looking around the room—"*friend* is not enough. I thought I'd be content with simply having you near, but I want it all and I'm not going to settle for anything less. I love you, Evelyn Amherst, and I'm not going to let you go." Lifting her angelic form into his arms, he heaved her over his shoulder and bounded toward the door.

Sully stepped in front of him, blocking his escape, and growled, "Where the hell do you think you're going, Barclay?"

"To the church on the corner, and neither you nor anyone else is going to stop me."

"I'll get the door for you," Señor Arolas encouraged, yanking it open.

"Don't I have a say in the matter?" Evelyn screeched as Justin strode out the door, Sully and Angel dogging at his heels.

"No." Justin adjusted her on his shoulder and headed down the carpeted hallway toward the front entrance.

"But she'll have to say I do," Angel commented, trying to hide his smile.

"She will."

"How can you be so sure?" Sully asked, following so closely in the tight hallway that Justin's hand brushed against his rough coat. Thankfully the man did not stop him; Justin would've hated to knock him on his ass.

"I believe she loves him," Devane commented from behind.

Justin stopped and turned, making Sully duck to avoid having Evelyn's feet crash into his head. "By the way, Sir Devane, I quit."

"But we need you, Barclay! We must rebuild after the damage Wheaton's done! The future depends on it!"

"Sorry, sir, but you'll just have to find a way to get along without me. I'm going to have my hands full raising our twelve children." He whipped back toward the front door.

"Twelve! Are you mad?" Evelyn shrieked.

Señor Arolas shouted from the rear, "I still have the Barclay diamonds, by the way."

"Good," Justin replied over his shoulder. "Evelyn will be needing them."

Evelyn tried to straighten, the blood rushing to her head, which must've been why her cheeks were so warm. "This is not the Dark Ages, Justin! You cannot kidnap a woman and make her your bride." Her heart was pounding, and the fear she tasted on her tongue was interlaced with the delicate spice of . . . joy.

"Of course I can," he countered. "I'm a rogue and a scoundrel, and I have a license in my pocket."

Her heart skipped a beat, and she thought she might expire from the elation thrilling her senses. To be Justin's wife, truly one with him in heart and spirit, was a fantasy for which she had dared not hope. It was too unreal, too delicate a chance to dream.

His grip tightened as he ambled down the front steps, jostling her against his shoulder. He murmured, "Don't worry, darling, I won't drop you."

And she realized she believed him. She trusted him. She trusted him with her person and her heart. She relaxed in his grip, letting him take the lead. It was not nearly as difficult as she thought it would be. Still, recalling her own parents' problems, she insisted, "But marriage can be trying. It has its own set of challenges."

"As if we've never faced conflict," he replied sardonically.

"I heard in parts of Italy it's customary for the townsfolk to place obstacles in the path of the bride and groom on the way to the chapel to see how they'll deal with difficulties," Angel supplied.

"Don't even think about it, Angel," Justin charged.

Loping along beside them, he shrugged. "Well, given I cannot participate that way, and since I'm Evelyn's closest friend and I can't be the maid of honor, I'll be the best man."

Trailing at Justin's heels, Sully grabbed her hand. "And I'll give you away."

Bemused, she chided teasingly, "As if you ever thought there was a man good enough for me!"

"Barclay seems besotted, and if he dares step out of line, he'll answer to me," Sully replied as they marched down the pavement, as bedraggled a bridal party as ever there'd been. "Besides, I've always wanted a herd of grandchildren."

"Is this a conspiracy?" Evelyn asked, the smile she was trying unsuccessfully to stifle lifting the corners of her lips.

"It seems, child, that they all love you too much to allow you to make a mistake," Devane commented dryly from behind.

"Put me down, Justin," she stated softly.

"No. I'm not taking any chances."

Her heart warmed with love for this brave man who had risked his life for those she cherished, faced his inner demons and trounced them, and taken her imperfect person into his devoted heart.

"But you are taking a chance, Justin, on me."

"No, I'm not. So long as we have no more spies, no more conspiracies, except for the one seeing us wed, no more bloody games. Oh, and you must promise to live as long as a hearty English oak. I don't want to spend a moment on this earth without you."

She was thankful he held her tightly, because she was so happy she thought she might fly from his arms.

The church bells rang and Evelyn's heart flipped over, so near were they to their destination. Did she dare assume the challenge, where her parents had failed so miserably? Happiness, fear, worry, joy all blended together in her belly in a combustion of sensations that felt like a cloud of butterflies fluttering wildly against her ribs.

Justin's grip tightened, and she bumped and jiggled on his shoulder as he ascended the stone steps. A door creaked open, and everything was suddenly shrouded in shadow. The scents of old stone and wax permeated the air of the tiny chapel.

As he carried her forward, the most glorious prism of colors washing the stone floor of the church came into view. Evelyn arched her back and looked up. The breath caught in her throat. The window was a mosaic of color depicting Daniel in the lion's den. She ventured she knew how he must have felt. Her heart began to pound, and her mouth had turned desert dry.

"What can I do for you?" a scratchy voice called.

Sir Devane stepped forward. "A wedding if you please, Vicar Kranz. We have a special license, and all is in order."

"Ah, if you say so, Sir Devane, but I do not have you on the calendar."

"I'm sure your coffers would appreciate your flexibility on this auspicious occasion."

"You've always been most generous, sir. But ah, pardon my query, is the bride, ah, ready for her wedding?"

Strong arms encircled Evelyn's waist and gently lowered her to the cold stone floor, steadying her on her feet. Warm hands cupped her shoulders, and she looked up into those exquisite green-gray eyes.

"Do you love me enough to marry me, Evelyn?" he asked gruffly, his gaze searching hers.

She studied that dear, beautiful face, and the vulnerability she saw there tore at her heart. Her lips split into a blissful grin as joy rippled from her toes to the tips of her fingers; she'd never been more certain of anything in her life.

"I do," she whispered, then stated more firmly, "I most assuredly do."

Epilogue

Sitting down on the sturdy tree limb, Evelyn adjusted her skirts and placed her parasol against her leg, just as she'd been taught so many years before. Sighing in relief for the shade, she could not help but smile as she watched her dear husband trying to teach their four-year-old son and two-year-old daughter how to fly a kite. Well, little Phillip was trying to learn, while Dina raced about the meadow chasing butterflies.

"Collect the twine, Phillip," Justin advised as the kite plummeted into the grasses. "I'm going to visit your mother."

Justin dropped down beside her and pulled her into his arms, planting a warm kiss on her brow. "The boy is good with his hands."

"Just like his father," she teased, laying her head on

his shoulder. Inhaling his familiar woodsy scent, she relished the affection of his strong embrace. She sighed with contentment.

He grazed his hand over her round middle. "How are you feeling?"

"About as big as this old oak." Shaking her head, she remarked, "I'll tell you one thing, Justin Barclay, I'm not about to go through this nine more times. Besides, you don't want to be an old codger when your daughters are coming out."

"Heavens, I hadn't thought of that. I certainly hope Sully is retired from the Branch by then."

She tilted her head to see his handsome features. "Why?"

"He's a crack shot, and I'll need all the help I can get keeping the rogues and scoundrels away from my innocent angels."

"Don't worry, I'll be sure to teach our daughters how to deal with them."

He beamed wickedly. "Oh yes, you always knew how to charm a rogue into behaving."

Drawing his head down so that his velvety lips met hers, she murmured, "Haven't you figured out by now, Justin? I like it when you misbehave."